Also by Stephen Swartz

Contemporary Literary Fiction

After Ilium

Aiko

A Beautiful Chill

A Girl Called Wolf

Exchange

Year of the Tiger

Fantasy & Science Fiction

The Stefan Székely Vampire Trilogy

I. A Dry Patch of Skin

II. Sunrise

III. Sunset

*Epic Fantasy *With Dragons*

The Dream Land Trilogy

I. Long Distance Voyager

II. Dreams of Future's Past

III. Diaspora

The Masters' Riddle

The Flu Season Trilogy

I. The Book of Mom

II. The Way of the Son

III. Dawn of the Daughters

Book 2

FLU SEASON
The Way of the Son

A Novel

Stephen Swartz

MYRDDIN PUBLISHING GROUP

UNITED STATES ◆ UNITED KINGDOM ◆ AUSTRALIA

ISBN-13: 978-1-68063-075-6

ISBN-10: 1-68063-075-X

www.myrddinpublishing.com

Cover design by Iris Schaeffer

NOTE

This is a work of imagination created for entertainment purposes and is not intended to convey any medical advice or provide health care information for readers.

What characters may state on the pages is solely a product of their fictional personalities and should not to be construed as the Author's own views on any particular facts and opinions whether accepted or contested.

FLU SEASON
a pandemic trilogy

Turn back and seek the safety of the shore;
tempt not the deep, lest...you come to port no more.

— Dante Alighieri, *Inferno*

Part 1

Exile

1

THE OUTERLANDS

What was that?

Another snap of a twig somewhere in this forest, just as dusk is creeping upon me. Somebody coming to kill us, or just a woodland critter? I'm not supposed to be afraid. Even so, I put my pen down and reach for Mom's pistol on the grass beside me, give it a pat.

The idea was to hide out where no one could find us. To be in a place where no one would just happen by and see us – see that we had food and supplies and try to steal them or, worse, kill us and take what we had. The chance was low of us meeting other people who might have the same goals as us: to survive this eight-year flu season and the virus that kept changing to kill more of us. Not sure people would also want to rebuild some kind of decent society we could live in. More likely they would want to save themselves.

So we left the cluster of abandoned buildings around the ferry landing, forgetting the island where we lived for nearly two years, and headed north, then to the west, through the foothills and up into the mountains, into the dark forest of a national park. It was a place where Mom took me when I was little, apparently to allow me to commune with nature but actually, as it turned out, it was because she liked the forest's acoustics when playing her tuba. A few deer, a fox, and a raccoon came to see who was making all of that racket. After all, she was playing a suite called *Forest Songs*, composed by her mentor Stefan Schweiz, but obviously without the piano accompaniment.

Mom liked to remind me that we were living in hard times, and that hard times require hard decisions. I'm hiding in these woods because of hard decisions. Mom had taken care of me all my life, but now she was gone. Now I have to find my own way through the woods. I can still hear Mom's voice urging me on. But the woods are full of viruses and variants that want to end humanity, and vagrants who prey upon survivors of the pandemic. They weren't exactly 'zombies', like so many people worried about, yet the effect was not too different: unthinking brutes whose aim was obtaining food, unconcerned with how they might treat anyone who stood in their way. Some had gone mad from the virus or from the vaccines. Others had simply let go of their humanity in a desperate attempt to live one more miserable day.

Resting my pen, I think over my description. Was it accurate? This is one of my tasks now: to record everything. A little each day, as I remember it. Another page of what happened to Mom. I don't know if this pen will run out of ink first or I'll run out of light as evening slips into night. Either way, my writing is doomed to end. The recording of our history will catch up to the present moment and that will be it. I will leave it as a record for the future.

The trees surrounding me block what light there is, so I perch myself up the slope, using the final cast of light to scribble on.

"Sandy?" my wife calls from down the slope, keeping her voice low. Everything echoes in these woods.

"Up here," I respond softly.

"I'm done," she says. "You can come back now."

"In a minute."

As she does every few days, she washes herself using a handful of precious water and a rag, standing naked out among the trees. When she's comfortable once more, she puts on the freshest clothes she has, although nothing has been washed for some time. We have to go to the stream for that. Can't do much inside our home – too small and can't risk getting anything wet.

She goes over the next hill whenever she needs to vomit up a bad mushroom or berries that aren't right. Over a different hill to squat over our poop pit, then toss some dirt in it and cover the spot with leaves. We cannot let anyone see that people live here.

As I continue expanding our dug-out home, we may get enough space to store more supplies inside rather than out in pits I've dug or up in trees out of the reach of animals.

Making sense of what happened should've been easier than it was turning out to be. That's why I wanted to record everything – from when Mom and I left the city because of the pandemic, when daily life became too unbearable, and our journey east, with stops along the way, on to the island. And our short life on the island, the reason we left the island to enter the dangerous outerlands, and what happened then that led us to this forest.

My legs ache, propping myself upon the hillside. I hold myself against the mossy patch, ready to slip and tumble down. With my knees a quivering desk, I scribble as fast as I can, forgetting a lot of the words I learned long ago in a different world.

Distracted by a fussy baby finally giving in to nursing, I hear Hannah telling her everything will be all right. I worry my wife will start singing, like she used to do, breaking into one of her pandemic pop songs. Of course, our baby likes the songs. But we have to keep quiet here.

"Are you coming?" my wife calls from down the slope. Hannah holds our infant daughter in one arm, braces herself with the other arm. "Isla's already falling asleep."

"Okay," I call down to her. "Just a little more."

I'm writing in the dark, only the orange glow cutting into the horizon, the trees all black silhouettes. The tall trunks remind me of the high-rise apartment buildings in the city we left, how Mom would sit out on the balcony with her tuba, playing sad songs while the pandemic kept everyone stuck at home. I had to attend virtual school using my computer and Mom did the same for her job. Life was very strict but we could endure it, waiting for it to end. But it didn't end. Two weeks – then two months – then two years. And more years, daily life getting worse. When food became scarce, fuel gone, criminals raging, and police running down anyone protesting the harsh conditions, Mom said it was time to go.

Where? I asked. To your grandparents' farm, she told me. But we had a lot of trouble getting out of the city, fighting through the desperate traffic, but managed to escape to back country roads. We got to the farm, but it wasn't as we expected. The pandemic chaos had spread. We found Grandma and Grampa dead: classic murder-suicide. We buried them.

Mom decided we should go to her older sister Laura's house. More bad things happened on the way. It seemed the whole world was a lawless frontier. Aunt Laura had her own way of getting by. Mom thought we should band together, yet Laura refused to come with us. So we left, headed to her other sister's house up north in another town.

That was where I met Aunt Jackie and, more importantly, her children – my cousins.

"Are you coming?" Hannah calls, her voice soft but insistent.

"Okay, almost done."

It's funny how we met. I have to smile as I think about how I'd explain it to someone. Aunt Jackie died so my cousins had to come with us. And things happened. Maybe it's not such a funny story, after all. My aunt was distraught over losing her husband to the virus and two daughters to violence. She wanted to go peacefully, so her little sister – my mom – helped her, promising to look after her remaining daughter and son.

Nothing in our journey was like it was supposed to be. The only good thing was meeting Hannah and falling in love. It didn't even matter that she was my cousin. People don't need to know that. We have different grandmothers, actually, but the same grandfather – because he'd been a real jerk, Mom told me on the island.

I close this notebook and make my way down the slope to our dug-out home.

Not much shelter available in this forest, a national park back when we still had a nation that had public parks like this, a wide swath of wilderness that nobody was allowed to develop. It seemed a good place to hide, waiting for the pandemic to end and society to return to something normal. Rather than putting up a lean-to tarp for the night, we found something better: a burrow in the hillside.

The scratches on my arms from the fox we evicted were healed now. It was narrow, but I dug it out more so Hannah could wriggle feet-first into it, then take Isla from my arms. I sat outside to sleep that first night. We hollowed it out more in coming days, enough for all of us to crawl inside. I got branches, broke them and cut them, used them to reinforce our home. We were sure to leave vegetation on the ground so nobody would see the area had been cleared, leaving it looking natural. I dug it out more, widening it, raising the ceiling. More supports, with tarps above and under us, a mat to sleep on. We gained more space, with an extra room to store Mom's precious tuba in its soft-side case.

We can sit up inside without bumping our heads now. Over the months we continued improving it, making it more comfortable: a warm, dry refuge from the rain and cold, good for the winter. We need protection from the harsher weather of this more northern location, and remain well-hidden from anyone who hikes through this forest.

I wriggle head-first in through the burrow's opening. Carefully turning around, I pull down the thick flap of mossy turf that serves as a door, then reach through the gap to move the bundle of bushy branches in front of the door to hide us. I hear the flick of a match striker and a flame glows from the stubby candle Hannah holds. A few minutes of nightly face time: regarding each other eye to eye, making certain each of us is who we expect to be in here and not a random stranger seeking shelter.

We're in this together, our eyes confirm.

Then we right ourselves for sleeping, share a kiss, and blow out the candle.

"What're you writing so much every day?" she asks, lips against my ear. "Your fantasy story?"

"No, not a story." This was our script. Hannah hadn't gotten to finish her high school because of the pandemic and I'd just started college when Mom and I left the city. But Hannah's smart. "I want Isla to know everything. Everything about her grandmother."

Hannah brushes my cheek with her hand. "I'll tell her."

* * *

Eventually Mom and I (she thirty-six and me nineteen), with my cousins Hannah (almost seventeen) and Nathan (ten), got to the island where Mom and her sisters used to go for family vacations long ago. It was a barrier island accessed by ferry at its north end, not in operation because of the pandemic, and a rickety bridge further south along the channel. They had a beach house there. It was on the beach: the backyard stretched out to the surf. We spent many evenings sitting on the back porch, watching the surf roll in, its steady roar numbing us to our fate.

It seemed as safe a place as any to wait out the pandemic, a flu season already six years running. But the people on the island had set up a community with strict rules. Mom passed off Hannah and I as a newly married couple to keep the lustful men from claiming her. We had to prove we were married by getting pregnant – which we did. But our hearts were full of love for each other anyway. And soon Isla was born.

Mom had struggled to balance her many roles on the island but eventually she lost her balance. She played along as best she could, planning for the day we would leave the island and return home to some kind of newly-manufactured normal. One man named Bucky we met made Mom happy for a while. They got along, but he went crazy. Then a sailor returned, a man who'd made her happy when she came to the island as a teenager. Mom confessed, awkward as it was after so many years, that this handsome sailor named Victor was most likely my biological father.

One day that crazy man got jealous of that sailor man and put a knife into Mom.

And so I shot that crazy man with Mom's pistol.

Fat Owen, leader of that island community, got the council to banish me from the island. They tried to stop Hannah from joining me, saying she needed to stay to help their breeding program now that she birthed Isla. Instead, she and Isla came with me. The men rowed us across the strait from the ferry landing, delivering us to the north shore. From there we were supposed to make our way through the outerlands to somewhere.

I'm sure the council considered it a death-sentence, the way a lack of food and ravaging marauders would make our journey dangerous. They would be rid of us, the good ones, without having to do any of the dirty work. I knew we would manage – we had to – thanks to all that Mom taught me and what I learned from the old Scout manual snatched from the community center library. But we weren't on a Scout camping trip.

The scene of them leaving us on the shore stuck in my mind.

"What're we gonna do? Where're we going?" Hannah cried once we were left alone on the mainland. She held a brave face through the transfer. She'd stood up to Owen, telling him off, insisting on joining me. She remained calm during the rowing. As the boat left, however, she let her emotions out. Tears dribbled down her cheeks.

"First things first," I mumbled, thinking – trying to think, but my head was full of storms, ideas crashing into each other, nothing making sense, no direction forward that wasn't already foggy and uncertain. "It'll be dark soon. We have to stay here – somewhere – for tonight."

We strolled around a while, making sure we were alone among the abandoned buildings. No telling if the shops were empty or if someone like us had chosen to live in them. I held up Mom's pistol as we looked in each broken doorway, surveyed each looted store. We listened for any noise that might indicate someone. But all was quiet – eerily silent. I felt nervous electricity surging through me as I carefully stepped among the shops, expecting to be attacked at any moment.

Gradually we relaxed, realizing no one else was there.

Nobody is here. We are alone. What should we do?

It felt like we were in a haunted house, where some guy in a costume would leap out to scare us and we would scream. I kept on expecting that. My heart beat faster with every step.

"Relax, will you?" said Hannah. She could always sense me off balance like I did sometimes.

A breeze blew in from the sea and we paused to breathe it. We were on our own. It was up to me to make hard decisions now, but I didn't feel I was trained for that kind of life and worried I would be wrong. There was even more at stake now than when Mom and I finally left the city.

"How about here?" asked Hannah, pointing to an alley.

"Okay," I muttered, relieved that I had her with me.

We found a good spot away from the wind, with good sight lines and defensible. Nobody could sneak up behind us. We set up our lean-to shelter between the shops, using a tarp folded up in the big pack. We made dinner of the food we were given. Isla got milk. I gazed at the stars, thinking of answers, glancing at Mom's tuba in its soft-side case, leaning in the corner.

"What should we do?" I asked myself as we made quick work of dinner. It didn't seem real that we were across the strait, homeless and at the mercy of any vagrants who met us. We had a pistol but that didn't seem enough. Before the pandemic we never expected the next person wouldn't be friendly, smile and wave, as we passed by. Now, that person would likely be hungry and see your bag of food as reason enough to kill you. Because if he didn't kill you, you would kill him probably for the same reason.

"There's a city up north," I said, thinking aloud. "But it's got to be worse than the city Mom and I left. It's been two more years. We would be competing with many others for what food they have left. More likely we'd get killed. I must protect you and the baby."

Hannah regarded me as the baby sucked. "I don't want to go to any big city."

"Okay, so we won't head north then."

I felt relief she didn't want that. I watched her nursing.

"We could go west. We could go back to your house," I said. "At least they have the Food Mart there. They were bringing food from the city every week, had a distribution center." I sighed. "But no way to pay for it. They didn't take cash and the only bank app that worked was restricted to residents." Then I brightened. "I could get a job there, at the Food Mart. Then we could get food. Yeah, food in exchange for my labor."

I stopped myself, thoughts of Aunt Laura intruding. She had lowered her standards and gotten by using the barter system. Mom and I observed her economic plan directly: men brought her food and she treated them to her bed. Yes, prim and proper Laura now a whore Mom found amusing, but we hadn't yet realized how bad society had become.

"You mean food for sex," said my wife so plainly, glaring at me. Visiting Aunt Laura was before Mom and I got to Aunt Jackie's and I met Hannah, so she only knew about Aunt Laura from what I told her. But we could see that situation unfolding every day on the island.

"No, I don't want that," I spoke firmly, hating the image that burned in my head. "Besides, out here, I doubt anyone will offer food for sex. They'll just take the sex and not give us food."

"But I would," she said, her voice low as though speaking only to herself, sounding full of sorrow for the years of youth she'd lost. "If we really, really needed food. Especially for Isla. Then I'd do it."

"You'd do that?" I asked, surprised by her words.

"It's just a silly little thing," she shot back.

"It is?"

"Yeah. Like your mother always said."

"What's that?"

"Something like 'Sex is just a sneeze, then you keep breathing.' Or something close to that."

"I remember." I could hear Mom's voice between sips of warm beer, sitting on the back porch of the beach house. "So you'd do sex for food?"

"What? It's a few minutes. It ain't like it would be for fun. Lotta unpleasant things people hafta do to get what they need. Like, say, work a shit job for a tiny paycheck."

"Yeah, I was a delivery guy at the start of lockdowns."

"But then I'd have some food to eat, and I could go on. Till the next time."

"Next time...?"

"But I'd share it with you, of course. Because we're a team, and I kinda like you."

"I hope you still like me when this is over."

2

THE OPPOSITE SHORE

There wasn't any fanfare for the start of our exile, not like they celebrated getting rid of us. When they'd delivered us across the strait to the mainland and rowed back to the island, we stood a while watching them. Only one acknowledged us, raising his hand as a farewell salute. A bit far to see clearly but I guessed it was Victor. Then he turned and joined the others as they started the walk south to the community.

In that first moment on the opposite shore my chest was tight, my breathing hard. The weight of the world pressed down on me. Late afternoon sun shimmered across the calm water of the strait. A lone crane took flight from the island, beating its white wings overhead, flying north. I turned to track its flight and noticed the businesses clustered around the closed ferry landing. It seemed an omen, a guide.

I regarded Hannah, standing with our baby in a sling against her chest. She regarded me: standing with Mom's tuba in its soft case on my back. We didn't smile. We didn't need to say any words. We understood there would be only hardships ahead. I was forced into it, but she had chosen to come with me, trusting me to protect her and our baby.

The next morning, we packed up the tarp and shared a granola bar and raisins we brought from the island. Swallows of water, boiled on the island and poured into a plastic bottle, to wash down breakfast. Isla got her morning milk as usual while I packed.

We started north, hiking up the road that brought cars down to the landing, a swath of pavement that stretched before us. A few cars and trucks sat abandoned along the road, still in cues from when the ferry stopped running. Other vehicles sat along the road going up the hill, a few with dead people inside. That was the new normal: people trying to escape, getting trapped at a ferry landing, waiting for a ferry that would never arrive. And they sat, waiting. Owen wouldn't have let them on the island. Only medically vetted visitors. Arriving with Mom, we'd crossed the old bridge further south along the channel, but it had fallen into disrepair and wasn't passable for vehicles.

At the top of the hill stood more buildings around the main intersection where a lone traffic light swung from overhead wires, out of order. Shops clustered there appeared abandoned: windows broken, doors flung open, dark inside, shelves bare, piles of trash. Being at higher elevation, we could look out at the sea, get a good view. I thought of that day when Mom went out on Victor's yacht to catch fish for the community hoard – which caused that crazy Bucky to get jealous.

"Sandy?" My wife gently called me. Sometimes I went to places in my head and had to be called back to reality. Part of my ASD, what some people called 'Asperger's syndrome' but other people called 'high-functioning autism'. Same thing, same effects. Mom noticed that about me when I was ten or so. I'm not stupid, I just think differently. And I have a little social awkwardness. My attention drifts away and that's dangerous in these times.

"Yes, Hannah?"

"You okay?"

I thought of Mom's typical response: "I'll never be okay."

Holding Isla tight in one arm, she put her other arm around me, gave me a hug.

"One of these stores might have supplies," I said, taking a step forward. "Or at least a roof over our heads."

"Maybe someone else already got there." Hannah was certainly the smarter of us. "And nobody's gonna want strangers coming in uninvited."

The world suddenly felt so enormous, overwhelming, and the three of us the only people in it.

"So we just walk, huh?"

I put my hand to my forehead to block the sun, staring as far ahead as possible. Being on top of the hill we could see a lot, but nothing very encouraging. No signs of activity, of life going on. No vehicles traveling, no animals roaming, no people outside doing things. Only this exiled family.

The road curved to the left as it went up the hill and then, from Hannah's memory, continued down the other side. It was the only way to the ferry landing, the only road to the next place if you were getting off the ferry. But we saw no movement. We seemed to be the only people left.

"Unless you find gas in one of the cars," she replied.

We knew the situation. We had come through it getting to the island nearly two years before. Mom meant well, but she hadn't planned for a pandemic to come along and ruin our comfortable life. If she had, she would've considered the need for us to drive out of the city. She would've bought one of the fully electric cars that could charge itself using solar panels, a new and expensive car, rather than relying on a gasoline engine. Instead, she had an old hybrid car. Mom liked to quiz me on where electricity for electric cars came from. Mostly from petroleum-fueled power plants.

We ran out of gas close to Aunt Jackie's. Then the battery died and there were no places to recharge it. We were able to switch to Aunt Jackie's big gas guzzler, which was technically illegal to drive on public streets. That car was hit by a truck, ruined. We took the guys' truck at gunpoint, after they tried to attack us, but the truck ran out of gas, too. So we were left walking, like now, and carrying all that we owned, plus food. And Mom's tuba. Now a baby, too.

The stores at the intersection appeared to have been closed for the season years ago, and left with little damage. No tourists so no business. Nobody would come down here if they knew the ferry wasn't running. The owners just left, never returned.

We found a few interesting things, took them without paying, but we couldn't survive on souvenirs. Not a lot of nutrition in the wooden carvings of sailboats. Or ceramic seashells made in China. Or t-shirts – but we did take a couple shirts each just to extend our wardrobe. Mine had a big marlin arching out of the sea. Hers had a sexy mermaid with seashells bra. And we got a bib for Isla which featured two smiling goldfish.

We went shop to shop, looking in the windows, checking doors, seeing empty shelves, the messes made by looters, souvenir stands tossed around, coolers leaking. We spent the day exploring, looking for anything we could use, especially food and drink (found some), a good place to stay until we could figure out what to do. We kept our eyes open for dangers (other scavengers). I remained wary of danger popping out from nowhere, which made me anxious. I kept patting Mom's pistol on my hip.

In one looted store, Hannah paused before a half-empty shelf of cosmetics. She'd never worn make-up on the island. She picked up a lipstick tube.

"You think I should get this?" she asked me like she had a budget to follow. She held up the tube, unscrewed it, brought out the bright red tip.

"You need that?" I grinned at her as our daughter, in her sling, grabbed at the lipstick.

"Mother never let me wear any." She picked at other kinds of make-up: shadow, mascara, blush. Previous looters had left those. "I was too young, she said. Then, with the pandemic on, with what happened, she didn't want me to look too nice. Maybe get raped by vagrants, you know?"

That shut me up. "I don't think you need that. You're pretty the way you are."

"So good enough for you, huh? Is that it?" She flashed a grin.

"No," I replied. "Take it if you want. I'll get some shaving stuff. Maybe you want a clean-shaven husband."

"I do, actually." She offered me a smile, then snatched it away. "You don't have much beard anyway."

Thanks, I thought. I tried so hard to be a man, but I'd only had Mom as my role model. Until I met Victor. Even being almost twenty-one, I still felt fifteen sometimes.

"I shaved a week ago. Before all this shit happened. Kinda busy with burying Mom and your brother, and getting us exiled, okay?"

She stopped, refocused. But I saw it hurt.

"I'm sorry."

She looked away. "Yeah, it happened. Can't pretend it didn't."

"Lots of things've happened...."

She came to me, hugged me with her free arm. "Sorry, hubby."

"Forgiven, wifey."

We took only a few minor items left in the store. Whatever we might pilfer was just more to carry. They'd given me time to pack before sending me off the island. I packed all I thought I needed, but that made a heavy load. I repacked with thoughts to camping. Every space jammed with some food. Then Hannah and Isla joined me at the last moment with her own pack.

"Shopping like this is so tiring," Hannah moaned. We exited the shop, started the next. "When I was little, Mother would give us a piece of candy or toy to keep us occupied as she went up and down every damn aisle."

"Not my mom. In and out. Before I could even know what she was getting. Or she left me in the car." I thought of the grocery in Hannah's hometown, the Food Mart, how Mom had to go in and get things when I'd failed.

"Now there's nothing much to buy – or steal," she laughed.

With a glance around, I saw it was getting late. "We better find a place for the night."

The sunset inched down the sky. I panicked that we wouldn't find good overnight lodging and have to set up the lean-to again. I was the man, Mom liked to point out, a father and husband now, so it was my duty to take care of my family, protect them from anything that may come at us, day or night. But I stayed a bundle of nerves, ready to fight at any moment.

Hannah came over to me, patted my shoulder. Her touch was always comforting. It was also a direct reminder that I had a lot of responsibilities now.

An old motel sat off the road, perched on the bluff overlooking the sea: *Tropic Isle Lodge*. A tall palm tree and rows of waves were painted on the faded signboard.

"Maybe they left a door unlocked." She shifted Isla in her sling, our infant getting fussy. "She needs to nurse. And I need to eat so I have some milk to give her."

"Okay, we'll stop here." We set down our packs, my sore back complaining. "I'll check it."

I tried a few doors, locked. Except one door. Swinging it open with an eerie squeak, I saw the room had been trashed. Someone had probably broken in, used it, and left. It smelled bad. I stepped to the next door. I thought of shooting the lock and breaking in but I didn't want to waste a bullet.

"Try the office," called Hannah from up the walk.

I went past her along the walk, on to the office at the end of the building. The outer door was unlocked. Inside, the office room was a mess but not too bad, not like someone had torn it up for fun, just normal clutter. Someone rummaged through it looking for cash maybe. That would've been a couple years before, when you could still use cash to buy things. Cash had no value now. In a pandemic nobody wanted to touch the money other people had handled. They used apps on their phones – until the grid went down.

Behind the counter was an old wooden desk with an ancient computer box and dusty monitor set up on it, like for checking in guests. It looked unused. Beyond the desk was a closed door.

I ducked out and called Hannah to join me.

With her behind me, I held up the shotgun she handed me as I reached for the door handle and pushed it open.

The room was dark, had no windows. My hand went for a light switch on the wall but, of course, there was no power. A soft *ffftt* – the glow of the lighter stick Hannah held up illuminated the room. We saw a dingy sofa with stained pillow and dirty sheet, two office chairs, a kitchen counter with old coffee machine and an empty water cooler on it. A round table took up the middle of the room. Beside the counter stood a full-size fridge.

After pulling a candle from her pack, lighting it, and placing it on the counter, Hannah sat on the sofa, holding Isla and cooing to her, getting her to feel safe. I kept the shotgun in my hands as I listened for a few minutes, expecting someone would've discovered this relatively comfortable place before us and be returning at any moment. The evening deepened. Time for all good survivors to take shelter for the night.

I closed the door, braced it with one of the chairs, like Mom showed me. Checking the cabinets against the wall, I found them stocked with cans, boxes, bags of food, bottles of water, cans of beer and tea. The fridge was not on, so it was warm inside but stocked with things that didn't need to be chilled. Showing the cache to Hannah, we shared a grin, believing we could make it.

We settled in and everything was so quiet. Too quiet.

After Mom and I were awakened at Grandma and Grampa's house by vagrants breaking in, I awoke at the slightest sound, expecting trouble. A window breaking was what woke Mom and me. Here, all was quiet. Hannah dozed off easily on that couch and Isla with her, but I had to stay alert. I sat in the chair by the locked door, nodding off every so often but jerking awake after a few minutes.

Then the noise came: a rattling of the door handle. Someone was trying to open the door separating us from the outer office. The rattling got worse as the person got more frustrated. Then a fist hit the door.

"Who's in there?" a man's voice demanded, adding a punch to the door.

I handed the shotgun to Hannah and grabbed Mom's pistol as I faced the door. When those vagrants had started upstairs, Mom swung the bedroom door shut, locked it. They heard that. When the first guy pounded on the door, she shot through the door, killing him. But I wasn't sure I was ready to shoot this one.

"I know yer in there," shouted the man, sounding a lot older than me. "Open up, ya hear me? Come on out. Or I swear I'll burn down this place, so help me God. I don't care. Won't get a penny of insurance but I'll burn it down anyway, with y'all inside."

3

THE OLD MAN AND THE SEA

I looked at Hannah but couldn't see her in the dark. She flicked on the lighter stick and lit the candle. In its faint glow I could see she was afraid. Isla started to cry.

"Open up, I said!" the man shouted, pounding on the door.

"Wait a sec," I called back, repositioning myself in front of the door. I waved Hannah to move to the side, out of the line of fire, and crouch down with Isla.

Then I reached forward and flicked off the lock.

"I got a gun," I warned the man.

"Yeah, well, so do I."

"We mean no harm," I said, holding up the pistol. "We don't want any trouble, just a place to stay for the night. We'll be moving on in the morning."

"I getcha, but this's my place. I own it."

"The night's half done already. Can't we finish it?"

A moment's pause. Shuffling on the other side of the door.

"It's only half past ten," said the man. He sounded more weary than angry. "But I can let you in another room."

I took a long breath. "Okay. Thanks."

The door opened a bit and light shone in.

As the door swung further, I saw a man of maybe seventy, white-bearded and nearly bald, dressed in a dirty, ragged shirt and a pair of blue coveralls. He held up a lantern which lit the whole room. The door swung fully open and he stood in the doorway like a prison guard, examining us.

"Youngsters," he cursed. "Just whaddaya think yer doin here? Nobody taught ya no manners? Just waltz on in, set up yer camp?"

"Sorry, sir." I lowered my pistol. He didn't have any gun like he said he did.

"This's my place," he said. "I own it. Long before this pandemic. I didn't just happen on it like you kids."

"We thought it was abandoned. Like other buildings here. We just needed a place for tonight."

"Well, this is my place." He tried to project anger.

"Okay, we'll leave. Give us a couple minutes to pack."

Then his mood suddenly changed and his eyebrows rose. We could feel the air in the room change.

"What's *that*?" he asked, his voice drawn out in awe.

Hannah had gotten up, standing behind me, holding Isla.

"Is that...a *baby*?" he said with wild-eyed fascination.

I stood firm before him, blocking his view of our daughter.

"Yes. Our baby," I answered, holding the pistol on him. "Stay away from her."

"Wow...a real baby." He stood admiring her. "It's real, ain't it? Not a doll? Ya don't see one o' them so much no more. Lotsa folks got the virus or got all them vaxxes, so they cain't make babies no more. I thought we's all doomed."

"Please don't hurt her," said Hannah, hugging Isla tighter.

With me blocking his way, he realized I would fight him if he dared come closer, so he stepped back, hands up.

"Nope. I sure wouldn't." The man shook his head, embarrassed. "No, I ain't no baby killer. Not like some folks. Not like them's that say babies taste the best."

Our first encounter with an outerlander and he talked about cannibalism. Mom expected that phase would come. I recalled Aunt Laura telling us what happened to her young son, killed and eaten by a gang of hungry marauders.

Seeing how innocent we were, the man relaxed. He lowered the lantern and set it on the counter in this inner office. He continued to gaze at Isla, a smile playing on his face.

"Ain't seen one o' them in years." He leaned forward, his finger extended, and touched Isla's cheek. Just a soft poke, like he was checking whether she was real. I moved to block him but he got past me. "A girl, you say?"

"Yes, our daughter," Hannah spoke.

"Aww," he sighed. "Might I hold her?"

"You're rather dirty," Hannah countered.

"S'pose I am. That's awright."

He continued gazing at Isla, who seemed to notice she was the center of attention and made a funny face, her pink cheeks aglow, her dark eyes curious. She squirmed in Hannah's arms, wanting to grab the man's long beard.

"She's a cutey, that's fer shore." His big smile pushed aside his beard. "Yep. Real cute."

"Thanks, we made sure to order a cute one," said Hannah.

I laughed at that. The man laughed, too. Hannah snickered and Isla gurgled.

"I guess you're no threat," he said and shoved his hand in his pocket, retrieved a set of keys. "Come on."

He stepped out as we gathered our things.

"I'm Quinn, by the way." Not sure if it was his first or his last name. We hurried after him as he hobbled down the walk.

He'd been out scavenging, he told us, his daily chore. He had no guests, of course. The motel rooms stayed locked, unused – except that one room somebody had broken into and trashed.

He led us down to the room on the far end and unlocked the door, let it swing open.

"Water's running but don't drink it. Not safe." He glanced back over his shoulder as the door swung open. "I'll bring you a bottle of water I already boiled."

"Same as on the island," Hannah shared.

"Island?" he quizzed, making a disgusted face.

"Umm...yes," I responded. "They voted us off the island."

"You're lucky," said Quinn with a chuckle. "Hell, you folks seem awright." He told us about others that had come across the strait: broken people, abused women, violent men. He had to usher them on up the hill and away.

"Thank you so much," I said to Quinn. I felt grateful and hated myself for being suspicious. Obviously not everyone was a criminal in this pandemic world. Hannah thanked him, too. "We'll leave in the morning, like I said."

"Oh, y'all kin stay long as ya like. I don't mind. Good to have decent folks ta talk to."

"We don't have any money," I said sheepishly. Actually, we had some old cash Victor gave us as we departed the island, thinking it might be useful. But there wasn't any reason to risk anything by divulging it to this man.

"No matter," he said, grinning. "Ain't worth nothing now. Hell, anyone that gots any money got it taken away by the gubment."

"If there's cell service," I offered, "I could use a banking app to pay you. We haven't used it for anything else so there's got to be money in the account."

"You deaf, son? I said, it's no bother. Besides, there's none o' that cellular service here. Nothing. Everything's off. And if you got any in yer bank, it's gone now, most likely, taken by the gubment."

"We should give you something...."

He kept his eyes on Isla, grinning like a grandfather presented with his first grandchild. "Seeing this little one is enough. Makes my day. Gives me some hope. Ya know? You folks gotta make it. For all of us."

"But we insist. Maybe I can help out around here. You got any work needs doing?"

He seemed to consider my offer. "Possibly. I'll think on it. But ain't got no electricity and no phone service. So no way you kin use those app things."

"I saw a computer in the office," said Hannah.

"You think that old thing still works?" Quinn screwed up his face in amusement. "Okee, yeah, it works sometimes – when I run the generator. It's not connected to that internet or anything. Just use it to play solitaire." He chuckled. "Lots and lots of solitaire, if ya know what I mean. Got some videos on it. But, hell, working up enough power just to watch one o' those ain't worth the effort."

I must've blushed. He saw that and stopped his joking.

"Thanks for the room," I said. "We'll keep it neat and clean. By the way, I'm Sandy. This is Hannah. And this li'l handful is Isla."

"Thank you, sir," Hannah added.

"No, thank *you*," said Quinn. "We kin talk more in the morning. Goodnight, kids."

He stepped out, started up the walk to the office.

Kids! I thought as he sauntered away. We were hardly kids, me being twenty, almost twenty-one, and Hannah eighteen going on nineteen. And we had a baby. We were a real family.

What an awful time to be a family.... It wasn't simple like go to work, come home, send the children to school, play with them, feed them, save for college – no, not like that. Now we had to scavenge for food and watch for vagrants. And the goddamn virus. I thought a moment. Quinn hadn't worn a facemask and he didn't insist we wear them either. He must think we're safe. Living alone here he wasn't worried about a virus. He knew anybody who was still walking around by now had to be safe or else they would've died already. I remembered the death counts reported every day before Mom and I left the city. Anybody left would've survived the virus, vaccine or not. Like us.

Hannah lit the candle again and in the faint light she was able to change Isla's diaper. As Hannah washed out the soiled cloth in the bathroom and hung it to dry, I wrapped a fresh cloth around Isla's bottom. I held her in my arms, nearly forgetting the reason for us staying in a run-down motel with a creepy old man admiring our child a bit too much. It seemed like a dream – or a nightmare.

I handed Isla back to Hannah when she came out. Pushing a straight-back chair against the door, I jammed it tight against the doorknob. Like Mom showed me. That Quinn guy knew where we were. He could call his buddies to come attack us during the night. I made sure the guns were loaded, ready.

"What're we gonna do?" asked Hannah as she sat on the still made-up bed. The room was stuffy, being locked up. Who knew how long it had been since the previous guests stayed here?

"First, we get a good sleep," I responded. "May not get a better place than this for a while."

"No, I mean after tomorrow."

"What is there to do? We stay or we go. Those are the choices. They will always be the only choices."

"We just have to stay off their stupid fucking island," she said. "Like we even wanna be there."

"So here is as good a place as any. No rule that says we have to go far away." I surveyed the motel décor, velvet seascapes on the walls, and sniffed the mustiness of the room. "It could be worse. We could live here. Yeah, I could see us building something."

"You mean start our own community here?" she asked, voice rough and disapproving.

I patted Isla's head. We had a start to a new community. We needed to secure a steady source of fresh water and food first.

"Sure, why not?" I replied.

"I don't even wanna be close enough to see it."

With a nod, I agreed, too tired for a debate.

The room had been locked up for at least a few years. Still had little bars of soap in the bathroom. Lots of folded towels, too. I unloaded the big pack and the other bag, then stripped down and went for a shower. Mom liked to shower at any excuse, careful to wash off viruses that might stick to her skin. Having to ration water on the island drove her crazy. Not literally crazy, not like that Bucky fellow, the man who killed her, but still a little insane. We all went a bit insane on the island.

"Maybe we should stay here," I said coming out of the bathroom wrapped in a towel. Hannah had Isla at her breast. "At least a few days. It's like a family vacation." I laughed.

"We're barely a quarter-mile from the landing," she noted.

"It's not like we have to go far, just off the island."

She frowned. "I don't wanna have anything to do with that island. Don't even wanna see it."

Like Mom and I did, Hannah and I developed our own script. But I didn't want to say the required lines, not tonight.

"I know." My eyes softened as I regarded her. "But my mom's buried there. So is Nathan. I don't want to go too far from them."

She choked up. "My brother never deserved any of that."

"I agree. Bucky just wanted to hurt Mom."

"By murdering a little boy?" she shrieked and Isla fussed at the disturbance.

"Apparently."

Knocking on the door startled us. Nobody would know we were in this room, not unless they'd watched us go in from some hiding place and were coming to get us, take what we had. Cradling Isla tightly in her arms, Hannah went over and peeked out through the curtains, then motioned for me to open the door.

"Who is it?" I called.

"It's me – Quinn – the motel owner."

"Oh," I said, swinging the door open. "Sorry."

"I'd be careful, too, if I's you." He presented the big case to me: Mom's precious tuba. "You left this in the office. I'm guessing you want it."

"Oh god yes!" I exclaimed, alarmed that I'd forgotten it. Mom would never forgive me if I left her tuba somewhere. It was an heirloom, passed down through four generations. In fact, Mom had expected Isla would be the next one to play it.

"You really carry that thing around?" asked Quinn.

"It's my mom's tuba," I explained, adding a short history of the instrument passing through our family and a list of music she'd played on it. I told how she'd taught music at a university before the pandemic and how she taught me to play it but discouraged me from becoming a professional musician like her. He hadn't heard of Mom's band the Tubafonics.

Hannah laughed at Quinn's reaction to my description of Mom as the topless tubist, playing her tuba on stage with only tassel pasties on.

"Yeah, I getcha," said Quinn. "Back in the day, I played me a mean guitar. Me and my buds, we had us a band for a time, too. Rockabilly ya might say. Yep, 'Sammy and the Sailors' we called ourselves. Then just 'The Sailors' after Sammy died – car crash, drunk, long before the goddamn virus come along."

Hannah perked up at that revelation. "I had a band, too."

"Ya did?" he asked, doubting.

"Kinda," she said. "Just me and a couple friends." She started to describe that time in her life. Our patient host sat enraptured by her tale.

"Oh dear," I sighed as they started discussing music.

I took Isla from Hannah's arms, continued rocking her to sleep on my shoulder as the two former band members sorted out the music world.

4

IN WHICH THE WORLD GOES MAD

It seemed strange to stay in a motel room for the night – what turned out to be several nights. Like everything was normal, like it was the usual thing to do. Just a family vacation. We forgot about abandoned cars, looted stores, dead bodies here and there, some on the ground decomposing or eaten by wild animals while others sat upright in stalled cars. Leaving the city, Mom and I had stopped at a motel the first night, unable to make it to my grandparents' farm the way the traffic was. But that motel was closed, nobody around, so we slept in the car, ever wary of vagrants coming for us. In the morning we drove on, arriving at my grandparents' farm in time to see the way the future would be.

I still remember Mom washing off at a spigot on the end of the building, stripping down, unconcerned with me seeing her. I'd seen her all my life; she was Mom, so it wasn't a big deal. I thought of that scene as I held Isla in my arms, her hand grabbing at my nose while I leaned in the bathroom doorway during Hannah's shower.

"You just gonna stand there?" she snarled.

"I like looking at you," I said.

"Can't a girl get some privacy?" She pulled the curtain harder toward the wall.

"Sorry."

Isla gurgled against my neck, resting on my shoulder, ready to sleep. I returned to the bed, setting her down on the sheet beside me, playing sleepy-eyed peek-a-boo.

When Hannah exited the bathroom, she waved her hand. The shower had cold water, but the room was warm and stuffy, no A/C and no fan working. She was happy to toss off her towel and join us on the bed.

"Kinda like a family vacation," I said after a while.

"Yeah, if we didn't have so much bad shit going on." She looked around the room. "It's not too bad, I guess. We were gonna leave anyway, weren't we? Your mom always talked of going back for Aunt Laura."

We both recalled that drama. No more words needed. I gazed at Hannah, realizing how much she was a part of me now, thinking my thoughts, feeling my moods.

"That's where we should go," she spoke up later.

"To Aunt Laura's?"

"Sure. And get her kid.... Betsy?"

"It's Bootsy."

"We could stay there, right? You think she'd let us?"

I pursed my lips, words pinched off before I could speak them. I tried to describe the large house, the grounds around it. I knew there was enough space for us, but I wasn't sure we would fit with the life Aunt Laura was living when Mom and I visited.

"Maybe for a short time," I replied.

"But she's got that big house, plenty of rooms."

"It's the same thing. Even if you got a nice place to sleep you still gotta do something. Like what about food?"

"Yes, but...."

Seeing her curious face, I reminded her of our visit there, me and Mom. I didn't leave out anything this time and she blushed.

"Well, yeah, I can see that," Hannah responded. "But like your mom said: 'Sex is a sneeze, then you go on breathing.' Right?"

I stared at my wife a long time but she couldn't really see me in the darkness of the room.

We'd only been off the island a few days, and not very far from it, either. I could almost see the shoreline from the parking lot of this motel, sitting on a hill above the ferry landing. Yet the island still seemed like a whole other continent. It was its own world. We had to leave here, I decided. We had to go somewhere. We couldn't stay at this motel the rest of our lives.

"Or we could go back to your house," I suggested.

Hannah shook her head. "Not with Mother still there under the blankets on her bed. I could never go there again."

We hadn't buried Aunt Jackie after she took all those pills. We were too afraid of anyone seeing us digging and calling the police. We hadn't realized there were no more police by then, none that would come to a resident's call. So we left her wrapped in sheets and blankets after she drank the special 'medicine' Mom prepared and never awoke from her sleep. We took Hannah and her brother Nathan with us to the island, like we were one happy family.

"One happy family...." Hannah had mumbled my thought. She looked up at me, smiled. We understood each other.

*　　*　　*

Quinn found a job for me. I cleaned out the trashed room while Hannah cared for Isla in our room, door open to enjoy the day. Sometimes they went out for fresh air but I cautioned them to stay close to the motel. The late summer days were hot, the sun bright, so they would soon return to the room. Or they'd go up to the office and Quinn would teach Hannah how to play the guitar. I could hear it. I was happy she got to play. Sometimes they would sing.

I brought out the broken furniture, tore up the carpet, gathered the scraps outside. I swept the floorboards. I carried all the mess behind the motel, tossed it in a dumpster there. From that spot I gazed out at the sea. The island spread into my peripheral vision and I wondered what people were doing there now that we'd left. What would someone who drifted down the coast think, seeing this dumpster on the bluff as the first sign of civilization? Then I went to work on the bathroom, which was worse than the main room. The folks that trashed it didn't seem to know what a toilet was for.

"I recall one time a family come down the hill, right past this here place," said Quinn one afternoon while I worked. "Didn't even gimme no look. There was an old fella, couple of younger men, a woman, and two young'uns. They weren't carrying much, like they weren't expecting to be away from home long."

He coughed a bit. It seemed to be getting worse.

"Anyways, I watch them just a few minutes and a gang of five men come running down the hill after them. The family scattered. Vagrants chased after'em, caught'em, and the slaughter began." He stared at the scene lingering behind him, over his shoulder. "Of course they took their time with the woman. And one took the girl. Guess she was maybe eight or so. Hurt them pretty bad."

I came out of the bathroom when he fell silent.

"Yeah, took'em up the hill there somewhere. Later I could smell something cooking, roasting, ya know. So I guess they was having a dinner. That's vagrants fer ya. No mind to treat folks like folks, like humans. Just like wild animals."

He looked at me, forced a grin. I tried to smile but inside I was shaking at the thought of my family getting attacked like that. Dare we even try to go in that direction?

"Odd thing how them vagrants weren't wearing facemasks, ya know? That family was, being so proper, following the rules n all. Still got killed. Ya just never know."

I took a breath – "Yeah." – and return to my work.

As evening came I joined Hannah and Isla at the office where Quinn had set the table, a fish dinner before us. After dinner he and Hannah played some songs, jamming, as I held Isla in my lap and danced with her as she giggled in delight.

"He's kinda like our grampa now, isn't he?" I said as we settled into bed. Hannah agreed. I remembered our real grandfather, how he'd been during my childhood visits to their farm. Mom took me to stay there when the Tubafonics toured, several summers in a row. Then Mom ruined it all by telling me what Grampa was really like, back when she was a girl. I understood Mom better, knowing all that history, but I didn't feel better.

"Well, Quinn's had a tough life," said Hannah, laying beside me. The room was too warm for a blanket. And Isla between us added warmth. "He told me stuff his papa did. And his mama, too. Lots of abuse. So he ran away from home and joined the Navy and sailed around. When his parents died he got the motel, he and his new wife. She was an island girl. Not our island but somewhere way way south."

"He mentioned that. How he got the motel."

"Yes, he told me about her. Inez was her name. He showed me a picture. I mean a real photo on paper. I guess he really loved her, but she broke his heart."

"Kept threatening to leave him," I said. "Then she did."

"Didn't like the motel life, I guess."

"I thought she met somebody, ran off with him."

"No, she ran off with *her*. Another woman. And took their two kids with her."

"That's sad," I said and sighed.

"Yeah."

"So he started drinking a lot."

"I guess I would, too."

"Then the pandemic came along," I said after a while.

"He said everything made sense then."

✳   ✳   ✳

Another evening Quinn came down to our room, rapped his cane at our door, invited us back to the office for dinner. We didn't expect him to offer dinner; we made do with what we brought from the island. But he'd caught some fish and grilled them. Actually, we smelled it cooking but didn't think to invite ourselves, even though we were hungry and the food we brought from the island was going fast.

"How's that sea bass?" he asked, waiting for us to swallow and give him our answers. "Fish tastes a lot better now there's plenty. The sea's filling up again. Practically jumping into my basket. And then ya open a can o' corn n a can o' beans, throw'em together in the pot n ya got succotash."

"It's a good time to be alive," I said, not knowing why I said it. I must've meant it was good to have a nice dinner. But they looked at me like I was stupid.

Hannah saw my reaction: me suddenly understanding that I'd said something stupid and freezing. She reached over, patted my hand.

"It sure is," she said, adding a smile. She turned to Quinn. "Sandy's smart, but he's got a kind of autism. Sometimes he says things that don't quite fit. Don't take offense, okay?"

"I weren't offended," said Quinn, sitting back in his chair. "It is a good time to be alive. What's the alternative? Being dead?"

"You're right," said Hannah.

"Sorry, everyone," I said. "Just slipped out. The food's great and I was only thinking how satisfying the dinner is. I forgot we live in hard times because of a pandemic. All those little viruses floating around looking for a good place to land."

"That's awright, young fella." Quinn got up and gathered our dishes. "No harm done."

"Let me," said Hannah, jumping up. She handed Isla to me. "We owe you so much already for your hospitality. I can wash the dishes. You sit down and relax."

Quinn gave a nod, returned to his chair. "She's a keeper."

"I intend to keep her," I responded, smiling at Hannah.

"Keep me barefoot and preggo, right?" she challenged.

"No," I responded. "Unless you want to be pregnant again."

She gave me that look. I wasn't getting her joke. But she did like going barefoot whenever she could. She walked down to the office for this dinner barefoot. And she had been so beautiful being pregnant. Quinn laughed.

She ran the water in the sink, washed off the dishes.

"It's good to have you folks here," said Quinn. "Gimme folks to talk to. It's been so quiet here.... Quiet since the pandemic made everybody stay home. Nobody come to the shore. That's the worst part. Nobody coming here. Nobody ta talk to...." He got emotional.

"I can't imagine that," said Hannah, her back to us, washing the dishes.

"I just had my mom to talk to," I shared.

Hannah broke into laughter. "And that's not a conversation you wanna have, lemme tell you."

"What?" I exclaimed.

So, of course, we had to discuss Mom's quirks, her strange ways of thinking, then on to how she'd let herself be tricked into doing all kinds of things she said she wouldn't do but did anyway. We suddenly realized how loud we'd gotten and stopped, noticing our host's consternation.

Sometime during our squabble, Quinn had taken Isla onto his knee, which was probably a safe thing to do.

"Sounds like helluva woman," he offered.

My throat tightened. "She was."

Hannah had finished the dishes. She came to me, gave me a quick hug and sat. "She was one of a kind, that's for sure."

I sat in the chair, numb as memories streamed through me. I couldn't stop them. Flashes of moments lived. Words from Mom. Touches. Scents. Seeing her again in vivid detail – with my eyes wide open. I couldn't speak.

"Sandy?" called Hannah. She glanced over at Quinn as though asking for his help.

Then I broke from my trance. I grinned, embarrassed.

"I'm okay." I took a few breaths. "Just thinking of Mom."

"I know," said Hannah.

I felt tears gather in my eyes, blurring my vision.

"It's okay, Sandy," said Hannah, squatting beside my chair and giving me a hug. "At least she don't hafta deal with this pandemic anymore."

5

THE CASTING OF LINES

Quinn got plenty of fish and set some aside for drying on the porch behind the office – hanging under the big sign facing the sea with an arrow pointing south to the island, as if shooing away boaters from landing on the rocky shore below the motel. The long strings of flesh twisted into jerky under the hot sun. But I had to swing a stick at seagulls trying to steal a bite. He said we could have some of it. He made a gumbo, too, with shrimp and crab, and beans, tomatoes, peppers grown by himself, and corn from a can in his collection. It was delicious. We patted our bellies for the first time in a long time.

"Shore is good ta have a full belly," he announced with both hands framing his expanded gut.

I followed, imitating him.

Then Hannah brought Isla up to her breast. She wasn't shy about rolling up her shirt. We watched a while. Quinn remarked how cute Isla was, keeping his eye ready to catch any glimpse of a nipple. He added how pretty Hannah was then continued his story.

"So there I was, the winning ticket in my hand, waiting for the light to change, and well, sonuvagun, here comes a garbage truck smack into me." Quinn shook his head. "Ticket flew right outta my hand, blowing away across the city, never to be seen again, not by me anyways. Somebody found it, but nothing I could do. A million dollars lost! That's when she done left me. I worked hard, promised to work harder, but she wanted a millionaire, not a sailor."

"That's so sad," said Hannah. She patted his arm. "Just over a lottery ticket."

"Well, there were other things, fer shore, but that lottery was gonna make things right again, ya know? Set us up for life, see. Wouldn't hafta rely on this motel n tourists coming down from the city, catering to all them snooty assholes."

"So what did you do?" I asked him as Hannah shifted Isla to her other breast.

"Why, first I had to sell the boat. No more taking tourists out to fish. Almost had to sell this place but then the pandemic come up and nobody wanted to buy it. Nobody even come down this way. No more vacations to the island. Everybody staying home. No tourists, no income, just hope n pray I kin catch some fish every few days. After the IGA closed, I couldn't get no more fruit or veggies, bread, or even booze. I stocked up all the cans I could get." He smacked his belly with his gnarly hands. "Look at me. I lost damn near fifty pounds since the pandemic started."

He did look thin; the baggy overalls gave him the appearance of being thicker.

"Same for us," I said. "Not getting enough to eat." I told him how Mom improved food production on the island, and how visitors brought supplies and some animals.

"Yeah, I had me some chickens, too, but eventually...yeah, they tasted better being roasted than getting eggs for breakfast, know what I mean?"

"I remember the first morning we had eggs on the island," I said, glancing at Hannah, who grinned back. She'd been so enticed by the smell of fried eggs that she'd walked out of the bedroom that morning before getting dressed.

"Seems yer ma was a real winner fer the island," said Quinn. "Shame y'all couldn't stay."

"Yes, real shame. But she...." I regarded Hannah, got her silent approval. "She was killed. By a man who used to be her friend. And I shot him for it. So they kicked me off the island." I turned to Hannah, holding Isla at milk spigot number two. "And she came with me, my wife and our baby. We're actually running away from the island. But not very far – obviously. We've been exiled."

"Exiled? Like that's a law?" Quinn chuckled.

"There's nothing there for us now anyway," said Hannah. "We have to make our own way now."

"So what're y'all gonna do?" asked Quinn, sitting up.

Hannah and I exchanged looks.

"I guess we gotta go back to where we came from," I said.

"Yeah? Up north?" he asked.

"No. Actually, west."

I told him more about my city, the way things had gotten so bad during the six-year flu season, bad enough that Mom decided we should leave. We waited that long because Mom kept expecting it to end any day. I hadn't said much to Quinn about it up to then. I didn't think it would be good to give out too much information, in case something might not sit well with him. I learned from Mom the benefit of holding back info. She'd grown ever more suspicious of everyone as the months went by. Now I gave Quinn lots of details, thinking he wouldn't mind hearing it. I described incidents of authority overreach, restrictions, empty stores, and violence. He nodded through my telling.

"Just like what I kept hearing from folks that drove down from the north. Sounded even worse than your city," he said, sadness in his voice. "Don't know what's gotten into folks. Big city's a bad enough place to live even in normal times. But me, I need the sea and the sun and lots of fresh air and nobody around – well, except nice folks like you, that is."

"Thank you for your hospitality," said Hannah.

"Yes," I echoed, "thanks again."

Deciding where to go, I thought of the city to the north, a larger metropolis than the city Mom and I left. It had to be worse off than our city. No, that was not the best destination. We had to keep to rural areas – which risked us encountering marauders – and small towns where there may be a few kind people to help us. Like the people joining together to make Pineville, a gathering of country folk who decided to found a new village in a pine forest. Mom and I met them on the way to Aunt Laura's house. Mom played her tuba for them. Maybe we could join a new community, one without the same harsh rules the island had.

"I been here the whole time," said Quinn. "Saw news reports on TV before it went off, but they's far away, ya know? Got my life here by the shore n that's good enough for me. Everybody else done gone away. Good riddance. Hah! Even run out o' facemasks, too. Sold'em for a pretty penny before folks stopped coming down here."

I smiled at his mention of wearing masks. "Mom liked to say all we needed was an island and some fruit trees and a garden plot, fish off-shore and maybe, if we're lucky, some chickens."

"And water," Hannah added. "Don't forget your mom made that distillation thing. Collected rainwater."

"Sounds like a smart woman," said Quinn.

I felt a knot in my gut.

"Sorry about what happened," he said in darker tone, chewing his lips. "Them islanders, not a good bunch. Too strict. Plain weird, if y'ask me. Them n their parties. I could hear'em whooping it up all the way over here. Saw fireworks shoot in the sky at night."

"They do tend to get rowdy," I said with an awkward chuckle.

"And too much sex," said Hannah. "I mean, they're so crazy about sex with each other." She stared hard at me. "We should've been leaving anyway – before anything could happen. If not for all their lame rules, your mom would still be alive."

Anger erupted in me. "It was Bucky who set her up, then got mad when she found out. He had no right to demand anything of her. It had nothing to do with Victor."

"So that's how it happened, huh?" asked Quinn.

"They got caught up in island politics." I had to admit it. "Too many mind games. But Mom play them the best, so the council had to cheat."

"That's too bad," said Quinn. "People can be the shits."

"They sure can," said Hannah and referenced a song by one of her favorite pandemic bands, Viral Dark: 'Black Lab, under a viral sky / Breathe in deep, you're gotta die / Cooking soup / Sneaky group / Spreading their poison all over the world' – meaning the *laboratory*, not the dog.

Quinn roared with laughter. "Them pandemic songs're so wild. Tell me more." He got up too quickly, caught his balance. "Lemme get my guitar. You can teach me some of'em."

The rockers jammed into the evening and I was the babysitter. But Isla loved hearing her mother sing, especially songs from the Wu Crew, Coronas, and Jewel Rhee. Quinn caught on, strumming his guitar to her singing.

They jammed late into the night.

I took Isla back to the room, changed her diaper, played a while until she went to sleep. I lay on the bed listening to the music at the other end of the building. They sounded good. But the pauses between songs got longer and longer. Then I didn't hear any music for a while and I, too, fell asleep.

When I awoke later in the night, Hannah was beside me on the bed, and everything became real again. In my dream I was back in the apartment with Mom and she was teasing me once more about us having to repopulate the world if we found we were the last two people.

Feeling Hannah against me, I knew what was real. There was a pandemic and we were on our own. Then an explosion in my gut and the thought filled me that *I* was alone. Actually, I was on my own. My wife and baby were extra, loved by me, sure, yet somehow on their own paths – paths which might diverge from mine at any moment.

It was time to leave, I knew. I could feel it the next morning, as the sun rose behind a bank of blue clouds, sending pink and orange rays down over the silvery sea. The trees on the hills above the motel shimmered in the breeze. Something was shifting. Autumn was arriving.

6

THE ANGRY SEA

For years Mom had teased me about us having to repopulate the world. Having me at sixteen, we were close in age and she was still attractive. But she would eventually be too old. It was hopeless. We both knew it, but she enjoyed teasing me anyway. Then I met my cousin Hannah. Doing our best to pretend we were married, we followed the strict rules of the island and produced a baby, the start of their breeding program to repopulate the island.

Owen, the island's creepy leader, begged Hannah to stay, had offered to lessen her daily tasks, but she came with me, accepting a harsh new life on the road – but then we settled in this abandoned hamlet just across the strait. She had to be wishing she stayed. She was scheduled to pair with Owen's nephew, Jackson, after me. He'd won her lottery. She would've been well cared for, I was sure. I wondered if she was thinking the same thing.

A storm was coming. I awoke early, sensing it. The wind was blowing hard against the motel walls.

I got up, kissed Hannah's cheek and Isla's tiny foot, and went out, careful to lock the door behind me. I made my way around to the back of the motel where I could watch the angry sea rant and rave. The sky was dark, clouds low.

The waves were foamy, crashing hard against the rocks below the bluff. I watched a while, knowing autumn was here. I breathed in the cool salt air and felt a thousand years old. It felt like we'd always been on this side of the strait and I couldn't remember anything that happened before.

I leaned against the wooden railing, elbows between vegetable planters. My work on the island with the community garden came in handy when Quinn gave me another task. He had me go around the hamlet pilfering pieces of wood from the other buildings. Then we built a few planters. We filled them with soil from bags he'd stacked in one of the motel's rooms. Then we planted seeds he'd saved and waited.

They were growing, I saw. They sprouted out of the gentle soil, reaching for the sun just as the cloudy days approached. Just when you think everything's going to be all right, clouds appear. Mom would've said that, with a smirk.

I could smell him before he spoke. Quinn liked to smoke the same stinky weed the people on the island liked. The sour scent stuck to him even hours later. It stuck to anyone near him, too. When they stayed up playing songs his smell covered Hannah and she brought it back, made the room smell like him. I guess I just had a sensitive nose.

"Couldn't sleep?" Quinn asked, sidling up to me. He rested his cane against the railing. We both leaned there, our eyes on the sea.

"A storm is coming," I spoke.

"Been coming for years," he said with a grunt. "Be coming plenty more years. Yep, long after us."

He wore a once-white t-shirt now soiled with brown sweat stains and spotted from cooking meals, and a pair of dirty, ripped blue jeans. He was barefoot as usual, his feet dirty and toes ugly, unkempt. His greasy beard fought the wind.

"Looks like this gonna be a bad one." He glanced at the motel, turned his head to survey the roof. "Your room should be tight."

I followed his gaze, looking for broken tiles. "I sure hope so." I told him about the previous year and the storms we endured on the island for several weeks of a southern winter.

"I remember...."

My eyes fixed on a white patch among the blue waves. It slid through them like a shark on the hunt. I recognized it was a boat. Actually, it was a yacht. Its sails pulled hard as it tacked back and forth, trying to make its way out to deeper water and away from the rocks.

"Look," I told Quinn, pointing seaward.

"Not a good day for fishing," he grumbled.

"Probably heading for safer water. I heard they like to be at sea during a storm, so they don't bash against the docks."

I stared harder. By its configuration and direction I guessed it was Victor's yacht, departing from the harbor at the south end of the island. He arrived months ago, docking his yacht beside the community center. They ran a cable from his yacht, with its solar panels, to power the community center for a while each day. He'd taken it out fishing a few times but mostly it stayed beside the wharf.

"I know that boat," I said to the wind.

"Yeah?" Quinn put his hand up to focus. "Lotta boats sail by, escaping from up north. Had one crash here while back. Hit hard, one died. The other tried to climb up the bluff."

"And...?"

"Oh, he got to the top." Quinn gave me a look. "I tried to be a decent fella, but this one, well, he weren't willing to accept my help. Not like you folks. Tried stealing from me. I caught him, told him to get on down the road."

"I guess he left then."

"You'd think. But, no. Yeah, he thought he could take me on. Returned at night, tried to get me." He made the motion of a knife stabbing his belly, then raised his shirt to show a scar. "I swear, it doesn't pay to be nice to some folks. If you're kind to a stranger, they know your weakness, and they can get you there when they wanna put ya down."

"I guess so." My head filled with imagined details of that scene. I regarded Quinn, counted his age again, wondering if I would ever be that old. Then I looked out at the sea, searching for that yacht among the waves. I could no longer see it.

"You folks can come down for breakfast," said Quinn, back stiff as he straightened up. "I'm fixing some biscuits."

"Thanks," I said as he stepped off.

Alone again, I had thoughts which disturbed me. I realized I no longer liked him. We had to leave, had to go somewhere else, make our own way.

Hannah was awake and getting ready when I returned. We went down to the office. It seemed normal but felt awkward – as though I could see things I hadn't been able to see previously, the light shining brighter.

"I'm sorry, but we'll have to be going soon," I spoke at the end of the meal, interrupting another conversation about bands. It felt like the wrong thing to say, out of place. They paused to give me a look, waiting for further explanation. But I had none and they continued their discussion.

"I wrote a ditty about how all the cemeteries would be full and what to do with the bodies then," said Quinn, ignoring me. He sang a few lines. Funeral pyres was the answer. His lyrics weren't any better than Hannah's made-up songs, but she liked it, laughed a bit, tried singing along.

"'Burn in Hell / My precious belle'," sang my wife happily. "'Your time is done / It was fun / Sucking on that gun' – like that?"

"That's purdy good, li'l missy," said Quinn.

I recalled Bucky saying 'little missy' when Hannah came out naked to the kitchen in our beach house that morning when the first eggs were fried for breakfast. Mom and Bucky were nude, too, coming straight from the bedroom.

I stared at Quinn. I looked at Hannah, grinning at their music.

"Hey!" I snapped.

"What's wrong?" Hannah barked.

"I said we need to be leaving soon."

"Heard ya," said Quinn, acting serious. "So where ya going?"

I lost my focus. "Somewhere. Not here. We have to go back and check on our other family members."

"That sounds fair," said Quinn.

"But you said we're fine here," said Hannah. "You said it's as comfortable a place as we're likely to find."

I had to change my tack. "Yes, it's been good. A chance to rest and make plans. But we never expected to stay here. Not across the channel from that evil island. Didn't we always intend to get Aunt Laura and Bootsy?"

Hannah nodded, thinking. "I guess so. But I thought we...that we changed our plans."

"Is this a good place to raise a child?" I asked her.

Quinn got up, put his guitar away. "Looks like a squabble for y'all, not fer me." He left.

Hannah and I stared at each other. Her eyes wondered why I said what I said. I reached for Isla, took her into my arms. Hannah got up in a huff and stormed away.

✳   ✳   ✳

I stayed firm in my plan to leave. The question was where to go or, more importantly, how to go. Jackie's house and Laura's house were in different directions. Coming to the island, Mom had taken a circuitous route, avoiding highways and main roads. If we went as directly as possible, how long would it take? We'd be walking and carrying our gear, plus a baby. And guns.

"Need a map?" asked Quinn, walking up to the open door of our room in the evening and overhearing our discussion. "I got some those paper maps in the office. Plenty of'em. Nobody use them no more on account of them GPS things on their phones. But I like to open them suckers up and get the big picture."

I looked up from where I lay on the bed with Isla beside me.

"Besides, they ain't got no GPS now, with the whole grid being down." He laughed.

Outside, behind Quinn, a light but steady rain fell but the cool breeze was delightful, a reason to keep the door open. He'd gotten wet walking down to us despite keeping close to the wall.

"Sure," I said. Hannah remained quiet, her mood sour.

"If y'all want dinner, I got sumpin I fixed up." He grinned at Hannah. "Might look like pizza but it might not taste like pizza."

We followed him back to the office and gathered around the table. He had indeed made something flat and round, covered with tomato pieces and pepper dices. A few shrimp in the middle. But there was no actual sauce and no cheese.

"You hafta use yer imagination. Made the dough all myself but getting low on flour." I tried to avoid imagining his dirty fingers kneading the dough.

It was burned on the bottom, sitting over an open flame out back where the grill was, the hood protecting it from the rain. But it tasted good compared to granola bars and dried apricots we had been planning for our dinner.

After we ate, Quinn took a map from a box of maps in a cabinet and we spread the map on the table.

"Here's us," he said, pointing to the spot on the map where the ferry ran in dotted lines to the barrier island. "Your island. So if you go this way...." He pointed to the black line beside the motel's location. "You can reach this highway in about an hour walking. Then you can either go right and continue to the big city, if that's your choice, or you go left and swing down along the coast for a ways before it turns west – there's a big hill to climb – and you go away from the coast after that."

"That must be the hill we came down coming to the island," said Hannah.

"I wonder how far it is to Aunt Laura's," I spoke, staring at the map. I told Quinn the town where she lived but it was off the map. He dug in the box, found a map for her state, opened it upon the table, continued measuring. "It took a whole day driving, and Mom was driving all around, not going directly."

"If yer going by foot it's gonna take some time, that's fer shore. Maybe a week or two. You kin only walk about twenty miles a day, at best. Carrying all you got, and hills."

"We'll just have to manage," I said, firm in my conviction.

"But why do we have to go?" asked Hannah suddenly. Then she brightened at a new thought. "How about me and Isla stay here and you go get Aunt Laura and Bootsy? You could travel lighter that way. Leave the tuba here. It'll be quicker."

"But what if I...."

We heard the rain hitting the pavement outside.

"What?" asked Hannah roughly.

"If something happens. If I don't make it...."

Hannah's face paled. "Don't you say that." Her color returned. "Besides, if something bad happened, you'll at least know your wife and baby are safe, right?"

Our eyes met awkwardly when I straightened up from reading the map. Something was different there.

"I guess so."

"Great," said Hannah, practically singing. "So it's decided. We'll stay and you go."

But it didn't sound right when she said it the second time. Too much cheer in her voice. I narrowed my eyes.

"I think it's best if we all go." My tone was firm. "Maybe we'll want to stay there. Maybe everything will be fine there. So I wouldn't want to have to come back here just to get you and then make the trip all over again. We have to go together."

Quinn stood outside the squared circle, satisfied to watch us scrabble. Hannah looked at him, maybe hoping for support, but he gave her no response.

"Anyway, we gotta wait for the rain to stop," she said, some sadness in her voice. "Probably be a few days."

7

AN AWKWARD TRUTH

A few days was right. We stayed in the room, mostly stayed on the bed. I thought we should make love again. It had been a while, but Hannah said she wasn't ready. She was still sore from the birth. Not knowing anything about that stuff, I had to believe her, even if I didn't.

"I'm afraid," she said long after we went to sleep.

I was trying to sleep but just tossing and turning, keeping her from sleeping. I gave up and opened my eyes, then scooted upright against the headboard.

"It's normal to be afraid," I said. "In these hard times, who isn't afraid? Anything could get you. Things you can't even see. Or even people that've turned crazy."

"All of that," she purred. I expected she'd scrunch against me, seeking comfort and security, but she didn't.

"That's why we have to stick together. Like Mom said."

"You and your mom."

"She was my whole life."

"I lost my mother, too, don't forget."

I reached for her in the dark, tried to wrap my arm around her shoulders but she didn't come closer to make it easy.

"We are both wounded souls," I said, not knowing where I got that line from.

Then she rolled against me, and we embraced. I could feel her soul slow-dancing with mine. We parted with a kiss.

"There's only one thing to do," I said, my voice gentle. "We just have to keep living. We have to hold on. We have to outlast this pandemic. And we need to raise Isla to carry on after us. That's our minimum job."

"So you expect she'll find a good guy and just make babies like I did?" Her voice had a hint of amusement. "So trad. I can't believe I'm even thinking that might be the only way. It's what Mother told me to do. No college and career for me. Get with a good, strong man, and take care of him so he'll take care of me, she told me."

"Hard times require hard decisions," I chanted. "Same for me. I suppose I was going to become a professor like Mom, but that path is gone now. I never thought of me being a father."

"I know we can't change our circumstances to be what we want. But we sure don't hafta give in so easy. I just want our daughter to do whatever she wants to do. As much as she can."

"But there aren't the same choices available now that used to be, like for my mom when she was a poor single mother with a tuba. She made her own way, no help from her family."

"Yeah, good for her. But Isla is different. Isla is special. I don't mean special like you are, Sandy. I mean, she's our little girl, so we have special ambitions for her. Other kids we don't care about — except they stay out of trouble for the good of the community."

"The community...." I had to sigh.

"Could we even start a community that would be the way we want it to be?"

"Owen used that science fiction book, well, used some of it but rejected other ideas in it. Like it was the Bible."

"He's a fat loser."

"But people followed his orders."

"They couldn't've been afraid of him."

"He did have a few buddies to enforce the by-laws."

"So he was a pathetic dictator with thugs."

I laughed. "Okay, that's him, all right."

"If we stay here, we could have our own community."

"Just us? It's going to take a long time to build it up. And what about Quinn? He'll die soon. Either way, we're going to need two or three other families. Then pair up the kids as they reach the age."

"Geez, Sandy, you sound just like Owen."

I huffed at that comparison. "It's social science. You need a few couples to have any viable community. I mean, genetically. People with skills, too. To do everything that's needed. Grow food. Protect the people. Raise the kids."

"Yeah, you got that figured out, huh?"

"Just following your comments." I took a few breaths, talking myself through the calming steps. "But we have to get Laura and Bootsy first. I promised Mom. She promised them."

"So, like I suggested...me and Isla stay here and you go get'em and bring'em here. That's the best way."

Aaargh! I could not reason with this woman!

* * *

It didn't take much to work myself into a rage. Mom knew it, knew what signs to watch for and could intervene before I went into a full-blown meltdown. If I got to that point I would lash out, unable to stop myself, raging like a madman until my energy was spent. So I had to catch myself before I reached that point. However, it was the small things that were most likely to set me off, like if my computer didn't do something like it was supposed to. Out here, I didn't need to worry about computers, just gangs of thugs or clouds of viruses or starvation. The big things I could handle.

Hannah knew about my Aspie traits, but she didn't know the signs to watch for to keep me from exploding, so it was up to me to be aware of myself and how things were affecting me.

So I made myself take everything I noticed and put them away in the right compartments. I wasn't being paranoid. There were explanations. Everything had to be logical. Yet I worried – worried about nothing, Hannah would say. But I kept it all inside, afraid to let any of my suspicions out in case it might make me look foolish.

"Don't be stupid," she would tell me, her usual phrase, then take it back when she saw how she hurt me.

It built up over the weeks. We talked often about going and we talked about staying, the age-old question. Is what we have better than what we might gain if we go to another place? Or could we die in the attempt? I fought with myself. I was afraid to bring them with me and afraid to leave them behind. Both were dangerous; it wasn't merely my mind freaking out.

Yet Hannah remained happy, as much as anyone could be after suffering at the cruel hands of the pandemic world and an island community that saw her as a breeding commodity. She wanted to frolic on the beach and sing songs like any teenage girl. But she'd been tied to me, supposedly to save her. She seemed to alternately resist it and embrace it. She was good to me. She was certainly a good mother to our daughter.

I could smell the old man's scent on her. It was smoky, like the grilled fish we ate, but there was something more. She returned to our room not as late as usual, so I asked why she was early.

"What do you mean?" she countered, acting like it was a dumb question to ask.

I pointed out she usually came back later, after I fell asleep. Like she was waiting for me to be asleep to avoid any risk of sex. I mentioned the period of music followed by the period of silence.

"You work hard," she said, sitting on the bed. "Of course you fall asleep early. I don't mind. Get your rest."

"It's not that. I would stay up for you."

"Oh, I get it." She fake-laughed. "You wanna fuck. That it?"

I was glad the room was dark. My face probably showed my frustration. Then she lit the candle.

"Well, yes," I replied. "It's what couples do. Okay, maybe not every night, but sometimes. We used to do that a lot."

"Yeah," she chuckled, "a whole lot." Sitting back, braced on her arms, her shirt stretched to show her bare belly. "But then I had a baby. That's a lot of stress on the parts, ya know. They need time to recover."

"How much time?" I shook my head, wanting to dismiss the bad question. "I'm sorry. Whenever you're ready."

Laying back on the bed, I stared at the ceiling. Discoloration marked where leaks had let rain through. Our perfect world with a stain.

"It's not like I'm avoiding you," she announced.

"Avoiding me? I never thought that." But I did think of that. "You're just never around. Like we live in different homes. You spend all your time with him."

"With Quinn?" She seemed shocked I'd say that. "Who else is here?"

"Me!" That blew out like an old tire. I couldn't catch it before it hit her.

"But I fucking sleep with you!" she shouted back.

"Yeah, sleep. Only sleep. Not 'sleep with' me."

"You're outta your freaking mind, Sandy. Don't be stupid."

She immediately tried to take it back, like she always did. She even scooted over to me, trying to give me a hug as she apologized. I curled my arms around her to complete the circle, but it didn't feel right. Too artificial. I knew it was when we parted.

"What's going on with him?" I asked plainly.

She studied me in the candlelight. "Nothing."

"What do you mean, nothing?"

"We didn't do anything," she growled. "Geez, Sandy."

"He's a dirty old man. I mean dirty like in doesn't bathe."

"He takes a shower...sometimes. That's beside the point really. He's been good to us. You have to agree. He let us stay here, in this room. He shares his food supply with us."

"I work for that. Do all kinds of tasks for him. My labor for our food. He pays us with that stuff."

"He's old. He can't do those things himself." Her face was tense. "And he's kind to us...."

I wondered why she said the last part. Kind how? What did she mean by adding that? I needed an example of this kindness.

"What did you do?"

"Do...?" She paused, fumbled for words. "He's teaching me to play guitar."

"But after the lessons? When I don't hear anymore music? In the silence."

She looked like a deer frozen in headlights. "Silence...?"

The room gave us an excellent example of silence.

"What did you do?" I said.

She got up from the bed, stood with her hand to her face, the other resting on her hip. It was a half-sorry, half-not-sorry stance.

"He's been good to us. What was I supposed to do when he asks for a favor?"

"What favor?" When she didn't answer quick enough I had to repeat my question in harsher tone.

"He said I was pretty and wanted to touch me. I said okay. He's been really good to us, so I thought it was fair. So I lifted my shirt. He said my stretch marks aren't so bad. They add character. He put his fingers on them. That's all."

"That's all?" I counted how many steps I had remaining before my meltdown. "Is it all?"

But she shook her head.

"He said it was a long time. He wanted one more time before he died. To lay with a woman. He said 'lay' and meant just holding, not sex. He can't do anything anyway, not at his age. He wanted to hold me a while. So we got on the couch there and he put his arms around me."

She began to sob. I didn't know if it was real or fake.

"But he's not very clean," I said.

"I know, but...he was so sad. I felt sorry for him."

My throat tightened. "How could you?"

"He had his arms around me, like we was spooning, ya know. Then he asked if we could do that but without any clothes on."

"What!"

"I got up and I took off everything. He watched me with such love in his eyes. Besides, he's seen my tits when I'm nursing Isla. I didn't think it was a big deal."

"But you were naked!"

"Like it's a big deal to you – you and your nudist mom."

"That's different."

"Is it?" She shook her head. "We got on the couch again, in the same position. He put his hands over my tits. He pressed against me from behind. He said my skin was so smooth and pure, and his was rough and dirty. Said it was the last thing he wanted, to be able to hold a beautiful girl in his arms before he died."

"Is he going to die soon?" It wasn't all sarcastic.

"Then he put his hand between my legs and I didn't mind. He said it was years since he was with a woman and would I mind laying with him, just holding each other. And since he's kind to us I couldn't say 'no'. So I did it. I held him in my arms. He liked that, and he thanked me for that."

"Just like that?" My eyes narrowed. "That's all? No sex."

"No sex. He can't do anything."

"Nothing?"

I shook my head, had to turn away. I couldn't decide if this was categorized as a betrayal or not. An indiscretion? I'd read stories, seen TV shows about this sort of thing. I had no idea how to handle it. When Mom took up with Bucky, I didn't feel betrayed. But I had Hannah then.

"Okay, you did it because he asked you. You felt sorry for him, so it was an act of pity, of...charity."

"Yeah, of course." She made a face like I was asking another stupid question. "He wasn't very clean. And smelling of all that weed he smokes. It wasn't like it was fun."

"I can smell that on you every night when you come home."

"You smell that way if you spend time in the same room with him. You don't have to lay with him for that."

"But you did...."

She took a long breath. "Yes. I did. Because he asked me."

"How far would you go...if he asked you?"

"I already said he's impotent. Can't do anything." She thought a moment. "Okay, he did get excited, being up against me. But..."

"But what?"

"He took care of that himself," she answered.

It was my turn to take deep breaths. "Okay, okay."

I felt my meltdown boiling but still under control. It was at the point where I could let it go into full-blown rage or still dial it back. It depended on what I wanted to do. Did I really want to explode? Would that make me feel better?

Or, on the other hand, did I want to be the wimpy kid again and let people walk all over me without me fighting back, without showing my displeasure at events? Who did I want to be? She had said previously, when we were on the island, that I could be violent when it was necessary but, because I was a 'good' man, I could turn it off when it wasn't needed. I could control myself.

In the light of one candle, I stared hard at her, this woman, my wife, then swung my hand. I intended to slap her face hard but, not measuring the distance accurately, only my fingertips struck her. Too light to hurt her, but she got the idea. Then I went out, behind the motel, scrambling over the rocks to the very edge of the bluff, staring out at the sea. I imagined how shockingly cold its depths would be if I were to jump.

8

A DISTANT DESTINY

Whenever Mom was upset, sad or afraid – or even happy! – or just needed time to think, she would pull Timmy into her lap and play, sometimes music from her repertoire, other times songs she made up as she played them. She was good, could pull beauty from that metal tubing in such a way you thought God was singing in His great *basso profundo* voice, filling the whole universe, frightening yet reassuring at the same time.

So following her example, I took out Mom's tuba and pulled it on my lap and blew long notes until my breath ran out. It was a kind of dying swan, I mused. Mom had taught me the basics, what keys to push for each note, and how to move my mouth and use my tongue, but I never practiced much. There was never time; Mom was always playing the tuba. But Mom was a professional, a full member of the Symphony back before the pandemic ruined it all.

I knew a few songs, simple tunes a child might sing, so I played those as best as I could remember. Repeated them. I got better. Gradually I felt warmed up and tried harder music like what Mom played. Nope – not for me. Mom could do it, had played the tricky passages with grace or, as needed, with bold verve. I returned to the simple tunes, feeling silly at daring to try something harder. I could never match Mom.

Before she was killed, Mom made up a few songs and wrote them down on staff paper I made for her. I took those sheets with me when I was exiled. How could I leave them? They were part of her. So I set them out and tried to play them. The result wasn't much better. I didn't have the skill to bring the notes to life.

"Is it enough already?" called Hannah from inside our room. "I'm getting a headache."

It was right in the middle of a song Mom titled "Sandy's Bride": a kind of hopeful-sounding waltz with phrases that kept landing in a minor key. Clearly the awkward flop on the final notes of the phrases was intentional, not a slip of the ink. Mom knew more than me, it seemed.

I tried to be kind, moving outside, to the far end of the motel, setting my chair there and aiming the bell of the tuba out to sea. With the weather cool and breezy, overcast, no one would notice a tuba blending in. But she was still annoyed.

Maybe I had played enough – enough to get some emotions out of me, enough to show my displeasure with her.

Displeasure is a funny word. Lack of pleasure, pleasure being the root, the main thing, the default position. Not having it was a mistake. Pleasure was the desired effect. She was denying me *pleasure*. The word made sense. But what was pleasure? Whose responsibility was it? Was it the same as *satisfaction*? Or some lesser thing? Was displeasure the equivalent to pain? Not having pleasure was not the same as its opposite. It was an absence of something.

Without a verbal response, I packed up the tuba and ended my pleasure. I understood the satisfaction Mom got from time spent with her little man, who she loved before I was born and all the days after, like he was my big brother.

Maybe Hannah hadn't done anything truly wrong. What were the rules anyway? Had we set any? I never expected I needed to make rules for *that*. She would just know what was allowed and what was not. She was my wife. She should do what was best for us as a couple. That was the deal we made. Did I need to say more to make that clear? I thought it was so obvious it didn't need to be stated. But we never had an actual wedding to share our vows.

I arrived at our room's open door only a minute ahead of Quinn coming from the opposite direction.

"You done with your homage to your mother?" my wife sneered. She seemed to get pleasure from that.

I didn't answer, setting the tuba in the corner.

"Hey, kids," said Quinn, appearing in the doorway in torn shirt and dirty jeans, a grimace on his face.

Hannah greeted him like he was always welcome – a reverent tone suggesting he was the boss you always needed to show respect to or you'd lose your job, but also the grandfather you loved no matter how bad he smelled.

I forced a quick smile, just to be polite.

"Heard ya playin that thing," said Quinn with a chuckle. "Ya sounded purdy good. Better'n expected."

"I need more practice," I responded, my voice flat.

I told him about Mom previously, so he knew the tuba's history. He wondered why we would want to carry the tuba around with a pandemic going on. Because it's special, a huge token of memory, I told him. There was still some magic to it.

"I don't know if I can stand more practice," said Hannah with a sour laugh. Clearly she got pleasure from teasing me.

Quinn laughed with her. "If yer still planning on leaving, you kin leave that here. I'll look after it. You won't hafta carry it."

He glanced at Hannah, who was holding squirming Isla, then back at me.

"Promise not to touch it," he said. "Heck, I dunno how ta play a thing like that. Take good care of it, anyways. We can lock it in the room and nobody'll touch it. You gotta be able to move fast out there. Can't let the vagrants catch ya."

Then he swept a hand over his head, through memories of the mop of hair that no longer lay there.

"Shore hate ta see y'all going. But I unnerstand, gotta check on yer folks. Gonna fret over ya, anyhows."

"He's right," said Hannah, her attention on Isla but giving me a glance. "Things are different now."

I wasn't sure what she meant. Different between her and me, or in the outerlands? Likely both. I felt that. Ultimately, if I were to die, I wouldn't care what happened to Mom's tuba. It was just a bunch of metal tubing. Melt it down, make bullets for all I cared.

"Hey, listen, kids," Quinn spoke up, excitement in his voice.

"What's up?" asked Hannah.

He grabbed his excitement, packed it away. "Oh...nothin much, just...." He gave me a sly look, jerked his head slightly to indicate we should go outside. "Canna talk ta ya a sec?"

Stepping out, he waved his hand for me to follow. Hannah got up, shifted Isla in her arms, acting upset that we men were going out without her, like we ordered her to stay home with the kid. That gave me a smidgen of pleasure.

"Be right back," I assured her.

"Whatever," she snarled.

Quinn led me half-way across the parking lot.

"Where we going?" I asked.

He glanced back at our room, waving for me to follow him.

When we were out of sight of the motel, he slowed, acted like his knee hurt, leaning on his cane.

"Listen now," said Quinn, stopping in the street as though he'd heard something and needed to check for another sound.

I stared at him, waiting for whatever might happen next. I felt the weight of Mom's pistol tucked in my belt at the small of my back. My hand slid behind, took hold of the grip, ready.

"What is it?" I asked in a low voice, as though vagrants hid around the corners of nearby buildings, ready to pounce.

"I just wanna say," he spoke softly. His hand scratched at his ragged beard. "See, I couldn't help o'erhearin y'all fighting."

"Fighting?" Glancing around, I made sure no vagrants were close enough to hear us.

"Yeah," he said and took a long draw of breath. "So I wanna set things straight. See, yer missus ain't ta blame. It were all me. All my fault. I just.... I'm a sad sack sonuvabitch. I knows it. Missed being touched, ya know? And she's...god she's purdy. Wanna just hold somebody. One more time in my life. What she done was pure charity. Act o' charity for a worthless ol' bastard. Don't be mad at her, okay? She's a good person. She's got a kind heart. You's one lucky sonuvagun."

That wasn't what I expected and my hand slipped down to my side, the pistol in it.

Seeing the pistol, Quinn stepped back, hands raised. "Hey, I apologize. There weren't no sex, believe me. I cain't do nothing no how. I'm soft as biscuit dough no matter what I do."

The pistol was in my hand, so I raised it, pointing the gun at him. I didn't feel any anger at him in that moment. But I did recall how it felt to raise the pistol when I shot Bucky after he stabbed Mom. It was so automatic, like my hand knew what to do and did it before my mind could reason through it and make a decision. Less than a heartbeat to act. This felt different. I was pausing to reason it through. Certainly if he had hurt Hannah at all, I'd feel differently.

But I lowered my hand.

"Okay," I said, and Quinn relaxed.

"I'm sorry." He lowered his hands. "This why I brung ya out here, away from her, so we kin talk man to man and she won't hear nothing."

"You're freaking seventy years old," I growled, not calm but maintaining control. "What were you thinking?"

"Well now, I'm actually *freaking* eighty," he grunted. "And I was thinking how nice it'd be to just hold somebody for a moment. One freaking moment, is all."

"But naked? She said you got her to take off her clothes."

"Yeah, that's right," he snapped back at me like it was the most obvious thing. "Cuz ya gotta be skin to skin for energy to transfer. Ever'body know that."

"Energy? Transfer? What?" I felt stupid, like I had no right to protest against something so profound as 'energy transfer'.

"Yeah, it's old magic. Folk stuff. See, people got energy in them and you kin transfer t'another person. I shore felt a lotta energy from that hug, being against her. Prolly gimme another year o' life. She's full of energy. But yew prolly knew that."

Oh, yes, I remembered. Once we'd finally gotten it done on the beach, she was constantly pulling me to our bed. I was tired from working all day yet there she was insisting we make love again and again. I barely got any sleep.

"Sorta," I responded and couldn't hide my grin.

"That's all it was," he said, his eyes looking sad. I believed his apology: he was sorry. And not just for getting caught.

"Okay," I said, studying his eyes. Mom said eyes never lie. "I believe you. And I accept your apology."

"Good, good." He regained his composure. "Anyways, I wanna show ya something. Call it a gift. On account of me being sorry to lay with yer woman."

"Without my permission," I added as he took a step ahead.

"Well, see—" He coughed. "On that matter she done told me she didn't need nobody's permission. See, I asked if it was awright n all. She said she was her own person, not yer property. I asked her the same thing n she said her body was hers n could do wit' as she pleased." Chuckles followed. "I's just the lucky sonuvagun she pleased to do with for my benefit."

That made whatever pleasure I got from his apology evaporate away. Everything was raw again.

He continued down the street, gesturing me to follow.

I remembered Hannah saying the same thing at the beach when we had the festival. She said she was with me because she wanted to be but that I didn't own her. She wasn't *mine*; she was hers but willing to be with me. And I suppose I was with her by choice, too. Each of us could walk away at any time. But now we had Isla so we had to stick together.

Quinn led us between a few buildings to another building left abandoned. *Shorty's Garage*, the sign read. It had seen better days, like most places abandoned through this long flu season.

We went inside, saw cars in the service bay. One sedan was up on the rack, no power to lower it. Another was down with its hood up, repairs underway. A third car, a small blue hatchback, looked like its work had been completed and was awaiting someone to claim it and drive it away. Maybe the car's owner had died and so never came to get it.

"This one's got gas," said Quinn, pointing to the hatchback. "I checked. Yeah, maybe it's old, but maybe it's good enough. Hafta crank it over n see. But I didn't wanna waste even one drop."

"We ran out of gas coming to the island," I reported, looking over the car. It seemed as old as Mom's car. Fully gas powered. Not one of the hybrids. Small gasoline cars were still allowed, if driven on your days of the week, indicated by your license plate number. I ducked my head inside to have a look. It was still fairly clean, the windows being up.

"If yer plannin' to leave, maybe it kin get y'all some o' the way."

That idea lit me up. If it worked, we could get to Aunt Laura's in a day instead of having to walk for two weeks or more.

"Been saving it in case I need ta get outta town fast." He stood back like he was showing off his prize hot rod. "Ya know, like if a hurricane come through. I kin just throw my bag in back n way I go, though I got no idea where to. Somewhere inland, s'pose, away from the storm."

"Got keys?" I straightened up from checking the interior.

Quinn reached in his pocket, produced his big set of keys.

"Here ya go." He pulled off the car's keys, tossed them to me.

"Thanks," I said, catching them.

"Yer lady's shore gonna light up seeing this li'l chariot."

"It *is* a chariot," I said, ready to laugh.

"A lady like her, gotta treat her right, if ya know whatta mean. She won't stand fer less."

9

THE GLOAMING

Hannah brought Isla outside when I drove the hatchback up to the door of our room, giving a honk as I shut off the engine. The fuel gauge showed just over half a tank. The engine had sputtered a bit at first then turned over. Quinn and I pumped up the tires and it was ready to roll. I backed out, drove like I had to get to the motel before it stopped running.

She bounced our baby in her arms, pointing to the car, talking to her about it. They both smiled like it was Christmas morning. That sight gave me pleasure.

"See what we found?" I called, getting out and shutting the car door behind me. "Now we can drive. Probably get to Aunt Laura's in a day now."

Hannah shifted Isla. "So you got it."

"Got it?" I was puzzled.

"Where's Quinn?" she asked.

"I left him over at the garage where I got this car, a few blocks that way." I started explaining how we would go, and the packing that was needed.

Now, having a backseat, we could take Mom's tuba with us. I thought the chance of returning to this dismal shore seemed more remote. That made me happy, too.

"If only we could find a car seat," Hannah said, cutting through my enthusiasm.

"You mean for Isla?" I hadn't thought about that.

"Of course. Don't you know about babies?" She laughed.

"You sit with her in back and I'll drive slow."

"That's not good enough," she countered in a more serious tone. "What if we get hit by a truck?"

That memory still shook us. Mom was driving, talking on and on about how music would save us, and a big black truck came out of nowhere, hitting us from the side. Her tuba was damaged. We weren't injured but one of the two men from the truck attacked Hannah. I put a pistol to his head, ordering him to get off her, but the gun went off, killing him.

"It was an accident," I mumbled, again convincing myself, and Hannah asked what I said. I waved her off. "You're right."

"Of course, I am." She almost laughed, like she wanted to laugh but dared not show me she was happy, catching it in her throat before it could get all the way out.

By then, Quinn had hobbled back to the motel. We turned and watched him approach. When he got to our room, he gave the car a loving pat on the hood.

"So, guess you kids'll be off soon," he said in a rough voice, then broke into coughing.

"Isn't that the reason you showed me this car?" I asked.

"I told you ever'thing. It was s'posed to be my getaway car for hurricanes." He looked over the car. "Besides, not my style. I need a vehicle that cuts through waves. Runs with the wind." He tried to laugh but failed. "Used ta have a real muscle car. That was long ago. When I was about your age."

I clapped my hands together, then recognized it as my mom's habit. "Then it's settled. We'll pack and leave in the morning."

"So soon?" Hannah and Quinn responded the same time, then glanced at each other.

"Every day we wait here, something bad could happen to Aunt Laura and Bootsy." Actually, I wanted to be away from this creepy old man. I wanted to take Hannah away from him. "We've been here long enough, haven't we? It's hardly an exile if we can still see the damn island." I turned to Quinn: "Of course, thanks for your hospitality."

"My pleasure," said Quinn, reaching out his gnarly hand.

After an awkward moment I extended my hand and we shook hands, man to man.

"Enjoyed havin y'all here. Gonna miss y'all, cain't lie." He got emotional, wiped his eyes. "Y'all welcome here any time."

Hannah gave me Isla and went to him, hugged him. Then he kissed her cheek and she didn't even wipe it away with her hand. Isla grabbed at my nose, gurgling words, like she wondered who that old man was.

"Are you with me?" I asked Hannah after they parted, and my heart fluttered as I prepared to hear her declare that she wanted to stay.

"I'm with you, Sandy," she responded instead but keeping a sad look on her face.

"Well awrighty then," Quinn said softly. "Good luck ta ya."

He gave a wave and limped up the walk to the office.

The rest of the day we packed our meager belongings. We got some food, supplies, and water from Quinn. We had to take some but I didn't want to take too much that it would make life difficult for him. I'd gotten the vegetable planters going, so he would have those. The distillation rig would replenish his water supply or he could continue boiling what came out of the tap.

The bathroom was a forest of freshly washed diapers, each awaiting its turn on a baby's bottom, catching deposits. Hannah worked on her hands and knees scrubbing them in the tub. I asked her if she wouldn't mind washing a few of my clothes for the trip and she accepted. I apologized for having her do that.

"That's what a wife is for," she muttered, sounding displeased. "Ain't that right? It's in the by-laws."

"No, it's not," I said, surprised she would mention that. "I just asked for a favor. I'm not expecting you to do all the household chores. There's nothing in the by-laws about chores."

"There's no fucking by-laws this side of the ferry landing," she grumbled, scrubbing her shorts in the tub.

I sighed, not wanting to get into an argument. "Okay, I'll do the laundry next time. We're a team, after all."

Watching her on her knees at the tub, wearing nothing but an old ragged pair of panties while washing the rest of her clothes, I remembered how we used to play in bed every night. I loved how we explored each other. I missed that time. Now there was always work to be done.

She turned, reaching back for the next item in the pile, and her hand hit my leg. She had to notice my attention on her. Gazing up at me, holding our daughter on my shoulder, a grin flickered across her face, like she could read my mind.

"If you wanna, let's do it," she said, getting up and taking my hand. "We got plenty of work to do."

She took me to the bed, pausing to drop Isla in her basket on the floor. Throwing off our garments, we rolled against each other and it felt so strange to kiss again. Like I was kissing someone new, someone for the first time. She seemed to agree and we went at it. We moved to make love and she pulled me in, held my face between her hands, kissing me. I moved against her until we finished.

Laying back, breathing hard, she grinned at me.

"Better now?" she asked, her voice thin, frayed.

"Oh, yes," I said, genuinely happy again.

"Good."

Then she got up, found her panties on the floor, put them on, and returned to the bathroom to continue the laundry.

I sat up on the bed, feeling unfulfilled. I wanted to cuddle with her – hold her, feel her heart beating with mine, knowing we were one. But I told myself we were adults now, not happy-go-lucky kids just playing adults. We had duties to perform and I realized she had performed one. She'd given her husband a moment's pleasure, what was necessary for her to get on with the daily chores.

Feeling bad from that realization, I joined her, kneeling in the bathroom beside her. I took clothes from the pile, began washing them in the tub, then passed them to her for wringing and hanging up. We were a team.

* * *

At night, with the car loaded up except for baby and tuba, we made love again, and it took longer and had more passion than in the afternoon. My wife. Her husband. A family about to hit the road, strong and determined. The new normal was us, free of masks and hazmat suits, with no viruses floating around. On our own, with no mother/mother-in-law to guide us. Mom liked to say every day was a challenge and if you get to the next day you win.

I awoke from a dream. Hannah was asleep beside me and the night was so dark. Even the crickets had stopped. Shaken by my dream, I got up, checked on Isla, splashed some water on my face in the bathroom, and stepped outside.

The sky was overcast, the breeze cool. Autumn had settled in and winter wouldn't be far behind. We had to get someplace where we could wait out the winter. Aunt Laura's house would be good, had plenty of rooms – if we could make our own arrangements for food. That thought stopped me, made my heart crash. How to get food? Aunt Laura gave favors in her bedroom. And me? What could I do? Manual labor? Dig a garden? Then it hit me: What would Hannah do? – do for us, her family?

Suddenly I didn't want to go to Aunt Laura's house. I would never let Hannah do things like that even to get us food. I wasn't sure she'd be willing to do anything like that. Hard times mean hard decisions, Mom liked to say, justifying some of the things she did. What had Mom done on the island? I ran down the list. What might Hannah do?

The image of Hannah standing naked before a leering Quinn filled my head. It wasn't part of a dream. It really happened. Then he'd gotten naked, too. The two of them in the office, on the couch, skin to skin. My heart raced, anger building in me. She said it was charity. He apologized. Yet it remained. *Dammit!* It would always remain, stuck in a loop that would play constantly, trying to kill me every day. But she's not mine, a voice whispered, she's with me only by her choice.

"Are you okay?" asked my wife, coming up quietly behind me in the doorway of our room. She hugged me.

I must've still been tense. She recognized that.

"Don't worry," she spoke into my ear. "We'll take our time. We'll make sure everything is safe."

I believed she meant our trip, but she could've referred to our marriage-without-a-wedding relationship. We had to begin again, so I turned and embraced her. I felt her arms press against me, squeezing out the pain. That felt good.

✳   ✳   ✳

In the morning we went to the office to say our goodbyes and thank Quinn once more for his hospitality. But I couldn't look at my wife. I would never look at her the same way I did when we first met, or when she took me down to the nude beach that night to give each other our Christmas gifts, or when we sat together so innocently during one of the island *soirees* while everyone else was going wild. It seemed my mind was forever cursed to collect vivid snapshots throughout my life and hold on to them, never allowing them to diminish or letting me delete them.

Yet I had to go on, had to hope everything would work out fine one day. It was like a game I had to try to win.

Hannah gasped when we entered.

We found Quinn on the floor, struggling to get up.

"Are you okay?" She crouched beside him. "What happened?"

He tried to chuckle then broke into coughing but swore it was nothing. Grinning, he pushed himself up on an elbow.

We gave him a hand, helped him to the couch. His breath was foul, as usual, but there wasn't anything harder than beer and weed in his back office room.

"You had a fall?" Hannah asked him, with a glance at me.

"I—" He tried to say more but in his eyes was frustration at not being able to form the words.

"You rest here," said Hannah. She got some water for him.

After clearing his throat, he tried to speak but only garbled words came out. He threw his hand forward. We didn't understand so he shook his hand, finger pointing.

I followed his direction, went to the cabinets. His finger angled downward so I opened the drawer below the counter.

"Open," he got out.

I lifted a spiral-bound notebook out of the drawer, like what I'd used for school before classes went virtual. It was folded open to a page full of scribbled writing, the marks of a shaky hand. *To Who it concerns*, read the larger writing at the top. He had gone over it repeatedly, making the letters darker and thicker.

"What's this?" I asked, turning back to him and holding up the notebook like it was evidence of a crime.

"That's...." He tried to finish, took a few breaths.

Hannah came over to have a look while juggling Isla.

"Now listen here, kids," Quinn sputtered. "That...."

Hannah took the notebook from me. "You mean this?"

He nodded, trying to take deeper breaths.

"A letter?" I asked Hannah.

"No." He composed himself. "It's muh dang Will."

"Will?" I asked.

Hannah went to him. "You're not dying. Not yet."

"Oh, wish it weren't true, missy." He struggled to breathe. "But it's gonna come someday. So I...."

"What?" I asked him.

"Bet I gotcher names right. But only half right," he grumbled.

He reached for the notebook and I helped him take hold of it, helped put the pen between his fingers.

"Now tell me, so I get it right, so it's official." He looked at each of us. "Whatcher full names?"

My wife sighed, then pursed her lips. "Hannah May Whistler – I mean Baumann. It's Baumann now. Yeah, old tradition, you see."

"And you, sonny?"

"It's Sandy. Sandy Baumann. No middle name."

"No middle name?" Hannah asked, concern in her voice, like I should've revealed that a long time ago.

"Well, Mom...she was a little weird, as you know," I spoke in a low voice to her. "She wanted to use Ludwig, she told me once, but then she decided not to use any name. She wasn't sure what bad things our ancestor might've done."

Hannah snickered at that.

"Got it," said Quinn, sitting back from scribbling our names at the top of the page. Bending over to write, with the notebook on his knees, left him breathing hard. He handed the notebook to me.

"There's no law offices around now, I bet. What do you want us to do with that?"

"Keep it," he blurted out. "It's yours."

"What? The Will?" asked Hannah with Isla being grabby.

"The whole dang thing. Motel, ever'thing in it, all the food put away, ever'thing. Yours."

We were surprised, glanced at each other.

"All yours...."

"How can you do that?" I asked. "What about your kids?"

"My kids? *Ffft.*" He shook his head. "Don't know where the heck they might be now. Don't know if they even alive." More breaths. "No, it's you two that're my family now."

Hannah handed Isla to me and knelt to help him into a better position to ease his breathing. "You're so kind."

"Not for kindness," he said. "Maybe nobody cares. If I leave it abandoned, somebody'll claim it. So...that...." He flicked his fingers at the notebook. "That'll give y'all some rights if it come down to legal matters. I signed it there."

"But you're gonna live a long time yet," Hannah said.

"Yeah, a lot longer," I added, and Isla waved her arm.

"Maybe. But I could be gone in a flash just as easy. Y'all know how flashes are."

Hannah turned and gave me a look like she was asking me if we should still leave with him being in such poor condition. But if we stayed, how long would we remain? How long waiting for him to die? If Quinn died, we'd be the owners of this old motel. If we stayed, how would our life go then?

We were ready, moments from departure. Nothing that might happen to this old man could stop us. Hannah looked at me sadly. My expression hardened. She pursed her lips, a clear message to me. I tightened my jaw, a reply.

"You kids...have a safe trip," Quinn said. "Be waitin fer y'all to come back this way."

The old man's grin was fixed on his face, his beard unable to hide it. Then he raised his hand again, flicking it toward the door. When we hesitated, he waved his hand harder.

"Go on," he grunted, sounding in pain. "Get on now."

I took the notebook and closed it. With a glance at Hannah, we stepped out of the inner office. Hannah, tears running down her cheek, swung the door shut and turned to me. I shared my sad face with her, to let her know I felt something. Empathy was hard for me but I was trying. She put her arm around my shoulders.

Isla, blissfully ignorant, was happy to bounce in my arms as we returned to our room. Our new car was parked in front. We got in, settled Isla, and backed out. With a pause by the office, a farewell honk, I turned the car out to the road.

10

THE ROAD OF RUINS

Mom was a professional musician as long as I'd known her. She played in a rock band called the Tubafonics when I was little, then became principal tubist in the Symphony. She was also a music professor: taught music theory, music history, music composition. She mentored the low brass students. She had three tubas, two at home: the B-flat and an F. She kept the monstrous C tuba in her office on campus. She also had an alto horn she said German folk bands played during Oktoberfest. She also had a euphonium which she inherited after her friend died. But it was the B-flat tuba she named Timmy and loved the most. Her great-grandfather Ludwig (Louie) had it made back in the Old Country, had an embellished plaque on the bell with the manufacturer's name and the place and year it was made. She named the smaller F tuba Freddie and the huge C tuba was Big Chuck or Charlie. But it was Timmy she loved the most, having family ties. She said he sounded the best and she played him nearly every day. She played all the favorite and famous music for tuba, as well as music originally written for bassoon, cello, or other brass instruments. Sometimes she wrote her own tuba music, but she never became famous. She was composing a tuba concerto while we were in lockdown because the pandemic didn't allow her to premiere the new tuba concerto written by a composer who actually was famous. She could play other instruments: horn, trumpet, viola, flute, even a little harp. Her college program required that they learn many instruments, so she did. But she never encouraged me to play an instrument; perhaps I was more valuable as audience. She did teach me the basics of the tuba, when I insisted, but I never got to play enough to become proficient. She didn't think I should become a musician, so when my college started I took Sociology classes, studying groups of people and why they do what they do.

Then the pandemic came – or returned, or continued but with a new strain, variant, subvariant, whatever, who knew? And we all went into lockdown again. Finally, Mom decided we should flee the increasing chaos in the city, get out early before the rush, and hide out at my grandparents' farm....

I thought of that as we drove the little hatchback along the road, feeling regret for leaving Timmy under the care of the ailing Quinn. The tuba lay upon the bed, safe in its soft-side case, valves freshly oiled, sheet pulled over it, the room locked. Nobody would know a tuba was in there.

Then Quinn handed us back the room keys.

"Keep'em," he said. "You'll need'em when you get back."

He had a master key, anyway, if he needed to get in any room.

The car struggled up the long hill. I was afraid to give it more gas, not wanting to use it up too quickly. The engine groaned, refused to move forward – but did go on. With additional gas from a can Quinn had saved, which might have been on the edge of being too old, we started with nearly three-quarters of a tank. In a small car like this, we could get all the way to Aunt Laura's easily, I calculated, going directly instead of the winding route Mom took getting to the island.

At the crest of the hill stood the hand-painted sign Quinn had made: *Ferry Not Running*. It let everyone know there was no point proceeding down the hill to the ferry landing, which would keep people away from his motel.

Quinn had drawn a line on the map he unfolded, marking the shortest, most direct route – which included highways bound to be congested, people stalled, jammed in, unable to move, and people would've died there. I told him about Mom's plan to take the lesser country roads, so Quinn marked another way to go. He explained his reasoning for that route, called it 'the way of the son'. Not the way Mom would've gone but a similar idea: keep to the back roads.

So we were driving it and staying well under the posted speed limit to save gas and always be aware of obstacles in the road and road conditions. The long hill going up from the ferry landing and its collection of buildings was the first test, the reverse of the long hill we had gone down when coming to the island. From the top of the hill we had a good view of everything: our former island home laying flat on the water, sun beaming through gaps in the clouds, one ray marking the beach house. No way to know what might be happening there, but we didn't care.

The road went through more clusters of shops scattered along the cracked pavement. Cars had stopped there, some right in the roadway, others pulling off the road. I had to weave through them, constantly glancing around in every direction for anyone coming at us to take our car or hurt us. I had my wife and baby to think of – but at least I didn't have to worry about Mom's tuba.

Hannah sat in the back seat and we fashioned a better basket for Isla since we had no official child seat to use. I could hear Isla goo-gooing in her basket when her mother teased her with finger games. We didn't talk; I was concentrating on the driving. Hannah never complained about missing the chance to drive. Her school shifted to virtual classes before she turned sixteen.

I had never been this direction. We came by the southern route, eventually going by foot over the old broken bridge across to the island. Maybe Mom had driven this way previously but I couldn't remember it. Hannah's family had come down to the island this way, she said, but that was a few years ago, during a lull in the pandemic when restrictions were eased. That lasted a few months. I kept the folded map against my seat, checking the route over and over until Hannah called me to pay attention to the road.

I didn't dare stop, not wanting to risk any attack from vagrants swarming out from behind buildings, or trees, or abandoned cars. That was my biggest fear. I kept Mom's pistol beside me.

Eventually, we passed farms – no livestock – and the people we saw alive waved at us as we passed. They weren't wearing hazmat suits. Only a few wore facemasks or face shields as they worked in the yards or sat in front of their houses. They seemed happy to see us: proof of life. I felt better seeing other people, especially when they were families. Things were getting back to normal. I could stop being so nervous and always expecting the worst. I had to shake off my training, conditioning. I'd taken on too many of my mom's traits – or maybe it was the Asperger thing affecting me in each thought and action.

"Calm down," Hannah said, sensing my anxiety.

The road became straight and flat, grassy fields on each side, treelines set back, old houses appearing abandoned further away. Overhead the clouds were large, drifting like white whales above us, not threatening but blocking the sun as we drove on. I slowed, made a turn, continued west on a new road which then started to wind around curves, got into a hilly forested area, then passed into open farmland. I felt better with open spaces; I could see trouble coming at us.

"Relax, will ya?" called Hannah from the back seat. "We are trying to nurse back here, okay?"

I slowed and heard the engine groan, refusing to cooperate. Something with the transmission. I dared not go too slow, thinking the engine might not want to go faster afterwards. No wonder it had been in the garage for servicing. I thought about the owners and what might've happened to keep them from picking up the car. Probably died. So many died, never getting to finish their errands. And yet, gazing around, there were few bodies laying about. Mom explained that most people who became infected would die at home or in hospitals, not out in the streets. Wherever there were bodies, I saw, they were skeletons, picked at by wild animals, or possibly hungry people. Mom was right: they had likely died at home, in their beds, after a prolonged illness. They wouldn't be out getting groceries and just drop dead in public. But if they were caught in traffic, or they met with violence, the bodies would be left where they fell.

"That's fourteen," said Hannah, counting the dead bodies here and there along our route. She counted only humans, not animals.

Then we came upon a pile of bodies on the side of the road and several smashed cars and trucks on the other side. It looked like some authorities had pushed the vehicles off to the side to clear the road while someone else had gathered the corpses neatly on the opposite shoulder. Three vehicles, smashed and showing signs of a fire, and maybe twenty bodies in the pile. One vehicle was a yellow school bus, broken into four sections, resting in the ditch along the road. A lot of the bodies, nothing more than skeletons now, were small, like they were children.

Hannah gasped as we slowed – but I didn't stop. Ahead was a small town so maybe they were heading there when the accident happened. Probably happened a couple years before.

"That's makes thirty-five," she whispered reverently.

We hurried on.

"If you go this way," I remembered Quinn saying, "it'll take ya about six hours. That's expecting the highway ain't packed. Lotta them folks got stopped. You best stick to the old country roads, like yer mama said. But you gotta be more careful out there now, more chance for vagrants ta get ya. Now if ya take this here way," as he traced the route over the map, "it'll be bout twelve hours, I figure, but gonna be safer." He pointed to possible detours I could take if I ran into problems along the preferred way.

The Way of the Son, I mused as I smelled the strong odor of Quinn, half sweat, half from the weed he smoked. I sniffed. The odor was not only in my memory, it was with us.

"Geez, you smell like Quinn," I said, looking up in the rear view mirror at Hannah.

"Huh?" She raised her eyes to the mirror. She'd long finished nursing Isla and set her down in the basket again. I was happy to hear her baby gurgles.

"I said you smell like Quinn."

"So? Anybody standing within six feet of him's gonna smell like him."

Within six feet. Yes, stay six feet apart, the mantra said. Social distancing, the new custom. That made me think of just how close they'd actually been. Skin to skin. His old wrinkly skin against her smooth pure skin. The wound kept tearing open. I had to complain again, not that the sour smell really bothered me so much, but that it reminded me of him, of them being together even for a couple minutes, and I wanted to rant.

Hannah argued back, with a warning to keep our voices low to not wake the baby. But Isla was still goo-gooing.

"It sticks to your clothing," I said.

"Okay, fine!" She tore her t-shirt up over her head and tossed it out the open window as we drove along. "Satisfied?"

That made me feel foolish, losing control that way and letting my displeasure feed my anger. I checked in the rear view mirror. The shirt lay in the road, dancing with the breeze.

"Yes, satisfied." I kept glancing in the rear view mirror at her – until she crossed her arms over her chest. I was about to apologize but decided I hadn't done anything wrong.

"Fine," she conceded.

Of course I felt bad. I didn't want there to be fighting between us. I wanted to go back to the first days of us falling in love, of our flirty playfulness, of the passion that made a child. I looked in the mirror again, saw myself and her in a single merged image. It was like in a movie, where the couple drives off into the sunset and the audience is left to imagine how their life will go after the scene fades to black. We were actually one entity, I knew. But she'd hurt me, and something in me wanted to hurt her, to restore the balance.

"I'm sorry," I muttered instead, then repeated in a louder voice.

"Okay, I heard you."

"I mean it." I shook my head, watching the road ahead, saw the signs at the intersection, turned and continued.

"I said okay."

"Honestly, I still feel hurt by what you did." I thought that was the best way: to be completely honest about my feelings. She would have to understand how I felt. She might even feel guilty, and that would give me some pleasure.

"What I did?" she snapped back.

"You and Quinn."

"I told you exactly how that happened. I don't feel bad for that. Besides, it got the car you desperately wanted. So you can drive home, or to Aunt Laura's house, whatever."

"You what?" I looked in the mirror again. "Got this car?"

"Yeah, I did.... But I sure didn't wanna go, lemme tell ya, so I didn't say anything. I knew you'd get all crazy and 'we gotta hit the road' like right this freaking minute."

"What?" I almost swerved off the road, turning my head to look back at her.

"Yeah, he told me there was a car. This one. He checked all the cars around and this one had gas and a key."

"No way...."

"Way. So he asked his favor. He'd already been nice to us, just some kids from the island. Lotta trouble, okay? He didn't have to do anything for us. So I did what I did. I did him a favor. For you, ya big stupid jerk!"

"No, it wasn't for me," I growled.

"It was! He said 'You do me a favor, I'll show ya something real sweet.' I asked 'What?' He said 'First the favor'. When he said what it was, the favor, it didn't seem so bad—"

"So you did it, huh? Just like that?"

"You think I liked being up against a smelly old man? Letting him run his hands over me? Touching me? It was gross. But I did it for you! For us! For this freaking car. I did it for us, Sandy. But you only ever think of yourself, about how you feel."

"No, that's not what I...." But I knew it was how I tended to do things. I'm the center of my universe, after all. I was the center of Mom's world. Why wouldn't I think of everything in terms of how the world affects me? But I knew what she meant and I could only claim it was some of the effects of my Aspie mind. I also knew it was time for me to expand my world. I was a man now, a husband and father with so many responsibilities and worries.

"So he showed me the car. This car. I said 'thanks' and didn't say nothing about it. I was okay being there. We were getting by. Same as on the island: he was catching some fish and you got the veggies growing."

"But I wanted to leave.... Okay, got it."

"I don't know why you're so desperate to leave. What else is out there? What the fuck's out there – out *here* – that's so important?"

I had slowed to half the posted speed, my attention not on the road as I tried to reason through her statements. I calmed myself a minute. I ran my lines through my head a few times, rehearsing.

"Mom promised to return for her sister. Now I assume that responsibility. I promised Mom that I would fulfill the promise she made to her sister, even though she refused to come with us the first time. Maybe they won't want to join us now. But maybe now it's us who need her. We could make it work there, staying in her big house. It's better than the island. Except there's no fish."

"Well, yeah, there *is* all those fish, thanks a lot."

That made me smile as I drove. I felt the car vibrating steady under me, the purr of an engine back in sync, humming along like the day it rolled out of a dealership, never expecting it would one day be used as a getaway car during a pandemic. But bless them for leaving the car in that garage.

"It's his family name," said Hannah, a few miles further.

"What?" I asked, shaken out of my driving trance.

"Quinn. That's his last name."

"Okay.... So?"

"His first name's Lucas."

"That's also okay," I said, eyes on the road.

She kept a serious tone: "Thought you'd wanna know."

11

A DESTINATION OF SORTS

The engine complained but we kept rolling along. I muttered some hopeful thoughts when it refused to work and threatened to shut off. I dared not stop and turn off the engine, fearing it might not start again.

Hannah sang songs in the backseat to entertain Isla. Some of them she'd sung before but others were new to me. She did have a beautiful voice but the lyrics were often quite bawdy. Isla wouldn't understand them, of course, not the way her mother smiled at her while singing. Maybe Isla would grow up thinking those bad words were how people were supposed to talk. We checked the radio, got only static. I had a few CDs that Mom brought but I didn't think Hannah would appreciate listening to tuba music.

Have to stay focused. Can't be lulled away by music.

The road was mostly flat, the pavement broken but level, no serious chuck holes. I could swerve around the ones I saw. It had been falling into ruin before the pandemic. When everyone stopped driving on the roads, there was no reason to repair them. Only the essential workers, the medical people and delivery people, were allowed on the city streets. I wanted to forget my days making deliveries on my bike after my school went virtual, always wearing my clothing as tight as possible, buttoned up, with facemask and hood. Now we had the windows down a bit and the fresh air blew in like an ancient god's breath.

There was nothing I could see, driving down this country lane, that made me think of death and destruction. The day was calm and bright – as though the world was way over there. I began to relax.

A line of trees on our left stood as guards separating the peace we felt from the chaos beyond. To the right the pastures spread as far as I could see, with only an occasional stand of trees or an old barn's roof appearing. I thought of Mom, the times she insisted on a quick swim in a farm pond to wash off any viruses that might've stuck to her. I smiled to myself but I guess a laugh popped out.

"What?" asked Hannah from behind me.

"Just thinking of Mom, how she—"

"Typical," she moaned.

"I was thinking how she made us swim in that farm pond after the truck hit us."

"Yeah, that was bent."

"It was the first time I ever saw a goddess...." I glanced at her in the rear view mirror.

"What, your mom?"

"No—you!"

I looked again and she had a wry grin.

"Eyes on the road." She'd pulled out another t-shirt from her pack and put it on, not wanting me to be distracted. "Are we there yet?"

That made me smile. Everything was going to be all right. Just keep going along this road and we would come to the intersection with a county highway, turn here, turn there, on to Aunt Laura's house. I checked the map beside me.

I looked up when Hannah gasped.

Automatically I slammed my foot down on the brake before I could look ahead. A few wolves padded about on the road before us. Another pile of debris and a burned out car husk. The wolves had been feasting, carrying away what they could. I expected them to move as we approached but they were bold, refused to flee, so I rolled slowly through them, parting them. One jumped up, clawing at the window as Hannah scrambled to raise it. The excitement disturbed Isla and she cried. I feared one of the wolves might get to her, so I hit the gas and sped off, hitting one of the wolves.

"That was close," I said when I couldn't see the wolves in the rear view mirror. "Never thought there'd be wolves out here, just coyotes. Guess they've expanded their range with all the people in lockdown."

We kept the windows up and the car got warm. I cracked my window, let in some air. We smelled something burning on the breeze. Maybe trash, something oily. Ahead fingers of dark smoke wafted across the road. When we got closer, I saw it was a pile of debris off in a field. People were there, monitoring the fire, but we didn't stop or wave to them, and continued on. Perhaps they were just another family getting ready to start a new life or burning the remnants of the old life.

Clouds moved in, blocked the sunshine, as the trees on the left became sparser and the fields on the right quickly filled in with trees. Houses sat among some of the trees, people who'd adopted a country lifestyle. They had little to fear from viruses, being away from the cities, surrounded by all those unclean strangers.

"We'll get there," I said to reassure my family.

Getting to the intersection with the county highway, we saw abandoned cars on the sides. One car had decaying bodies sitting upright in it. They obviously were infected and died, never left their vehicles. Hannah gasped at the sight, turned away, complaining how awful the world was. The county highway was littered with vehicles but not as much as the state highway had been when Mom and I were leaving the city. Enough of them remained so I had to drive slowly to maneuver through them.

I immediately wanted to turn around and go another way, but the vehicles thinned out and the road ahead was open. I picked up speed, glancing at the fuel gauge. No *E* flashing yet.

In the rear view mirror I saw Hannah was watching the world go by outside the windows. Isla lay in her basket, her mother's hand caressing her while she slept. I felt good, felt important.

* * *

My dreamy thinking took me away from my driving focus. I nearly missed a sharp curve. The swerve of the car awoke all of us. Apologizing for the jolt, I promised to pay more attention. Hannah asked if I was tired and needed to pull over for a rest, but I repeated my concern that we not turn off the car's engine before we arrived at Aunt Laura's or ran out of gas.

Hannah mumbled a curse, then sang a few lines of one of her songs under her breath – like she wanted me to hear them but not let on that she wanted me to hear them.

"It's okay if you wanna complain," I said, eyes forward. "I know I'm not perfect. But I'm trying, okay?"

Hannah sat up straight in the back seat. "I know you're not perfect. But you're good enough. Anyway, life's pushing us so I'm gonna buckle up and fly right, as they say."

"What's that suppose to mean?" I had to ask, my foot slipping off the pedal as I half-turned to glance at her. The car jerked to a slower speed.

"It means...." She looked away, as though thinking thoughts she didn't want to show on her face. "We were just, like, thrown together. If not for this pandemic, we would probably only see each other at some lame family reunion like every five years or so. We sure wouldn't have a baby."

I confirmed her idea. Like Mom, Hannah was more right than wrong. It was a glorious turn of fate for us to meet when we did, each of us at the age we were. Pandemic or not, it was time for us to meet a special someone. That we were cousins was only a matter of statistics.

"I should've stayed," she said, tearing me from my daydream. "Shoulda stayed on the island. We had everything working there. Yeah, I coulda slept with Jackson, winner of the sacred lottery. It wouldn't be so bad. I woulda been queen of the island someday, ya know, after Owen died."

"What?" I couldn't believe what I was hearing. Maybe she was teasing me. Sometimes I couldn't tell if someone was fooling me or if they were speaking straightforward. That was part of my Aspie curse. "What do you mean by that?"

"I mean that...all we've been through...."

I had to keep on driving, holding my eyes on the road.

"All we've been through...I dunno if it's worth it. And now we're going to who knows where...and...."

"We're going to Aunt Laura's. To save them, her and Bootsy. Because it's the right thing to do."

"Sandy, you're so lame."

"Lame?"

"You can be so freaking lame sometimes." She leaned forward up against the seatback. "Hey, I don't mean you're stupid. You got some smarts, book smarts, but...."

"But what?" I let the car slow further.

"I'm just saying...everything woulda been easier if I stayed on the island."

"Now you decide?" I swallowed hard. "Okay, easier for you. I still had to leave. By-laws and all. I told you to stay. It's dangerous in the outerlands. Then you chose to come with me. And I love you for that, for taking the risk with me."

"Risk, huh? But we went a whole quarter-mile from the ferry landing, is all. What's the difference? I mean, *boyfriend*, it's like we didn't really leave. But we started over—"

"But we're leaving now, aren't we?" I shouted back. "Will Aunt Laura's house be far enough away from the island for you?"

She fumed, crossing her arms. Then she exploded into a loud conflagration of cursing that made Isla cry.

I put my foot down on the brakes, the car stopping in the middle of the road. I shifted to Park, the engine still running, and turned to her.

"We gotta get one thing straight," I shouted over the seatback at her. "You and I have done what we've done. It's history. Fact. Now it's up to us to stay together and work together because... because, dammit, we're all we've got. I can't live without you, *girlfriend*, and you can't live without me. And Isla sure can't live without both of us. We have to stay partners and make this work. It's pandemic time. We need each other. Geez, I need you. Not just for sex but for love, for helping do what needs to be done for our survival. I will fight for you, to save you. Mom told me if she ever got attacked that I should just run away, save myself, because if I tried to help her we both might be killed. I was supposed to run away, but I never could. Then...then she was killed anyway and I couldn't do anything. Nothing!"

I had to stop, breathing too hard to keep shouting.

Hannah put her hand on my arm as it bent over the seatback.

"There's a lot that's fucked up—" and she shrieked.

I quickly turned forward. A group of rough-looking country folk had gathered around us. Vagrants! Six of them, four men and two women, all older than us, dressed in mismatched clothing that had been worn for years, now dirty and torn. They looked intelligent, not like mindless zombies. They carried farm tools as weapons. The man in front of the car glared at me through the windshield, his lips twisting in a snarl, holding a sledge hammer in his hands.

Hannah screamed, grabbing Isla to her chest.

I shifted out of Park, moved my foot to the gas pedal. But they blocked the way. The car lurched forward a bit. They slapped at the windows, kicked at the doors, shouted at us in words I couldn't understand. One man picked at the hatch in back, hitting it with something hard. I froze, half amazed at how they managed to survive and half in terror of what they might do.

I grabbed Mom's pistol, held it up to show them I had it. The woman by my window stepped back. But the man in front, raised the sledge hammer in his hands, pulled it back ready to swing it.

My foot hit the gas and we shot straight ahead, knocking him aside, and charged down the road. I saw the hatch door fly open, swinging up as we pulled away, blocking my view of them. Hannah continued screaming, with Isla crying. I had my foot all the way to the floor and we hit 70 down that county road, swerving to avoid abandoned vehicles, before I thought we were far enough away to let the car slow down.

My chest ached from my pounding heart. My hands merged into the steering wheel. I had to pry them off, one then the other. Hannah settled down, but Isla still cried. The road was straight and level, trees away from the road, a good place to pause. No way those vagrants could catch up to us.

I set the car in Park and got out, engine running, and checked the back. One of our packs was missing. Probably the vagrant had taken it, or it had fallen out as we raced away. Same result. Most of our belongings were in that pack – clothing and food, boxes of shotgun shells. The shotgun was still there, lain against the inside wall of the trunk space. A box of shells Randy gave us at the ferry landing when we were leaving the island thankfully had been put in Hannah's small pack which was inside the car.

Closing the hatch, I gazed down the road in the direction we came, my hand to my forehead. I couldn't see anyone at the end of my vision. Shadows obscured my view. Sunshine streaked through the trees along the road. I detected movement. Could be them.

I got into the car, locked the doors, windows up, and checked on Hannah, who gave me a grimace as she held Isla, trying to calm her. They were clearly frightened.

"We lost the big pack. But we should get to Aunt Laura's soon anyway." I grabbed the map, studied the route, located where we were, measured how much further it was. "Maybe two hours more. If we don't encounter any more distractions."

"That was so freaking scary," said Hannah.

I shifted into Drive and continued on at a reasonable speed.

✳　✳　✳

I drove slower, checking the folded map frequently, not sure of the right direction. Hannah sat in back with Isla, not saying anything whenever I seemed uncertain. She trusted me to go the right way. I had to demonstrate she could trust me.

We tried to discuss our next move: what we would do in this new normal in general, not for only the next few days. But we got increasingly angry. I think we were more angry being forced into these circumstances than at each other. We wanted to be carefree, have nothing to worry about, just enjoy life. Our circumstances, forced us to consider doing things we didn't want to do. Youth was finished. With a baby to care for and trying to survive in a new dangerous world, I felt like crying. But I would never let Hannah catch me crying. Mom would give a snarky remark that would dry my tears instantly, but Hannah would giggle and, although she wouldn't say it, she'd think I was a stupid kid.

I was so inwardly focused that I nearly missed a big curve in the road. The car scraped against the guardrail. Hannah shrieked, held on to the front seat as I straightened the car and kept going. We rolled down an incline on the road, around another big curve. The road leveled out, became straight again as the pines thickened on either side of the road.

"What the fuck're you doing?" Hannah barked after we again were stable. "We better not crash!"

That was it. I swerved to the side of the road and stopped, put the car into Park, left the engine running. I noted the fuel gauge: one-eighth tank remained. The area around us didn't look familiar but my last map check indicated we were getting close to the town where Aunt Laura lived.

"Why're we stopping?" she asked in a mean voice.

"I need a break!"

I shut off the engine for the first time since we left the motel. I was too angry to worry whether it would ever start again. I opened the car door and climbed out, stood tall, stretching my back.

"Fine!" she snapped.

Isla started crying; amazing how she could sleep through our arguing but as soon as we stopped she would awaken and, hearing no more angry words, decide to cry.

"We have to do *something*," I said after a moment of breathing. I looked around, noting how low in the sky the sun was. We were wasting time arguing. We were almost to Aunt Laura's, needed to get there before dark.

"But what?" cried Hannah.

"This isn't the way things are supposed to be. It's not what we expected. Not what we want. But it's what we've got."

"I know, I know."

She got out of the car, stood by her open door.

"But you don't hafta act like a freakin jerk about it," she said.

"I know you got issues, but...but you're treating me like I'm the child, a child you gotta take care of, not your partner. I choose to be with you, don't ya forget. Geez, Sandy."

Standing by the front tire, I turned to face her, standing by the rear tire. Movement in the dark woods off the road caught my eye. Probably the breeze. I stayed focused on my wife.

"You're right," I said. "I'm sorry." I had to breathe again. "My whole life has been one endless lesson in how to be the kind of man Mom wanted me to be – doing it without a father as an example. I told you about...*him*," meaning Victor.

"Oh, Sandy...." Hannah came to me, took hold of my hands as we gazed into each other's eyes. "You're doing okay. I know you worry about everything you think you have to do. But we're in this together, okay? You do you and I'll do me. Okay? Together, we'll make it."

We were right on the verge of embracing, finally coming to an acceptable reconciliation, back in love. Reaching for each other, I caught more movement in the corner of my vision.

I pushed Hannah back, reached for my pistol on my hip – but it was in the car.

As they came out of the treeline I tried to scramble around her to dive into the car for the pistol but she was in my way. I shoved her aside, but she didn't see the vagrants coming. I tripped trying to dive into the car, hit my knee on the door runner as I fell across the driver's seat, reaching for the pistol on the passenger seat – but the pistol dropped on the floor, sliding under the seat.

I stretched my hand for the pistol but couldn't get hold of it.

Then they were pulling me out of the car by my ankles. They grabbed Hannah, one big man wrapping his arms around her as she squirmed and screamed.

An old woman, her gray hair messy, wearing vintage clothes in layers, face and hands dirty, reached in the back seat of the car for the basket where Isla lay crying.

"Such a purdy child," said the old woman.

12

THE CAMP IN THE WOODS

More of them gathered around us as my heart was ready to burst: this would be our end. I really should have considered staying at the motel with Quinn instead of daring to traverse the dangerous outerlands, where any people who had survived the pandemic were desperate and hungry, where there would be no law enforcement officers to save us, where there were no laws. We were on our own and having a pistol just out of reach wasn't good enough.

The group wrestled us away from the road and back into the woods, two big men pushing me, one man ushering Hannah behind me. The old woman carried Isla in her arms. They spoke to each other as we went through the woods, saying how it was their lucky day. It appeared they had a camp deep in the woods, a place where they would be hidden from the police I prayed would come looking for us. These people intended to remain hidden. And it was their good fortune that an innocent young family happened by.

"Better'n our usual trap," laughed one man who had my arm, looking back at the old woman.

"Not as good as th' ol' wounded granny trick," she snickered. "They always stop to help, then we grab'em."

"This time even easier," said the man.

The woman cackled in delight.

"Nobody come down this road no more," said the man pulling Hannah along.

We were ushered through the woods, down a narrow trail with

bushes slapping at us. I scrambled to pull myself together, thought of words, and finally spoke them. I tried to negotiate with them. I asked them what they wanted with us, saying we didn't have much of value but they could have it if they let us go. Just let us walk away. They laughed at my suggestions. They knew what they had. They'd done this previously, it seemed by the way they talked, but it was my first time, and now to have my wife and baby involved! I couldn't handle it.

"This one talk too much, don't he?" laughed the man.

They discussed among themselves what to do with us, but their speech was too country for me to follow. I got bits of it, mentions of Uncle Jed and Cousin Timothy, nephews Danny and Cal, aunts Flo and Meg, and Pa-Paw up in Heaven, and how happy they'd be to see what these folks had caught. References to losing their farm, taken by the government for refusing to get the vaccines. Hatred for the virus, disdain at the long flu season, absolute loathing for police and tax men.

As we arrived at their camp, an older man stood like a sentinel before us, looking like a wizard with his wooden staff in one hand and a white beard falling to his waist. He put the staff in the crook of his arm and raised his other flannel-shirted arm, pointing at me then Hannah, said we weren't wearing facemasks.

"Most likely they anti-gov like us," said the old man. He moved his wooden staff around in front of him, then leaned against it. "So they's suitable for joining the family." None of them wore masks or other protective garments. But they kept to themselves.

The camp was dark being surrounded by forest. Above, through the treetops, the sky was well into sunset. Maybe we could escape in the darkness, I thought.

A plain-looking woman roughly Mom's age joined the group, singing out her praises for a loving god who continued to bless them with new life, meaning Isla, in this new village they were building. They were beginning with a gathering of people to build it, I guessed, both its structures to live and work in and at the same time populating it.

"Praise the Lord!" sang a man coming from a poor make-shift

shelter, half tent and half wooden lean-to. He was younger than the old wizard man and greeted the group. He looked us over, eyes staying longer on Hannah. "But first we gotta see if'n this one'll hold up. I don' mind givin'er a trial. Muh pleasure. Do the break-in fer ya."

"Yew gotta be wed first," the white beard man sneered.

"Not fer romancin," the other man responded. "It's what they call recreation."

"We do it proper," said White Beard.

I wasn't tied up, just made to kneel on the ground, with one of the adult brothers watching me from a step away. I tried to think, make a plan, but I was overwhelmed. I couldn't process what was happening. Mom had tried to teach me what I needed to know. If I had the pistol I'd shoot them. I had to become a monster, I knew, but I was a sniveling mouse. I tried to not let the tears in my eyes cloud my view. Had to stay ready – for what? My words had no effect on them – ignoring me, laughing, or shouting back at me.

"Yer time's comin, boy," the biggest brother called. "Cousin Timothy, he like them skinny boys."

I could no longer try talking them out of holding us. There was no reasoning with them. They didn't think logically, fixed in their own world. So I would have to fight – to fight for Hannah and Isla, knowing I might lose one of them by even the best of my actions. Or lose myself in the attempt. I had to become a wild animal, acting on rage not reason.

I got to my feet, caught by the brother guarding me. I managed to wrestle myself from his grip and rushed to Hannah, grabbed at her arms, tried to break their hold on her but failed, then went straight for the creepy old woman cradling Isla in her arms but got blocked by another man who easily knocked me down with a swing of his hand to my chest. I crumbled on the ground. More laughter, this time directed at my desperation.

I scrambled up, got knocked down again. I got up. The men stood amused, daring me to do more. They would keep slapping me around. They knew I couldn't best even one of them, as big as they were, much less all of them.

"Settle down, boy," said the biggest of the men before me.

"He's wiry sort," said another man. "Y'all got his nose bleedin.'"

"Serve'im right."

"Like it says in the Good Book, yew kin work off your bond in... what's it? five years?"

"Yep, five years labor."

"Then he can leave."

"This'un? She gonna be a mama five times over."

"But she'll not leave us. Nor her young'uns."

"That's how we build a village," the ghastly old woman wailed with Isla clutched in her arms.

"The Lord done blessed us!" shouted the middle-aged woman. A ragged kerchief covered her head, apron hanging around her waist over a well-worn grandmotherly dress with faded flowers. She glanced at me; our eyes met. She was merely playing a role, I detected. Maybe she didn't want to be there any more than we did.

I felt something in that connection. But I'd lost my breath in getting roughed up. I couldn't hear more because of the pounding of heartbeats in my ears. If ever I wanted to cry it was at that moment, unable to think what to do, feeling ashamed at letting us get into this predicament. One man saw my tears, laughed, and shoved me further down on the ground, my face to the grass, as two other men held Hannah between them.

"This one's mighty fine," said one of them. I couldn't see which with my face to the ground. I slowly rolled onto my back and saw the branches of the trees overhead, looking like prison bars.

At gestures from the creepy old woman, they sat Hannah down on a log they used as a bench. The old woman, a hag if ever there was one to Hannah's innocent Snow White, sat down beside her, began telling her the rules, what she would need to do for them, now that she was theirs.

The old woman called for the middle-aged woman wearing the kerchief to take Isla. She stood, acting maternal, bouncing Isla in her arms, calming the frightened baby. My wife cried out, begging them not to hurt her. We're survivors like them, trying to get by.

"Please let us go," Hannah begged. "Please...."

"Please?" laughed one of the brothers. "Ya say ya wanna please us, zat right?"

Hannah burst into sobs.

"She gonna do plenny fer us," the biggest brother declared. He looked in his forties, wore dirty coveralls and ragged shirt, had a scraggily black beard down to his collar, wore a hunter's cap over his long, greasy hair. He seemed the oldest, could be the son of the creepy old woman.

"Yew get a man's woman, he gonna obey ya," said the other big man, standing behind Hannah. "But yew get a man's woman n his babe, too, n there ain't nothin he won't do fer ya."

"Gonna work that boy to the bone," laughed the big brother.

"Now, boys, we gonna do this proper," the old woman spoke.

Hannah squirmed in the grip of that man, standing behind her. He put his hands on her shoulders, leaned down to sniff her hair.

"Let her go!" I shouted from my position on the ground.

Big Brother, standing at the end of the log, went up to Hannah. Then, as if in defiance of my demand, he grabbed her t-shirt at the collar and jerked it down hard so it ripped open. He liked what he saw. He grabbed her breast through the tear, got milk on his hand and stepped back in surprise.

"Whad ya 'spect? She's new mama," said the old woman in her creaky voice. To Hannah: "This one's yours? Not stolen from nother family?" To the brother: "People tend to do that, make new families from the remnants of the old ones."

"Yeah, like us," Big Brother responded. He looked over at the middle-aged woman in the kerchief, then back to Hannah. "She gonna be muh new wifey. So where's Uncle Jed when we need us a preacher?"

"They's out huntin," the brother guarding me said.

"This one yers?" asked the old woman again.

Hannah confirmed Isla was her baby and begged again for the woman to give her back. Instead, the middle-aged woman lowered Isla to the arms of the old woman.

"Rather like holdin purdy babe again," the old woman said with a chuckle, and tried bouncing Isla in her arms. "These three, they weren't purdy, not to nobody," and she cackled.

"Maw-aw...," said the second brother.

Big Brother, snickering, eyes never leaving Hannah as he stood in front of her, laid his hands on her shoulders. The second brother standing behind her stepped back. She shook them off.

"Please let us go," Hannah whimpered.

Big Brother looked around the camp, as though seeing who was watching him, as he made a rabid grin with his tongue wagging.

"This one gonna be so fine," he laughed, putting a dirty hand to her cheek in mock caress.

"Let her go!" I shouted from where I lay on the ground.

The man guarding me gave my shoulder a boot-shove and the command to be quiet.

I tried to get up, got pushed back again by the brother guarding me. Dressed like a farm boy, he was shorter than Big Brother or Second Brother, but they had a resemblance. With me posing no threat, he turned his attention to the other brothers' harassment of Hannah.

I counted six men of various ages, all but one older than me, in their thirties and forties, looking as though they were brothers. Or cousins. The old woman they called Maw had to be seventy. The middle-aged woman who shouted praises and a younger woman barely out of her teens stood back from the circle. They seemed to be tending to dinner, cooking something in a large pot over a fire.

Big Brother called out a woman's name.

At his call, another young woman appeared, pulling her dress on as she climbed out from under a lean-to shelter, pausing to fix herself. A naked man rolled over on the bedding as the canvas flap fell back closed. She hurried over, looking scared. He cursed at her. She carried a hank of rope, brought it to the two men standing by Hannah.

Second Brother jerked the rope out of the woman's hands. She recoiled at the rope burn she got but he laughed.

"Now y'all be kind," Maw chided them. "Yew got no learnin how to treat womenfolk."

"Shore's a skinny thang," said Big Brother, looking at Hannah.

"But we kin fatten'er up quick enough. Then she kin handle us." He glanced around the circle of kin. "All o' us. But me first."

"Then me," demanded Second Brother.

"Y'all best mind yerselfs with a young'un like this," said Maw. They seemed to respect her; she had some control over them. "She ain't gonna handle y'all no how. Gonna tear apart. Y'all try that n she'll die on ya. Then whaddaya got?"

"Then it's dinnertime," said my guard with a snort.

"Yessiree," called another brother or cousin from the edge of the group, "first the fuckin then the feastin!"

"Watch yer mouth, boy," Maw chided.

"Well, heck, don't want'er dyin," said Second Brother, who had moved behind her again. His hands squeezed up and down her. "Gonna need more babes. Now ain't that right, Maw? Three or four, at least, ain't that right?"

"Men need wives," said my guard, eagerly nodding. It was as though Owen himself had snuck off the island and transferred to this forest enclave, rewriting the by-laws once more. Like Quinn told me: 'When society collapses, if men are hungry they want food. If they're not hungry, they want sex.' That was the law of the post-pandemic jungle.

I repeated my request to let us go, trying a gentle, polite voice. Perhaps I could play on Maw's motherly sympathy.

Ignoring me, the old woman cackled, apparently amused as she adjusted her kerchief around her wrinkled face. She ordered the middle-aged woman, whom she called Sally, to place a blanket on Hannah's shoulders, showing some kindness by giving her cover for the torn shirt. Maw looked between Hannah and Isla, now held by this Sally whose long dirty hair fell down over her arms and shoulders. Possibly she was a sister, or a wife they'd stolen. Either way, Sally acted as Maw's helper.

Hannah pulled the blanket around her shoulders, pinched the sides together at her throat, keeping her eyes down.

"Don't yew be 'fraid now, child," Maw spoke. "We's good folk. Just got in trouble wit' them gubment enforcers. But we's all safe – healthy, I mean. Never got the virus, not to my eyes. Kept away from other folks – which's fine ba me, the ways they be carryin on bout this jab n that boost, like crazy folk."

Hannah looked up, evidently relaxing some, and gazed past the old woman. Her eyes appeared to focus on me across the camp. I tried to look strong for her but perhaps she no longer believed my act, didn't have any trust that I could free her.

"Yew heard them boys jawing," Maw continued in her rickety voice, "but don't yew fret, child. They'll treat yew right. Yew just gotta treat them right. They ain't bad boys, just percocious, n at their age, they gots sum feelins need released." And she went on explaining the rules of their village. Her voice got lower as the evening darkened and I couldn't hear most of it.

I could imagine the old woman describing something like what we experienced on the island.

"Yew kin call me 'Maw'," said the creepy old woman, "like they do. Now what's yer name, child?"

"Hannah," she muttered, head down again.

"Well ain't that a purdy name. But that's my name, too. So I'm gonna call you...Ruth. Yep, from now yer gonna be Ruth."

"Okay...."

"Say it: I'm Ruth. Part of the Morgan clan now."

"I'm Ruth...."

"Ruth. Part of the Morgan clan. Say it."

"Part of the Morgan clan."

"Now yew be one o' us. Hallelujah! Ah, it won't be so bad now, child. Why, yew be like me one day, old n gray, but in a big house by then, with a brood of grandkids ta mind. How yew like that?"

Hannah nodded as if required to.

"What's the babe's name?" asked Maw next.

"We named her Isla," Hannah responded, her voice trying to be polite to win over the old woman. "She was born on an island." She spelled out the name.

"Tha' don't make no sense," said Maw. "Let's call her Lila after my dead sister. Lila. Good name."

Hannah was becoming resigned. "Okay...."

"Or we kin jus call her Baby Ruth," and she cackled for a while.

The brothers had stepped away, bored with not being able to bother Hannah, but their attention returned at Maw's cackling.

When she calmed, she gazed at me across the camp.

"What's yer man's name? Though he hardly a man yet, more like one them young scalawags."

"His name is Sandy," said Hannah.

"What? For a boy? That ain't right."

"It's short for...Alexander."

"That's better, I reckon. But too long. From now on he'll be Lex. Lex, the helper boy. Doin our chores. Yew don't mind him workin fer us, do ya? Five years, then he's free. Yew kin see'im ever' day, course. But yew's a free girl now. Free ta choose one o' ma boys."

Maw pointed around the camp. "That tent's Harley's. He's ma eldest. Prolly best yew go wit him. Won't cause no trouble thatta way. Cobb stays in that there tent. Him n Harley don't get on. Mine's o'er there. The gals o'er there. Nancy and Sally. Uncle Jed in that one. Cousin Timothy and his boy in that lean-to. Silas and Jake, my younger boys, in that one. When yew settle down with one o' ma boys yer gonna live together in his tent."

"But...." Hannah muttered but Maw heard her.

"What're ya sayin?"

"But I'm married already," Hannah spoke in a low voice.

"What's that?" asked Maw, not hearing clearly.

"She says she's already married," said Second Brother. He had come back, standing behind her again. He leaned down.

Maw cackled, shaking her head. "Them outsiders don't count. We don't recognize them marriages. Y'all kin start fresh now. Pick one o' ma boys as yer husband. New husband. Or let'em decide among themselves. They all're mostly same, one good as the next."

"But...I don't know them," Hannah muttered.

"We got time, child. Time enough fer ya ta get ta know each o' them," said Maw. "Yew kin spend sum time wit each o' them. See which o' them ya like. Which o' them treat ya best. Take a week or two. We ain't goin no place."

"But I...I can't choose," said Hannah, in a calculated tone.

"Shore ya can. Look at'em. Pick yer poison." Maw cackled. "Yew better choose soon cuz when Uncle Jed gets back, he can perform the vows. Then y'all kin go on to the consummationing."

Little Brother, standing by me, laughed out loud.

"If'n yew asked me, I'd pick Harley fer ya. He's a hard worker n he's one most likely ta get mad he don't get his way. Gonna cause heap o' trouble if yew pick another brother."

"I ain't gonna cause no trouble," Second Brother assured Maw.

"Yew say it now, but we knows different."

"I swear it." Second Brother straightened up, resigning himself to not getting the girl.

Listening carefully to the old woman's prattle, even I might've been persuaded to join their extended family.

A twiggy noise arose from outside the camp as Uncle Jed and Cousin Timothy returned from their hunting trip, a rabbit and a brace of quails in hand. A teenage boy followed them, dirty like he'd swum through mud and not looking too happy. Then I saw his hands were tied in front, the tall man leading him by a rope leash. They pushed him out of my view, into the darkness of the woods, telling him to wash up. Maybe he had to go after the game they shot, into the swamp, a go-getter, just another person captured by this family.

They forgot about Hannah a few minutes while the uncle and cousin recounted their adventures. They gave the carcasses to the younger woman for preparing. She knew what to do, didn't need instructions. The other woman, Sally, went with her to help.

Uncle Jed saw Hannah sitting forlornly on the log and went over, squatted before her to have a closer look, nodding, then stood up grinning. He gave his approval to Maw: she looked healthy. He suggested Maw check her for the rashes some people got from too many jabs and boosters. Maw would inspect her in the tent, away from the menfolk's eyes. Uncle Jed glanced at Isla, bouncing in the old woman's arms, but he had no reaction.

Cousin Timothy, tall and thin, with a hooked nose and beady eyes, gave me a look. I sat on the ground, my legs crossed. After a moment he stepped closer, leaned down to give my cheek a caress as though checking that I had whiskers, then left.

They went out of my view, but I added them to the camp's men tally. There was no way I could do anything with all of them around us. But I had to do something. *Think!* Even if we might pretend to want to join them, I would lose Hannah to one of those men. I would be little more than their slave, doing menial work as I watched my wife birth another baby and another. By then I'd want to die, maybe try running away, maybe even get away – but I'd have nothing to live for. Hannah would survive. She could give in, let them welcome her into their family.

"Already got this here babe," Maw spoke when the uncle and cousin retired. "She gonna be real purdy sumday. We kin build up our village again."

"Men need wives," my guard repeated, his voice low like he didn't want Uncle or Cousin to hear.

"And I'm gonna go first," growled Big Brother, thumbing at his chest. "Maybe second, too. And third, hah!"

"But you got Nancy," said Second Brother, pointing to the tent behind me.

"Ah, dang it, she ain't no fun. Don't do nothin but cry. Cain't stand it." He regarded Hannah. "But this one, she's just right. She ain't gonna cry." He leaned down. "You ain't gonna cry, are ya?"

"Yew too dang rough on her," Maw responded. "Donna up n died cuz you too dang hard on her. Same gonna be for Nancy, yew keep on her like ya do. She ain't young no more. Naw, son, this'un, she ain't gonna last long if ya don't take it easy."

He made a sad face. "But, Maw...."

She repeated her words and her son listened, standing up and nodding respectfully.

"Yes'am," he responded at the end.

I understood their situation, wanting to rebuild. I wanted to shout to them, offer my message of the new normal and how we should work together. Better to do that than take what you can get for now and not have it any longer. Like rationing food. You could eat it all at once and feel full and satisfied, or you could stretch it out, eat a little each day and have it last longer.

"The kid makes sense," said my guard, Little Brother. He stood aside so I had a clear view of Hannah and they of me.

"Dang whippersnapper," Maw grumbled. "I knows a school boy when I sees'im. Them's the smarties tha' got this pandemic going."

"Awrighty, we kin keep'er purdy," said Big Brother. "She kin do sum work fer us."

"Now yer thinkin," said Maw. "If we's gonna feed her, she gotta do sum work."

"So we kin have her a real long time, yeah?" confirmed Second Brother, chuckling. "She kin work on her back."

Maw cradled Isla who cried at the strange interactions. She kept reaching for her mother who wept until the old woman finally handed Isla over to her. Hannah hugged her baby, kissing her, as Maw sighed at the display of motherly love.

"Yew boys play nice." Maw gazed at Isla, secure in Hannah's arms. "This'un looks ta be just few months old. Y'all gotta be patient fer this one ta grow up. That be twelve years...if'n any us still round by then."

"We ain't got no food fer these folks," said Little Brother.

"We'll make a new town no matter what," said Big Brother.

"We kin start wit this here girly," said Second Brother, waving his hand. "She still young 'nuff to push out three, four more. And they's gonna be all mine."

"No, they's gonna be mine," Big Brother challenged.

"Yew boys gonna hafta share," said Maw, holding up a hand to stop their bickering. "Every other babe, awrighty?"

"But I go first. Ain't that right, Maw?" He seemed desperate for her confirmation.

"Dang it, boy! Where's yer head? Life ain't about sleepin with gals. Y'all gotta build things. Do things. Man things." Maw turned her wrinkled face to her son, showing disappointment. They stared at each other a moment. "Harley...."

"Yeah, Maw?"

"You're the eldest so yew get'er first."

Big Brother showed a smug face to Second Brother.

Maw called to her helper, who hurried over.

"Whaddaya think, Sally?"

Hannah juggled Isla in her arms, but when Maw reached for Isla, Hannah, thinking better to comply, handed her over.

"Shall we let'er grow on up here n be one o us, or else make us a fine stew? She's mighty plump."

Hannah shrieked: "Noooo! Please! Let her be!"

I jumped up. My guard's attention was on the old woman. I charged at Maw, knocking her off the log. Isla tumbled on to the ground, momentarily shocked at falling then bursting into a loud bawl that filled the forest.

Second Brother rushed to me, swung his fist into my jaw as I tried to get to my feet. Shaking numbness from my head, I reached for Isla, got her in my hands before being kicked in my belly while my arms stretched out, holding onto Isla. As I rolled over, I managed to pull Isla to my chest, wrapping her in my protective arms.

"Let'em be," said the old woman. "Ain't no harm done."

"Nobody hurts our maw," snarled Second Brother. He gave my belly another kick. I lost my breath but held tightly to Isla.

"Please let us go!" Hannah cried out. "Please! And we won't tell nobody about you, I swear."

I tried to look at her from where I lay on the ground but the brothers blocked my view. The third brother stood by me, his boot in the small of my back.

I realized I could scramble up, push Little Brother aside, and run as fast as I could through the dark wood and maybe get away from them. With Isla in my arms, I might be able to dash out of the camp. I could reach the car and drive away. I would've saved myself, like Mom said. I'd have Isla. But Hannah would be lost.

I couldn't do it.

"Ya wanna run, boy? Go on then!" shouted Big Brother. "Ain't gonna get far. Nothin out there fer ya no how. A lotta death, viral death, is all ya gonna find out there. And wolves."

I could only lay on my back, gut in pain, as this Sally took Isla from my arms and handed her to Maw like a carnival prize.

Maw cradled Isla once more, cooing at her, talking so casually how that chubby leg could be mighty tasty.

Hannah screamed in fearful rage for them to let us go. To let her have her baby. To not hurt us. That she would do anything if only they would let us go free.

"Zat right?" asked Big Brother.

She gave a nod. "Just let me and my baby and husband walk away."

Everyone stared at her.

"N yew'd do anythin fer dat, huh?" Big Brother confirmed.

She froze, realizing what she'd said. But gazing at Isla held in the old woman's arms, she muttered: "Yes."

13

THE SACRIFICE

The camp was quiet when I came to, only rustling leaves whenever the breeze blew. I found myself tied up, my back against a rough tree trunk, darkness around me but for the low fire in the center. The brothers took their time beating me, forcing Hannah to watch, until they managed to knock me out. When I awoke I was already tied to the tree, facing the campfire.

I tried to shake the numbness from my head and not let my arms and hands fall asleep.

Got to stay focused, I kept repeating, half-forgetting what the words meant. *Focused on what?* I had no plan. I couldn't think straight, my mind raging like a hurricane knowing Hannah was in one of those tents, fighting one of those brothers, and there was nothing I could do about it.

I recalled Uncle Jed, who they said was a preacher, standing before one of the brothers and Hannah. She wore a nice dress they'd given her and a thin white cloth over her head like a veil. Uncle Jed said some words, holding open a thick book. Everyone cheered when he finished. They passed around a jug and shared a few bottles. The beating before the ceremony was entertainment. It let Hannah know I was no longer in her life.

Glancing around the camp, the night enveloping everything, I tried to guess who went to which tent, who was still awake, a faint candle showing against tent canvas, or unlit tents full of moans and grunts. I didn't know which tent Hannah was taken into – not that it mattered now. What was going to happen had happened. I could only imagine the worst.

Have to think of her. Have to let her go.

Everything was finished for me. My gut was a coil of knots, snakes ready to strike, if I could just get free. Even my standard meltdown wasn't enough. It alarmed a few of them but in the end didn't result in any sympathy.

"What an odd boy," Maw remarked, turning to tearful Hannah. "Now ain'tcha glad yer no longer wit' tha' queer fella?"

She put her hands to her face as the beating began – just boys being boys, Maw cackled.

What to do? I had to come up with a plan. But I had to get free of this rope first. My body too sore to move, I knew I had to. So I squirmed against the rope, loosening it a little but unable to free my arms. And when I got free, then what?

My mind was a racetrack of thoughts, with constant crashes. I fought with myself, trying to hold my mind still. Hannah was in one of the tents. Isla was in the old woman's tent probably; they'd talked about her staying there. How to save them both? How to get all of us away? Which of us would be sacrificed?

Thinking hurt my head, made me numb. I couldn't do anything but feel drowsy, too much energy expended. My body ached. Blood from my nose had dried on my lip.

Before I could nod off, someone came up to me, stopping and standing between my outstretched legs. I looked up to see Little Brother standing over me, holding a torch. He had a small plate in his hands. With a smirk on his face, he squatted and studied me, holding the plate up. He moved the plate close then pulled it away, teasing me.

"Maw says we gotta feed ya. Gotta keep ya fit fer workin," he said, then shoved the plate at me, forgetting my arms were tied back. He figured it out and picked up the drumstick, what actually was a rabbit haunch. He thrust the leg forward until I bit hold of it. "There ya go, boy."

I tried my best to keep hold of the meat as I chewed on it, teeth gripping the bone, but it fell from my mouth.

"Yer bout as clumsy as muh kid sis, Mariah," he said with a sneer. "Dead now three years. In the end she couldn't do nothin, had ta get help fer ever'thing. Off ta th' A&M she goes, to get sum higher learnin, but they got'er all wrap up in politickin...." He got choked up, took a long breath and looked away. "S'pose that's how she got hooked on vax, whatever they's pushin back then, from the start. Wouldn't let ya do nothin lessen ya got the latest jab. So she got'em, got'em all. Couldn't get enough of'em. Never felt safe from the dang virus."

The drumstick dropped from my mouth and he retrieved it for me, held it up so I could bite again.

"By the time she come home she was too sick to do anythin. No gubment relief neither. Her body all twisted up, cain't walk, skin pricklin with rash, boils poppin, pus bubblin. Lawdy, she gone blind first, then guts runnin all day n night, screamin in pain—"

I dropped the drumstick again.

"Sorry," I said, meaning about his sister.

Getting annoyed, he plopped down on the ground within arm's reach. He picked up the leg from my lap, shoved it in my mouth again, treating me like I was a stupid child.

"So what's yer name anyways?" he asked me, ignoring the fact I had rabbit meat in my mouth.

After I swallowed some and let the bone drop in my lap again, I answered him: "Sandy."

"That's a girl's name."

"It's short for Alexander," I lied, following Hannah's lead.

"Then why ain'tcha Alex?"

"I don't know. Mom always called me Sandy."

"Well, they call me Silas. Or just Si." He gave me a long look before he picked up the bone, not much meat left. "So where's yer maw now?"

"She's dead," I said bluntly. "Killed."

A minute went by.

"Virus?"

"No. Knife."

Another minute of deep thought.

"Knife, huh?"

A half-minute more.

"Murdered," I replied.

Two minutes.

"Whadda shame."

Making himself comfortable on the ground, crossing his legs, he remembered to feed me again. He put the bone up so I could bite.

"Still got our maw. She too feisty ta e'er be killt. Not like some. Like Uncle Jed. He done lost his maw from the virus, way back, ya know. First wave. Before they even give it a name."

He continued rambling on about his family, farm folk who lost their farm because of government mandates which kept them from working. Mandates! They had bills to pay yet couldn't earn money being locked down, even out in this rural area where nobody was close to them at all. The county sheriff brought the order one day: foreclosure. His maw argued they should be allowed to farm their corn, sorghum, rye, and raise their pigs, chickens, and dairy cows, especially with food shortages causing protests nationwide.

"We ain't bad folk," said Silas, pausing to contemplate his fate. "Just got swept up in this whole goddamn pandemic shitstorm. Ya know? Lotta folks same way."

Trying to get by, I understood, to survive. *Survive.* Got it. Mom and I, and my cousins, were trying to survive, too. We expected people would want to band together and help each other. But we were wrong.

"I got hired into th' army then," said Silas. "But all we ever did was fight against our own citizens, ya know. When they's protestin shit. No food, no gas, no medicine. Just stay home forever, they said, like food grows on trees but yew cain't go out n pick any of it. Course folks gonna rebel. I woulda. Sometime we gotta shoot'em. That was our job. Ya know?"

I nodded. Mom and I lived through that in the city before she decided we should leave. We never joined any protests, however. Mom never liked to get involved that way; she thought it best for us to wait it out. Wait for what? The bad to end? What if it didn't? What if it never ended but got worse day by day, month by month?

We were waiting for something – something that gradually became only a fantasy. But waiting was the new normal.

"My cousins, the whole Bodine family, they got wiped out by the virus. Ones that didn't got rounded up, their farm confiscated, turned over to the gubment, n they's taken to quarantine camps, never seen again. And my gramps, he lived in the city up north, kept getting his store broke into, everybody high on all kinds o' vax, goin crazy. Money no good, yeah, so ever'body stealin what all they need. He wanted to sell his shop, get outta town, but who'd wanna buy it? So he burned it for insurance money, ya know, and headed up north – I mean way way up north, away from ever'body, into the woods, by a lake. He's fishin all day, I reckon."

I spit out the bone. "Done."

"I know they got troops along the border now," Silas continued. "Keep folks from crossin. Some states don't want folks from other states, neither. Heard they got more pandemics going in the big cities, don't want nobody to get out, don't want nobody to come in. They been gatherin up folks, lockin'em in quarantine camps. Say it's all worse now."

He let out a long, painful sigh, then gazed at the stars through the treetops for a minute.

"Yeah, couldn't put up wit none o that, so I up n quit."

He looked at me, a captive audience.

"Don't mean I signed nothing. Just walk away, ya know? Didn't tell nobody. Better I go back n help Maw than go round up folks I don't even know n put'em in camps fer who knows how long."

"That sounds right," I mumbled.

"Did whatta had ta do," he said. He got up with a grunt, stood over me.

The rabbit bone lay between my outstretched legs.

"Then that dang Philpot! Yeah, always spoutin his rules, sayin food's on the way, just vote fer him. Fuel comin soon, so vote fer him. Vote fer him else y'all gonna get round up n put in camps, sayin he done got mandate from some global high-ups like he made himself God."

Silas shook his head, remembering.

"Can't you just let us go?" I asked, words tumbling out before I put breath behind them.

"Maw, she always complain 'bout them bigwigs wanna cut the population down, keep just enough for slave labor. Keep the good stuff just fer themself, none fer us. Philpot's one o' them, yeah, n he wants ta be *president!* Of what? There ain't no damn country no more. But he worked with some higher-ups like Birdwell and his bunch of crooks. Now there's a real asshole. They got their fenced-in compounds with their private armies, got ever'thing yew kin dream of. Maw thinks it's all sum plan they got fixed. Just gotta hide away, start again, make a new world—"

"Can't you let us go?" I asked in a firm voice, then looked up at him. "Please."

With a half-grin, he looked down, his face half amused and half full of pity for me.

"Where ya gonna go?"

He took the plate and left. I noted which tent he disappeared into. Only his brother or cousin in there with him.

The night was suddenly much darker, creatures stirring.

*　*　*

My body ached, head sore. Pain was meant to give me strength, to urge me on. But I was more used to mental pain, losing a video game kind of pain, not sports field pain. Still, I knew I had to fight to my final breath, no matter if I lived or died.

I wondered which tent Hannah was in, and who she was with. There wasn't anything I could do about it. I hadn't heard screams or bawling. It was me who was in pain, unable to act, paralyzed by my fear of losing everything.

No, I had to save myself, I suddenly decided; I had to ease my own suffering – knowing how selfish that seemed. This wasn't the city with virtual classes and Mom close by for anything I needed and it was all right if I had a meltdown. I was protected. This was real life – the 'RL' the kids in my virtual school laughed about, like they would never have to experience it. I was right in the middle of

RL. If Hannah was lost to me already, then I had to save myself, maybe find a way to start over, go somewhere I wasn't known.

Stop it. Don't give up.

I was as useless as a knob on a tree trunk – which kept poking my back, irritating me.

My mind crashed around a corral of hard ideas, each scenario worse than the previous one, imagining all sorts of awful things, picturing one of them on top of her, having no concern for her, hurting her, taking her as his wife. A firestorm raged through me and I couldn't make it stop. I felt hurt for her. Yes, it really was always about me, like Hannah said. But at least I tried to fight them earlier, showing her that I would try to save her. Even if I couldn't, she'd know I tried. I'd gotten beaten up for her. Maybe she would remember me that way: a martyr.

I teared up. *Stop crying, special boy.*

Drops of moisture hit my face. I thought it must be my tears at first, the cool breeze blowing them back at me. Realizing it wasn't, I feared it was something from a bird up in the tree. But it was rain. I could smell it in the air, the earthiness of sacred relief. I let the drops revive me, licking my lips.

Let me get wet, catch a chill, develop pneumonia and die. Then my misery would end.

As the patter of rain grew, I heard rustling behind me, then a tug on the rope. I couldn't see what was happening on the other side of the tree. It must be some woodland creature come to nibble on my hands. I couldn't feel anything but tugs. Would this misery never end? One thing after another.

I wanted to cry. I wanted Mom to somehow come and save me. *But you're a man now, right?* I nodded. *You want to prove you're a man, right? Then act like a man—*

"Stay quiet," said a voice – light, feminine.

Suddenly the tightness of the rope released and I could pull my arms around to my chest. I shook them out, letting the blood flow again. My hands regained feeling.

The woman who helped Maw crawled around to me.

"You!" I exclaimed in a hush.

She had a six-inch knife in her hand, used to cut the rope. She put her finger to her lips.

"You're Sally, right?"

"I let you go," she spoke softly, "so you take me with you, okay?"

I quickly nodded. "Okay."

"Here." She gave me the knife, handle toward me, and pointed at one tent. Her chin jutted in that direction.

"Hannah?"

She nodded, putting her hands together to make the gesture of a wedding ring on her finger. I understood, although I shuddered at what I'd find there. And worried how I should get her out.

Sally made a gesture of cradling a baby and pointed to the old woman's tent. I knew Isla was taken there. Sally would get Isla while I took care of other business.

"Got it," I whispered.

Now it was up to me to act violent. I felt rage boiling in me. I waved my hand in the direction of the road where the car waited and her eyes went there. I hoped they hadn't gone back to see what else they could take. We lost most of what we started with when we encountered the first set of vagrants. I hadn't heard the engine since they captured us so maybe they hadn't bothered with it, thinking we ran out of gas, another abandoned vehicle. I made the motion of turning a steering wheel and she nodded.

"Thanks," I whispered, holding up the knife.

Sally scrambled away on her hands and feet, keeping low, her knees not touching the wet ground. I understood her plan. The old woman trusted her to care for the baby. She'd nursed Isla earlier in the evening as Big Brother took Hannah for his bride before the clan, then took her to his tent as the family cheered.

It had to be done. Or else I would die trying. No other choice. Lightning flashed through my head, and just as quickly was gone, leaving a spot of clarity: I could get up and run and be free all by myself now. I could get to the car and drive away. But the rest of my life would be hell if I did that, if I left them. I wanted to shout at Mom: *No, I won't run away. I won't save myself!*

I stalked up to the tent Sally indicated, knelt outside to assess the situation. They were awake inside, talking in low voices. The moaning and grunting was done.

"That awright?" Big Brother said, his voice strangely gentle. "Don't mean no harm. Just we lost our home, see, gotta stay in the woods, but we's gonna make us a whole new farm, big house, a barn, ever'thing all over again. Yew gonna be mighty comf'table, promise."

"I get it," Hannah replied. Her voice was soft and dreamy, not at all like she was in pain or angry. "Same for us. Just trying to get by, find a way to survive."

"Sorry if'n I got too rough, heh heh, just my way. Don't know ma own strength. Tried ta be gentleman-like. Ain't used ta no lady like yerself, purdy n all, city gal fer shore."

It sounded like a kiss.

"Mmm, excuse me," Hannah said with a cough.

"That a viral cough? Sound like."

"Huh-uh." Her voice sounded rough. "It's the cold air."

"Oh shoot!" Big Brother erupted. "Gotcher blood, huh?"

Hannah cleared her throat. "Looks like it."

"Well, we kin finish nother time. Yer gonna be round here long time, make us a whole village of kinfolk. I kin tell yer a fer-*tile* woman. Mmm, look at that soft belly."

The tent flaps lay closed, one edge over the other. I couldn't see inside. I used the knife to slip one flap off the other, creating a gap.

In the soft glow of a candle set on a footlocker, I saw them side by side. Hannah lay on her back with the man on his side, facing her. Big Brother, who claimed her first. A ratty blanket lay over her legs, drawn up to her hips, leaving her belly uncovered. She lay with her arms folded over her bare chest. His meaty paw slid back and forth over her belly. He had the same shirt on as before but his dirty overalls and nasty undershorts were pushed down to his ankles with his feet still in muddy boots. It was clear what had happened. I fought against myself, keeping my rage in check lest I give away my position.

I could burst in, knife aimed. But then what? He was a big man and I couldn't just wrestle with him. I had to strike quickly – one thrust, like Bucky did to Mom. With a belly stab, she suffered for several minutes. For this man, he would wail in pain, letting his brothers know what was happening and they would come to help. No, I had to go for the throat: kill him and cut off his shouts in one act. I ran that scenario through.

When the candle went out and they lay quiet a couple minutes, I figured they'd gone to sleep. I fixed their positions, worried that, in the dark, I might stab Hannah instead of Big Brother. I listened again, determining she would be to my left as I entered. Straight into the tent would be the brother.

I pinched the tent flap, crouched, knife ready.

In one swift motion I burst in, slicing between the tent flaps and leaping atop Big Brother, one hand feeling for his chin, holding his lower jaw against his upper jaw, the weight of my body trying to hold him down as he startled. My other hand thrust the knife into the side of his throat, behind his windpipe. I sawed through his larynx, then went for an artery. I twisted the blade to make a mess. As he squirmed, hands on my neck, I pulled out the knife, feeling blood spray everywhere and on me. His hands grabbed his throat. I shoved the knife up under his chin, pushed it in as far as the blade would go.

He lay still, hands dropping to his chest.

At the first motion, Hannah scrambled to her knees, afraid she was being attacked herself. She gasped in fright, about to scream but stopped herself.

"It's me," I spoke in the dark of the tent. "Let's go."

I left the knife in place, wiped blood from my face and hands on the blanket, then tossed the blanket aside.

Taking her hand, I pulled her up and we rushed out.

Outside Sally waited, rocking sleepy Isla. She came out of the shadows, surprising me. I jerked my head in the direction of the car and we all ran together, but not at full speed because we had to dodge branches.

After a hundred yards of slapping brush and splashing through a small stream, we broke from the woods several yards down the road from where the car sat. It was still there! We hurried to it as the rain continued to fall, light but steady.

Getting to the car, I heard shouting behind us.

I opened the back door for Hannah and she dove inside, laying across the back seat. Sally, carrying Isla, rushed around to the passenger side and got in. I threw myself into the driver's seat.

Swinging down between Sally's feet, I reached under her seat and found the pistol. They'd been too busy capturing us to bother checking the car further. It wasn't going anywhere, they figured. I brought the pistol up, looked to my left.

More shouting. They had either discovered Big Brother or else they were awakened by the noise of our escape through the woods. Or Maw found the baby missing. It didn't matter: they were on us. They held a couple torches as they emerged from the trees.

I turned the key still dangling in the ignition and the engine groaned then sputtered. I tried again, looking at the fuel gauge: enough. I gave it another try and the engine kicked over. Weak but running. I fed it some gas as Hannah in the back took Isla into her arms from Sally.

Breaking from the treeline, the torch light showed two hulks, one with a big axe leaning on his shoulder and the other bearing a good stick of pine in his hands. They saw us sitting in the car, the dome light coming on with the engine. I reached up, turned off the light as one shadowy hulk raised up beside my door and slammed the big pine stick down on the windshield, cracking it.

If they found Big Brother, they wouldn't be content to capture us again. No, they would need to punish us.

Another blow to the windshield—

"Go! Go," Sally urged.

The other brother and two more men got to the road, with the rain coming down heavier. With my door window down I swung the pistol up, aiming at the bigger of the shadows and squeezed the trigger. I hit him just below his ribs. He fell back, dropping on the ground, then got to his knees, hand over his wound, screaming. Another man came into view behind him.

Little Brother Silas stopped, his pine stick up and ready to swing against the windshield. He looked back at his brother. Then, cursing, he swung the stick down hard, again and again, breaking through the windshield. Shards sprayed the interior as I ducked. My head lay in Sally's lap as she cringed against her door.

"I was nice ta you!" he cursed.

Bent down like I was, my hand smashed the gas pedal down to the floor and the car launched forward like a rocket, weaving as the road dipped. We hit potholes, wheels spinning on the loose gravel, fishtailing as the car charged away from the camp. Sitting up, I took hold of the steering wheel, jamming my foot to the pedal as I wiped spots of blood off my face.

"She cut me loose, gave me the knife," I called back to Hannah as I kept my eyes forward, squinting through the windshield and the rain falling in the headlights. "I agreed to take her with us."

I steered around a pair of abandoned cars in the road.

Sally turned to look as we passed them, saying something the engine noise drowned out. One of the cars was probably hers.

The headlights dimmed, battery fading. Enough to see the road ahead. A curve came at us which I maneuvered successfully. When we were straight once more we found the state highway, packed with vehicles, silent and dark in the night, the rain obscuring my view, everything frozen in the pandemic world.

14

THE WAY OF THE SON

The car's engine complained and the noise of the rough road made it hard to hear anything inside the car, but I thought I heard her say from the back seat something that sounded an awful lot like the words *He raped me.*

My mind was fixed on one thing: getting the hell out of there. I would never stop again, not until we ran out of gas, which would be soon. We had to put as much distance as possible between us and the vagrants. We had to get as close as we could to Aunt Laura's place before we were forced to walk. I kept to a high speed, as much as the car could handle on the rough road.

Maybe it's only a voice in my head. Maybe it didn't really happen. Maybe it's just my imagination tormenting me.

We came to the state highway, four-lane divided, packed with various vehicles frozen in time, weathered over the long flu season. It was difficult to see clearly with rain sprinkling on the concentric circles of the windshield after the pine stick smashing. Most cars had pulled to the sides so I tried to weave our way through them but finally we reached an impasse, couldn't go forward any further.

There were a few people, destitute, carefully working their way through the jam, checking cars for anything useful. They spied our car, seeing that we were alive and the car operating, and started to come toward us. I had to back our way through them, crashed into a couple cars as I did but I didn't care. Get us out!

Backing until I found a wide enough space, I got the car turned around, hating the gas wasted in that dead end. We headed down the highway going in the wrong direction but there wasn't anyone coming at us. I turned off at the next exit, found another road.

I made a wrong turn, had to double back after a mile, went the right way, found the correct highway – the sign post had been bent down so it was hard to read. I knew from the map it would lead us directly into the town where Aunt Laura lived. She actually lived outside of town. I hoped we could skirt the town, which had been in full riot when Mom and I got to it two years before.

I heard the words rattling in my head once more as I slowed to steer around more abandoned vehicles. People had gotten stopped, then walked away. A few people still sat upright, dead in their seats, the process of decay in various stages. Some had blood splatters on the windows, as though they'd taken matters into their own hands. Couldn't take it, put a gun to their heads.

"Are you okay?" were the first words I spoke since we left the camp. I'd thought of asking her in the tent but I was glad now I didn't. The answer was obvious.

I glanced at Sally in the passenger seat, as though my words were meant for her. She said nothing but her eyes still showed shock. She turned to look out the side window. My eyes went to the rear view mirror. I saw Hannah had lain across the seat, holding Isla tight in her arms. Maybe she couldn't hear me with the noise of the car and the road so loud.

The yellow light was blinking, illuminating the letter E on the dashboard. The countdown had begun. Outside, dawn was a slice of orange rind behind, a threatening gray limbo ahead, a warning to find a good place to hide for the day.

The town came up and I veered away, took the by-pass. I gave the town a good look, everything quiet, blackened. Lots of burned buildings standing like dark husks. No industry operated now, no shops open, no offices welcomed anyone. Vehicles sat where they ran out of gas, filling the streets, trash and debris everywhere from the rioting, looting, protests, and fires, the remnants of society's mad dash to extinction. I could imagine our city, after Mom and I left, how much worse it would be now. And to think I'd seriously considered Hannah and I going there to start a new life after exile from the island. Yes, after the pandemic finally ended, when they gave the all-clear. Now there was no one to give the all-clear.

I found the boulevard Mom had taken before, remembering the way and felt better. This parkway was about the same as before, untouched by the violence in the town. I felt hopeful as the engine rumbled, the car shaking as we drove along, the last drops of gas spurting through the system, waving farewell to the tank.

The road leveled and the car slowed, but we rolled to the start of a slope and as the engine sputtered and ended, we coasted a bit. The avenue leveled again and we came to a slight incline where we had to stop, unable to coast further.

I pulled to the side, in the shade of some trees that formed a line along the yards of the fine homes standing there.

With a quick check of Hannah, glance at Sally, I got out and stood by the car, gazing in every direction to get my bearings. After a minute's survey I located Aunt Laura's house, way up the avenue. It might be a ten-minute walk to the gate, then another few minutes going up the curving driveway to the house.

"We made it." I almost laughed from joy, feeling relieved.

With a deep breath, I went to the open window.

"Can you walk?"

Hannah gave a quick nod, her face tense. I guessed she might be in pain. I didn't know what to do. I thought the house might have some medicines or other products she would need.

"We can wait, if you want." I watched for a response.

She remained motionless.

"I'll stay with her," said Sally, turning from the front seat.

"Should I go up to the house by myself?" I asked them. "No, I'm not leaving you alone, not ever again."

A long groan filled the backseat.

"Sandy, you never left me alone," Hannah muttered, trying to put some breath behind her words. "We were together when this all happened."

"Well, I think we should stick together. I have the pistol now." The pistol Mom got from her grandfather held seventeen rounds, and I had – ejecting the magazine to count them – ten remaining. There were two boxes of ammo, one in the big pack which we lost and one in the small pack Hannah kept on the floor in back.

I opened the door, eased her feet aside and knelt down to feel for the small pack. It had been shoved forward under the driver's seat. I got hold of it, wrestled it free, and set it on the seat by her.

"Thank goodness," I muttered.

"I kicked it there," said Hannah, with pride in her tone, "when we got attacked the first time."

"When they got the big pack."

I checked the hatch. It was empty. No bags, no food packs, but the shotgun lay up against the inside wall of the hatch, jammed in.

"Good thinking," I said, returning to Hannah.

Sally stood outside, her door open, as she scanned the area.

"Thank you again," I said over the roof of the car. "We couldn't have gotten away without your help."

She gave a sideways nod. "Welcome."

"And we got you away, too. What will you do now?"

I immediately thought it was impolite to ask. Maybe she had no plans, nowhere to go, no one to rejoin. So it would be rude of me to ask her. I didn't want to force her to think of bad memories.

She shook her head, looked away.

"Sorry," I said. "Didn't mean to trigger you."

She coughed, cleared her throat, and spit on the ground.

"It's not triggering," she said, looking off in the distance. "I'm used to it." She seemed to be searching for a horizon out of view. "Yeah...." She turned to meet my eyes. "Every day I'm reminded of everything that's happened. Those Morgans the worst of it."

"How long were you with them?"

"Feels like all my life, but about three years, I guess."

"Oh, that's terrible." I didn't know what to say, or when to shut up. "Were you captured the same way we were?"

"I don't know how you were, but our car ran out of gas. We passed it on the road as we left. We saw an old woman, looked hurt, ya know, so we stopped to help. Right thing to do, yeah? Next thing we know we were swarmed by those brothers."

She looked away.

I regarded her in a different light. "You said 'we'...."

She wiped her eyes, kept gazing off. "Yep, me and my little girl." She turned to me. "Missy was her name."

I couldn't let myself ask what happened to her.

Her eyes narrowed, closed, then opened. "She was twelve. Old enough for them. Hurt her too much for her to keep on living. And me...I couldn't get away, nowhere to go, always tied up. First year anyway. By then, they believed I could be trusted and I wasn't tied anymore." She tried to chuckle but coughed and spit instead. "Of course they took turns with me. Got me pregnant but I miscarried. Thought I did it on purpose and beat me for it. After that, well, I was just a slave to them."

"I'm sorry." The first words to come out of my mouth whenever someone would say anything sad or horrible.

She looked away. "Yeah, me too. Sorry, I mean."

"What will you do now?" I asked with genuine concern.

She wiped her eyes. "I'm free." She gave a little laugh like she couldn't believe it. "Goddamn free at last."

I waited for more but she didn't speak another word. After a while she sat in the car, breathing deeply, holding her hands in her lap like a good church woman.

Checking on Hannah at the open rear door, I saw that Isla was awake, looking around like she wondered where we were. I picked her up, gathered her in my arms, stood up outside the car.

"See? Over that way is your, uh, what's she called? great-aunt? Your grandma's sister. Her name's Laura. Actually, it's Lauraline. Like your grandma Polly is Pauline. You have to remember these names. You have to write them down and pass them on to the next ones in our family. Your sons and daughters. You listening?" She was grabbing my nose, finding delight in the moment, blissfully ignorant of everything that happened around her. "And your name is Isla. That's Isla Augustine. Because you were born on an island in August." But don't remember this day.

✳ ✳ ✳

Already the grass covering the extensive lawn had grown calf-high after being untended for years. A herd of sheep would be well-fed mowing that down, I mused as we arrived at the wrought-iron gate and gazed between the bars.

Above the gate, the iron letters spelling *Ironwood* still curved over the arch. A few autumn leaves had caught in crooks, others collecting at the stone base. Overhead, the sun fought to push its rays through a haze of growing gloom, dark shadows draping the silent house ahead. A shudder swept through me.

I suddenly worried that Aunt Laura might not be there. She might have left with her friend, Big Earl, the corrections officer, when her situation got worse. Or else, I worried, she was no longer alive, having succumbed to the violence of one of the men who brought food. That had been her means of survival. Her degree in Economics didn't help her in hard times. Nor did her husband who spent lockdowns stuck in his secretary's apartment. I'd gotten the full story from Mom.

I helped Hannah up, got her to her feet, weak and in pain. She wore the big sweater Sally gave her, which swept down to her hips like a short dress. She'd mended herself, insisting I stay away as Sally helped. They'd dealt with the bleeding. There were stains on the seat, but I doubted we'd ever drive this little car again.

Sally and I took an arm and got Hannah walking.

"I got it," Hannah barked.

But I kept my hand to her elbow and Sally stayed a step behind to catch her if she should falter. Hannah said she was fine, but the walking made everything in her body move around, and cramping was the main problem. We paused to let cramps pass.

All I could think of was what Mom told me about the day I was conceived. She liked to tease me with the story. The man who was my father had come to her and they'd joined together after a consensual gaze. For years I thought it was rape only to learn from her drunken confession one night on the island that she wanted to be with that man, more than twice her teen age, mostly to get back at her abusive father. And, of course, she got pregnant. It almost had a happy ending when that man returned to the island while we were there – Victor, the yachtsman – and he finally understood he had a son, began treating me as his son, only to see Mom killed by Bucky, that crazy old man.

Shaking my head, I realized I'd gone down another memory hole. I glanced at Hannah, who leaned against Sally.

"Better?" I asked. "Ready to continue?"

Hannah nodded, took a hesitant step. Sally followed.

With one arm bracing her, I carried Isla against my chest, her head rising above my shoulder where she could survey the world. If she'd been told she would enter this world of hard times, would she have consented to the transfer of her soul into this baby? Or would she have declined the offer. We could promise her loving parents, but not much else.

I let out a sigh. *Made it. We goddamn made it.* Mom would be proud of me. But not the part where we were captured by those country folk. I glanced back at Hannah. Her eyes found me but her face showed no emotion.

"We made it," I said, hoping to cheer her up. "Aunt Laura's. We finally made it."

As we stood looking through the bars of the iron fence at the big house up the gravel drive, I took a deep breath. If only we hadn't stopped to argue on the road. My gut boiled. If only.... Then we would've arrived last night. And without injury.

I gave the iron bars a slap. "We almost made it the whole way. Now we have to walk up to the house."

Sally smoothed her garments, a plain skirt and blouse, granny boots probably snatched from Maw. She'd clearly dressed up for an escape. Her eyes showed cautious joy being away from her captors yet wary that she wasn't entirely free and might be recaptured at any moment. She posed with her hands in front, like a habit.

I regarded Hannah resting on the ground. She gazed at me, a mask of pain on her face. She tried to hold Isla for a moment, then returned her to me. I cradled Isla as she wavered in drowsiness, then broke into a cry of discomfort. She had a full diaper.

With Hannah resting, I opened the small pack slung on my

shoulder and retrieved a fresh cloth. I laid Isla on the ground.

Sally pushed my hands away, flashed a grin as she took the cloth from me. "Let me."

So I stepped back, watched her gently speak to Isla, soothe her, while carefully removing the dirty diaper, wiping with the clean edges as she did. A skilled professional.

Hannah seemed uncomfortable by the way she didn't want to move. I wondered if she was injured. If we could get to the house there would be more we could do to ease her pain. But first, the most important thing had to be done:

"I'm sorry," I spoke in a solemn voice. "I am so sorry. It was all my fault. I am supposed to protect you."

She gave no reaction, as though her mind was elsewhere.

"We have to walk on up to the house." I regarded the curving driveway. "About a hundred yards. I'll help. We can make it."

The words seemed ironic to me. I should've done more to help her. I did all I could, got beaten for my effort. There was no way I could take on those brothers, but I had to try.

"Can you think of a song?" I didn't know where that stupid idea came from. "One of your favorite bands?"

She came to life. "You mean like 'Blessed Babe'? Callie Odem's song? Or the Coronas' 'Ravaged'? Those?"

"Yeah, sure. If it takes your mind off...."

She seemed to slip inward, hearing the tunes in her head as a faint humming emanated from her throat.

I should've said that earlier, when we were trying to get her up out of the car. With a slow nod to my suggestion, her mouth a tight grimace as if feeling pain, she paused for a couple breaths. As she rose to her feet I placed my hands around her waist to help steady her but she shook them off with a grunt.

"Leave me alone," Hannah snapped at me.

I didn't know what to do or say. My mind raced with thoughts. I recalled how Mom had reacted after the vagrants attacked her in my grandparents' house. She fought them until I got the pistol and fired. But Mom was tough, could handle it, shake it off. Hannah was gentle, although she could be snarky just like Mom. I could imagine Hannah growing up to be like Mom in all the strong ways. I mean *wrong* ways. Freudian slip, Mom would say. Maybe it's the result of being forced to deal with bad experiences: either let them crush you or fight through and survive. I couldn't say which.

15

THE MEANS AT THE END

"A child!" cried the woman at the door. She'd taken a peek through the smoked glass on either side of the twin doors, then swung one of them open. "Why, I never! I wouldn't've ever dared presume, not after such time as this. Well done, nephew."

Aunt Laura seemed bright and cheerful in that first instant of greeting, her voice as syrupy as before. She looked as fit, too, so she must've been getting enough to eat. She'd met us in a silk robe previously, as though she expected a different guest than us.

This time she appeared in a ratty bathrobe. Everything seemed different. But I didn't have time to assess her condition.

"She needs help," I said darkly, holding up Hannah, with Sally steadying her other arm.

With a glance, my aunt immediately seemed to understand. She took over, pushing me aside and ushering Hannah down the hallway to another room.

I waited, listening but not able to hear much. I could make out Aunt Laura's voice but not her words. Time stretched out until it lost all meaning, only the angle of the sun outside marking change. It might as well have been years.

Holding Isla, awake and curiously studying this new place, I looked around for Bootsy. I thought of calling out for her but didn't want to detract from our focus on Hannah's well-being. My little cousin would come out when she was good and ready. Meanwhile, I could think about everything I'd done wrong, make a list of all my failures, and plan how to make amends, and beg Hannah to forgive me for allowing us to fall into that horrible situation.

"She seems okay," I said to Sally, referring to Isla. "I guess you didn't have any trouble taking her. Nobody stopped you?"

She shook her head. "The old hag was asleep. I just picked her up, ran out." She seemed to want to say more but stopped herself.

"Can't thank you too much for saving our little girl."

She gave a nod, like it was obvious. "It's good to be away from them, the whole lot of them."

"I wonder what alerted them to our escape. Did we make too much noise?"

"Doesn't matter." She gave a satisfied grunt. "That old witch. She was snoring. So I pinched her nose till her mouth opened then poured a handful of dirt in, held her mouth shut as she choked. Good riddance. I hated being her servant for three damn years, cleaning up after her. And rubbing her feet. God, her nasty feet! And the crazy spells she was always conjuring. She had the evil eye, too. So I put a stone to her eye after she was good and dead and punched down hard, then the other—"

"Wow," I muttered. "You killed her?"

"Wouldn't you?" She narrowed her eyes. "Didn't you want to?"

"Well, not her so much," I replied. "She didn't do anything. But the brothers definitely."

"She told them what to do, what to do to your wife."

"Yeah, I think I would've killed her then."

"She deserved it." With deeper breaths, her anger evaporated. "First person I ever killed."

"I killed the big brother," I confessed. "I'm guilty."

"Justified." She chewed her lips a while. "No, mister, thank *you* for saving me." She kept shaking her head like she couldn't believe she was free.

"I've killed five," I muttered, seeing them crowded together in a field in my mind, looking half-decayed yet grinning at me.

"Oh, yeah?" she asked, perking up.

"Let's not talk about it," I said. "It's done now."

"Agreed."

"I wasn't there but a couple days but I sure hated them, too."

"And your wife got the worst of them...."

Her words echoed in the room, hitting me repeatedly, until I begged for silence to return. I listened for any sounds coming from down the hall, hoping for something good.

"That's my aunt," I said, being obvious again, so afraid of the silence that hung around us. Dark thoughts multiplied, stacked up, rose to the surface in the silence.

As I waited, occasionally glancing over at Sally as we both sat on the floor, backs against opposite walls, I took time to consider Aunt Laura's house. The large lawn was overgrown, as expected, paved drive worn, broken, not unusual for the situation everyone had gone through. The house needed paint. It looked abandoned – with some windows boarded up as though the glass was broken – a lot more than when Mom and I visited. We'd arrived in our little hybrid car and, getting no answer knocking at the front doors, we went around to the back porch. Mom shouted up at the windows and finally we met my aunt.

The woman we found back then dressed in a fine silk robe and received deliveries of food and supplies from men she entertained upstairs. Mom smirked a lot, reminding me how her older sister by ten years had always been uppity, looking down on delivery people. She'd married, had kids, followed all the trendy social movements and said the right pronouns, trying to always do the right thing. Then the pandemic came. In the lockdown her husband got stuck at his secretary's apartment. They made a baby. So did my aunt, with the gardener. The pandemic went on and living became more difficult. Times were tough. So she eventually embraced the barter system: food for sex. Or sex for food, as Mom defined it.

However, now she was clearly sick, obviously wounded, not half what she'd been two years before. She greeted us in that bathrobe, unkempt, seriously thin. She hadn't been eating well. She wasn't expecting us, or anyone, thus hadn't made herself presentable – a big *faux pas* in her world. Two bandages marked her gaunt face, skin thin enough to tear easily. She had bruising around her eyes, like someone punched her. She hadn't smiled, but when she spoke

I could see a few teeth were missing, affecting her delightful honey voice. Her hair was all gray now, unwashed and hanging down her shoulders, uncut since our visit. She appeared to have aged ten years in the two years we'd been away.

I felt sorry for her. Mom had offered to take her with us but she thought it better to stay in her house and fend for herself. She never trusted her baby sister, who always got in trouble.

What the family's reputation was before the pandemic didn't matter much *during* the pandemic. Everything was about survival, waiting for the bad to end, the good to return as soon as possible. Rich became poor, and poor became poorer. It was the uneducated, hard-working people who survived most easily. They knew how to get by with less, to endure, to play the games their 'betters' refused to play or reluctantly tried to play yet always lost for lack of skill. Mom had done the same. She made her own way, rejecting most of the assistance her family members offered.

Aunt Laura had been caught unprepared two years before, but she was still too proud to let her little sister take charge. We saw how she got by. And she had a new man in her life, apparently, a corrections officer named Earl who seemed to treat her right. She was happy, so we left for my Aunt Jackie's house in another town.

I gazed down the hallway, hoping to see Hannah coming out of the room, fully recovered from...whatever happened.

Sally sat on the floor, feet tucked under her like a kindergarten pupil. She watched me like I was an actor on stage. I noticed her attention sticking to me, annoying me. I thanked her again. What else did I owe her? We'd saved her, too. We were even.

I flashed a smile, enough to let her know I saw her staring at me, an acknowledgement of her existence. In this depopulating world that was a significant thing.

Then it hit me: something I missed in our initial moment of seeing Aunt Laura opening the front door. Perhaps she was also recovering from the same thing Hannah experienced but she hid it better. Someone had been violent with Aunt Laura, undeserved no matter how she presented herself. As she'd said previously, a deal is a deal. But Mom pointed out how not everyone would honor the deal. They would simply take and not give their share in exchange.

"She's way too thin," I muttered, then realized I'd spoken.

"Got a nice house," Sally responded, keeping her face plain and unemotional, like she was speaking only because it was required.

"It was nicer two years ago when we were here." I looked down the hallway once more.

We arrived in mid-morning. We sat waiting until it was noon outside, the rooms in shadow, so empty and echoing every footstep and random creak of the house.

I wondered again about my little cousin Bootsy, who was five when we visited before. Aunt Laura had claimed she was mentally handicapped but as I played with her she didn't seem abnormal to me – but who was I to make a determination like that, me being 'mentally handicapped' with my Asperger's syndrome? It wasn't a matter of intelligence but certain social behaviors. Mom guided me, taught me how to do things despite this flaw. She suggested once or twice in my early years that it was the result of having an older father – though she never told me who he was, not until we were living on the island and Victor arrived. That was awkward.

Aunt Laura appeared from the room and stepped lightly up the hallway to where we sat on the floor in the main room. All the furniture was gone, or remained only as pieces stacked up beside the fireplace. The ceiling's Baroque painting had faded badly. The room had a dusty smell, a bit smoky, with a hint of sourness from ...from unwashed bodies?

The odor arrived with my aunt. She stood between Sally and me. Clasping her hands in front of her closed bathrobe, she looked every bit a grandmother although she was only forty-eight or -nine by now.

"How's she feeling?" I asked.

Aunt Laura made a face, letting me know I was being stupid. She knew the whole story of my conception, birth, and childhood. She knew I was a 'special boy', as she put it.

"It's not as though she caught a corona virus," responded Aunt Laura smugly. Her hand went to her face, either checking one of the bandages or wiping away a tear. "So what happened?"

I was surprised. She had to know just by checking Hannah. It should be obvious. Perhaps she wanted a second version and then could compare the two and decide the truth.

"She's going to be all right, isn't she?" I asked hesitantly.

"We shall have to see."

I felt like she was accusing me of something, of not acting quick enough, of not preventing what happened. But I had already found myself guilty. Everything was my fault.

"I think she was raped," I replied, lowering my eyes.

"You think...?" Aunt Laura took a long breath.

"I mean, I wasn't there." More stupidity from my mouth. Why couldn't I just stop talking? "I don't know what to say."

"What happened?" she repeated.

So I told her, everything from Hannah and I finding a car with gas and trying to head to her house, then being attacked by that clan of country folk. I tried to negotiate our release but they were determined to have Hannah as their new wife. They threatened to kill Isla so Hannah gave in.

"Then Sally, she untied me and got Isla while I freed Hannah. Then we ran to the car and drove off. But they chased us and I had to shoot one of them."

"Hannah?" asked Aunt Laura. "Jackie's daughter?"

"Yes. That's her." I pointed down the hallway. "Didn't she tell you?"

Her face got sterner. "Hannah, your cousin?"

My throat tightened. "Yes...."

"So you married your cousin?"

"Yes." I pouted, feeling ashamed. Then I grew stronger. "But it was the only way. Mom was okay with us being together."

"And you had a baby...."

"Yes, of course. We had to. They made us – those people on the island." Again I filled with shame and couldn't understand why. Aunt Laura had the same gift as Mom: power in the tone of her voice. "But we love each other. We really do."

My aunt frowned, blinked. "Why, how Southern of you!"

"But actually...." I thought of an out. "Mom said we're only half-cousins. She said you knew all about that."

"I do...?"

"About how grampa.... Well.... You and Aunt Jackie are only half-sisters to my mom."

That made Aunt Laura blush.

"Even so." She stepped closer to have a look at Isla, asleep at last on my shoulder. "I fear for her. Her life. Whether she will have all her proper faculties. It happens to siblings who reproduce. For cousins – even half-cousins – I'm not sure. It's dangerous, Sandy. Were there no other girls on the island who struck your fancy?"

"No." I looked up at my aunt. "Hannah is the one. The only one. I knew it the moment I first saw her."

"Indeed. And yet, you can't always have what you want. Didn't your mother teach you that? Seems Polly got what she wanted, unlike the rest of us."

"Not really...." I couldn't say more.

"Hannah was, let's see, sixteen when you met her two years ago? Is that right?"

"But almost seventeen."

My aunt pouted. "And you were nineteen?"

"Just by a few months."

"Close but no cigar. As your mother likes to say."

"But Mom was sixteen when she.... When she had me."

"Two wrongs don't make a right."

"But it's love!"

I started to feel tears gathering in my eyes, afraid I'd be locked up for my crime. But I dared not wipe the tears away or I'd look like a stupid child. Dammit, I had killed to save Mom and killed to save Hannah. I'd shot men. I fought with men. I *was* a man! And no old woman was going to make me feel like I wasn't!

"There is no such thing," said Aunt Laura in a voice hard as concrete. "Love is a chemical. A good bottle of gin. False words that lead to bland sex. A beautiful sunrise that brings storms. A long night of the soul you awaken from and realize you're still alive and feel disappointment. It's a fear, a regret, a deep ache that never ends. It's someone you wouldn't kill in their sleep; you'd let them awaken first. It's memories you're happy to forget. An angry bird that shits on you then flies away. That's what love is, boy."

"Okay, okay," I said, retreating and feeling bad for it. Isla was stirring at our noisy confrontation. "We love each other. I did what I could do. We got away, didn't we? Thanks to her." I gestured to Sally, who pursed her lips at getting credit.

"Why were you coming here?" my aunt asked after an awkward silence. "What were you expecting?"

I was dumbfounded. After all we'd suffered to get here!

"We had no place else to go. And Mom made me promise to come back for you. For you and Bootsy. To save you. I mean, give you another chance to join us. But...well, I guess we're here to join you now. Because you have a big house to live in. If you wouldn't mind. I'm willing to work. I can dig a garden. We have some seeds. Mom thought we could make it work, but...."

"But...? Where is your mother, by the way? Why didn't she come with you?"

"Because...." I gazed up at my aunt with tears again filling my eyes. "Because she's dead."

My aunt blinked hard. "Dead?"

She lost her poise, slumped. She tried to drop herself into a sitting position, evidently in discomfort, yet unable to stand after that news.

I lowered my head, just as Isla was waking and getting grabby, and spoke as calmly as I could:

"She was murdered. On the island. By a man she met there. She liked him but he tricked her, got her to do things she didn't want to do, so when she discovered what he did she kicked him out, out of that beach house. Then, when my father returned — that's a whole 'nother story, but he's the man Mom said was on the beach that day — the man she kicked out got jealous, and kept harassing her. He eventually stabbed her. And in this new normal there wasn't any doctor or medic or hospital or ambulance, nobody who knew what to do, and she bled out, died right inside the community center, with all the members gathered for a meeting she was going to lead, and nobody did anything to help. Except me.

I went out, found that man, and I shot him with Mom's pistol. So the council ordered me off the island. Exiled. And Hannah chose to come with me, her and Isla. I told her it would be dangerous but she insisted. If she stayed, some other man would take her for his wife, according to their damn by-laws."

Aunt Laura was slowly nodding her head, as though it all made sense now.

"I'm sorry," she said, reaching across the floor for my hand and clasping my fingers. "Your mother could be a real bitch, pardon my French, but often the sweetest person in the world. Anyway, she never deserved that. Besides, she's family, and we never reject our own, no matter what they do. You did the right thing, Sandy. I mean shooting that man."

✳   ✳   ✳

And there I was, holding tight to my daddy, my chubby arms not meeting around his tense neck as he talked with his aunt and the woman from the camp whose milk I'd sucked in that witch's tent. I remembered being taken from my mama and fearing I would never see her again. But I did get her back, wounded perhaps yet alive. I was little more than a toy at that point, someone who mattered only in the future, when tough decisions would need to be made. For now, though, I could simply observe: 'watch and learn' that old man at the motel liked to say to my daddy.

He tried his best, I'm sure, to deal with our circumstances. I know he wanted to support my mama but didn't know what to do or what to say, got frustrated, blamed himself, talking about the things he'd done wrong in his life, how he missed his own mama, how he wasn't good enough for my mama. And his aunt, the tall, thin, older woman who looked ill and would die soon, told him hard truths he didn't want to hear, lessons about life, women's lives, the reality of their existence, the good and the bad, and what men could do, both the good and the bad, and how she herself had experienced the same thing too many times through the hard years of the pandemic, believing she could live on through the kindness of strangers and the barter system, yet soon enough realizing it could work for only so long before breaking down into the chaos of greed.

My mama rose eventually and came out to us. My daddy got up from the floor to meet her, handed me over to the other woman. He remained stuck in his place, his arms reaching for my mama, welcoming her and hugging her tightly, as we watched. I saw her crying streams as they parted, still holding each other's hands and gazing at each other.

I heard his aunt spouting pearls of wisdom in a honey voice: "There's nothing you can do, not in these hard times. No doctors about. Y'all going to have to live with it. However, get it stamped into your heads that it's neither of y'all's fault. It was a bad man that did it, and he's gone now – dead, she said. Paid with blood. So it's done. Best you move on now, as though it never happened – though y'all know it did."

And my daddy cried as much as my mama. The woman holding me cried. She had lived a rough life with those people, too. Thanks to my daddy she was able to escape from that camp, but she could never escape the things that happened to her there. My daddy's aunt teared up, thinking of the times when she was made to obey at the hands of a bad man, full of fire and temper, and because of obeying, she could keep going in these hard times – the result of a pandemic from a simple virus that no one should have ever been burdened with but, because of the mindless labyrinth of tortuous bureaucracy and the personal enrichment involved, went on to overwhelm the world. They messed up big time, my mama's aunt said.

I regarded these people from the arms of the woman they called Sally, seeing from the height of her shoulder a world of pain into which I had been brought, into which I would struggle. I had no clue how I was able to see everything: past, present, and future. I could not, however, change anything. Eventually it might become possible. That was the power of this strange woman's milk, filling me with a potion that sparked powers I didn't know how to control. Straight down the line from an old Appalachian witch. I only knew that I was yet a baby who had to continue acting like a baby until such a time as I could spring forth into my new form. Then I might be able to save the world, or a good portion of it. My grandmother spoke of a special child, a magical thing, born maybe once or twice in forever. It could yet happen. And she would blow a great horn to summon all to rise up. That would be the sign.

However, now it was time to play the part of the baby and fill the cloth around my bottom with my waste. They would be amused and care for me even more. They would feel needed and that would make them happy. I would let them care for me.

"Here," said my daddy's aunt. "Give her to me. Let me take care of that. Y'all've had enough stress already."

16

HARD TIMES

I listened to my mama speaking to my daddy: "He didn't hurt me, but he did force himself on me. I mean, didn't punch me or choke me to make me give in. His words were threats. Kept reminding me of my baby. So I had to let him or else something bad would happen to Isla. And he must've finished, I guess, by the way he acted, and the blood only came when he pulled out. He thought he busted me, but I reminded him I had a baby, gave birth already so it couldn't be that. Stupid man. No, it was my period starting up again. He was shocked. Guess he never saw that before. He apologized for hurting me. I acted like I was glad he apologized. I said I'd be his woman if they'd let my husband go. I'd keep my baby, of course, and raise her in their family. I said all that to put him at ease. But it wasn't good, I want you to know. I didn't enjoy it, didn't want it, but what could I do? I couldn't fight him. If I tried to fight him it would've been a whole lot worse. I tried to talk to him, get him to wait. If only my period came sooner, maybe he would've held off. But it didn't. He said things he thought would make me happy, compliments, saying I was sexy even though I was skinny, as he rolled on top with all his weight to do what he wanted. I wanted to scream, like it hurt, and I guess it did. I wasn't ready – but more so he'd think he was the big man doing his thing to a poor girl. It was like that. I said 'no' – had to, part of the act – made it sound real, but it only made him more excited. I played like I enjoyed it, but that made him work harder till it really did hurt and I complained. I tried not to cry. He said he was done and rolled off me. And then he saw the blood and thought he was something special. He asked if I liked it and course I said 'yeah' and he laughed, said we would do it again in the morning. Then he moved up against me and was quiet for a time, holding me in his arms with his b.o. stinking up the tent. He was asking questions, like where I'm from and all, and I answered, but I kept thinking when he fell asleep I would run out and get my baby from that old witch and just keep running till I couldn't run no more. That would've worked. No need to kill him like that."

"I didn't know what else to do," said my daddy, his face wet.

"I didn't know what they did with you. If you were even alive."

And my daddy held her tight, wouldn't let her go, repeating "I'm sorry, I'm so sorry," over and over until she made him stop.

"It's done," said my mama, wiping her eyes.

The woman named Sally held me while they talked, tried to turn me away from my mama and daddy crying, maybe to save me from their trauma. However, it would never be enough to protect me from what they endured to save me from the clutches of that witch and her evil plan, from the evil brothers who did her bidding, from the spell she laid upon me, a simple spell which would bend and twist me into a wild creature they could never control. Only my mama and daddy could ever do that, yet they would not wish to do that, because I would save them one day, long after they had forgotten what happened to them in the woods.

* * *

Aunt Laura kept staring at me and I finally asked her why.

"Because you look terrible, Sandy," she said.

"Well, they did beat me up pretty good," I responded. "My face hurts. So does my back. And my ribs. And my legs feel like rubber. Charley horses, you know."

"Here," she ordered, "come with me."

I got up and followed her. She led me into another room in the long hallway. This room had furniture and she gestured for me to sit down on the old chaise lounge. I felt like a prince lazing on that half-couch.

"Shirt off," she directed. "Sit up."

It was rather difficult pulling my shirt off over my head with everything hurting. Sitting in a car, driving for hours wasn't so bad. I hadn't noticed the pain while we were fleeing, focused on our escape. I guess adrenalin took over. Now I could feel each wound clearly and sharply.

Aunt Laura gasped at the marks on my body. "That's a beating for sure, bless your heart."

She had a tube in her hands, squeezed out ointment. Her hand was cold on my skin but soothing. She pointed out each bruise and I winced when she touched them. My face required a more delicate touch but I let her go ahead, not resisting. Thank goodness she had no mirrors in there or I'd know how ugly I must appear to Hannah, who rested in another room.

"Don't you worry." She continued massaging my wounds. "I'm sure you two'll be fine. You and your cute baby."

"Where's Bootsy?" I blurted out, my thoughts leaping into my mouth unchecked.

Aunt Laura froze, finger right over a sore spot between my shoulder blades. She seemed to give her answer some thought.

"You mean Bethany Anne...."

"Is that her real name?" I asked in a nicer voice.

"Yes, Bethany Anne. Yet she could never have lived up to that name. My late husband's dear grandmother, the matriarch of their industrial concern. Impressive woman. No, 'Bootsy' was a childish nickname. From the way she tried to say her name."

She chuckled, seemed to relax a little.

"Where is she? Playing in her room?"

"No."

Her massaging continued in silence. Then, reaching the end of my back, she could delay no further.

"Like your mother, Bootsy is also dead, I'm sorry to say."

"What?"

I enjoyed meeting my five-year-old cousin previously. I played

Mom's tuba for her. We shared a game of hide-n-seek. She came to me in the night with a soiled diaper that needed changing – only to have my aunt grab her away, telling me not to touch her, like I was some kind of pervert.

Aunt Laura sat on the chaise lounge beside me, her hands in her lap. The ratty bathrobe fell open a bit too much, revealing a boney figure and frightful lesions across her breasts. She stared down at her hands.

"She wasn't going to make it," said Aunt Laura in solemn tone. "It was better she went quick."

"Virus?"

She shook her head. "Earl took care of it."

"Big Earl? What'd he do?"

"He...took care of it."

"What do you mean by that?" I was getting worried.

A few sniffles ensued. "He ended her life. But it was quick. She never suffered."

"But why?"

She turned to me, her face flushed and tears streaming.

"You don't know what we went through. It was awful. Horrible! We were trapped here. A gang was terrorizing us, surrounding the house. We couldn't get deliveries. It seemed it would never end. I tried to go out but they chased me back in. A gang of teens – pre-teens, twelve or thirteen maybe, maybe twenty of them, like a herd of jackals." She paused to breathe.

"You were attacked by a gang of kids?"

"Forget their age. They were vicious. No hesitation killing. Earl tried to reason with them but they attacked him. He lost an arm: grabbed him, wouldn't let him go, and another one brought a saw up to...."

"Pandemic monsters," I cried, shaking at the image.

"I got him tied up awright so he wouldn't bleed but you know there's no doctors nowadays. So he got infected, then.... It's hard to say. He died. That's why I don't go upstairs. He's still there in the bathtub, covered in sheets and some cement I mixed up. Easier than digging a grave. I couldn't go outdoors, too dangerous."

My eyes went to the ceiling. In my previous visit, I'd never had reason to go upstairs. That was where she took her visitors for an hour.

"What about the gang of kids? We didn't see any when we got here."

"No, they're gone, thank goodness." She looked at me, deciding what to say. "Earl didn't show up at the corrections institute, so someone came looking for him here. Two of his...his colleagues, I suppose they're called. I explained his injury, the infection. But they didn't care. They decided to try what Earl'd gotten. I fought them as best I could. And poor Earl was too weak to help me."

"But the gang of kids?"

"Those two shot them. All the marauders. Used shotguns. Got them all, one after the other. None of them escaped alive, they said – while they were taking me as they wished, treating me harshly. That was the one good thing in an ugly afternoon. Getting rid of those vicious feral kids. They returned other days. A few times they brought others. It was horrible. And no food deliveries, either. Occasional sandwiches from the corrections institute sometimes, a prisoner's meal all it was."

I didn't know what to say. She'd had a difficult time since I last visited, no doubt, and I could understand her appearance.

"They won't be back," she muttered. "They made it clear I'm no longer attractive. I don't look good to them nowadays. They worked me over too much, I suppose." She tried to laugh, failed. "That's my fate. As your mother predicted."

"So you know how Hannah felt...."

Her face tensed.

"We all know. It's the way of the world, young man. Don't you forget it." She shook her head, recalling. "Earl and I turned this house into a fortress. Boarded the windows, barred the doors extra tight. Manned them with what guns we had. He would take shots at them. They broke in a few times but he shot them. They even climbed up to the second floor, feet on shoulders, to break in through a window there but Earl chopped their hands with an axe and they fell."

"But there's no bodies out there...."

"He gathered them, dragged them back behind the barn. Now I suppose some wild animals may have fed on those corpses since then. It's been nearly a year. He did that with only one arm, bless his heart."

I couldn't breathe, hearing her story. Nothing was going to be better in this new normal everyone was praying for. How could this be the normal anyone wanted? Every man, woman, and child for themselves, the only goal finding food to get you to the next day. And brutal, forced sex if you're not hungry.

"This is what you left that island for?" she asked. "You should have stayed, no matter what rules Hannah said they had."

I shook my head, then looked up at her.

"So they killed Bootsy, too?"

"Oh no." She flashed a weak smile which seemed inappropriate. Maybe she was embarrassed. "Earl killed her, like I said."

"But why? Was she sick?"

"No."

"Then why?"

"Because we were hungry!"

* * *

We rested into the evening, the only sounds the occasional sobbing from my aunt in a room far down the hallway, or Isla stirring and wanting to play. After what would've been supper time, I went in search of food, nervous at the thought of finding only something I would deem inedible.

I went downstairs into the pantry, found shelves of canned food there. Shelves of jars containing vegetables and fruit. I already knew there was an electric can opener in the kitchen, but with no electricity, that was only an antique curiosity. Thirty-nine cans of vegetables, fruit, and a few of chili, tuna, Spam. A plastic box held lots of packets of microwave rice, noodles, potatoes. Another held microwave dinners which had all gone bad with no refrigeration.

Wondering if my aunt knew there were cans down here when

she and Earl dined on her daughter's body, I brought a few cans upstairs, showed them to Sally. She brightened at the sight of the food. Yet I felt sick thinking of my aunt and Earl preparing their sacrificial dinner. Perhaps they'd gone insane, even for a few days, driven mad by the attacks, fearing the end. Perhaps they expected they would die anyway. Food in jars and cans was their long-term ration, I considered; fresh meat wouldn't last too long so better to consume it quickly. My gut tightened.

Sally and I managed to make a decent meal from a can of peas, one of potatoes, and a can of chili-no-beans. Thankfully, there was a manual can opener in one of the kitchen drawers. We put out plates, divided the food.

Aunt Laura joined us, no doubt alerted by our commotion, and immediately shrieked that we weren't allowed more than one can per meal.

"We have four people," I explained. "Three cans for four people is fair. And Isla needs milk, so Hannah's gotta eat."

"I've got milk, too," Sally offered, a hand cupping her breast. "They kept me nursing their babies in the camp down the hill from the one you was at. I need to empty them."

"We all need to eat something," I said.

My aunt's nasty robe had fallen open in her consternation. We saw the lesions, red and purple, ugly as heck, but not like rashes some people got who took too many of the vaccines and boosters.

"What's that?" asked Hannah, perking up at the sight.

Aunt Laura snapped her robe closed. "It's nothing."

"No, it's something," I said. "I saw it when you were massaging my sores."

"Well, you got your massage, so there's really no need for any further questions."

"But what is it, Aunt Laura?" asked Hannah boldly.

Our aunt stood firm, her face a stone mask. She glanced at Sally, holding Isla, who looked at me.

"I suppose it's God's punishment," said my aunt.

"Punishment?" I asked. "For what?"

"For what I've done. Everything."

Hannah started to ask what that might be, daring her aunt to name her sins, but I clasped her hand and she understood not to ask more.

"It's cancer," said my aunt. "That's my self-diagnosis. However, there are no doctors anywhere, much less a competent oncologist."

"Breast cancer?" asked Hannah, shocked. "Mother thought she had it, too – years ago – but she got a few treatments and it went away. I guess it was early stage."

"No chance of that now, dear," my aunt replied softly. "It's in God's hands. And He seems to have decided the result in my case. 'This one I won't be saving.' He told me so."

"It doesn't work like that," I jumped in.

"You know what I've done." My aunt addressed me. "Of course your mother didn't approve. Yet it was the only way. We had to survive until things return to normal. But she said...your mother said there would never be a return to our kind of normal. At least not in our lifetime."

"We wanted you to come with us," I spoke up.

"To that island? To the beach house? That awful place?"

"It wasn't so bad.... At first."

She waved her hand around the room. "I have this house. I wanted to stay here. I just never expected things to get so out of hand as they did. I had deliveries of food for a while. I even had Earl taking care of me. In the end, however, it all fell apart – as you well know."

"We know—"

"It's like in one of my Economics courses way back, when we studied market trends. Talked about rats in a cage. Pent up, they went mad. Then, when they were released, they savaged their lab neighborhood, not for any economic reason but to let off steam, as it were."

"Sounds more like Sociology than Economics," I cut in. "I was taking Sociology in college before—"

"Think of humans in the same situation: locked up, forced to stay together, with no hope, no expectation that it will end soon, and with limited food and other necessary supplies. Then everyone is released from confinement. They burst into rage at everything and everyone around them. Again, not for any economic reason – they're not searching for food – it's merely to vent the energy they've built up."

"That's sounds like science," said Hannah in serious tone.

"Ready to explode – at each other within their lockdown space or in society once they're let out into it."

"Definitely science," Hannah confirmed.

"I stayed here. With my youngest, Bootsy, who'd never survive out there. I don't know what has happened to my other children. Except Kenneth." She glanced over at me, who knew already, then turned to Hannah. "He was grabbed by a wild gang of men. They butchered him! Right there in the back yard. Made a bonfire and barbequed him, cut into separate pieces, laughing as I watched from the window." She pointed up and my eyes followed.

Hannah sat shocked, then threw her hands to her face.

"José came by and got his kid in the early days. He wanted to take his family back to Mexico. He thought it wouldn't be as bad down there. I haven't heard from them in all the time since."

"I'm sure they're fine," I offered.

"How can you be sure? They may not have gotten there, what with all the violence on the roads nowadays."

"I'm hopeful."

My aunt gestured at Hannah. "Still hopeful?"

I hung my head at that.

"You nearly lost your wife and child," she continued.

"I have to stay hopeful – hopeful everything *will* get better."

"You keep on repeating that mantra, nephew, up to your final breath."

"I will."

"José is...?" asked Hannah cautiously.

"Her gardener," I quietly replied.

"Really?"

"The twins, Sammy and Tammy, were away at their boarding schools. Sammy was ready to transition, I was told, going to be Samantha. Tammy, they said, was turning into a fine dyke. Better for them to go with the trends and survive, I believed. Yet no word from their schools to this day. And Bootsy...."

Hannah was quietly sobbing. No doubt the memories of her own siblings weighed on her. Her two younger sisters were dead. We had all lost someone, we soon discovered once we were on the island. It was a sanctuary of survivors trying to start again – but in a decidedly weird way, based on ideas in a science fiction novel the community leader liked. My wife lost her brother on the island, hanged from a pier by the same man who stabbed Mom.

"It's a terrible time to be alive," I said to the dark corners of the room. "Yet here we are: still alive. Somehow. Despite everything we've been through."

At that, Isla perked up, gurgled a message to us, squirming in Sally's arms, reaching for my aunt.

She took Isla from Sally's arms, held her against her shoulder as Isla waved her arms as if in triumph.

"I was always a little envious of your mother," said Aunt Laura. "As the baby of the family she received all our parents' attention, and that of other family and friends, no matter what achievement I earned. And she was musical."

I looked up at my aunt, feeling glad she confessed.

"I was supposed to be the one to lead our family. Make us a good family – after what your grandfather got away with. I got to go to a big university, get a degree, two of them, in fact. Then I did something foolish: I married a man from a good family who had no business sense and tried to run his family business. He preferred the trappings of success without doing the work. He liked to dally with his secretary, and you know the rest of that story."

"You could've been something," said Hannah sadly.

"I was something, niece," my aunt snapped. "I ran his company – till this pandemic changed everything. However, I always envied your mother's freedom. She had you, which was not an easy time, certainly, but then she was free to do as she pleased. She wasn't the eldest child who had to take on family responsibilities. No, she could learn to play that god-awful horn and go on tours, dancing half-naked on stage, bless her heart. At least Polly found a career playing in the orchestra and teaching music, right? That certainly was something: a landing for a fast jet that had soared through the clouds, her boy in tow. I suppose she realized the need for a good stable environment for you, Sandy."

"Yeah, guess so." But I felt sad hearing about Mom.

"Now she's dead. As we all shall be soon enough. It's only a matter of time. One way or another. Praise the Lord. I can hardly wait for my final breath. To let this pain end."

17

THE ROAD TO RUIN

In the days that followed, I went around the large house and its extensive grounds, noting unfortunate flaws to the kind of idyllic landscape I'd wished for. I checked behind the old barn, just large enough for a pair of horses that no longer existed. I saw the pile of bones behind the barn, skeletons of young humans disturbed by wild animals. I opened the barn doors and stood back as the musky air wafted out, then went inside with a cloth covering my nose and mouth. I gathered a few tools for later.

Work made the day pass better, and having an excuse to stay away from Hannah and Isla helped us heal. Sally brought me a drink, stayed to chat. She had no plans, she said, so I told her we might as well stay here. Plenty of rooms, some with secrets, others closed for our own good, yet enough remained for us to lodge in – like the motel across the strait from the island.

When she left me, I paused to contemplate the island, the ferry landing, and the motel, wondering if Quinn missed us. He no doubt missed Hannah – and the thought filled me with anger. Him! And those brothers in the woods! A crow flew by, cawed at me like it was leaving me a message. *Yeah, get over it*, it seemed to say.

In the normal life we were denied, Hannah would've grown up, met other boys, tried a few sexual experiences of greater or lesser success and pleasure, and when she finally did meet me, both of us being older, she would welcome me not as her first but as her last lover. I wouldn't care that she had experimented. Or, if I were to be truly honest, we might never meet.

I gazed at the sun, feeling its brightness burn into my eyes a moment before looking away, the intense fire blazing in my mind.

You're a fool, I chided myself, continued examining what in the barn might be useful, taking it for the next phase of our journey.

We can't stay here. Too many bad omens. Something is going to happen. I can feel it—

A shot rang out from the house, echoed across the yard.

I went to the open doorway, staring from the barn to the back porch. The memory of finding my grandparents sitting in chairs on their back porch after their murder-suicide returned to me. The back veranda was empty, though, the French doors ajar. I took a few breaths, preparing myself for what might happen next.

I ran to the house, burst through the doors into the main hall.

I heard a scream from down the hallway.

Rather than run, I walked, measuring my steps so I did not arrive too soon.

It was my aunt's room, what she used as her room now, the one with the chaise lounge. She sat upon it, comfortably lazing as a queen in her parlor, leaning back against the end panel with her head tilting away from my view. But I saw the result of her prayer.

"What happened?" cried Hannah, rushing to the doorway.

We saw the blood. Mom's pistol hung on Aunt Laura's finger, drooping on the floor.

I retrieved the pistol, regretting not carrying it with me while I was outside. I put the safety on.

"She was in constant pain, she said." I turned to Hannah. "I guess she didn't want anymore of it."

I found some rags and cleaned the blood, sending Hannah out to take care of Isla, who was just getting to know her great-aunt. Sally helped me transfer the body onto a sheet so we could slide her out of the room, down the hallway, and out the back doors. I got her to the end of the yard where I left her covered with the sheet while I began digging her grave – just like Mom and I did for my grandparents.

I hadn't planned to dig a grave when I awoke that morning, but things needed to be done. Always some task. Routine helped keep me balanced. Physical labor kept my mind from freaking out. The toil held off my meltdowns. I could think more clearly as I worked my still sore shoulders and back, using the pick and the shovel I'd taken from the barn.

Now what? In a twisted way I supposed that in some greater scheme, I inherited the house. Unless Laura's ex-husband claimed it. There wasn't much left anyway. It harbored too many disturbing vibes. Besides, a big house like this one just invited marauders and scavengers searching for anything useful. Nobody would bother breaking into a poor-looking house.

When I'd finished digging, I cleaned up and called the others to join me for the ceremony. We said some kind words about her. Isla wasn't having it and cried like she didn't want to be there. The sun shone, the cool breeze calmed us, and the pandemic seemed far away. Sally had cut some flowers from a patch at the end of the house. They had grown on their own without need of our attention, a reminder that life would go on no matter what we did.

I pulled the body to the side, eased it down into the grave, then said a prayer that had been underlined in Aunt Laura's childhood Bible. I found the book on her nightstand. In the front were pages where someone had written the names and birth/death dates of family members going back four generations. I saw my mom's name and birth date – no death date – and mine.

Beside the grave, Hannah gave me a firm one-armed hug while holding a fussy Isla in her other arm, then returned to the house with Sally as I filled in the grave, made a nice mound. I wished Mom were here to see off her big sister.

Now it was only us who survived: the remaining generation. And Isla representing the next generation, so busy watching and learning. Someone had to survive. Someone had to carry on, try to make things right. "So where do you see yourself in five years?" I was asked at a job interview four years before.

*   *   *

"Do you have anywhere to go?" I asked Sally after dinner, using another pair of cans. Hannah had taken Isla away for nursing.

"My home is far away," she replied in a sad voice.

"No relatives around here?" I wasn't trying to put her off, just trying to get an idea how we could help her.

"No, we were going to my parents' when we got stopped."

She got emotional, wiped her eyes.

"You think they're okay?" I asked after a moment.

"Who knows? It's been three years. No way to contact them. They could be dead – either from the virus or like your aunt. They never knew what happened to us."

I nodded, trying to understand. "Well, of course, you're welcome to come with us. I just wanted to check with you, you know, if you had other plans. See if we could help you."

She sniffled back tears. "Plans? I guess I didn't think that far. I only wanted to get away from them. You were my ticket. Thanks for taking me with you. God, it was just a few days ago I was their slave girl – and now free! Can't believe it. No, I don't know what to do. I'll try to help out, take care of your baby, clean up, things like that. At least I'm not getting raped now."

I almost choked, caught myself, and took a long inhale.

"If you want to get rid of me, it's okay, too," she continued. "I'll go. I can walk somewhere, see what's there. Make my own way. I don't mind. Whatever you want."

"Well, Isla seems to like you," I offered, thinking how she had resisted being shifted from Sally's arms back to Hannah's. "Seems you two get on fine."

"And she's gotten some of my milk, too, so she knows me. They had me nursing little Clyde and Caleb over at the camp in the next hollow. And a newborn, just before you arrived. Mariah, I think they called her. Nursing them was my only time to get any rest."

"Milk is milk, I guess." Another stupid thing to say, I realized by her *humpf*.

"My mama said her milk was special – different somehow – and that's why I was smarter than other kids. We come from poor stock but I got into university. I guess even milk gets passed down."

"Oh, yeah?"

Just making conversation, but I began to wonder if there was anything true to that idea. Mother's milk was made from whatever the mother ate, I knew from school. Mom had insisted Hannah get as much protein as possible, which on the island came mostly from fish, although later we got eggs from the community's chickens.

"That old witch, heathen at the worst, though they all played at being Christian. Folk stuff, mixed together," said Sally. "I feared her. Always threatening me. In her tent she had a lot of pagan things. Artifacts, tokens. Voodoo stuff. Like for casting spells."

"Oh, that's just fake." But I wasn't sure. The stuff of movies to scare people. The pandemic made everything real. Horror movies were made right outside your door now. "She may have believed it, but I doubt anything ever changed by her doing some ritual or saying a spell."

"I'm not so sure," said Sally.

"Well, I don't believe any of that. My mom was a professor. She taught me to look at the truth of things, think logically, not go for magical beliefs. Have to see things with your own eyes, experience it directly. Scientific method. Like they did with the virus, figuring out its structure so they could make a vaccine."

She seemed taken aback. "Did they? I mean about the virus. We heard it was fake. Oh, the virus was real enough, but it was made in a lab – cobbled together from other viruses. They wanted to use it to get control over everyone. So they could push the vaccines on everyone. That's the real pandemic: those so-called vaccines. Then they could control us. Like how you had to wear a mask just to demonstrate your compliance with their rules. A mark of the devil, Maw said. Play along with—"

"Now hold on," I said, hearing Mom's voice in my head.

"It's like a witch's spell: believe it or don't believe it, it may still work on you whether or not you're aware of it working on you. That virus is like that. What's it really doing? Who really knows how things would've been without the pandemic going on? If it was all planned, then it worked perfectly."

"But it...."

I didn't know what to think, Mom's words coming back to me. She never believed it was as serious as they said, not that she was a scientist. But she was smart. She could read reports like anyone could. She might've been only a music teacher but she knew how science funding worked, how you play the game, giving the results that those funding it want. She ranted about colleagues on campus 'dealing with the devil' and their questionable research projects. She mentioned her doctor friend – she tutored his son on tuba. She admitted, when I pressed her on it as we traveled, that we hadn't actually gotten the vaccine. None of them. We had fake vaccine cards. Yet we never got sick, either, not to any degree. Nothing too different from a common cold. We still wore the masks when required and kept away from other people.

"Why would anyone want to kill off so many people?"

Sally grinned, looking half pure evil and half a carnival barker. The way the evening light struck her face affected my perception. She moved to get out of the sunset glow.

"To make the world easier to rule," she replied.

I scoffed. Then I nodded, thinking about what she said but also drifting into my own world as Mom's words echoed around me. It was six years of the long flu season with all that messaging, news reports, countless medical discussions, and the masking, keeping apart, restrictions of what you could do and where you could go, how many people allowed in one place, and the vaccines, one after another, and booster shots, and whatever other medications people thought would help – before Mom got to the point she decided we should leave the city, believing it wasn't going to get better any time soon. And we got to the island, living in that beach house for almost two years.

"Well, it's been eight years now," I muttered. "And everything's collapsed. Nothing to go back to. Gotta start over. Doesn't matter what we believe anymore."

"What I'm saying is the same thing they – the government and health officials – were telling us isn't believable any more than what my granny told me about what certain herbs and minerals, and the right spells can do. If you're raised on magic, you believe in magic. If you're raised on that science, you believe that."

"Well, you gotta believe in something," I said, realizing how stupid my rebuttal was as soon as I said it. "What I mean is.... How do you know? Are you a scientist? Or a doctor?"

"You don't need to be a scientist or a doctor to read what scientists and doctors publish. Of course, what gets published is based on the gatekeepers shutting out any opposing views. It takes intelligence to understand what they write about, what they say. Technical language. You still have to read it yourself."

"That's what my mom said. She said grants are always subject to the researchers getting the results the grant funders want."

"You're mom was right." She took a big breath, like she was reloading for more debate. "You wouldn't know it to look at me now, but I used to be a model. The kind of model who posed in let's say provocative poses for photographers. That was a long time ago. But before that, I was a medical student, working to be a doctor. I studied all that stuff. It was my granny who got me interested in nutrition, herbs, all that, how to treat people holistically. So I read lots of articles, tons of them. I learned all that."

"No, I never would've guessed," I said when she paused.

"If not for a fucking cheating scandal, I would've completed my degree, started residency. I would've been right there on the front lines when the pandemic started. I would've been treating people – maybe catch it myself, maybe die. Maybe my daughter would've died that way, instead of how she did. Her dad might've given a damn. He wouldn't ever accept her as his. Said I slept around. But I didn't."

"You're right," I said, only partly joking. "I wouldn't believe you were a model. No offense intended."

"None taken. I'm thirty-three now. I think. Looks go. Especially living rough in the woods. Anyway, that was ten years ago. When they kicked me out of med school I grabbed the first job that came my way. I had student loans to pay, but without the career to pay it off. A guy offered me money for, you know, *posing*. Which led to more photography. I'm not saying I was real sexy or anything. More the girl-next-door type. But nude. Flirty, not slutty. Wearing bikinis, lingerie, acting flirtatious. But not actual porn. Never did any sex on camera. Gawd, that was a lifetime ago...."

"I'm sorry."

"Sorry for what?" She pursed her lips, staring at me.

"Nothing. I always say that." I had to grin at her. "My mom got me into that habit."

"But here we are, in tough times, barely getting by...."

I pondered our situation a moment.

"We need to get a bunch of people together. I mean good people who'll share the work that's necessary to rebuild society. We need to get a farm started, grow crops, raise livestock. Like olden days."

I regarded her a little too long and she looked away.

"But we keep running into bad people who are determined to hang on to the last scraps of the old society, just taking what they want, waiting for the end—"

"Instead of admitting we need to start again," she cut in.

"My aunt has a good amount of land here. If only we could find a tractor to plow it. We have seeds. Then we need a few chickens, maybe some goats. They practically raise themselves. A pig would be good to have for the manure." Our eyes met. "We could make it work here."

"As long as gangs of feral kids don't come back," she said in a serious voice, then broke into laughter.

I didn't understand. "She said they were all killed."

Sally shook her head, looking down. "There will always be feral children searching for food. The pandemic killed off the elderly and regular adults a lot more than the kids. Lot of orphans out there. Hungry orphans. And they will form bands, working together. It's kind of like that *Lord of the Flies*."

I pondered a while, then: "What's flies got to do with it?"

✳ ✳ ✳

She was right. When she wasn't helping Hannah take care of Isla, Sally poked around the house, found a lot of secrets to avoid. The house had eight bedrooms and five bathrooms. Four bedrooms and two bathrooms were off-limits because of what secrets they held. It seemed that not all who arrived to exchange goods for services left the house. She called me to confirm her investigation.

"I really can't say. Maybe they mistreated her and she just responded with equal violence. Tit for tat, as they say."

"Tit for tat?" Sally cracked a smile.

In the bathroom where Earl rested, we could see the hump in the concrete where his half-arm lay atop the rim of the tub. Nothing else gave away his final resting place. I saw the floor had sunk a little with the added weight.

There was another bathroom which held someone in a similar way. And the bedrooms had been locked, but we found keys and opened them to horrors we hadn't expected. On the beds lay bodies wrapped in plastic, covered with cloth sheets and blankets, blood stains on the beds and carpet. One room had sets of handprints on the walls, as though the victim had been trying to escape. The flies didn't seem to mind the stench.

"I guess that's what I've been smelling," said Sally. "Just like the cadaver lab in med school."

"Yeah, I just noticed it."

"I never would've thought she could be so violent."

"I wouldn't ever have believed she could be so damn strong," I responded. "Fighting those men."

"Maybe it was her man friend who did it."

"Earl? ...Maybe."

"They simply closed the doors to rooms they would no longer be using."

"Looks that way."

We discovered a cedar chest at the end of the bed in the last room on the hallway. It had a horrible odor leaking out. And the body of a child, not yet fully decomposed, lay inside. It was missing legs, as though they'd been cut off, amputated – I hoped after the child had died, but I couldn't be sure. Perhaps there had been an accident and the legs needed to be removed. Then, once removed, they decided not to waste the meat.

I recognize the decaying face as my little cousin, that little girl my aunt considered a burden. Mentally handicapped. She wouldn't be able to survive, she'd told us.

"So they only ate her legs," said Sally, staring hard into the cedar chest.

I closed the lid, replaced the padlock, got up and practically leaped to the doorway to catch my breath.

"People can be so evil," she said, joining me for fresh air. "A pandemic can bring out the worst of our humanity."

"Humanity? What's that?"

I had to leave, had to walk away and be alone a while, a chance to decompress from this revenge tour.

We suffered a lot just getting to my aunt's house, thinking we could make a go of it here. But what we found here wasn't very inviting. I couldn't sleep well after finding what we uncovered in the house. It was a mortuary now. I imagined the spirits roaming the halls, looking for revenge. We were the only ones available to be their victims. Sure, we could close the doors, but we could never forget what lay behind those doors.

Another day, at the end of the hallway I found a nearly empty room – old paintings stacked up with other unneeded decorations. At the corner of the room an ornate spiral staircase coiled down to the first floor. I went down, stepping lightly as the wrought-iron structure rattled. At the bottom another room awaited. It was full of useless electronics: old televisions, videotape players, a stereo system with five units, several game consoles, a record player turntable and boxes of vinyl albums. I gave the albums a brief look, flipping through them, finding they were music from way before my time, old songs from the '80s.

The door at the side of that room appeared to be a closet, so I had to look inside, hesitating in anticipation of a skeleton hidden there. Instead, the door led to the garage.

Three vehicles sat there: a large gold Cadillac sedan, an open-topped green jeep, and a camper van. A fourth parking spot was empty except for a few bikes stacked against the wall.

The van got my attention. Orange flames went down the sides. Across the rear doors was painted: *If it's a-rockin' don't come a-*

knockin'. Otherwise, it looked like the kind of van people could live in for a short trip. I saw the layout of table and padded benches, a mini fridge and cabinets. If desired, the roof could be raised up to make more headroom. It smelled stale, but it had been locked up for who knew how long?

On the side of the garage was a gray metal box fixed to the wall. Inside were rows of hooks, some with keys hanging. They were clearly labeled, as though someone had anticipated this day when a stupid kid like me would come to try out the vehicles.

I went to the Cadillac first and sat in it, put the key in and waited. I admired the meticulous interior, its plush upholstery, the special touches only a luxury automobile would have. It must've been my uncle's pride and joy. I turned the key and the engine did nothing. I tried again, then gave up. Probably the battery had died long ago.

I went to the jeep next and got a groan from the engine. It started eventually. I quickly noted the fuel needle sitting on E and shut off the engine. I wondered how much gasoline might be in the Cadillac, if it was viable now, and how I could get it out. I looked over at the van.

Sitting in the driver's seat, facing the garage doors, I had a strange feeling. I saw the unmistakable trappings of a corrections officer inside. This must be Earl's van. I thought back to the day he pulled up in front of the house and Aunt Laura gleefully ushered him upstairs with hardly more of an introduction to me and Mom than that he was her 'beau'. They stayed upstairs and he left the next morning.

Evidently he kept returning, eventually backing his vehicle in the garage attached to the house by a kind of man cave my uncle had built. That made sense: the garage next to the 'man cave', all his entertainments close together, all at one end of the house to be away from his shrew wife. I smiled at the thought.

I turned the key in the ignition and the engine cranked over, rattling a bit then found its groove and churned steadily. The fuel gauge showed a half-tank. I shut off the engine, felt the van shake. I didn't want to waste another drop of gas. Thank goodness there was something positive about this place.

Thinking of Hannah and Isla, I imagined the three of us going in this van on a camping trip to some state park. We would set up the roof, cook our own meals. I might catch some fish in the lake. Isla could commune with nature, maybe chase butterflies, splash in the creek, hike over trails beneath a shady forest. We would be a happy family. If only we could make that dream real.

The reality now was that if I were to take my family out for a weekend's camping, we would most likely be set upon by a roving band of hungry people, possibly feral children. There was no more camaraderie among campers. Vacationers were on their own. No more friendly greetings, no hands waving from passing cars. No sharing of a cup of sugar or of coffee. No singing songs around a campfire. Now campfires would be only for cooking whatever food they had managed to kill, animal or human, depending how skilled they were, how desperate they might be. And some of them might even carry the virus or one of its variants so a single cough caught on the breeze might bring it into our noses and that would be the end of us. Just like that.

No, a van was useless.

But a van with gasoline had possibilities....

18

VAN LIFE

In that moment I couldn't help but grin at the sight, grinning like I hadn't for too many harrowing days.

"Ay? Ay...?" I gestured down at Isla in her makeshift diaper, propped up on the driver's seat in Big Earl's van while I turned to see Hannah's reaction. "Isn't she cute?"

"Really?" my wife remarked, unimpressed, with arms crossed over her chest, head tilted to the side in judgment.

"What?" I waved my hands. "Hey, she's cute. Admit it. Besides, she'll be driving someday. If they ever get around to refining some more gasoline."

"Please don't have our baby sitting where Earl's butt was."

"She's got a diaper on."

"I doubt that's enough."

She stepped away, pulled a shop rag off a cluttered table at the back of the garage where a few auto parts sat, forgotten.

"Here, raise her up." She laid out the cloth, no cleaner than the seat's cushion, and smoothed it. "Okay, you can sit her down."

I lowered Isla to the same spot. She gazed up at her mother as though wondering what all the fuss was about. I took her little hands and tried to stretch them up to the steering wheel. We got only to the lower rim. But Isla wasn't having it and began to cry.

"You need to spray down everything in here," said Hannah. "Like your mom did with that truck those men drove. We could've gotten real sick from their coughing. But, hell, your mom made us swim in that pond to wash off."

"I remember...." Actually it was a wonderful memory, despite the man chasing and tackling Hannah, trying to assault her, and me having no choice but to shoot him. Actually, my finger slipped and the pistol went off. Maybe it wasn't such a good memory.

"That's where you first saw me. Saw me plumb naked for the first time." Her eyes seemed to twinkle at me.

"And you saw me, too." I smiled, a little embarrassed.

"Hah! Pervert!"

"Pervette!" I countered, not sure if it was a word.

With a moment's gaze at each other we threw ourselves into an embrace, locked in a tight kiss, before I could even recall what had happened to her and pull away in disgust. I didn't want my lips touching the lips that *he* may have kissed. Or lips that may have done more than I dared consider.

I drew away. She seemed surprised at first, then appeared to understand. I felt bad.

"Sorry," I moaned.

"It's okay," she muttered, stepping back.

We stood quietly beside the van, with Isla calm again. Then she let out a squeak, seemed to enjoy her ability to make a noise and tried it again. We laughed at her effort.

Hannah came to me, put her hands up to cradle my face, held me firmly, and planted a big wet kiss hard on my mouth.

"There," she declared proudly, dropping down, feet flat on the floor. "Those lips are mine. They belong to me. I'm still your wife. Got it? No matter what happens. Okay?"

"Okay, I believe you."

"And you're my damn husband. Always. No matter what."

"Okay," I mumbled, stunned. "Thank you."

"I didn't do anything to hurt you. I only wanted to save us. Or you and Isla, at least. I begged them to let you both go free. So forget it. I did what I had to do."

"I will," I snapped back at her.

"Good."

Catching my breath, I realized she was right. She was always right. She was my compass, my home port, the air I breathed. I couldn't imagine what she would think if the reverse happened. Suppose I was forced to go with Ana Maria back on the island, the way we'd been scheduled to pair up by the council? How would Hannah feel about that? What would she do?

Isla's gurgling broke me from my rabbit hole trip.

"I know you don't wanna stay here," I said, just to completely change the subject. I felt immediate relief.

"What makes you think that?" Hannah retrieved Isla from the driver's seat, cooed at her.

"Because," I spoke firmly, "you're always saying 'I hate it here' and 'This is a house of horror'."

"Oh." She had her attention on Isla.

"I get that it's a creepy place," I responded with as kind a voice as I could muster. "But it is a house. With a big yard. Plenty of land to farm. We could make it work."

"You would plow it? Plant seeds? Tend them? Harvest them? With no tractor? Breaking your back? Would you?"

"I would." Sure, maybe I'd give it a try for a while but then I'd give up, being too much work for one man. Even with a wife to help me, it would be too much. I'm a city boy, after all.

"Would you?" She had Mom's snark sitting on her face. In that instant I both loved the memory and hated the response.

"Yeah, I'd break my back for you – you and Isla," I replied. "If you would massage my back every night."

"You know I'd do that anyway. You just have to ask."

We stared at each other a moment too long and I worried she'd try to kiss me again. I was being stupid, I knew, but couldn't stop. I took a deep breath.

"Well, what other option do we have? We have to do something. We have to start over if we're going to survive."

She sighed. "Survive.... I hate that word."

"I know, I know. You wanted to be a rockstar."

She laughed, a true guffaw that filled the garage. Isla giggled in sympathy.

"Listen," I said gently, "we can just keep those rooms closed off and never go to this end of the house. Plenty of space on the other end, with the kitchen and all. In time we'll forget there are even any bodies over here."

Her mirth flipped to anger. "That's the craziest idea I ever heard!"

I stared at her, watched her calm down blink by blink, and now felt like kissing her. My eyes shifted to her lips as she spoke:

"Now we have a means to an end." She patted the side of the van with her hand.

"This van?" I wasn't sure what she meant.

"Yes, this van." She grinned. "You said it's got gas. We can go somewhere. Back to the motel. Is that okay?"

"To the motel? Okay? To see Quinn? Isn't there any other place we could go?"

"Listen, Sandy," she began, mocking my way of speaking, "we came all the way here to Aunt Laura's and what did we find?"

"It was a legit destination," I said, losing my urge to kiss her. "This big house. The property. It could hold several families. Plus our aunt...and Bootsy. I mean, Mom made me promise—"

"But the reality is very different from your expectations, wasn't it now?"

I lowered my head. "Yeah, I guess so."

"So let's go back to the motel. We know what to expect there. Quinn is giving it to us anyways when he dies. Everything was working out there."

"But it's too close to that damn island," I said with a snort.

She held out her free arm, with Isla trying to grab her hair, an invitation to a hug. I stepped up to her, gave her that hug, let her mouth perch by my ear. I heard her say the magic words:

"And what about your mom's tuba?"

✳   ✳   ✳

When Mom and I got to Grandma and Grampa's farm after fleeing the city we saw there had been a fire. Someone had been using the fireplace in the living room to cook and the fire had gotten out of hand. But they managed to put it out. The room was damaged though, but Mom and I still stayed upstairs in the bedrooms, having nowhere else to go. I slept in the same room where I'd stayed during summers when I was younger, with Mom across the hallway in what was my grandparents' room. After the vagrants broke in.... We just left. Drove away. So it didn't seem wrong to let Aunt Laura's house go, too.

I gathered everything from the pantry – all the cans and jars – things from the kitchen and garage that might be useful, and put everything in Earl's van. I cranked the garage door up by hand and drove the van out to the front of the house. Hannah and Sally packed blankets, sheets, towels, and clothing, all of Aunt Laura's hard-won women's supplies, into the cabinets of the van. The tools I laid on the floor. We found the two benches could be unfolded and when braced would join over the aisle to form a full bed. I realized what the *come a-rockin'* was all about.

Then I stacked pieces of broken furniture in the fireplace of the main hall and lit it. I was getting good at making fire. Mom would be proud. But pride had nothing to do with our decision. Whatever happened in the future, this was not going to be a place we would ever return to. There was plenty to hide in the rooms: evidence of a world gone mad.

We got in the van and took our seats. Me, the driver. Sally in front. Hannah with Isla in her basket on the bench behind me. I pulled the van up to the gate where we paused to look back at the flames starting to reach the roof. The flames would spread out in each direction, running to the ends of the long house.

"I guess that's it," said Hannah mournfully and gave Isla a big hug, kissed her head. "Say goodbye, li'l Miss Isla. Try to remember this visit to my aunt's house."

"It's a pity," said Sally.

I had no words to share, feeling like I'd betrayed my aunt and maybe my mom, too. This was our family's property, after all, and I shouldn't abandon it. If we were leaving it, however, burning it down was the right thing to do, leaving no evidence of the crimes committed there.

Out through the gate, under the *Ironwood* arch, we drove, into a new normal we never asked for.

Over several nights Hannah and I came to an agreement to return to Quinn's motel near the ferry landing. We believed it was our best hope for survival. A place where we could live a long time and raise Isla to adulthood. We had gotten things going there, had a daily/weekly routine, able to get enough food – enough that we also had some leisure time. Besides, as Hannah liked to point out, Quinn had given the place to us in a handwritten document.

"I don't mind," said Sally when we announced the plan. "I want to see someplace new. Never been to the coast."

"It can be real pretty," said Hannah, sounding excited. "Sunsets and sunrises. They got a nude beach on the island, but of course nobody goes there. Everybody's so skinny now."

The ladies laughed together.

"I just want to lay out on some sand and let the sun bake me into a soufflé," said Sally. "Right now, there's nothing else I want. And a nice cold can of beer. Or a margarita."

We drove along the same avenue that led out of town, onward just as Mom drove when we left two years before. My heart beat strangely, hands tightening on the steering wheel as the van rolled smoothly along. I realized we were coming upon the place in the country where Mom and I found that deputy's car on the side of the road. Down the slope lay the female deputy, badly raped and tortured, left for dead. Mom ended her pain and it seemed to haunt her the rest of our trip. That was our first real confirmation of the new normal: a world without laws or law enforcement, everyone on their own.

I slowed as we got close, surprised I still recognized it. As we came over the hill, I saw the car remained on the shoulder, dirty and weathered, although the doors which had been wide open on both sides previously were shut now. I almost stopped beside it – instead only slowed, gazing through the open windows, broken out glass, through the car to the grass beyond, down the slope, but I couldn't see anything from the road, not even the mound where we buried her and hid with loose brush.

"Why are we stopping here?" asked Hannah.

I realized then I never told her what happened to Deputy Alice Alton. It was too frightening. After all that we'd experienced since that day, it would only make things worse. I still couldn't believe what I saw, the cruelty people could do to another person. Mom told me to look away but I couldn't.

"What's this place?" Hannah asked.

"We passed it coming to your house," I told her.

She moved up front with Isla in her arms to have a better look. She gave it a good look. "So...?"

"When Mom and I were passing by, that car was here. There was a female deputy.... She was attacked."

"Ohmagod," Hannah gasped, understanding.

"She was barely alive. Mom tried to help."

"Help? Were there any doctors available back then?"

"I could've helped," Sally offered. "I was almost a doctor."

"No," I said sternly. "Nobody could've helped her. She was too badly hurt."

"So what did you do?" asked Sally, concerned.

"Mom ended her pain," I said and listened to the silence for a minute. "With a bullet."

"Geez," Hannah groaned, then got choked up.

"New fucking normal," Sally muttered.

I drove on, got up to the speed limit, keeping an eye on the fuel gauge. We had plenty if I didn't speed too much. But an old van like this wouldn't get very good mileage. I checked the map every few minutes, turned here, took the fork there, kept going as I watched for marauders awaiting victims. Eventually I recognized the area.

"This county highway goes by your town," I called to Hannah. "We could stop at your house, grab anything you need."

She moved to the front, gazing out. "Are you kidding me?" An alarmed face appeared in the rear view mirror. "Mother's still there."

"I know, but...."

What haunted Mom was when we got into town and stopped at

the small Alton Food Mart for some supplies, she discovered that the deputy we buried was the grocery owner's daughter. Mom felt guilty about that, like the sack of food was blood money.

Here were the apartments we'd checked first. Mom learned my Aunt Jackie and her kids didn't live there any longer. They had moved back to the house where they'd previously lived. Mom tried to explain things to me but I wasn't clear on what had happened. Domestic trouble, she moved out with the kids, got an apartment. When the pandemic first started, my uncle and my aunt reconciled and lived in the house again.

But with lockdowns and other restrictions in the early days, my uncle and second daughter Kristin had gone out to get groceries, got taken to the hospital where he died. Kristin disappeared at the same time. Hannah knew about that. And how her little sister Julia was killed by vagrants. And her brother Nathan, who went with us to the island, betrayed by Bucky, the fellow who taught him to fish. And before we went to the island, her mother, Jackie, distraught over everything that happened wanted out.

Hannah managed to put voice to some sad songs she made up as we drove.

Actually, she found sheets of music that Mom wrote while we were on the island and put words to some of them. For example, a tune about Owen, the island community's leader: 'You're just a fat old man / With a pervert kinda plan / Get on home with your big ass / You got no brain and no class!' And others. When she laughed to herself, her voice was tinged with pain, losses quivering there between her vocal chords like a breeze that portended a storm.

"That's nice," Sally offered. "You have a nice voice."

"'Everything's nice'," sang Hannah, face to face with a grinning Isla. 'You're fire and ice / But twice the price / You're a dirty whore / Who's gotta have more.'" She paused. "Are we there yet?"

Sally chuckled nervously, unsure how to take Hannah's song.

"I'm just happy to be on the road. Haven't gone on a road trip in three years."

"...when you were captured." I had to add the obvious.

"Yes," Sally replied, sounding annoyed I mentioned that fact.

Awkward silence.

"Wonder how the house is," said Hannah. "Maybe it's not there now, torn down. I wonder if they'll find Mother, and go looking for the murderers." And she broke into a lullaby: "'She took the pills / For her ills / Laid her head down / With a frown / Never awoke the next morn / Another stillborn.' Well, yeah, okay, that doesn't make sense, but anyway...."

"It makes sense," I said, then considered if I was wrong.

"You kids are funny," said Sally. "How did you ever meet?"

Hannah gave an awkward laugh.

"It is a funny story," I said, trying hard to see some humor in the details. "We visited them, the place we're going to now, and her mother was suffering from severe depression and had a concussion after fighting vagrants. So at her mother's wishes, my mom helped her die, gave her a lot of pills. So they had to go with us, her and her brother. They couldn't survive if we left them alone."

"Well, now we'll never know," said Hannah sadly.

"But we lost my mom and her brother," I added and got a frown from my wife.

"And the rest of the story is this beautiful li'l baby, aren't you li'l Miss Isla, goo-goo-ca-choo," Hannah teased and Isla responded with a huge grin.

"And then we had to leave," I said to conclude our story.

The wind had picked up outside, blowing hard against the van, making it shift on the road. Overcast skies. Dark clouds moving in from the coast. More strong gusts made me tighten my grip on the steering wheel. A storm was coming.

I found the apartments we stopped at before, but headed on up the main street, driving slowly to be able to watch for dangers. The small town seemed even quieter than before, possibly because of the approaching storm, the darkening skies.

Ahead was the Food Mart. We decided to stop and see what they had, even though we had loaded up the van with everything we could from Aunt Laura's house. I was unsure how we'd pay for it. As we got to the intersection where the store stood, it was clear the store was closed. High wire fencing stood around the building and the parking lot, its windows and glass doors smashed, debris piled up outside. More like it was out of business permanently.

At our previous visit, they managed to keep food stocked by bringing a truck down from the city each week, but had to impose limits to ensure the supply would be fairly distributed. Everyone had worn hazmat suits and there was a strict curfew in effect.

Now we didn't see too many people out at all. Those we saw looked homeless, wandering aimlessly, wearing only facemasks as protection or, by now, just a habit.

"This is it?" asked Sally, leaning forward, staring hard out the window. "Looks old."

"They were getting by," I said. "But that was two years ago."

A sturdier fence extended across the street going past the store, all the way up to the SuperMart where Mom and I tried to get the last drops of gas. We found they were out. We managed to drive over to Aunt Jackie's house on battery. We had used Jackie's large sedan to continue our trip to the island after moving Mom's useless hybrid car into the garage.

The black metal fence ahead of us looked serious, rising as high as the roofs of single-story houses, looking as sturdy.

Along the fence stood men in camouflaged military uniforms, helmets, olive-drab cloth facemasks. They carried assault rifles. One of the soldiers turned as we approached, held up his hand.

We slowed to a stop.

The soldier waved his hand more urgently to signal us to halt. We couldn't go anywhere with that fence in place, anyway. I wasn't sure what to do so I stayed where we were, halfway into the intersection, like I was preparing to turn into the Food Mart's parking lot.

"What do I do?" I asked my van mates as the soldier, rifle ready for action, came up to the car.

"Be cool," said Sally. "Just be cool."

19

WAR ZONE

I cracked the window an inch as spits of rain started spotting the glass. The swarthy soldier had his hand on his sidearm as another soldier with long black hair stood warily behind and to the side of him, rifle raised, aimed at us. Both wore cloth facemasks.

"You must not be from around here," said the darker one, name tag: Hendricks. He took his hand off the pistol at his hip, placed it over his rifle, holding it across his body, hand on the trigger guard, a long magazine curving down. "You should know there's a curfew on right now."

"We just arrived," I said, sounding anxious. But it wasn't fake anxiety. "We're from here." I thumbed behind me. "She is. My wife, I mean. Her family's house is just a few blocks over that way. Any chance we can go there?"

"Where?" asked Sergeant Hendricks. His buddy, the corporal, stepped closer, keeping behind him, rifle aimed at me as I lowered the window fully and leaned against the door. No doubt a gaudy van like this was suspicious on its own. Any vehicle able to drive was suspect now. Where were they getting gas from?

Hannah came forward, carrying Isla, and told the address.

"This whole area's off-limits," said Corporal Cheng. "You hafta go back."

"Back where?" I asked. "We're hoping to find a safe place here."

"Please," Hannah begged, leaning against my shoulder. "We got to get home. My mother's worried." She held up Isla. "And we gotta show her this baby. You know how new grandmothers are."

They were not persuaded, shaking their heads.

"She's a cutey," Sgt. Hendricks said in a serious tone. "But it's too dangerous there. You're practically on the front line."

"What's with the fencing?" I asked.

"You don't know?" asked Hendricks. "This is the front line. The rebellion? I guess no way you can get news now, huh?"

"No, everything's down. No power. No cell service." But I saw a few generators running, sitting on a trailer beside what looked like a command post. If only we could get our phones recharged.

"There's some service here," said Cheng.

"Your house, that address." Hendricks glared at me. "It's pretty close to the front line. That fence, it divides the whole town, west to east. Holding back attacks from rebels."

I gazed as far ahead as I could, through the fence grid. The sky growing gray limited what I could see. Haze in the distance.

"How about the SuperMart?"

"SuperMart's long been closed. It's enemy territory now."

"Enemy territory?" My eyes widened. "Who's the enemy?"

"Them folks from the north side," Hendricks replied.

"North side of town?"

"North side of the country!" He became annoyed. "Look, I get it that you don't know nothing about this. Long story short: once the police put down the riots, we were called in to keep order. But they formed an army, brought down people from the city to fight. We're trying to hold on here, maintain this side of the town, waiting for reinforcements from cities south of here."

"Like a real war," Hannah muttered behind me.

"Not a real war, ma'am," Hendricks spoke up. "It's folks ain't following official mandates versus folks that did. They're pushing back, you could say. Wanna take the whole damn town under their control. Goddamn freedom, they say."

"Freedom'll get us all killed," Cheng echoed. "There's two kinds of freedom: the kind where we're in charge and the kind where nobody's in charge."

"I see." I turned to Hendricks. "And north of town?

"North all the way to the next country. All under mandates and subject to law, with the president in charge."

"I thought the president died. From the virus, back a few years ago? About the last thing we heard before power went down."

"True." He glanced at the command post then lowered his voice. "But the succession.... Well, the last cabinet secretary died so they elected a new president from themselves, from surviving members of Congress. So it's President Philpot now. The senator from our state. He's in charge, ordered out the Guard to maintain control. We'll fight back once we get reinforcements."

"But everybody's the same now, aren't we?" I asked, wondering aloud. "I mean, living in survival mode. Hunkered down. Waiting it out. Negotiating the new normal. I mean, hardly able to spare a husband or father to man the fences."

"Are you a soldier?" Hendricks asked, narrowing his eyes.

"Naw, too young," I responded, then got a poke in my back from Hannah. I caught her worried face with a twisted frown. So I told him: "I'm not eligible on account of I got a form of autism."

"Autism?" Hendricks screwed his face into a fist. "We just need warm bodies that can hold a gun."

"But we gotta get to my house. Gotta see my mother," Hannah said behind me, holding up Isla where the sergeant could see her.

"Okay, I guess you folks ain't rebels," said Hendricks, giving a satisfied grunt. "We have to check everyone. And you should know, nowadays all fuel is appropriated for official use. Like government or military. We could confiscate your wheels – but I won't, seeing's you're a decent family and all."

"Thank you, officer," said Hannah.

"It's sergeant."

"Okay, sergeant, sir. Thanks."

Hendricks turned, pointing at the fence. "Everything from First Street on north is enemy territory. From west Tyler, all the way across to the east side, County Highway Six. That's the border. Your house is a couple blocks south of the fence, so be careful."

"Be careful?" I asked, not sure what he meant.

"Sometimes they'll take a shot at somebody walking by," said

Cheng. He stepped up, rifle lowered. "The way the barriers are set up you can't drive straight over there. Gotta loop around. Gotta go all the way over to Rogers, then turn north. See, the whole town's divided. There are folks trying to take over."

"Take over?" I asked, acting amused. "Who would want to take over this little town?"

Hendricks shook his head: another stupid kid. "Like I said: there's a war on. Kinda like the North versus the South all over again. So it's Albright in the north, Philpot in the south. And that Winston in the middle, too, if you wanna count that tiny territory. But he's siding with Albright these days. So different governments and the territories meet right here. We held them off but it's week by week."

"But we're the legit gov'ment," said Cheng proudly. "Them's the rebels, sneaky bastards. Plumb vicious. Cannibals, some of them. So don't get captured by them."

"Your house is in the safe zone," said Hendricks. "Barely."

Cheng cut in: "You maybe have to walk, once you pass through the checkpoint."

"Checkpoint?" I asked.

"Yeah, we're checking everyone going through."

"Checking what?"

"That you're our side." Hendricks scoffed, tired of talking to a stupid kid.

I wanted to say we weren't on anyone's side. We were on our own side. Just trying to make it through to where the new normal was. Why did everything have to be about sides?

"You got your vax cards?" asked Hendricks, seeing his superior watching him from the command post. Cheng perked up, too, reset his rifle. "Got IDs?"

I knew what to do, how to act. Mom had taught me well.

"Oh, man, nobody's got those anymore. Life is too rough. We barely escaped from a camp of vagrants with the clothes we got on." Then I went too far. "We were lucky to find this old van with some gas in it and tried to make it here to her house. Whatever we had we lost long ago."

Hendricks shook his head, like he'd been fooled again.

"Gonna have to ask you to step out of the vehicle." He motioned for other soldiers to come over to check us out. "Need to make sure you're clean. Got masks?"

"No, we ran out of those, too," I said.

One soldier handed a couple masks over to me, the medical-style paper ones. I put one on and handed the others back. Hannah put the other one on. Sally scrunched down in the seat.

"Okay, now step out."

"Really?" I asked. "We're no harm to anyone. In fact, we were already captured. By some country folks. We're just trying to get home. It's been a harrowing trip, let me tell ya."

"Look, man," said Hendricks with a sigh, "don't gimme no shit. Just doing my job. I don't wanna be here no more than you guys."

"I know. And thanks for your service," I said. "But we really do not have IDs. We lost all those things when we were escaping from the vagrants. Escape meaning I was tied up and my wife, she...she was assaulted by them."

"I hear ya. We need to check your vehicle for any contraband."

"And what contraband would that be?" I wondered if farm tools would be considered weapons and we might be arrested for them. Better to be open about it. "We have some tools, but they're strictly for farming. We mean to start again, make a farm."

"Step out," he repeated.

I opened my door, slowly lowered my foot outside, still gripping the steering wheel. Trying to remain calm, I worried most about being taken away for some vague reason and never seeing my wife and baby again.

"You should know, I do have a pistol in the van. It's my mom's actually. Well, she got it from her grandfather. He was in Vietnam. You need protection traveling out here nowadays, am I right? Too many vagrants ready to jump you. And we got jumped!"

"Yup," said the Private looking inside the van. "Yup. Here it is." He took the pistol from the center console, held it up by its hand grip, like he didn't want his fingerprints on the metal.

"That little thing?" Hendricks said, grinning. "Loaded?"

"Yes, about ten bullets left," I admitted.

"Keep it. Just don't shoot us. I know it's dangerous out there."

"They have a shotgun, too," said the Private.

"But no shells," I explained.

Someone was calling to Hendricks and Cheng from over by the fence, by the trailer of humming generators. At the same time, the van's rear doors were opened from outside and gray daylight filled the cabin. Hannah, holding Isla, cringed against the side bench. Sally leaned away, sinking in her seat. The soldier jostled the tools, grunting about their possible use as weapons.

"Spade, couple shovels, a hacksaw, wood saw, wooden stakes, assorted wrenches, hammer, screwdrivers, box o' nails," the soldier called out.

He backed out, closed the doors, and reported that he'd found nothing important.

"Where'd you find the gasoline?" asked Cheng, pushing against me with his rifle lowered but hand on the pistol grip.

"It was already in it," I responded.

"This ain't your van?"

I laughed. This was like our fifth vehicle since they stopped delivering gas to the stations.

"No, it used to belong to my aunt's boyfriend. But he's dead, killed by a band of feral kids. My aunt's dead, too. Nobody else going to use it. We're just trying to get home, like I said – to my wife's house – see if we can make a go of it here. We're just trying to survive like everyone else is."

"Survival, huh?"

A third soldier was standing on the passenger side, looking in through the closed window at Sally. He tapped on the glass and she looked up. A flash made her turn away and rub her eyes. It was a device he held up to the window, snapping a photo. He poked his finger a few times on the device as he stepped around the front of the van.

Hendricks and I were talking about what a family needed in order to survive in the woods, before a farm could even be started. Needed to build a shelter, like his family had done. Wife and three kids in a dug-out home. Had to wait out the war there, he said, hide away for a while. That's what his family was doing while he was forced to be on duty with the Guard, protecting the town from rebels. He described how he made it, finding a good location, the specifications, how he braced it with boards and used tarps to seal out moisture, made it nice and warm, comfortable, protected from weather and hidden from hikers. And only he knew where it was.

"Sounds good," I responded, genuinely impressed.

The soldier coming around from Sally's side of the van held up the device so Hendricks could see the screen. Both men smiled. I caught a glimpse of the screen: a nude woman on a bed. Meantime, other soldiers arrived at the passenger door, rifles ready. Others looked over Hendrick's shoulder at the image on the screen.

"That's a fucking match, Sarge," one soldier said.

"Sit tight, don't move," said Hendricks.

Other soldiers forced the passenger door open, grabbed Sally, who resisted, screaming "No!"

They pulled her from the van, dropping her on her bare knees on the pavement. She didn't feel that pain, too busy fighting hands grabbing her hair, taking her arms.

"No! You can't do this!" she screamed.

"What's going on?" I asked, not knowing what to do.

"She's registered," said Hendricks.

"Registered? What does that mean?"

"It means she's on the list. She was arrested before," he replied. His attention was on the soldiers wrestling Sally away from the van. They dragged her kicking and screaming over to an old yellow school bus parked beside the Food Mart fence. It seemed to have been abandoned but was being used for detention. A few people gazed forlornly from its windows.

"Arrested? For what? She didn't hurt anybody," I argued. "She wouldn't hurt anyone. She was captured by the same country folk as us. In fact, she helped us escape."

"She has ties to the rebels. Her husband is a local commander."

"What? That's crazy talk," I responded.

"You related?"

"To her?" I acted surprised. "No, we don't really know her. She was captured by those vagrants before us. She said she'd been with them three years. But she helped us escape after they captured us. We're just giving her a ride because she helped us. But...we don't actually *know* her."

"Sally Winston? Never heard of her?"

"No. She didn't tell us anything about herself. Just that she was captured along with her daughter. But her daughter died, she said."

"It's protocol. Need to question her."

A soldier came up beside Hendricks, held up the device, flashed at me. He checked the results. "Clean."

"Clean?"

"No criminal record," Hendricks explained.

If only they knew how many I'd killed during these two years, saving Mom, protecting my wife and baby. It was justified, every one. But in these hard times, a lot didn't get reported.

"But her?" I asked, looking at the yellow bus.

"Assault. Some drug charges."

"That's nothing these days," I tried to argue.

"Still need to question her on the rebel ties."

"But I can vouch for her," I dared say.

"You sure you wanna do that?" asked Hendricks. "Might be better for you to just move along, forget her."

My throat tightened. "Okay, yeah, sure."

Hannah started to say something out the open window of the door, but I waved her back. She pointed to the generators sitting on a trailer with a trio of solar panels unfolded, aimed up at the gray sky, sitting on the flatbed of a truck. She gestured like she had a phone to her ear and I nodded.

"I see those generators," I said, only partly as distraction. "Any chance we could charge up my phone? See if we got any messages? Just a few minutes. It's important these days, you know. Checking if your family members are alive."

Sgt. Hendricks glanced back at the generators.

"Ten minutes would be enough," I suggested, then leaned down and spoke in a lower voice: "And my wife's MP3 player, if possible. She was raped by those country people. Listening to her favorite songs would really improve her mood, you know?"

Hendricks gave a nod. "Okay."

I waved at Hannah and she gave me the phone. When I looked at her, I remembered our food stash from Aunt Laura's pantry.

"Tell you what, Sergeant. We got some goodies you and your men might like. Food things."

Hannah took my cue, set Isla down on the bench, and got out a couple of the family-sized jars, brought them up front. She handed one to me through the open window. I showed it to the sergeant.

"Whoa! What's that?"

"We got…succotash," I said, reading off the handwritten label, "and we got some kind of bean salad." I smiled; Hendricks' smile matched mine. "It's Lima beans, red bell peppers, onion, corn, and spices. Looks good, doesn't it?"

"Sure does." He glanced back at his squad. "Fresh?"

I inspected the lid, still sealed tight. On top was a wire twist with a date tag. "Not opened since she made it."

"How about that one?" he said, chinning at the bean salad.

"You don't have to choose. We'll give you both for a charge-up. This bean salad's got green beans, the yellow wax beans, and red kidney beans. Plus garbanzos, but they're not really beans, I think. Or are they?"

"Hush now, you sold me," said Hendricks.

"Give you guys both of them for ten minutes charging. Deal?"

"Think we can spare some juice." He called over to the soldiers by the generator trailer. "Taylor!" The guy was busy chatting with another soldier. "PFC Taylor!" The soldier turned. "These folks here can get ten minutes to charge a phone. One phone. See to it."

"Thank you so much, Sergeant. We appreciate you."

I took the phone to the generators. The phone was dead, not enough power even to turn it on. I got the cord from Hannah and plugged it into one of the generator's outlets. A soldier's phone was also charging there so I didn't feel too bad about using their power. It all came from the sun, after all, even on a drizzly day. I slipped

Hannah's MP3 player into another outlet.

As the generator did its work, the soldiers were discussing an attack expected any day, comparing what was coming to what had happened previously.

It felt strange being at the Food Mart with the world different from even two years before. I shared a few tales of my adventures with the soldiers and they shared their stories with me. Most of them were young, my age or not much older. I worried they might press me into service. One man, Sergeant Sadler, said he had a similar kind of van back home and asked about ours, but I couldn't answer him, not knowing any of the specs.

"My mom's car is parked at the house a few blocks from here. It's one of those hybrid cars. Any chance I could charge it a little?"

"Oh, that's way too much juice to give away," said Sgt. Sadler. "Can't authorize. Besides, without gas you're not going very far."

"Well, thought I'd ask," I said, hoping for pity.

"But thanks for the food," Sgt. Sadler responded.

"My aunt's a good cook," I said, although I didn't know if she really was or not.

Sadler, looking about forty with a week's growth of beard, was the most laid-back of the group and started talking in an amused voice about the rebels out there, his younger brother among them. "Kinda like the Civil War all over again," he said, and described how groups of protesters took over the north side of the town, setting fires, looting. Not enough police to restore order, so they called out the Guard, but most of them had to be rounded up going door to door. Ordered to erect the fence that now divided the town, they stood watch and sometimes exchanged gunfire. Bullets were in short supply but the rebels made some bows and shot arrows over. Others launched spears, threw rocks and bottles.

"Okay, there you go," said PFC Taylor, unplugging the cord. "Went a little long, so we're gonna need some dessert." He laughed, his eyes going to Hannah in the van.

"There's no dessert," I said firmly, stepping back.

"Kidding," said Taylor.

Sgt. Sadler gave Taylor's shoulder a slap. "Cut it out."

I grabbed the MP3 player with one hand as I held up my phone with the other hand, making a distraction. My phone blinked on, showing 11% power available.

I clicked over to Messages, fearing there would be none, that no one was left alive or had a working phone to send any messages. I found two: one from Mom that was only a test (*How's it going, Sandy?*); I recalled when she sent that on our trip – and one from Victor: *I hope this is correct number, going away, too much trouble here, best wishes.* That explained seeing his yacht sailing out that day, which I saw from the back of the motel.

On a whim I typed out a simple message, sent it to my contacts list: where I was, that we were going to my Aunt Jackie's house, and hoping everyone was doing all right. It was a date stamp for the future: On this day, at this time, in this town, we were alive.

I was about to power off, to save the battery, when I got a reply and a soft *ding*. I froze, staring at the screen. Glancing over at the van, I saw Hannah sitting in the passenger seat with Isla.

With a nod, I thanked the soldiers for the charge and got in the van, holding up my phone.

"Look at this," I said to Hannah. My message must've gone to Aunt Jackie's phone, although I'd never called her. Just added her number after getting a Christmas greeting years ago.

Hannah reached for my hand, her fingers digging into my wrist as she focused on the screen:

I'm here

Her chest tightened, gasping for breath, as tears ran from her eyes. She handed Isla to me and put her hands to her face.

"I just sent out a message to everyone and got this reply."

Hannah tried to catch her breath. "She's alive...."

20

HOMESTEAD

They had plenty of time to check us but nothing showed up in their database. It seemed nobody was looking for a middle-aged female tuba player and her teen son, and his cousin/wife and baby.

"I get it," said Hendricks with a disappointed scowl, standing beside the driver's side window. "You fleeing from rebel territory, ran out of gas or whatever, captured by forest folk. Then you got free, found this van with gas, headed here. Got it." He flashed a grin. "Okay, noted. You're clear to go."

The sounds of gunfire rattled down the street.

"What was that?" I exclaimed.

"Rebels letting us know it's dinner time."

More calls from the guys positioned at the fence, more gunfire coming from that direction, sounding like it was a few blocks away.

"Damn fools wasting their precious ammo."

"Thanks for the food," said Cheng. He rushed to the fence.

"You better go," said Hendricks. Gunfire echoed up the street. "Go over to Third and turn up Benton. That's as far as you can get, I think. Walk the rest of the way if you need to." He waved me to get moving. "Good luck. We got another attack coming."

Backing the van away, I made sure to not look at the school bus detention center. Maybe Sally would be looking out. Hendricks was right: we didn't know her, not really. She could've killed us in our sleep and taken the van, gone her own way, maybe to the other side to join her ex-husband. Have to be more careful.

I turned at the intersection and went east as directed.

We went down a debris-strewn street a few blocks then turned north, a different route than what Mom and I took when we visited two years before. The neighborhood had fallen to ruin.

"Can't believe they took her," I said, eyes on the street ahead.

Hannah had moved to the passenger seat with Isla secure in her lap as I drove slowly around abandoned vehicles.

"Good thing they didn't have anything on us." I had to chuckle, still nervous. "I thought being related to Mom would've gotten us arrested for sure." I meant that as a joke but Hannah didn't laugh. "Guess we fooled them, huh?"

"They scanned us?" asked Hannah.

"I saw them run their device, pointing it at each of us. But I checked out, no bad marks. I guess you didn't have a record since you never got a driver's license."

"I didn't turn sixteen till the pandemic was in full swing," she said with a regretful sigh.

"I know. But I'll teach you to drive—"

"She didn't do nothing," Hannah erupted. "Just being related to somebody that did something." She looked out the side window as though believing she could see Sally blocks behind us.

"We don't know her," I insisted.

"We're just going to leave her?"

"We have to." My hands gripped the wheel, determined to get out of there as quickly as possible. We had a short drive through a trashy residential neighborhood but I feared thugs could pop out from between the houses at any moment.

"She helped us. We have to help her."

"Hannah, it's the new normal." I glanced at her. "We could be arrested ourselves if we tried to help her. Besides, we really don't know her. What could we do, anyway? They have guns."

"We...." She fell quiet, thinking. Putting her hand to her face, she wiped tears away. Isla began to grab at her hand and after a few grabs Hannah batted the baby's arm away. Isla began crying.

"She helped us escape. And we helped her escape. We're even," I said, driving us from the checkpoint. "We got her to this town.

Not our fault they arrested her. What happens from here on out is not part of that deal."

Hannah sniffled, holding Isla tighter.

My heart was beating fast. "I mean, I hope she'll be all right, and everything, but...."

"What an awful world this is," Hannah muttered.

"But your sister is alive," I reminded her to change the subject.

She wiped her eyes, pursing her lips. "Yeah, at least that."

"That's great news."

"If it's true."

I maneuvered the van through the streets, abandoned vehicles, trash and other debris blocking the way as the rain fell steadily.

Strangely, all I could think of as we pulled against the curb in front of Hannah's old house was Mom's tuba, under blankets in a locked room of that motel by the ferry landing. By then the fuel light had come on. The rain had picked up. The wind blew harder. We hunkered down in the van, trying to forget what happened. It had been a terrible week.

I folded the bench seats into the bed so Hannah could lay on it with Isla. I sat on the bed, leaning back against the cabinets. I put my arm around Hannah as she began to nurse Isla, who had been getting fussy. Hannah tilted her head against my shoulder. I felt her heartbeat vibrate through me as I looked down at our hungry baby sucking away with the patter of rain on the roof. Suddenly it all made sense and I felt peace surrounding us.

"Everything is hard now," I spoke, barely above a whisper. "We always have to put ourselves first." I felt her nodding against my shoulder, heard sniffles. "Family first."

"I know...."

The wind rocked the van, rain hitting the roof louder.

"Must be a hurricane blowing in from the coast," she said, soft as a baby's breath.

The tintinnabulation on the van's roof gradually lulled us into drowsiness. Too much stress during the past several days, but we were safe now, waiting out the storm in Big Earl's hippie van. I got a blanket we took from Aunt Laura's house and wrapped it around

Hannah and Isla. We napped until the rain let up, which was all the way to morning.

*　*　*

I rested in my daddy's arms, against his chest, his shirt wet from sweating despite the cool air in the camper van. I rose to see what my world had to offer and saw that my mama had gotten out of the van. My daddy held me tight, staring out the front window.

"Easy now," he said as I pushed against his restraining hands. I wanted to see where my mama was going. I worried like before that she might not return to me.

Instead, I saw her standing in the yard, the rain falling down around her. She held out her arms as another woman came out of the house. The door swung shut after her as the woman rushed to my mama. They embraced, so tightly they seemed like one person to my little eyes.

My daddy took a deep breath and tears slid down his face to my arm. I shook them off my hand as I continued to watch my mama and the other woman.

"That's your aunt," said my daddy. "Her name's Kristin. Aunt Kristin to you. She's younger than your mother...by two years."

I looked harder at the two women hugging in the yard, rain wetting them. They looked different, my mama with long dark hair and the other woman with short yellow hair. Then, out from the same door, came two children, hurrying to the woman and calling "Mama, Mama!"

My mama took a step back, letting them hug their mama, the woman with the short hair. Everyone hugged everyone, then they realized they were getting wet and turned to the van. My mama led them over to us, opened the van door, and in crawled the two children. They weren't babies. They were older than me, like they were born a while ago, before I was born.

They settled in the van but the other woman stumbled on the gardening tools on the floor. Her kids managed just fine and sat on the benches. My daddy had folded up the bed and made benches after we awoke. Sitting in the driver's seat, he turned and greeted them.

"This is my sister, Kristin," said my mama to him.

"Yes, I figured," said my daddy. "Nice to finally meet you."

"Hi," said the one called Kristin. She pointed to the older boy, who did not look much like her, having dark skin and curly hair. "This is George." And to the younger boy, looking like his brother, she said: "Can you say your name?"

"Gway," he said with a lispy sputter, smiling at his success.

"Nice to meet you," said my daddy to the boys.

"His name's Clay," said Kristin.

And they paused, a moment of silence that said so much.

My daddy held me up like his favorite prize. I tried to speak but I hadn't learned how yet; I could only watch and learn, as the adults liked to say. The two little boys were chattering in their excitement.

There was a lot to share in those first minutes of reunion. Everything wanted to come flooding out all at once but they both understood they had plenty of time to talk, to share. They weren't going anywhere.

But there was a detail that needed to be shared.

"There's a family living in the house," said Kristin. "I guess they'd be called squatters. They found the house and nobody was at home, so they broke in and been living there."

My daddy complained, reminded her it was their house and the squatters should leave. But my aunt said she didn't mind. They were decent people. She told them when she arrived that it was her house. They asked her to prove it. She pointed to the pictures on the walls, pointing to her and other members of her family in the photographs.

The two boys laughed at her telling the story.

"So I said they could stay," said Kristin. "They have four kids. Had their me-ma, too, but she died not long ago. No virus in them. I mean they had it already and are clean now."

More questions about how she was doing and what she's doing now from my mama and my daddy.

"I can't talk about what happened," said Kristin, looking down at her hands folded in her lap. "I try to forget, but here are these boys to remind me." She smiled at them, put her hand out to ruffle their hair. Then she looked at me. "And who is this little one?"

My daddy passed me over to her and she gathered my chubby baby body into her arms, held me up face to face.

"Isla Augustine Baumann," said my daddy with pride.

"Wow, Hannah," said Kristin, her eyes wide. "Baumann, huh? You and your cousin? I never woulda thought...."

"It was a love match," said my mama.

"Love at first sight," said my daddy, which was what I had been sensing since the day I was born.

"Well, I'm still Whistler," said Kristin. "Never did get to marry their daddy." She looked at her sons. "Can you say 'Isla'?"

They repeated my name, the younger one giggling after.

The woman called Kristen handed me to my mama. As I settled into her loving arms, the two women cried. I felt at home among them, like we were all the same family, though our circumstances had made us take the long way home. Now we were together.

"Let's go inside," said Kristin.

✳   ✳   ✳

A break in the rain gave us the opportunity to run to the house, bursting through the doorway like we were our own storm. In the main room, as Kristin said, a family was gathered about on the furniture, making the living room their camp. They looked like my mama and my daddy except they were older and had badly worn clothes, like they had pulled them out of a trash dump. The smell in the room didn't agree with me and I tried holding my breath until my face turned red. I failed and began to cry.

"Aw, what's the matter, Isla?" asked my mama.

I made a pouty face. Mama raised my bottom to her nose and sniffed for a dirty diaper.

"Nope, she's clean."

"Must be the new surroundings. She's been through a lot," said my daddy. He was half-right.

"Too many strangers," said my mama with a wave of her hand at the new people.

"Let me introduce everybody," said Kristin. She gestured to the older man, bearded but looking sickly. "This is Dale. He used to be an office worker. Copier repairman. But then he came down with the virus. The company closed during the lockdowns." She turned to the older woman. "This is Barb. She's like his wife now. They met on the road." She pointed to the two girls, maybe thirteen and ten. "This is Janie and Penny. Janie is Dale's daughter and Penny is Barb's. They're a road family, like I said." She pointed to the two boys, looking eight and five. "These two little squirts are James and Howard, but we call him Howie." The boys greeted us.

I had never seen so many children. I thought I was the only one in the world. A camp full of dangerous adults, yes, but not younger ones. That both frightened me and made me giggle. And the two boys that ran out in the rain, named George and Clay, barely able to run as young as they were.

"There. See? She just needed to know who everybody is," said my mama.

"Now there's a bigger family," said my daddy.

Dale waved his hand, forced a smile to be polite. Barb smiled better, like she was glad to meet us. The children were hesitant.

"Like I told you, they found the house with nobody living in it."

"That's right. Your mother, she sure weren't living," said Barb softly, like she didn't want Kristin to hear.

"Yes...." She pursed her lips. "We've been here for six months. After we escaped from that quarantine camp. I'll tell you more later. Anyway, I saw the note you left, about going to the island, but no way I could get there on foot."

The sisters hugged again, getting teary-eyed.

"I just hoped you guys would have a safe life there."

My mama laughed, wiped her eyes. "Not really."

"We had to leave," said my daddy, juggling me in his arms.

"So we got Mother buried proper out back," said Kristin with a tear rolling down her cheek. "And we tried to do what we could in this house. Sure as heck don't need the whole place for myself and my boys."

Everybody was staring at her sons, probably thinking the same thing: Who's their daddy? She must have understood the silence so she addressed it.

"Their father is Malcolm. He was.... Let's say I met him at the quarantine camp, after me and Father were rounded up."

"And you never came home," said my mama, "even after Father died there." My daddy knew that part of the story, it seemed by the way he reacted. My mama pressed for more but was told she would get the details later when they were alone.

"So, anyway, Malcolm died. Shot as we were escaping. But he helped us get out. It took about a month to get here. Then had to hide when they checked if we came back to this house." Kristin turned to the family sitting around the living room. "Thank you for covering for us." To my mama: "We hid down in the basement and they brought us food."

"That's great," said my mama, and the sisters hugged again.

"But you...." My daddy started then stopped. I guess he realized everything would come out eventually.

As it was, we were in a house, safe from the storm outside. We discovered the power was still being rationed, a couple hours each day, so the lights went out promptly at seven. They continued to talk in the dark room, however, and I got bored with all the words. I was falling asleep upon my mama's shoulder.

*　　*　　*

I held Isla in my lap, sitting with the Carter family, listening to them breathing, watching them watch me. It seemed we were all assessing the likelihood of each of us carrying the virus, looking for signs. Or they wondered about my story. Who is this guy? Who is that woman, his baby-mama? How is their arrival going to affect our staying longer in this house at the edge of the war zone?

When Mom and I visited two years before, we slept in the room that was Kristin's and Julia's bedroom. We slept on the twin beds because the daughters were no longer there. Now Kristin returned.

Being the oldest, Hannah had a room to herself when Mom and I visited earlier. It was there the two sisters shared their stories, hugging and crying together. I couldn't hear much from the living room. I dared not go stand outside their door, which was closed. Occasional sobs or surprised exclamations came out of that room, but I tried not to think about what information might've caused those reactions. Hannah was overjoyed to find her sister – yet also sad at everything that happened to her. Now we had the chance to save someone else. We had failed so badly with Aunt Laura.

Isla had tired of showing off for the strangers and fell asleep on my shoulder, her tiny breath puffing against my neck.

"'Tain't fair ta have a child in these here hard times," said the father, his eyes staring blankly like he was blind. The flickering candlelight didn't improve his appearance. "Gonna hafta grow up in constant terror."

"Well," I said, winding up for a long rant, "we're expecting that everything will calm down any day now. Then we can start over. We didn't have a baby just to have another mouth to feed. We expect her to save the world someday."

The kids started in with their questions. The two girls asked the most, speaking in cheery voices more out of politeness than happiness. The boys were quiet but asked one question each at Barb's urging. Have to be polite to this man who's related to the girl whose house it was, they seemed to accept. Otherwise they sat forlornly on the couch and chairs, waiting for time to end.

Kristin's older son, George, wanted to know about this magical island everyone was talking about – where there was plenty of food and warm sunshine all day and no viruses. I told them gently that it didn't exist. He insisted it did; his mother talked about it. Even in a paradise, I explained, there could be terrible things to confront you. There never really is a safe place, totally safe, and you always have to be ready to act. I held up my hand, thumb up and finger out like it was a pistol. The boys were impressed.

The father grunted, shook his head. "Fool," he mumbled.

"I think it's a wonderful story," said the mother, smiling as best she could, showing her naked gums. "A baby means you ain't given up. You're planning for the future, one that'll be good for her, good enough, anyways."

"Shut up, damn woman," the father snarled.

She fell silent, made a face like she knew she'd done wrong, and retreated into her soul.

"Anyway, things happen," I said. "And we deal with them as we need to. Every day's a challenge, my mom used to say." I paused to think of her. I imagined her sitting beside me in this room, happy that Kristin had returned. "If you get to the next day, you win."

We resumed our staring mode until Dale sensed the time and commanded Barb to fix dinner. She got up and went to the kitchen, waving the older girl to follow. I waited with the father and kids, mostly in silence. When one of the kids asked a question or made a comment, anything that broke the silence, they would look at the father like they needed permission.

Knowing the time was important: an hour of electricity for preparing dinner. You could set your clocks to it: 6:08 to 6:51, as I measured. Dinner consisted of canned and packaged food that was either put in a bowl or had to be heated over a small countertop brazier. The food was served on plates around the table. For the extra people who arrived, the mother put plates on the counter; we'd have to stand there to eat.

The mother sent the daughter to get Hannah and Kristen, and they joined us for dinner.

Hannah had a warm expression when regarding me, which I interpreted as meaning 'everything's going to be all right'. As we stood side by side at the counter, eating, she leaned toward me, bumped my side like we used to do on the island. I gazed at her. She wiped her eyes occasionally but wore a smile. Suddenly she set down her fork and took my face in her hands, stretched up to kiss my cheek. Everyone saw.

I gave Hannah a one-armed hug as we continued eating the meager rations the family shared with us. Thank goodness for the technology of canned food. And real hot dogs! They had mustard in restaurant packets, a whole drawer full of them. It felt like an ordinary dinner in the old normal. I thanked Barb, said it was good, better than we'd had in a long time.

They weren't the friendliest of families, but we all handled the pandemic in our own ways. At least they weren't cruel. They didn't insist on us doing anything other than assuming traditional roles. Hannah and Kristin, getting wet in the rain, had dried off and changed clothes before coming out for dinner. Hannah looked so pretty in the new dress she wore, with her dark hair combed out, hanging straight down her back, like an angel.

I thought back to my first glimpse of Hannah, greeting us at the door when Mom and I arrived, not knowing anything that had happened. She'd been solemn, so serious in her manners, taking over responsibility for the care of her ailing mother and younger brother Nathan. We eventually sat on the back porch, gazing at the fallow yard, talking about everything we missed because of the pandemic. She told me about her favorite bands, sang a few songs, then suddenly she kissed me.

"Sandy?" I heard someone call me from my trance. "You okay?" It was Hannah, noticing I was lost.

"Yeah, okay."

Later, Hannah helped clear the dishes from the table. Kristin helped wash them using boiled water collected in glass bottles. I played with Kristin's sons while Barb held Isla. Then Hannah and I met in the same room Mom and I had stayed in. Kristin went to Hannah's old room, where she'd been staying with her sons since her return – except for the weeks they hid in the basement. When we first met, Hannah and I had sat together on the bed with the lights out, listening to her MP3 player together, one ear bud in her ear and the other in mine.

We did that again, remembering those special moments before bedtime. We found comfort in returning to the same place. I pulled out from my pocket her MP3 player and slid it into her hand in the darkness.

"What's this?" she asked, turning it in her hand.

"I got it charged when I charged my phone."

"Ohmagod!" She kissed me, then uncoiled the ear pieces and

pushed one in her ear and the other into my ear.

In a few seconds we were listening to the Coronas' hit song of four years ago: 'Alone Together' – followed by the Wu Crew's ballad 'Sub-Mission'...as in the 'sub' mission of the pandemic mission was to destroy everything and hand over complete power and control to the world's council of evil overlords. "They were way ahead of their time," Hannah had said two years ago.

We sat head to head, shoulder to shoulder, and by the time the next song played, Callie Odem's 'Lay Me Down', we were locked in a kiss, our tears melding us together. Isla noticed and cried for attention on the opposite twin bed. Hannah and I parted, laughing, and turned off the MP3 player to save the charge. She brought Isla up to her breast; Isla hadn't been hungry at our dinnertime.

"Bet you never thought two years ago we'd be here, doing this, with a baby," said Hannah. "But, hey, I'd never wanna go through a pandemic with anyone but you, Sandy."

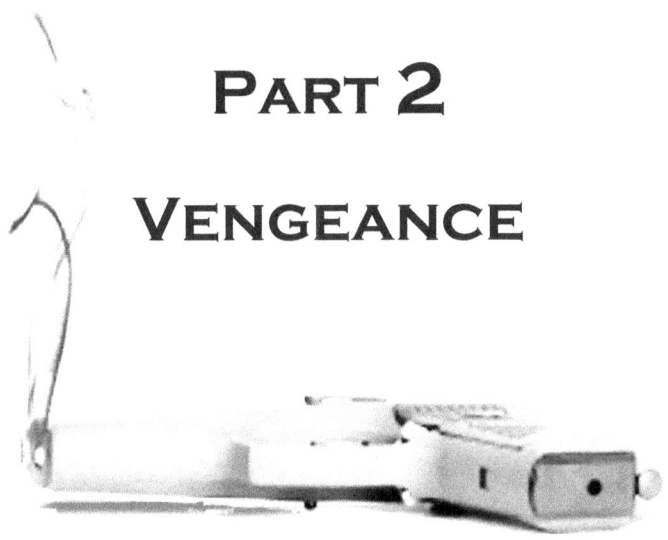

PART 2

VENGEANCE

21

THE PASSAGE

"So, you're from around here?" I asked too innocently of the Carter patriarch. A stupid question, but the silence of the evening was too deep. They were happy to sit and stare. Dale, the father, did pull out a book and read for a while, but the kids knew they had to be absolutely quiet while he was reading or risk a scolding. Barb, the mother, could speak but only in a low voice whenever she needed to say something to the kids. Sometimes Dale would grunt at being interrupted and Barb would apologize in a meek voice. I would've offered to take the boys outside to play, toss a ball around maybe, but the rain continued.

"You wanna know, I'll tell ya," said Dale, turning his book over on his knee. "This is crap anyways."

I thought he was referring to the book he was reading, with a cover suggesting a vampire story. Those were the books available in this house.

"Nice job, office in a high-rise. You know, up north in the city. Good salary, plus benefits. Had a nice house in the suburb. Good schools. Then all this crap. Pandemic time. You know what that was like, the first days, during the first lockdown, everybody not knowing what was happening, not knowing if or when it would end. People got caught with no food or supplies, hadn't stocked up. Run outta toilet paper first off, everybody scared shitless."

"Yeah," I said, remembering how it was for Mom and me in our city, but we lived a simple life anyway.

"We stayed in, as ordered, but my oldest couldn't handle it. She tried to kill herself. Stopped her the first time, but she succeeded with the second try. Maybe that'll explain why I'm so bitter. None of it mattered, we come to learn. Not that bad – okay, yeah, sure, to some people, mostly the elderly and people that already had underlying conditions. But for most of the rest of us, it was just a big exercise in population control – and they liked what they saw, how we reacted, how most people were all too damn happy to bow down and submit to every damn lie they broadcast."

"Okay...."

I could've guessed he was one of those resisters just by the way he presented himself, but now I knew for sure. Mom and I took it seriously at first, too. Nobody knew anything. Then Mom changed, started not believing everything the authorities said, suspicious of what was happening. Everyone had a sad tale to share, or a tragic story that needed to be told.

"Sorry about your daughter."

"Yeah, well, what're ya gonna do? Teenagers. They do what the hell want, am I right? The pills didn't work good enough. But the kitchen knife did. Almost cut her whole hand off—"

"So you left your city? Like we did our city."

"You betcha. Like lotsa folks, we thought it'd be better in the countryside. Like a camping trip. Went to a park and set up camp. Others there, too. Everybody trying to start fresh. But as the news got worse, some people panicked. They didn't wanna work together to build something new. Naw, they had to take what they wanted, needed, maybe thinking if not now then they'd never be able to get it. Not even any things for survival, just whatever was shiny and pretty. Bobbles and trinkets. Big-screen TVs and gaming systems, like we even had electricity. Hell, I'd've given 'em a can of food if they asked."

"Something happened?"

"My wife – first one, not Barb over there – she tried to protect our Janie from a man breaking into our tent. She got a knife in the gut, my wife, Myrna, I mean. She bled out right there in the tent. Nothing you could do. Well, I grabbed the knife and stabbed that sonuvabitch all I could, maybe fifty times, up and down his body till I run out of strength."

"Wow," I exclaimed but in a weak voice. I was thrown back to the day Bucky stabbed Mom, how she fell and bled out, and nobody could do anything. And the tent in the woods, killing Big Brother Harley. But I didn't want to share either story with the Carters.

"So me and Janie and the boys packed up and run away, eventually got to this town. We looked around for a nice house and here we are. Oh, and on the way we met up with Barb and her girl. Her husband, a cop, died fighting rioters. Anyways, the girls got along fabulous, so we decided to stay together. We made a new family. Guess we'll stay a family till the end now – whenever that might be."

"That's great," I said unconvincingly. "I mean, uh, I'm glad you found each other. It's kinda like how Hannah and I met, right here in this house, two years ago. Mom and me, and my cousins kinda made a new family, too."

"Is that so?" asked Dale, accusation in his tone.

"In a pandemic, you get with who's available," I said before I could form a good rebuttal. "But for us it was love at first sight."

Dale laughed and for the first time since we arrived seemed a regular person. He picked up his book, turned it over to read again, shaking his head.

"Same damn thing in this book. First sight crap. Crazy stuff. *A Dry Patch of Skin*, huh? This guy is turning into a vampire. First symptom is dry patches on his skin. Well, I guess it's supposed to be realistic – says it's 'medically accurate' – but it's vampires, huh? Bunch of devil stuff, ya ask me."

I let him go back to his reading as my thoughts turned inward, remembering everything about our previous visit, Aunt Jackie's death, leaving with Hannah and Nathan for the island. I chewed my lips, deciding I should write everything down in the notebook I got from Quinn. I went to our pack and retrieved it, opened it to a fresh page and began writing.

* * *

In coming days we kept away from the Carter family as much as we could. They did their own thing and we did ours. Hannah and Kristin spent a lot of time alone, catching up, and I didn't get the story of what happened to Kristin until later and then only a brief version.

"I know you don't wanna hear all she told me," Hannah spoke in a soft but serious voice as we lay together on her old bed in her room. Kristin and the boys took the room with the twin beds. "I mean, it's pretty bad. Not easy to hear."

"Does it help you to tell about it?" was all I could say.

"It's not like I wanna tell her secrets, but you and me, we're a family so that makes her your family. So maybe you better know. Just don't go telling anyone else."

"I'm just glad she's alive. And, hey, she's got two sons."

"Yeah, let's start with them, okay? I never expected my little sister'd have two kids before I had one. Well, she met Malcolm in that quarantine camp. Neither of them had any symptoms, just tested positive on a test, false positive, and didn't get any re-test. Off they were taken like so many people. Government going crazy, rounding up anyone they thought might be trouble, virus or not."

"Yeah, Mom worried about that."

"She said it was like an army camp, tin roof huts, girls and guys separated, family groups together. Sick people all around her but she never had more than a sniffle. But time came for people to do what they want and some men tried to get with the girls, ya know? Malcolm was one of them but he knew how to fight, at least, so she chose him as her protector. And that's how she got his sons. First one, George, was born in the camp. The other, Clay, was born while she was on the run from the camp. Had him come out of her while she was hiding in the woods. She eventually got to the house here but found that family living here."

"The squatters...er, I mean, the Carters."

"The bad part's more at the beginning. At the hospital, I mean. Father was in ICU dying, full of all kinds of drugs and in a coma. They didn't know what to do in those days so they did everything all at once and that killed him. Kristin didn't know that. She was already gone by then. She didn't have symptoms but they kept her there. She got tired, went for a walk inside the hospital. But she got stopped by a man in a hospital uniform, asking where she was going, ya know, like she wasn't authorized. He pushed her into a restroom, into a stall, ya know, and...."

She had to take a few breaths.

"He was assaulting her but she stabbed him with the pocket knife Father made us carry just in case. He fell against the stall door, screaming in pain, but his weight against the door kept her from opening it so she crawled on the floor under the door. She ran out of the building and hid in the woods behind the hospital."

"Good for her," I blurted.

"But she was afraid of getting arrested for what she did."

"It was self-defense."

"There was vagrants in those woods and they saw her, grabbed her. She tried to talk them into letting her go. Instead they sold her to some others for food and they took her away in a van, kinda like Earl's but packed with other girls. They drove them to the city, put them in a house, together in one room. And every night they were taken to other houses for customers, then picked up and brought back to what she called 'the mansion'. It wasn't really a mansion, just a big house."

"I've heard of that sort of thing. Sex trafficking. Wow. Even in a pandemic—"

"Then they got raided. When they checked everyone, they took them to the quarantine camp. But they didn't separate them from their abusers so she had to keep on fighting them. So Malcolm, he stepped up to protect her. She treated him good, she said, and she got pregnant easy, like right after getting with him."

"Okay, that's enough," I said, my voice weak, throat tight. But I wanted to shout out my hatred of the world, rage about how people can be so cruel to others, especially while a pandemic is going on.

"She was like eleven and a half when she went with Father to the hospital. About thirteen when she was taken to the quarantine camp. Now she's got a boy three years old and a fifteen-month-old toddler. Coulda died a bunch of times during the years. But those boys' father is dead, shot by guards. He was able to lay across the razor wire, holding it down for them, and ordered them to run over his body to get away. I guess he bled to death there. She said they didn't look back, just assumed he died."

"No matter what he was before," I said, feeling choked up, "that Malcolm was a hero at the end."

"Sure was." She wiped her eyes. "And she had a big belly then, hard to run, taking her boy by the hand, going as far and as fast as she could. Government health inspectors came around the house looking for her."

I knew some of the story: "And the Carters lied for her, said she hadn't come back here. They hid in the basement and the Carters brought them food."

"When the Carters arrived, they found Mother wrapped up on the bed. They saved the note I wrote when we left. They gave it to her when she got here, so she knew what happened. About us going to the island. Then I told her what happened there, about you and me, and li'l Miss Isla coming into this world, this awful world. I told her everything. Like what happened to Aunt Polly. And what happened to me at that camp in the woods. And about Aunt Laura."

My heart was burning. I had to calm down.

"She's all caught up now," I said, fighting with all my strength to hold back a laugh at my clever comment.

"Lemme just say one thing, Sandy," she began, then paused to give me a quick cheek kiss, to soften me up for whatever she was going to say. "I wanna repeat what I said to you before, so we're clear. I did what I did to save us. It wasn't noble, though. It wasn't fun, neither. It was two minutes of stupidity, him grunting like a pig, thinking he was making me feel good. Nope, not at all. I really don't know why you guys fight over it. Or why you'll do damn near anything just for the chance to do push-ups for a couple minutes. I mean, does it feel *that* good? I can't believe you guys want it so bad you'll do crazy things, criminal acts, to get a chance to fuck. I don't get it. Didn't do anything for me."

"Well...." I had a rebuttal lined up, ready to launch as soon as I heard what the topic was going to be, but then decided not to say it. I was going to tell her how I felt being with her. And I know for sure she felt something. I could see it in her eyes, and feel how she responded to me. But I guess that was because we were in love and we wanted it. But others, I mean the rapists, the abusers, how could they find enjoyment in someone else's fear and pain? It didn't make sense. Why couldn't the virus knock them off instead of the good people trying to get by in these hard times? I decided I had to say it, so I did.

"Yeah...I know," she eventually responded in a whisper.

I took a big breath. "She seems all right now, anyway."

"She's not all right. She was abused, a lot worse than me. Had to do all sorts of things no kid should ever be forced to do. But she's a smarty, like you. She learned right off how to survive. Have to give'em what they want so they won't hurt you. And Malcolm, he protected her. Like in prison movies: find the tough guy and make him your friend. Nobody touched her after she took up with him. She got by, survived, okay...but she's sure not all right. She puts on a happy mask for her boys."

"We have to take her with us," I said, the thought popping into my head.

"With us? To where?"

"You keep saying you want to go back and live in the motel by the ferry landing."

She took a long, long inhale, let it out even slower.

"Well, I guess so. But she has the house here, and electricity sometimes and it's my house, too: my bed, my stuff still here."

"But it's where your mother lay dead for two years. It's on the front lines of the revolutionary war. You can hear guns any time of the day and night. Rebels could break through, overrun us here on this block. We can't stay if there's going to be street fighting."

"Maybe you're right."

"For once." I chuckled. We needed to end on a light note so we could sleep well, not be so tense after hard stories.

"Don't worry," said Hannah with a snicker, "I know you'll be

213

right again sometime. I'm sure of it."

There was a tapping on our door and I sat up on the bed.

"Yeah? What is it?"

Barb swung the door open a bit, peeked in, carrying a candle.

"There's someone come to see you. At the front door."

"Now? It's after midnight," I said, climbing out of bed with just a pair of shorts on.

"No, just eleven."

"Who is it? Government agents?"

"No, just a woman. Looks kinda beat up."

"What?" Hannah responded, getting up.

We went with Barb to the front door. I took Mom's pistol with me, just in case.

The woman on the front stoop, soaked from the rain, was Sally. A grin broke across her face when our eyes met. She pinched the plastic sheet she wore over herself a little tighter below her chin as she stood dripping and barefoot, her thin dress of little comfort.

"Sorry to wake you. Can I hide out here?"

"Sure," I said, giving her a quick look. "Hide out?"

"You escaped?" asked Hannah, waving her in.

I held the door open, not even thinking what the consequences of harboring a fugitive might be. It seemed all of us were fugitives now, some more fugitive than others. She stayed by the door to try to contain the dripping. Barb went to get some towels.

"Saw your van outside. Sure can't forget that one, with orange flames down the sides." She chuckled as she accepted the big towel from Barb. "I see you found your house. Good for you. Got a big family, huh?"

"How'd you escape?" I had to ask.

"Escape? Hah. They let me go. Done with me."

She shifted the tarp carefully off her head and shoulders as she wiped herself with the towel. Bruises on her face were revealed as Hannah raised her hand, adjusting the candlelight as needed.

"They wanted to make sure I wasn't going to go help the rebel leader, my ex-, the notorious Frank Winston. I told'em he's always played at politics, always wants to get involved, protest anything, even use violence to get his way, and that's why I left him, left him years ago. I told'em I'd just as soon kill him as look at him."

She paused, took several deep breaths, shivering from the chill. I also shivered, standing in just my shorts. Hannah wore her usual t-shirt and panties while Barb had on a bathrobe.

"Is your face okay?" I asked, focusing on her black eye.

"They had to make sure I wasn't acting, so slapping me around a bit kept me honest. I'll be awright. Some bald guy in leather coat, calling himself 'Commissar of Truth' or something, acting tough. He wanted to do more, I could tell. But a soldier called him out and he laid off."

"We're glad you got away," said Hannah.

"Seems I'm getting used to getting away. Anyway, they treated me better than those Morgans did. No sexual abuse, I mean, just a rough pat-down to check for hidden stuff."

"Please make yourself at home," I said, like I had any right to make that offer. "There are fresh clothes somewhere here."

"Right," said Hannah, giving the candle to me and exiting as Barb continued wiping down our visitor.

Hannah brought out a fresh dress, told me to turn away as she and Barb helped lift the wet dress up and over Sally's head, as I watched the shadows on the wall, then they toweled off her body. I didn't look as they slipped the new dress on her.

Hannah said I could look again. Barb got another towel to wrap around her wet hair.

"You gonna catch yer death o' cold, dear," said Barb.

"Just happy to be indoors," Sally responded.

"Oh – Sally, this is Barb. Barb, Sally," I said.

Barb gave a nod as the women continued cleaning her up.

"Sally helped us escape from those country people, like I said before. They arrested her at the checkpoint by the Food Mart. But they let the rest of us go."

"Then they'll likely come by here looking for her," said Barb as she squatted to wipe Sally's bare legs and dirty feet.

"No, they're done with me. I'm nobody," said Sally. "Gotta be a nobody. If you try to be somebody they'll put you down."

"They know you came in that van out front," said Barb.

Sally turned to me: "That van of yours is easy to spot."

"Maybe I should move it," I thought aloud.

"Ya think?" Hannah sneered. "It makes our house a target."

Nodding to myself, I went to get the keys from the bedroom and get dressed for going outdoors. I had been so close to being ready to make love with Hannah when she started telling me all about her sister. What she went through. That ended my interest in sex. It took all my will to push away the image of Big Brother laying over Hannah in that tent.

I sniffed back a tear, coming from either sadness or fear, as I returned to the front door wearing jeans and a flannel shirt.

"I'll drive it over a few blocks and walk back." I gave Sally a quick look as I pulled the tarp she'd used as an umbrella over my head and shoulders.

Stepping out into a light but steady rain, I was glad we weren't still on the island when this hurricane hit. The north side of the strait wouldn't fare any better. I worried about Mom's tuba.

As I paused on the front stoop before making a dash to the van, a scenario raced through my head: me going out on a mindless task and never returning, getting swept up in some police action, put in a camp, never to see Hannah or Isla ever again.

But I stepped off the stoop anyway.

22

WINTER OF DISCONTENT

We live in hard times, and hard times require hard decisions. It's what Mom liked to say, maybe a little too often during the past few years of this pandemic and the chaos that's come about because of it. I believed her on and off, being just a boy then a teen, until I got her final lesson and I made a hard decision. In that vast instant, however, it was easy. I think of Mom. I miss her. We were always a team, her and me against the world. I think of how she raised me, cared for me, encouraged and protected me as I grew into a man. But then she had to go away – like it was a rule.

Sitting inside Earl's van, I ranted and raged, angry at myself and angry at the world for this mess. Everything had been turned on its side, thrown out of balance. If not for this pandemic these people I'd lost would still be alive. And I would be in some college classroom, studying how people in groups behave, heading toward a career in social work, most likely. I'd have my own place but I'd visit Mom, listen to her playing Timmy, whatever she might be working on for a recital or a concert with the Symphony. Maybe I would meet someone on campus, fall in love, do the usual things, have children and grandchildren. That would be my life – without the pandemic coming along and raking half of everyone into the grave.

If not for this pandemic I wouldn't have met Hannah, and we definitely wouldn't have Isla. I had to laugh, thinking of how that unfolded. But, gee whiz, I sure loved her. I could never imagine being without her. My mind ran with a twisted scenario, seeing us as old people living on a farm, surrounded by our grandchildren visiting us in the summer just like I did with my grandparents, and wondering which of us would go first. Each path ripped my heart. If I went first, she would be left alone to finish out her life. If she went first, it would be me suffering through my remaining days. Probably we would die within weeks of each other.

Outside, the rain had lessened but continued rattling on the van's roof. I hadn't gotten very far driving it away from the house. I'd planned to park the van between other abandoned cars in the parking lot of a strip mall we passed going to the house. The pizza shop, nail salon, and two other stores were abandoned, windows broken, looted. No one would return for more so I planned to fit the van in tight to hide it. I wanted to keep the hideous orange flames running down its sides out of view. We'd come back another day to collect the gardening tools and other supplies.

I started the engine, the fuel light shining bright in the dark. I left the curb right away, not wanting to waste fuel idling. Down to the end of the block, toward the Great Fence of the South, hearing a few pops of gunfire in the distance. Turn left, another block, turn left again, another block, then the shaking of the van as the engine gasped and sputtered, and the engine stopped.

Realizing it, I veered against the curb where I was, parking in front of someone else's house. The houses along that street were all dark, power shut off for the night. The house where I parked gave no indication it was occupied. If it was, they'd awaken to see this odd vehicle sitting out front and wonder where it came from, who it belonged to, and more importantly whether it had any gas left in the tank. Food and fuel. That was all we thought about.

More gunfire, further away. I took my time ranting inside the van, looking like a madman. I didn't shake my fists but I slapped the steering wheel a few times in my rage. It was good I was alone. Eventually I calmed and settled back into a new normal. I made a plan. I put the words together to propose it to Hannah. Memorized it. Spoke it aloud a few times. Satisfied, I got out, locked the door, and walked back to the house through the dark rainy streets, the scent of the last gunfight in the air.

I passed a couple shady characters, hoods up, hands in pockets, going down the opposite side of the street. They didn't look over at me, hurrying to their appointment. Turning the corner, I saw other people here and there, sitting tightly under cover, wrapped up like that was their home now, watching me. One figure I couldn't tell was a man or woman gave me a nod as I passed and I waved my hand. A few shots rang through the air as I reached the house.

The adults were up, talking quietly in the kitchen, the Carter family camped in the living room as usual. Hannah got up when I walked in, hugged me like I'd been out on some great adventure with my return uncertain. Sally frowned, watching us hug. Kristin sat at the table, looking like she'd just rolled out of a deep sleep, while the candle flickered. Hannah sat again and I leaned against the wall.

"Ladies," I greeted them. "I think I have a plan."

They looked at me like I was some kind of idiot. I'd had plans before, of course, and look how those turned out. The Way of the Son wasn't always good. I stood up straight and told them my idea, then sat in the last chair while they discussed what to do.

*   *   *

In the end I was outvoted. Despite the awkwardness of living with the Carter family, having rebels shooting nearby, limited food and electricity, the gals voted to stay. After all, trying to go from place to place hadn't worked out very well. We always found trouble. That was my fault.

My plan was to get Mom's car charged up and drive us back to the ferry landing and live out our remaining days there at Quinn's motel. My plan would work only if we could charge up Mom's car, obviously, but that remained a challenge. But I had a plan for that.

"Every day's a challenge," my mom liked to say. "That way you stay alive."

Right. But what if the challenge kills you?

Mom would have a snappy answer, but I couldn't think of one.

The house was barely enough space to keep us from bumping into each other going about our daily tasks. And what were our daily tasks? We were definitely homebodies. It was too late in the year to start a garden but I took a stab at making one in the back yard. We would plant in the spring. Otherwise, a little cleaning inside the house: the usual, as much as limited water forced us to cut back on laundry. Isla had other plans; her diapers needed to be washed in order to be reused. And dinner was always a challenge. I made the walk over to the distribution center usually with Sally, wearing a cloth facemask and a floppy hat to hide her appearance.

Sometimes I went with Dale or Barb and carried back the bags or boxes of cans and packets we could carry. There was never fresh meat or milk, only jerky and canned sodas. Everything we got was leftovers saved from before the pandemic. Nothing was produced. Eventually the last can and packet would be handed out and that would be that. The end. Some people fought over items but soldiers guarding the distribution center made sure we maintained an orderly process. Other people went hunting. The neighborhood was free of cats and dogs, squirrels and rabbits, and fewer birds.

We got by somehow. The evenings were filled with dark silence, sitting together swapping stories of woe. Hannah and I listened to a song or two on her MP3 player each night until the charge failed. We charged it during our hour of power each day. My phone lasted longer because I didn't check messages often. None came through. However, I sent a message out every week, hoping for a response.

Hannah and I took over the room with the twin beds, made it ours. Kristin and her boys took Hannah's old room, all in one bed. The Carter family occupied the living room, as though they'd found a suitable campsite, Dale sleeping on the couch and Barb on the loveseat, their children on the floor. Sally had to make do with the room where Hannah and Kristin's mother had lain dead for two years. She put new sheets on the well-scrubbed bed, of course.

The kids played together mostly in the basement, sometimes in the back yard. We warned them to be quiet outside to not attract attention. As winter came on it was easy to stay indoors. Outdoors seemed colder than we remembered it being in our childhood. We remembered when everyone was worried about the world becoming too warm. Dale rattled on about 'global warming', laughing at the end of every sentence.

There were never many people out. Where did they have to go? Everyone seemed to hide inside their homes. I understood that: if there are people, they might have food and supplies we could steal or take by force. Or we could make a meal of them, disgusting as it might be, because we're hungry and there aren't burger joints open any longer. Or if they're girls, we can grab them and rape them. So people hid their children.

Kristin and Barb made a plan to pair the daughters and the sons when they were old enough – assuming we'd survive that long – but it was just talk to fill the hours. The kids hated that kind of talk, the girls thinking boys were yucky and the boys too young to know what they discussed. I thought of telling them what my mom was always suggesting to me as I was growing up: about us having to repopulate the world – but I couldn't say anything after Howie complained quite loudly that he would never 'marry' his sister. By then we'd have a better homestead, either making do here using a back yard garden, or elsewhere in the country. We would be able to go on, surviving into the next generation, no matter what life was like. Maybe we'd join with other families and found a village, call it Newtown or Pandemia, something cute. I would name our village Pollyville, after Mom. Always on our minds, of course, would be security from marauders, vagrants, and rebels.

The first day seeing a little snow fall in this southern clime, I felt amused by Dale's 'global warming' bugbear, something people worried about before they had any pandemic to worry about. The pandemic stopped industry, halted traffic, ended pollution, and left the Earth to green up again. Some people cheered that: proof that mankind was a pestilence upon the Earth and good riddance to the excess population that died during this pandemic.

I stood on the back stoop, right where Hannah and I had first talked, where she kissed me. I watched fluffy flakes drifting down, not enough to cover the yard, melting on contact with the grass. After a while Hannah came out and wrapped a blanket around me, then slipped inside so we could warm each other. Like old times: sitting out back, talking, waiting for time to pass. She sang a song she made up: "'Hey, snow, can you just go away? / Don't wanna play / Come again another day / Long after we're gone / Would that be so wrong?'"

I had plenty of time during the winter weeks to work on Mom's car. I learned a lot about how the system worked, going through the owner's manual page by page. Lots of time for reading. (I even read that vampire novel Dale finished.) Lots of time for writing in my notebook, too, writing down all we were doing and had done, making a record for Isla. I found the cable for charging Mom's car but with only a couple hours of electricity each day it would take forever, and we wouldn't have any power for household chores.

The hurricane that blew inland when we arrived here left some damage. A few trees were broken and bent. A neighbor's tree had fallen where we'd parked the van in front of the house. If I hadn't driven it over to the other place, it would have been crushed. And to think we might've been sleeping in the van overnight! With an empty tank, it remained where I left it. I walked back and forth retrieving tools. In fact, walking around the neighborhood looking for anything useful was my daily task. Sometimes Sally went out with me; she wasn't afraid. Hannah and Kristin dared not go out.

I often wondered what might have happened to Quinn's motel when the hurricane passed through. Maybe it was destroyed. Or damaged enough so it was no longer a good place to live. I worried about Mom's tuba. I thought of the island. Maybe the hurricane had damaged houses there. I smiled, pondering those people and the community they formed. What would they do now? Did they know how to repair things? Replenish their food? Now they'd want someone like me to direct the reconstruction, lead them into the new normal. Maybe I should return and claim it.

The soldiers continued to hold the line along the iron fence, and manned checkpoints here and there. We could go out as we liked but they advised us to stay indoors. Rebel gunfire could erupt at any moment. A stray bullet could hit us. They hadn't made further inroads, hadn't moved the border, but they continued harassing our side. Sgt. Hendricks rotated out, went back home to his family sheltering in a dug-out he'd made, replaced with another sergeant named Gage who was more strict. Sgt. Sadler remained, a lifer, and often shared information about the world, whatever he heard from the army communications band.

We weren't the only nation in civil war. Many places around the world faced eruptions of violence as governments broke down and people rose up. Of course, there was constant rioting over food shortages, lack of fuel, and more repression. Nations threatened war to grab scarce resources, similar to ancient times when most fighting was for survival, not glory and medals. It was coming here, Sadler said, evoking the wise old sage, rubbing his stubbly chin. I replied we already had that, citing conditions in the city Mom and I left and the presence of the rebel bands on the north side of this town.

"Don't quote me," said Sadler, "but they're talking of a big bomb, using that as a threat. Don't make no sense. 'Give us your food or we'll destroy your food'? Crazy politicians. Stupid generals. And the rest of us just have to wait and see just how we're gonna get fucked."

I had to agree. "Maybe they won't work. It's been a long time, right? I mean, after sitting around for so many decades."

"Don't wanna trust that, though," he said.

No telling what tomorrow would bring. I had to keep my plan active in the back of my head. We had to be ready to flee – and it would become necessary soon. Needed to get Mom's car charged.

"He's a real asshole. By the book," said Sadler about the new sergeant. "He went to all the seminars, kissed asses up and down the battalion. No way he'll let you charge up a car battery."

"How about if he doesn't know about it?"

Sadler laughed, others turned to look, and he stopped.

"If I could get the car here...but *over there*...and used a long cable...hmm...? It just might work."

Sadler grinned, glanced back at Gage across the street at the command post. "Sure. It could work."

"Thanks," I said and slipped him a small jar of pickles brought from our stash.

"Ooo, pickles. And these are the good ones."

"Sweet pickles, not those Kosher dills."

"Great." He opened the jar, wiped his hand on his pants and plucked out a pickle, bit off the end. "So what've I got to lose, huh? They gonna send me home? I got no home now anyways."

"You know where we live, right? You're welcome for dinner any night. Come on over. During the electric hour."

"May hafta be later. We're supposed to monitor everything here while the power's on."

"Whenever," I said. "You'll be welcomed, so come on over."

"You betcha."

✳ ✳ ✳

Sgt. Sadler grinned, acting shy when he encountered Sally in the living room. She happened to be the one closest to the door when he knocked. Not expecting to find her in our house, he nodded at the nice dress she wore from Aunt Jackie's wardrobe. Had her hair washed and combed, looked nice.

"You're that woman," he said, searching for the right words, "they put in the bus, ain't ya? The one related to the rebel guy."

She gave a curt nod, apprehensive about this soldier coming to the house, his broad shoulders filling the entryway, even though I'd told her he was coming for dinner.

"I'm sorry, ma'am," he said. "They shouldn'ta done that. Ain't right. That's why I made him stop, that hardass bastard. I know you didn't do nothing. Hope they didn't hurt you bad."

"They roughed me up pretty good," she said, lips tense, "but at least they didn't rape me."

"Yeah, I hate when they do that."

"It wasn't you," she said, a hard edge in her voice.

"I still hate it. Ain't right."

Her face softened. "You ever...?"

"Nope. Never. I was taught to treat women right. A Southern gentleman and all."

"That's mighty kind of you."

"I lost my missus going on five years now due to the virus," he said, "either that or too many vaccinations. Valerie was a kind of jab-aholic. Couldn't get enough, afraid she would miss one. Even when her light brown hair turned premature white, started falling out. She died soon after. Haven't cared much about anything ever since."

"You poor man," said Sally, patting his shoulder.

We sat around the kitchen table, Hannah and I together on one side, Sadler and Sally together on the opposite, Kristen at one end, and the other end empty or given to the spirits of the house. The Carters ate in the living room with Kristen's boys joining them. Isla had fed earlier and napped during dinner. We chatted casually on topics of no consequence, all safe subjects, tried to make a joke or two. We avoided talking about our pasts – even though talking about our future was harder. We pulled out a few extra jars and cans for this dinner, and we all enjoyed it immensely.

"I was wondering," said Sadler at the end of dinner, "if I could... really hate to ask but...maybe take a shower? You can say 'no' and I'll understand. Just wanna be clean if I'm a guest in your house."

Sally burst into laughter. "Sure. But only cold water."

"I don't mind. It's been a while."

"Then go ahead," I said, waving my hand toward the hallway.

"Cold shower's what I need." He gave Sally a long look and she turned away, blushing. "Keep me thinking straight, ya know?"

He had an odor, barely covered with sprits of air freshener. He had battlefield scruffiness, too, but maintained his dignity, taking pride in being a protector of the community. I had to admire him for that – a little like Victor the yachtsman who was my father.

He got up, glanced back. "I won't mess up anything."

"Sally can show you the way," I said.

She smiled and led him out of the kitchen.

"What're you doing?" Hannah asked me when they exited.

"He's fixing her up," said Kristen with a giggle.

"Buying a charge up for Mom's car battery is what I'm doing," I said boldly. "I invited him to dinner as part of the deal. Nothing else. But if they like each other, it's okay with me. It's dinner that's the deal, not.... Well, not anything else."

But the girls laughed together. I didn't get their joke.

"You did good," said Hannah, patting my arm.

"What did I do?" I asked and they giggled again.

It must've been a sponge bath, as long as it took. The water pressure being low, you basically had to wet yourself, then soap up and rinse off. That took maybe two minutes if you focused. Had to save water for other people. We couldn't hear the shower running from where we sat in the kitchen but we did hear the door to Aunt Jackie's room close with a creak. We didn't see them for a while, neither Sally or Sadler, whose first name we learned was Buck.

Just as I was about to fall asleep in the chair, there was Sadler standing over me with a big smile pasted on his clean face, looking refreshed and ready for anything in the candle's glow.

"Thanks again...for...the dinner," he said in a low voice, late as it was. He glanced down the hallway.

"You're welcome," I responded.

He started toward the front door, paused. "Almost forgot."

Digging in the side pocket of his camo-patterned army coat, he pulled out a handful of something.

"Here." He opened his hand and I saw four shotgun shells. "For defense. All I could get. Mark your target."

"Wow, thanks."

"I'll get some guys to come over and help you push your car. I'm sure we can get it charged up. Now, finding some gas is gonna be the hard part."

The lights had long been out by that hour. A few candles lit the rooms. The Carters were content to slip into sleep, their candle almost out. As I passed down the hallway, I saw Sally lying on the bed, a naked leg sticking out from the coverings. The candle on her nightstand showed a scene of contentment. She stirred, rose up to blow out the candle, and fell back.

"Hey, Sandy?" she called, seeing me there.

"Yeah?" I responded, stepping into the doorway.

"Thanks." She settled herself among the bed covers.

"Okaaay." What was everybody thanking me for? It was just dinner and I didn't even prepare it.

Joining Hannah in our room, I felt like a king. I'd achieved something good. My plan, my directions. My success. Rolling onto the narrow bed beside her, she pressed against me, told me I did a good thing. Of course, I mused.

"I got us a charge for Mom's car, so we could get out of town."

"No, silly." She gave my chest a playful slap. "You brung people together."

"That sure wasn't my intention." That part was an accident, I decided. "I mean, I really never thought they would, ya know, get together like that. Or do whatever they did."

I noticed my wife had stripped to her skin under the sheet. She scooted up to me, kissed my cheek.

"Guess it's been a while for both them," she said.

"Yeah, guess so." I let out a big exhale, ready to go to sleep, my work done.

Hannah rolled against me, her hand going to my face, cradling my jaw. "It's been a while for us, too, you know."

"Yeah, I know."

It had been weeks since the incident. It stayed in the back of my mind, but no longer poked into my daily consciousness. I could look at my wife and not see her with that country yokel. But I was afraid to go where he'd gone, even though she said it was all right. She'd had three periods since then, she offered as reassurance.

"If you wanna...." She ran her hand from where it rested on my chest down to my groin. "Then I wanna...."

I could only sigh. "I don't know if I can." Honestly, I'd been so busy every day, worrying about everything, that I lost my interest in all that sex stuff. Or maybe that was all bullshit, a trick of my mind. "I mean...I *can* but I can't. You know?"

"No, I don't know. You don't want to, or you physically can't do anything?"

"Oh, I dunno." I sighed out my frustration. "I'm too stressed by everything."

"Stressed is what it's suppose to fix," said Hannah, giggling, "or so I've heard. Let me try, okay? You can stop me at any time if you feel uncomfortable."

"I guess it's all right."

She climbed on top of me and nothing felt uncomfortable. Not at all.

23

WAR ZONE, PART 2

The soldiers got to know me, the boy who brought them pickles and veggies in jars. "Hey, Pickle Boy," someone would call when I approached, "what you got for us today?" I laughed it off. They were helping me, after all, so I rewarded them.

Over the spring weeks three or four of them, or a different three or four, would help roll Mom's car up the streets, heading to the Food Mart, a little bit further each time. Eventually we got it close to the generators trailer. Sgt. Sadler ran the cable over at night so nobody would notice. It took some time, of course, only being hooked up a few minutes every other night or so.

Meantime, I went around the neighborhood every day with my canvas bag. Inside the bag was a five-gallon plastic gas canister, the bag hiding it from the view of anyone watching me. My task was to find gas in abandoned cars and collect it. Sally gave me a hand pump she found in the garage. When I was sure I was alone, I would pry open the fuel door with a crowbar, wrench the cap off, and run a line down to see if it hit gas. If there was any, I drew it up, depositing it into the canister. That, too, took time.

We did these tasks under sporadic spouts of gunfire. Some days were more dangerous than others. In fact, shots hit the pavement near me once and I had to dive into a row of bushes in front of a house to escape. Another time I was crouching behind the truck I was siphoning from and a stray bullet hit the side panel near me. A little closer and it could have set off an explosion. I worked more at night, when I could go about without being seen. Hannah would wait up for me to return.

Sgt. Sadler kept coming by, acting like he was on patrol and checking we were safe. Sometimes he visited openly, seeking Sally. She seemed alternately pleased he visited and annoyed he visited so often, as though she worried what the pious Carter family might think of her. Sure, she'd done some glamour photography in her past but they had no way to access any of it. Sally went out with me some nights on gas collection duty, keeping watch as I worked. We talked about her future; she had no ideas. Taking it day by day, she said. Other times she cared for Isla so Hannah could get some rest or do the dinner prep.

When I was in the house and my chores had been completed, I would sit and write by candlelight in the living room, which tended to be the brightest place.

"Whatcha scribbling about there, young fellow?" asked Dale as he turned his latest book over his knee. Another rainy night forced me to stay home, so I wrote in my notebook.

"It's a diary, I guess. Everything we do. What we've already done. I want Isla to know when she gets older."

"You sure you want her to know all that?" he asked, raising an eyebrow.

"Good and bad. It's history. Gotta record it. Just being honest."

"Hard to be honest if yer writing 'bout your own life, things you done, even good ones."

"I'm trying to be honest," I said, and meant it. "She can decide for herself when she's old enough."

"By then she'll be doubting you."

"Maybe." I glared at him. "But if I don't write it she won't have anything to decide about."

He scoffed at my idea, returned to his reading.

"I'll be sure to mention you and Barb, and your kids," I added.

"Don't you write a damn thing about us, you hear?"

"Okay, no Carter stuff."

"Damn right."

Instead I wrote about our stay with Aunt Laura, Mom and me,

the first time, and Earl visiting her. I tried to describe everything without getting into a story; just the facts. Finishing that chapter, I started on the Alice Alton chapter but had to stop. I turned over a few pages and started fresh describing our arrival at Aunt Jackie's house and Hannah opening the front door. I filled a couple pages describing my thoughts and feelings seeing her for the first time and then the two of us sitting on the back stoop while her brother Nathan played catch with himself in the yard.

Gunshots interrupted my writing.

Dale pinched the candle out and we sat in the dark. More shots and we slid to the floor. Barb and the girls huddled in the hallway. Dale, the boys, and I crowded among the living room furniture. Hannah and Isla were in the bedroom hiding with Kristen and her sons under the bed. Gunfire rattled our windows, the percussion hitting the glass. The kitchen window broke out.

The next evening while I went out on gas collection, I saw the big metal fence which used to be two blocks away had been moved closer. Now it ran just one house away.

Sgt. Sadler came by with his squad in the morning, knocked on the door to announce the shift of the border and tell us we should consider leaving. I reminded him the car wasn't fully charged yet, nor had I filled the gas canister.

"You may not get to charge it all the way," he said, looking over my shoulder as if searching for Sally inside. "One gallon'll get you out of town, at least, where you'll be safe."

I got annoyed by him looking over my shoulder. "She's not here. She went to pick up the rations at the distribution center. Not back yet. You know how those lines can be."

"Oh," he said, seeming genuinely disappointed.

"Look, I know she likes you. Don't worry." I had to grin. "But maybe she's afraid of commitment, you know? Life hasn't been too good to her, so she doesn't want to put all her eggs in one basket."

"But I just need one egg," he said, his whiskered face smug. "I got the bacon already." He laughed.

Then I saw her returning at the end of the block. Sadler noticed my eyes shift. He turned, seeing Sally and Barb carrying the box of supplies between them and a clear plastic jug of water that was given to residents, one set per family per week. We combined what we got, of course, and shared it among everyone in the house. Like an extended family.

"Evening, ma'am," Sadler said, tipping his helmet to Barb as the women arrived. They set down the crate on the stoop, their arms tired. Barb took the water jug on inside. "I was just coming by to check on you," he said to Sally, who stepped around him to get to the front door. I moved aside and she entered, following Barb. "I'm sorry," he called after her.

"You're excused," Sally called back, not staying by the door.

I grabbed one handle of the crate and Barb returned to take the other side and we carried it in.

"What's wrong with her?" Sadler asked when I finished with the crate and returned to the stoop. "I've been treating her right. Perfect gentleman."

I found one of Mom's smirks stuck to my face. "You're asking the wrong person if you wanna know about women." We shared a laugh.

"Yeah, awright," he said, disappointed. "I'll check on you guys tomorrow. Tell her I'll be by, okay?"

"Sure will."

He turned to go, his squad waiting patiently in the street.

* * *

"I can fix a copy machine but not a car," said Dale. "We used to just take it in to the dealership for maintenance. Every three thousand miles, like the dealer said."

I had coaxed him out of the house to help me with Mom's car. We were close to the army generators but needed to keep the car hidden well enough that soldiers wouldn't be suspicious. Only Sgt. Sadler knew.

"I think learning how to repair a car is something they should teach in preparation for a pandemic and the complete collapse of society," I responded. "But, then, nobody expected a pandemic."

"Nobody expected gas shortage, neither," he said. "No need to fix a car if there's no gas."

He was right, but I had to keep to my plan, to be able to leave any day. Already rebels had pushed south a couple blocks, making our house dangerously close, the target of stray bullets. Everyone had to stay indoors and away from the windows.

"We can't stay here," I insisted to Hannah and Kristen. "It's a literal war zone."

They relented and gave consideration to my proposal again: to return to the motel by the ferry landing.

"But what about that big hurricane that went through last fall? It had to've done some damage," Hannah countered.

"True. We don't know if the motel's damaged or not. But we do know this neighborhood is getting more damaged. We already had the kitchen window shot out."

"He's right," said Kristen, a sad look on her face. "You guys left here before. It's not so hard leaving home. It's not exactly the same house we grew up in. Not no more."

"I wish we could go back to the way things were eight years ago. That would be nice."

"Eight years?" Kristen laughed. "When you were, like, twelve? And me being ten. We barely got started on life. No way we could imagine the way things've gone since then."

Hannah felt a tune in her head, had to mutter the lyrics: "'So long alone / You lost your home / Now it's time to roam / In the wilding gloam / You'll find the way / Some fuckin' day / A new world sits in the palm of your hand / dust into dust, sand for sand'" and she just hummed the rest of the Wu Crew's famous song 'Road Ode'. Kristen knew the song and hummed along. They broke into harmony, smiling at each other.

I let them enjoy the moment, happy the girls were together again, acting like sisters.

Then gunfire interrupted our musical moment. We dropped to the floor and Kristen shouted for her boys, to locate them. After a minute they crawled into the room, crying, continued straight on under the bed.

"Dang rebels," Dale screamed from the living room. He'd been hit by glass from a broken window. Barb fashioned a bandage for his arm.

After that, he was ready to help. The catch was that there was no room in Mom's car for their big family. They could keep the house, if they wanted, Kristin agreed and wrote out a deed of sale, but they had to be willing to suffer the consequences.

"We'll obey whoever's in charge. We can be subservient, meek. Then we'll inherit the dang Earth," Dale offered. "We shall abide."

What if the rebels gained control of the block the house was on? What new rules would they have to obey? Or would they finally be 'liberated' from the 'oppressive' regime of President Philpot? The rebels promoted Albright, a state representative, as their leader. She promised a kinder, gentler existence but only after the enemy was vanquished. Hard to say which would be worse. Each side offered a certain degree of order against continuing chaos, the last fragments of a dying civilization. It was at least something which could be used as the foundation for a new society. Like a phoenix rising from the ashes of itself, reborn.

✳   ✳   ✳

The woman called Sally held me in her arms, rocking me as she stood in front of that soldier they called Sadler. I was used to him because he came by often, always wanting to talk to Sally. It was dark and they stood in the entry of the house. I didn't know what they were saying, me being just a baby, but I knew I was hungry and if she wanted me to go to sleep she had to feed me.

So I rooted against her chest and finally got her attention.

"Okay, baby, okay," she said, and unbuttoned her blouse.

The soldier seemed surprised but pleased, smiling as though he liked seeing me nursing. He must be concerned that I was getting enough nourishment. Sally had large nipples, which were easy to latch onto, but her milk was less sweet than my mama's. Even so, I felt better with this milk, maybe because she was older. I don't know, I'm just a baby.

234

"That baby sure does like to suck." The soldier grinned. "I wish I had a kid. Never got to have one. Lotta people lost kids after the vaxxes. What they called 'adverse effects', ya know."

"I lost my girl," said Sally, gazing down at me, shifting me into a better position. I really liked that, got more milk at that angle. "Violence, not virus."

"I know. You told me. Sorry."

"Yeah, sorry I mentioned it again." She seemed to read between his lines. "I'm too old to have a child now. Pushing forty."

"I wasn't, uh, saying that." His smile slipped into smirk. "But you do look good for pushing forty, I mean."

"That all that matters now?"

"Heck, I guess. What else is there? The rebels? The fence?"

"Yes, the whole world."

"Fuck the world – oh, excuse me, ma'am. What I mean is—"

"Things are different now," she said in a sad tone. The milk slowed. "It's the afterglow of horrendous mistakes. Look around. I don't see anyone wearing masks. Except at checkpoints, which I get, because you never know who's coming up to it. But the rest of us, nobody has the virus anymore. Or cares about it. So why can't everything just go back to the way it was?"

"Because everything's been destroyed now, and nobody wants to fix it, not unless they can be in charge now."

She grew tense and the milk shut off. I bit down.

"Hold on, Isla!" she responded. She caressed my head, got me to go on nursing.

"Her hair's really coming in now, ain't it?" said the soldier, and I wanted to tell him I look just like my mama at the same age – or so my mama said.

"Everyone now either has immunity because they got it, or got over it, or else they got the vax, one of them at least, maybe all eight shots. And all the boosters. So who's left? Only country folk that were never close enough to anybody to catch it. But it's not eradicated. It's out there, floating around, waiting for a good inhale to find a new home. Still, most of us are stronger now for getting it. We can fight it off. Our bodies are toughened up. I mean those of us who survived it."

That soldier was staring down at me, watching me suck, like he wanted some, but it was all mine, all for me. I wasn't going to let go of the nipple.

"That's a beautiful thing," he said.

"What? Getting immunity? Hah." Chuckles rumbled through her chest, disrupting my latch. We had to set it again. "Oh, I get it. You mean seeing a baby nursing. It's a perfectly natural thing. Hmm! Ah, I guess you mean seeing my tits. Like it's something unusual."

"I didn't mean it like that," he said. I could sense his growing impatience. But I wasn't going to leave any milk for him. He had to find his own breast.

"But now the big problem is not keeping safe from a virus but keeping safe in your neighborhood, from those people who survived and have nothing now. And they never learned how to do anything so don't know how to start again from scratch. That's the problem, right? As you and your troops know." She reset me at her nipple.

"Yep, law and order is totally wiped out. Even police wanna be at home to protect their families, can't be spared to protect other people. And don't get me talking about the Guard. We had another go AWOL last night. No show at morning muster. These young fellas, they just walk away whenever nobody's watching. No sense of duty, or loyalty."

"I saw one cutting through the backyard last night."

"Oh, yeah?" He had her describe what she saw, which matched what the soldier knew about the missing man.

Suddenly a shout from down the hall interrupted us.

"So who left a big turd in the stool?" my daddy called out. "You don't flush after number one but you sure as hell do flush after a number two! Got it? James? Howie? Dale?"

Sally laughed, breaking my latch, then repositioned me.

"That was me," said Sadler. "Low water pressure. I thought it went down."

"Can't blame him, your AWOL," she said. "The way things are, I'd be heading home, too."

The soldier smiled, nodded. "Yeah. Thing is, I ain't got no home to go to no more."

"The problem now is everything that's happened on account of what we did because of the pandemic. I mean, you can't shut down everything, keep people locked up, ordered to do this or that, and then flip a switch and it all goes back to exactly like before. You can't expect civilization to pick up like you left the game during a commercial break and it's on again when you return to the TV. People aren't like microbes."

"Microbes, huh?"

"You know what those are, don't you? It's all the microscopic things: bacteria, viruses, other material. We're like microbes. We join together, fight each other, grow and die in minutes or hours. We form a society, kinda in a way. And the Earth is our host body."

"Earth, huh?" The soldier chuckled, but not in a good way. "I swear, you're talking like one of them death cult wackos. Save the Earth. Kill the people."

"No, I'm not one of them." She shifted me to her other breast and the milk flowed easily there. "Strange how those people called for population reduction but never started with themselves."

He laughed and I relaxed, knowing that these two were going to make it.

"Yeah, them first."

"I'm trying to keep it real," said Sally, voice a little stressed. "Like it or not, this is what we've got now, no matter what all's happened during the past eight years. This is us now...surviving. Like it or not. Now we have to do clean-up on aisle one through a million."

He laughed again at her words. I sucked, feeling tired, wanting to be cradled in warm arms and go to my happy place.

"Well, Sal, I'll protect you," said Sadler. "If you want me to. Not so good at cleaning aisles but I'll give it a try. If you want me to help out, I'm willing. I'll stay with you if you want me to. I know I want to. I mean I like spending time with you. I mean the times we been together, ya know?"

"You just like going to bed, I'm guessing."

"Well, heck. Sure I do. Cannot lie about it. You got a fine body under that granny dress, but I see more of you than that. I see how you care for that young couple's baby. I see you helping out. You're a good woman, the kind any man would wanna be with."

"You sure about that?" she said, rocking me to slumberland.

"Absolutely sure. Heck, I'm even willing to be a farmer, if that's what you're wanting, but I'm better at bringing down a whitetail."

The milk stopped flowing then but I was too sleepy to care. All I remember is being squeezed between them as they leaned in for a kiss. I had no idea what they got from putting lips to other lips. It was not as though they got any milk that way.

"Come on, baby," said Sally when they parted. "Time to put you to bed with your mama. Now you're full of my magic milk, you can have sweet dreams."

She took a step toward the hallway.

"And sweet dreams to you, too, Sal," said the man, letting out a long sigh. "I swear we should just leave, just walk away from here, you and me, or with your friends. Go someplace far away. Let's do it, Sal. We can start fresh. I put aside some supplies—"

"Goodnight, soldier boy." She went back to give his rough cheek a peck and my hand swung up to pat his whiskered chin.

Then my eyes fell shut.

24

THE BREACH

The Way of the Son is fraught with danger, menace at every turn, and a lot of stupid mistakes that pop up when you least can handle them.

That was the last sentence I wrote in my notebook, right before climbing into bed beside Hannah. I wasn't sure what I meant by it, only that I'd made mistakes and promised not to make any others. But I knew I would.

The next morning the spring sunshine was struggling to break through gray morning clouds as I headed out on my daily rounds to see what I could find. I would try to gather more gas from an abandoned car or two. Mom's car had gotten charged probably as well as it could be, about 60%. Mom complained it was barely able to charge up to 80% when we were leaving the city. I managed to put a couple gallons of gas in the tank, little by little, unsure if it was still good. Sadler said to mix the old gas with some new gas and that would refresh it and then it would be fine.

As I headed back to the house, a squad of soldiers marched up our street in a tight square with rifles ready. The fence had been moved south during the past week, right along the house beside us. Seeing soldiers on our street wasn't too unusual. We actually felt a little safer.

Sadler went to the door anyway, knocking like a salesman, his rifle resting in the crook of his arm.

I saw Sally come to answer the door. "Hey there, sailor."

239

He grinned, then got serious. "You guys need to leave. Like right now. They're coming, Sal. We offed their commander a couple nights ago, lucky shot. No telling how bad it'll be."

"It's Sally," she said, ignoring his warning. There were random acts of gunfire for weeks now. "Sal is my father. Salvador. Call me Sally. Sal-LEE!"

"Sal-LEE, get out now!" He raised his voice. "All of you. You're way too close."

"Okay, I'll tell everybody."

"Right now," he insisted, then pushed past her, poking his head into the house. He shouted his message to get out, loud enough I could hear it from across the street.

Hannah came out, asking what all the shouting was about. She held Isla, squirming and fussy in her arms. The women talked as Sadler stepped back and directed his men into position. He left the front stoop as Hannah sat down there to talk with Sally about whatever Sadler had told her.

If not for his warning and the presence of soldiers, it would've been a lovely scene: pretty young mother and her cute baby out enjoying the warm spring breeze.

And that was all I thought of when the big horn blared, louder than Mom blasting her lungs through Timmy, like that Tubal-Cain summoning the universe to worship, with the ground shaking of heavy movement, and the soldiers taking aim as thunder from the north end of our street roared over the horn and the sirens from our side wailed around us, the civil alert system engaged from the backup generator, and me screaming over to the house for them to get out *now! Run! Get away from there!* Only Hannah holding Isla hearing me, sitting on the stoop, then jumping up and pounding on the door to get everyone's attention – and Sally realizing what was happening, Kristen bringing her boys out and immediately seeing what the emergency was: the monster dump truck bulling through the heavy metal fence yards away, huge wheels churning, tossing sections of the metal fence aside, flung into the air, as the beast exploded through—

Soldiers sending a spray of bullets through the windshield,

easily striking the masked driver, causing the truck to veer off the street, across the yard and right toward the front of our house, right behind everyone fleeing—

Sally rushing out, her go-bag in hand, Sadler seeing her, seeing the truck charging, pulling her to him then, recalculating, giving her a big shove away from himself, backward against the concrete stoop, just as the silver grill of the huge truck struck him, catching him under the chin, tearing his head off his shoulders as the truck rolled forward, grinding his body into the muddy yard, the giant tires rolled up his leg as it plowed into the brick wall of the house.

Screaming in horror, Sally dared not look – we shouting for her to run to us, to forget him, but she being too overcome with shock, the noise of the truck and the horn blocking our voices—

The truck halted, caving in the front of the house, crumbling bricks right where Aunt Jackie's bedroom was. Sally dropped her bag, kneeling on the ground, anguished at Sadler's death – with more desperate calls from us, caught herself, located us, got up, started toward us—

From the dump bed of the huge truck a dozen people clad in full hazmat suits with face shields and gloves, sprang up, tossing glass containers that looked like test tubes and other small jars, which shattered on the pavement, sending the contents flying into the air – as we wondered what was in them they were so eager to break open in front of us while they were protected, and Hannah's scream making sense: "Virus!"

I grabbed her hand, jerked her along with me, running up the street as fast as we could go, away from the truck and the virus containers being smashed – more rebels in hazmats breaching the gap in the fence like raging terror, stabbing with their homemade spears anyone trying to escape—

"Go!" Hannah screamed, and we ran, her carrying Isla, then me and Kristen holding her toddler and taking the other boy's hand, dragging him with her, getting to the end of the block and turning the corner as more soldiers raced past us, toward our house, to the horn's blare – me shouting to them about the hazmat suits and the smashing jars of virus, and Sgt. Gage with his rifle ready nodding but not doing anything to protect himself but pull up his balaclava over his mouth and nose, ordering the others to do the same, and me not believing that would help them.

Reaching Mom's car parked near the generators trailer, we all scrambled inside, one big pile, me climbing into the driver's seat, Kristen beside me, the boys in back with Hannah holding Isla, and my hand fumbling for the keys always in my pocket and fearing I'd left them in my other jeans – but finding them, shoving the most important piece of metal in the world into that ignition slot, and turning, hoping, praying, hearing the crank and the hum and the grind, the churning, vibration, energy flowing, the engine starting, the car shaking, not caring what might be behind us but backing straight out and wheeling around in a half-donut—

"Wait!" cried Hannah.

It was Sally, jogging toward us, one hand over her nose and mouth, the other waving at us to stop.

My heart beat too loudly to hear her shouts, but I waited all of one second, then took off toward her, slamming the brakes in front of her. Hannah opened the rear door and Sally dove in across the back seat, over the others' knees, as I hit the gas again, the car spun around and zipped down the main avenue, pedal to the floor.

All of us were sighing in relief but holding our breaths until we were well out of town, heading to nowhere, as long as we were out of the town, with no time to pack or prepare or think through what our next steps would be. We passed the apartments where the girls had once lived with their mother, and found the county highway and turned south, then southeast.

I suddenly understood the way we must go: the Way of the Son, who thinks he knows best or at least as good as his mom, or his wife, or his baby, because everything and anything could pop up like a dump truck in the morning haze with the crazy world ready to swallow you whole and not even choke.

The miles stood up and frowned at us, then seeing we had no fear, lay down and let us pass. The fields did not wave. The forests did not nod at us as we passed. And none of us spoke a word, only George complaining of his arm hurting from the way Kristen had dragged him behind her. Isla remained alert but calm, too curious to be afraid, not knowing what it was she saw happening. Perhaps she would not remember it as she grew older.

Eventually, we seemed to catch our breath, could relax some, and slowed. We were somewhere between a fallow crop field and a thin wood, a fallen barn off to the far end of the field, a stone cairn back among the trees. The skies continued to cover us with dark overcast but let a few rays of sunshine cut through, giving us hope.

We rolled down the windows for some fresh air, now that we were far enough from that town to breathe again.

"Where are we?" Hannah asked quietly, looking around.

"The middle of nowhere," I replied.

A bird cawed, flew away. The breeze touched the car, continued on. The grass bent, then bent back. Time had stopped.

"We're awright," Kristen offered. "We got each other."

"But not much else," I said.

Only then did we pause to think of the Carter family huddled in the living room, and me wanting to go back to get them but nobody saying it made any sense to try, that we had no more room in the car, that they would be all right – as long as they survived the morning's assault. They knew how to take care of themselves, and we wanted to believe it, just so we could sleep at night.

✳ ✳ ✳

Mom always told me if I ever left the house, referring to our beach house on the island, I should be sure I had my keys and the pistol. She would say it like I was still five years old and I hated that. But I listened to her. We are alive because I listened. I had the keys in my pocket when we needed them and the pistol in its holster which we would've needed if we hadn't been able to leave the town.

"We have to assume they're dead," I muttered as we drove, but only Kristen in the front seat heard me. "The way that truck hit the house, the way the rebels were attacking everyone. There's no way they got out alive."

Kristen *shush*ed me.

"So close," I mumbled. "So damn close...."

"We all coulda died," said Kristen. "But you were ready."

Sally was in tears when we finally stopped. We hadn't run out of gas yet but we needed to pause and assess our next move. It was late afternoon by then. We'd driven along county roads, avoiding the interstate packed with long-abandoned vehicles. We found an open area to pull over, and I dared shut off the engine.

We piled out of the car and Kristen consoled Sally, hugging her and speaking soft words. Kristen had lost her boys' dad during her escape so she understood how it felt. Hannah and I never thought Sally and Sgt. Sadler were that close, although I guessed he 'had a crush' on her. I bit my tongue, remembering how he was crushed by that dump truck and vowed never to use that word again.

"Don't worry," I announced, going around to the trunk with the keys in my hand. "I've been sneaking around collecting gas. Got a can right here: two more gallons. Good time to fill the tank." I gave a long look to the four directions, all relatively flat land, crop fields going wild. No other people in sight.

Opening the trunk I saw the orange plastic canister and let out a thankful sigh. I also saw things I didn't expect. A brown paper sack held several small jars of pickles and other veggies and fruit, like what I'd given to Sadler to share with his squad. But he hadn't shared, apparently, and was returning them to us. Was something wrong with them? Beside the sack was a big cardboard box stuffed with the green packets of MRE meals, a couple dozen of them, that he and his soldiers usually ate. I wondered why he put them here. Was he intending to go with us? Behind the MREs box were two boxes of ammo, one of shotgun shells and one of bullets. In the back of the trunk was the shotgun I brought from the van. Under it, wrapped in a green army blanket, was a black assault rifle like the soldiers carried. The curved magazine laying beside it had to hold fifty rounds. It was full.

I stepped back in amazement, then grabbed one of the plastic bottles of water from the case Sadler had put in the trunk.

"What's all that?" asked Hannah, seeing my animated pose.

"I dunno." I shook my head. "No wonder the car was sluggish, weighed down with all this. He must've stashed these things when I wasn't looking. I gave him the spare key so he could move it if anybody got suspicious. But he...."

Kristen's sons wanted to look so I lifted up Clay and George peered over the lip of the trunk.

"What's that?" asked Kristen, her arm around Sally's waist.

I turned to Sally. "It's Sadler's gift. I didn't know he was doing this. He stocked up the trunk with the stuff he knew we'd need to survive. Food and ammo."

Sally came up to me, threw her arms around me, sobbing.

"He must've been planning to go with us. He talked sometimes about what he'd do when his time was up, like going with us."

"That's what he wanted," Sally got out through her tears.

Bursting into fresh sobbing, Sally reached for Kristen.

"I'm sorry," I responded, thinking what I'd said that upset her. All right, got it: 'when his time's up'; but I meant his army service. He was about to complete his tour and rotate out. I told Sally and she shifted her teary hug to me. I rubbed her back, let her wet cheek rest on my shoulder.

"He never expected to die," I said to her. "He wanted to be with you. He told me. But he saved you. I saw him push you away, out of the way, not at all thinking of himself. It could've been both of you killed. Or you rather than him. He sacrificed himself. For you. For all of us."

She broke from her sobbing. "I know, I know."

"We can remember him as a hero," Kristen added, coming over and caressing Sally's shoulder. "I know you two were close."

I stared at the cases of canned veggies and fruit stacked in the corners. "How're we gonna open all these cans?"

Sally looked up suddenly. She reached deep into her pocket. "Here," she said, holding up a small silver hooked device. "Sadler gave me this. It opens cans."

"Oh." I examined the small thing, a clever artifact of the army. "Never forget a can opener when you're in a pandemic."

I rearranged the trunk. We didn't get to bring extra clothes or feminine supplies when we fled. Sally had come out with a bag but dropped it as she ran. We didn't bring any diaper cloths and Isla needed a change. I pulled off my shirt, then my t-shirt and donated it to the cause. The breeze was cool on my bare chest as the women got Isla smiling again, wrapping a strip of my t-shirt around her clean bottom as I put on my outer shirt again.

Hannah picked up Isla, sat in the car to nurse her. The boys watched with great interest.

"Mama, I'm hungry," said George.

"You are?" Kristen replied, amused. "Guess it wouldn't hurt to give you some. If I still got any." She picked up Clay and went to the backseat. Rolling up her shirt, she set the toddler in position. George crawled onto the seat, leaning to her. Hannah smiled at her sister.

"Snack time," I mumbled, then turned to scan the landscape.

Outside the car, I leaned against the closed trunk beside Sally, waiting for the kids' snack time to be over. In a small way, she reminded me of Mom, being about the same age. But she had a different vibe. She'd been through much worse than Mom. I told her she reminded me of my mother.

"Oh yeah?" she said, looking askance at me. "Well, I'm sure not breastfeeding you." She turned her back to me.

"That wasn't at all what I was thinking," I said. "What I meant was whenever I got upset at something, Mom would hug me, hold me until I felt better. And if she got upset, I'd hold her, too."

Sally turned then, pursing her lips in apology, and wrapped her arms around me, laying her head on my shoulder.

25

THE ROAD TO NOWHERE

Calculating the distance and choosing the best route, I guessed we could make it to the ferry landing on the gas we had. It was the only destination now, others being ruined or unknown and risky. Everyone agreed on the plan. Hannah told the others about Quinn and the Tropic Isle motel. They could each have their own room. The boys liked that idea.

I thought about the hamlet around the ferry landing. I worried about the damage the hurricane might have done. Maybe it would be too much for us to live there. I wondered about the island, if anyone was left there. How much more desperate would vagrants there be? How more alert did I have to be?

"I wish we could wake up and find everything different," I said to myself as we drove along.

"What?" asked Hannah, sitting in the passenger seat.

I wished we could walk casually down a country road without fear of marauders rushing up to kill us or vagrants capturing us. I wished we could go anywhere with nobody wanting to take what we had. Wouldn't it be great if we could walk down a road and maybe another family would see us, wave their hands, welcome us to their camp? Maybe they would offer us some of their food and drink. We would talk, and we wouldn't get angry or jealous or try to hurt each other. They might suggest we join them, helping build a village. That could happen. More likely they wouldn't trust us. We wouldn't trust them, either. Instead we'd see each other as a potential threat or a happy accident and kill the other.

"I have to protect us. I have to find us food. I have to be sure we survive."

Hannah asked what I was mumbling, and I said: "Nothing."

After a while, I sat up straight, realizing I was drowsy, shook my head. The others had fallen asleep in the backseat. Hannah was awake beside me, watching the road.

"We could go over to the island," I said right out of the blue as we drove along.

"Now why the heck would you wanna go there?" Hannah asked pointedly and made a face.

"I dunno. Maybe there's some things we could use." For a few minutes I made a mental list. "That hurricane probably damaged a lot of things. People would've left. I could scavenge for whatever is useful. You know, build some planters. I could dig up the garden, bring it across to our side."

"You got it all figured out, don'tcha?" she challenged.

"I have a life for us figured out," I said firmly. "All of us. I have responsibilities. Taking care of you and Isla, as well as our other family members. I'm the only adult male. I'm in charge."

"Oh are you?" she said but laughed like she believed I was only teasing. I was, in fact, totally serious.

The others awoke at her laughing, asked what was happening.

"You can be in charge if you want," I came back at her. "But I still have to do the things that are appropriate for a man to do, what only I can do. Building, procuring food, protecting."

"Okay, Sandy," she said with that edge to her voice I think she picked up from my mom. "I, Queen Hannah of the Motel, do hereby command you to do all things necessary for our comfort and safety for as long as we shall live at the Tropic Isle motel. That includes Kristen and the boys, and Sally."

"Thanks," called Sally from the back seat, Clay on her lap.

"I will serve you faithfully," quoth I with a polite flick of my hand in formal oblige.

"Done, Lord Knight! Sir Sandy of the Island, noble sire of cute princess Isla, protector of the queen and her court."

"I accept, Your Majesty."

She started singing: "'You bow to your queen / Come when she calls / Play in her bed / But don't let it go to your head / When midnight falls / Off to your room unseen!' Got it?"

"Yes, Your Majesty," I confirmed.

We all laughed but George, who remained confused, then asked what it meant. Kristen explained to him how life was going to be from now on, from when we arrived at this new place. He asked if his daddy would be there and she sadly told him he wouldn't.

"Is Sir Sandy my daddy now?" asked George.

"Well, he could be. At least a step-father. Or a surrogate dad."

"Just call him Uncle Sandy," Hannah told the boy.

✳   ✳   ✳

The hilltop had the same view as when we drove away. What was different was the damage we saw. The roofs were torn, a scattering of shingles, corrugated steel panels tossed about, trees broken or batted down to the ground. I eased the car, which was about to go on battery, down the slope, steering around debris left on the road. We rolled into the parking lot in front of the motel.

Shutting the engine off, we burst into celebration at reaching our destination.

"We're home," I sighed.

"This?" asked Kristen, unimpressed.

"It does need a little work," Sally observed.

"I wonder if he's still here," said Hannah in solemn tone.

We climbed out, stood stretching beside the car. I surveyed our surroundings, pistol on my hip. Seagulls cried but otherwise only an eerie silence. I dared not honk the car horn, not wanting to let any hidden marauders know fresh victims had arrived. I cautioned everyone to be quiet and keep their eyes open.

"We made it," I said proudly. Being in charge, I had a lot on my shoulders. "We'll stay here, if we can. At least for a while, see what we can do. There should be some fishing gear in the office. We can try for a seafood dinner tomorrow."

"That would be nice," said Kristen.

The battery in Mom's car was down to 1% with the gas tank having only fumes. We wouldn't have made it if not for us pausing at a few traffic jams along the way to draw out the last few drops from a dozen cars. If you could ignore dead bodies sitting inside the vehicles. You had to wonder what they were thinking driving off, getting stuck in the mass of evacuees, unable to get away, choosing to stay and wait, maybe already infected, and dying as the engine idled away to nothing, the sun of summer baking them inside their cars. Now the car was finished. Good ol' Mom's car!

"I'll go check on him," said Hannah, handing Isla to Sally.

Kristen picked up Clay, held George's hand as she watched her sister go up the walk to the office. Hannah didn't rush like she hoped to jump into his arms nor lagged like she feared finding him dead inside. I thought I'd better go with her. No telling who might be inside there instead of Quinn.

"Wait," I called and jogged up to her.

"I'm okay," she growled, continuing.

"No. You wait." I insisted. There was no way was I going to let my wife walk into a potentially dangerous place with no protection.

"What's the big deal?" she asked when I caught up to her.

"We don't know who's inside. Maybe it's somebody different living there now."

She paused, thinking. "Okay, right."

We proceeded to the front door, my hand on the pistol at my hip. The door was jammed but we could see through the cracked window that the furniture was broken, the ceiling hanging low, gray insulation billowing out through the gaps, hanging down. The door to the inner office was closed.

"Looks like hurricane damage," I said.

"Hope he's okay," said Hannah. "Maybe he left in time and he's not here now."

Quinn said the hatchback we drove away in was his get-away vehicle in case of hurricane, and I felt bad that we took it.

I bulled my way in, forcing the door aside. With pistol held up, I called out for Quinn, waited for a reply but got none. There were no sounds of someone scrambling up to confront us.

"He's gone," I announced.

With Hannah's help, we moved some of the debris away, made a path to the inner office, and tested the door. Locked, of course. I reached in my pocket, retrieved the ring of keys our host had given us, tried three of them before opening the door. As expected, more debris blocked the door but I worked it open an inch at a time.

"Seems worse in here," I told Hannah, looking inside.

It was dark, having no windows, but light streamed in from the outer office. The inner office was packed with boxes and supplies he'd managed to stash, hunkering down from the hurricane. He'd packed the room tight. But it was the odor that made me back out.

"Smells like death," I said to Hannah.

She didn't believe me, of course, had to take a sniff for herself. Pinching her nose, she turned away.

I pointed to where the couch was.

"That's probably him. Asleep on the couch, as usual. Under all that insulation that's fallen from the ceiling. I'm afraid to look. No way to know if he died before the hurricane hit or if something happened to him because of the hurricane."

"He had a bad heart," said Hannah. "Maybe cancer."

"He was plenty old."

As best I could see, the ceiling slumped, like in the outer office, the rain coming through enough to dampen everything and, with the weeks passing, turn the room into a pungent terrarium. It would be a lot of trouble to clean it up, but we could salvage the supplies he'd stored and move them out.

We backed out and took deep breaths of fresh air.

"He was almost dead when we was leaving." Hannah teared up as we exited. "That's why he wrote that letter giving us the motel."

We just stared at each other a moment.

"So now we're motel owners, huh?" I responded, feeling sad.

"Guess so."

Other buildings had lost some of their roofs. I worried about the motel rooms, whether they were sound enough to be habitable. I worried about Mom's tuba.

STEPHEN SWARTZ

We returned to the others, who had moved into the shade of the eaves. The sun had broken through the clouds, shining bright and warm. I remembered the summer spent on the island and gazed in the direction of the island but couldn't see anything from that spot. I remembered other, previous views, felt previous emotions. I knew I would have to return, just to satisfy my soul and visit Mom's and Nathan's graves.

"He's dead," Hannah told the others, "but he was like real old anyway. Like older than grandpa age. He might've died before the hurricane. But he left us the motel. He wrote a Will for us. Sandy's got it in his notebook."

"That's great," said Kristen, still unimpressed. "But coulda left you a nicer place, ya know?"

"It wasn't bad before the hurricane," Hannah replied.

"Before the pandemic," I added.

"Well, you get what you get," said Hannah.

I gave Hannah the pistol, winking at her. I took the assault rifle out of the trunk, checking the magazine before inserting it.

"You keep an eye out," I told them. "I'll go around back, look at what damage there is."

"Can you go ahead and open the room already?" asked Hannah.

"Let me check the back first, see if there's any damage, before we enter, okay?"

"Yes, sir!" Hannah snapped a salute.

My eyes went to Sally, who startled at the military behavior. Hannah picked up on that, dropped her hand.

"Be right back," I said.

From the end of the motel I worked my way around or through all kinds of debris blown up against the wall, pushing some of it back, stepping over broken panels and tiles. I kicked some things off the edge, let them fall to the rocks below. Getting over to the veranda where the planters were set up along with the rainwater barrel, I found they'd been tossed about but weren't destroyed. We could rebuild. I straightened them as I thought backwards through the previous months.

Standing at the end of the veranda I gazed seaward, feeling the spray, smelling the salt air, filling with memories so large I could not contain them. Almost three years before, Mom and I started out for what was supposed to be a sanctuary. A safe place to wait out the pandemic, although we'd already endured six years of it. I was still a kid, even at nineteen. Two years later, when we had to leave the island, there was still no sign of the pandemic ending.

I was a man at twenty-one, not just by age but by experience. Thoughts of the day I shot Bucky returned to me. And the brothers in that camp in the woods. I didn't feel anything. Certainly not guilt for shooting them. Was that the measure of being a man? To kill justly and have no regrets? Or was it that we now lived in a different time with new rules? I couldn't decide. However, the rear veranda of this motel was a good place to contemplate all of that.

I realized the time that passed and rushed back to the others. They sat in the shade, talking out their plans. Isla was a happy camper in the new place. Maybe she remembered it. Kristen's boys seemed wary but they'd been through a lot already.

"I think we can make it work. The planters can be repaired," I told them. "The rain barrel's still there. Not too much damage. The roof looks intact. Didn't see any significant damage, other than in the office. Anyway, I can clean up everything – hah, like I helped Quinn do before."

"Home sweet home," sang Hannah, sounding cheery.

"A lot of things blown against the wall," I said.

"I've seen worse," Sally remarked.

"Well, I think Mother would be happy," said Kristen. "The way we've fended for ourselves, gotten by, survived."

"Yeah," said Hannah, nodding. "But I wish she knew you were alive before she chose to go away."

"I think she knows," said Kristen.

I regarded our little group. We had the start of a village. Three women with three kids and a man. Would've been better if Sadler had made it. One man wasn't enough to do the work or adequately protect everyone. Take out the man and the others are defenseless. It wasn't a hard-and-fast rule, just cold reality. If Mom were here, she'd be in charge. But we could make it work. I would teach the women to use the guns. Obviously the next generation would have to be Isla and Kristen's boys – something like they tried to do on the island. With Isla not yet at her first birthday, it would be many years before we could think of the next generation.

Mom was right: we would have to repopulate the world, or at least our corner of it. We had to assume we'd stay together, not add anyone, and build our own life here. We had to stay healthy, avoid injury and illness, not take risks. Maybe get a little mean to hold everyone accountable just so we could survive.

I stared at the door to the room Hannah and I had lived in. It was the room where Mom's tuba rested on the bed. After sitting a few months, the valves would need oiling. In my head I could hear Mom playing it, maybe the Hindemith sonata, or the somber solo from Mahler's 10th symphony. Or the Effie suite. I wanted to hear something, anything.

"Let's see what we've got now," I said, holding out the key ring, selecting one, acting dramatic as Mom had done when we arrived at the beach house on the island.

The door swung open, the room dark, but on the bed was the big mound I expected. Above it was a water spot on the ceiling but no break-through. The blanket that covered the tuba had gotten wet but was now dry. It had a dank smell so I pulled it off and tossed it aside. I regarded the soft-side case: a few water spots on the vinyl but otherwise good. I lifted it off the bed with an *ugh*.

Kristen peeked in, her boys beside her, curious eyes examining the room. "And you guys lived here?"

"For a few weeks," Hannah replied. "Then Sandy decided to go on a road trip."

"And the rest is our history," Kristen finished for her sister.

"Hey, Kris, don't worry," Hannah snickered. "Sandy's writing it all down. Then Isla will know everything."

✳ ✳ ✳

First thing was to move in. I opened all the rooms, checked them for suitability and comfort, aired them out. Hannah and I took our old room. Kristen and the boys took a room two down from us. We moved everything from the car into the room between. Sally chose the room on the other side of Kristen's from us, but over time she stayed more often in the room with Kristen. I saw them growing closer. Sally helped care for the boys and sneaked a smooch with Kristen whenever they thought nobody was looking. Didn't matter to me.

Despite Sally being the oldest, I felt I was the one in charge. I had to do things that only I could do. I had to protect them, most of all. And provide food from the planters and fish from the sea. So I was tired every day, but I had to keep going. Until the kids were grown up and could help. I never expected the women to help; they had a lot to do taking care of the kids. I only wanted some comfort at the end of the day. Most evenings Hannah would rub my sore shoulders, say soothing words, make me feel loved.

Next task was clearing out the office, both the outer, which was easy, and the inner, which took a more delicate effort. After taking out lots of fallen debris, I got to Quinn's decomposing body. He had a board stuck in his belly, likely something falling from the ceiling. Or he was outside and the hurricane wind blew the board straight into him, then he crawled inside to die. Probably he died from that wound instead of it being his heart or advanced age. With his body wrapped in a sheet from a spare room, I moved it outside, dragged it to the bluff, found a good place among the rocks to deposit him. Hannah came to say a few words, never looking under the sheet.

Yet that didn't seem the best way to resolve it. The sea birds would snack on the body. There was no place to dig a grave there. So I found some rope and tied him up, attached to a heavy section of the damaged roof. I put him into a small boat I found bouncing against the broken dock below. After rowing him out to sea, I said more words and slipped him over the side.

Rowing back, I gazed south at the island, wondering what was still there, who had survived, and if anyone would remember me. I wondered if I might be welcomed back. Who would be in charge now? Maybe they needed someone to help rebuild. I considered the resources we had there. I decided I should go check it out, retrieve what I could.

Meantime, I went around the abandoned damaged buildings to see what might be useful. My new job title: scavenger. I cleared out two stores: all the cosmetics, t-shirts, decorative souvenirs, some artwork.

And I cleaned Mom's tuba. I oiled the valves from the bottle in the pocket of the case. I polished the dull silver metal with the cloth in the pocket. Then I set Timmy in my lap and put my lips to the mouthpiece, and blew a long, low note, like a fog horn in the mist, almost expecting to hear another horn reply.

Hannah patiently listened, didn't say a word, not even when I tried to play a song. Isla paid attention, her eyes bright at the new sounds. Kristen's boys came down to listen. Even Sally stopped by out of curiosity. I played a song I knew from childhood that Mom had once played for me. When I finished, I felt better, and there was slight applause.

"When you're older, I can teach you to play," I told the boys. Isla already knew I would teach her.

An hour playing Timmy, then some private time with Hannah, got me through the days of labor, work that needed to be done to survive, not simply to earn a buck or two. And being appreciated for it helped a lot.

I thought of that as I paused in the strait where the ferry once ran. I could see the fragility of the motel on the bluff as the boat bobbed in the water. A roof and walls equal shelter. Fresh water and food was the next thing to secure. Then what? What do we do for the next many years? Just live. And do what? Grow food, collect water. Try fishing again. My second job would be food procurer.

I'd put the rainwater collection system in working order. The jars and cans of food would run out eventually. The MREs we were saving for an emergency, if we had to flee once more or if weather or other dangers prevented us from getting food otherwise. And if we had to ration, we needed to make sure the kids got enough food so they would grow up healthy. Otherwise we wouldn't be able to rely on them to take care of us later. Dining on breastmilk was convenient but it couldn't last much longer. Isla was ready to try solid food.

Returning to the motel, I gathered everyone in the spare room we designated the meeting room. We shared our meals there, too.

"It's going to get worse before it gets better," I spoke as we sat back from our meager meal of the food we brought. "A lot worse. We have to get ready – ready for the next disaster, whatever it is. Storms, vagrants, sickness, anything."

Everyone stared at me like I said something stupid.

"I mean, we're here, and fairly settled. That's good. But it isn't the end. We need to keep working. Every day is a challenge to get food and avoid injury. Every day we survive is a day won."

"Geez, Sandy," said Hannah, "way to tell a joke."

"It's no joke."

"What he means," said Sally, "and I know he's right, is we can't just sit back and think we're in paradise here. We have to work every day to get something to eat. It'll be hard."

"Exactly." I was glad she put into words the idea I was trying to get across.

"I know there won't be no more grocery stores," said Hannah. "We gotta do for ourselves."

"Now that we're here," I said. "Now that we've gotten things set up, we need to establish some kind of routine, to make sure everything gets done."

"What needs to get done?" asked Kristen.

"Getting food. Job number one. That means fishing and tending the garden planters. That means collecting the rainwater. We can make it work, but we all need to chip in."

"We can do that," said Kristen.

"We'll make a chart, list the tasks, assign duties," said Sally.

"Good," I replied, glad they understood.

Hannah almost choked. "So are you happy with going on your excursion?"

"My excursion?"

"Yeah, to Aunt Laura's." Her tone wasn't happy. "And then to our house? And here we are again. Back to the same place we left. Got your wanderlust out of you now?"

"We got your sister, didn't we?" I was surprised how I shouted at her, then calmed myself. "Okay, we couldn't save Aunt Laura or Bootsy like I thought. Sure, that was the plan. Anyway, Mom made me promise to get them. So I tried."

"Your mom made you do all sorts of things," said Hannah like she was invoking a curse. She held Isla, who sensed the change in mood and pouted, unsure what to feel. "Now it's our turn to fuck things up."

"Fuck up what?" I quizzed.

Kristen told her boys not to repeat my words.

"We're back where we started. Just like if we never left. We got worse than we gained by your trip," said Hannah.

"The hurricane wasn't my fault."

"I don't mean that."

Kristen tried to intervene, failed. I bowed my head.

"Yeah, I know. We could've died several times. But we didn't. It was risky but we made it back. With your sister. And her kids."

"Yeah, that's a good thing," Hannah responded.

"I could've made it even if you didn't come," Kristen offered, but I didn't know whose side she was on. "I really thought you guys were living large on the island."

"And they helped me escape, too," said Sally.

"That's another good," I counted.

"We never were living large," Hannah said to Kristen. "That island was full of fanatics. Crazy people. Trying to make their idea of a paradise. But the hurricane's taken care of that."

"At least we had a little power in the town," said Kristen.

"And rebels attacking," I reminded.

"But we had to leave everything there."

"Your point?" I asked her.

"The point...?" Hannah breathed loudly. "We've got nothing."

"Listen, if we—"

"Don't 'listen' me!" Hannah shouted.

It was so raw the boys shrank back in fear. Isla bawled.

"If we stayed here we would've had to deal with the hurricane. Could've killed us, too." I had to take a breath.

Kristen held up a hand. "Guys, please stay calm, okay?"

"Every damn day is a challenge," I went on. "If we get to the next day, we win. And we play this game every fricking day. We don't have a choice now. The point, my queen, is to stick together, try to make a decent life here, hope for the best but prepare for the worst. And the worst will come sooner or later. There's a lot we need to do to secure this place. We must protect each other and our home. Our new home."

Hannah sighed. "Our new home...."

"It could be worse," Kristen offered. "I'm glad you guys came. I'm glad we could reunite. You did good, Sandy."

I nodded. "Thanks."

"You take his side?" Hannah was angry so Sally took Isla, held her, tried to calm her. "Listen, Sandy. You know what I want. And I know I can't have it. Not now. Not ever, the way things are. But the alternatives aren't so great. Gimme a break, okay?"

"Sorry." I pursed my lips, not knowing how to respond.

"Everything's different now," said Kristen. "I accept that. We all've been through a heckuva lot. Can't go back, can't return to a childhood cut short. We have to move on, no matter how we hate doing it."

Hannah pouted. "I guess...."

Pointing to the spot on Hannah's shorts, Kristen got up, helped her sister up. Her period had started so they went out to take care of it, having no supplies and making do with substitutes. The simplest necessities, unavailable. It seemed unfair. Sally glared at me, as though it was my vault. I hadn't anticipated the shortage and stocked up for them ahead of time.

They went out. Sally played with Isla's hair to pass the time.

"I think I should go over to the island," I announced when they returned. "You know what supplies they had there. Maybe they're still some left."

"I don't know what it is with you, Sandy," Hannah spoke in a low voice. "You're hung up on that place. Is it about your mom? She died there, I get it. But me and Nathan, we had no choice. Your mom dragged us there, made us live there, no choice, and we had to like it, like everything she did there, too."

"But...." I took a long breath. "But that's where we...you know... made Isla. Where I fell in love with you. Where we...."

Hannah shook her head, like she was acknowledging her error.

"Yeah, I get it. You have fond memories of us in bed, or on the beach, but that's done. A memory. Now what've we got?"

"We've got a family." I tried to meet Hannah's eyes but she kept turning away.

"Now you guys need to remember just how much you love each other," said Kristen, looking at one then the other of us.

Our eyes met then, a second, then looked away.

There wasn't going to be any more debate tonight. She got like this sometimes, blaming me for the state of the world. I wasn't getting what I wanted, either. That was the deal we had in this new normal. Nobody got what they wanted. You had to fight for everything and always came up short.

"Like I said, it's gonna get worse long before it gets better," I said to summarize. "So I should go over there and see what I can find and bring back." I stared hard at Hannah. "You can come if you like. Or not."

"I will never step foot on that island again," she said through gritted teeth. "And don't you dare bury me there."

26

ISLAND OF DREAMS

We've read the stories where everyone we know disappears except for a chosen few. They must face the harsh reality that exists for them. They search for water and food, try to find good shelter, and protect themselves not only from illness, wild animals, storms, but other survivors. We've read them, but we always knew they were fiction, just entertainment for dark, lonely nights when the wolves didn't howl and the gunshots fell silent and even our own breaths were stuffed down our throats because we didn't know what was around the next corner, or what might happen the next minute, or where we might end up a heartbeat after we took the arrow or the spear or the knife in the gut and couldn't cry out for our kin but only think our final thoughts and a prayer for a mother long gone, when you were sent on your way, far away, because of a quickly invented law.

I have never gotten over that, the way they concluded I had to leave the island, that I was the criminal. It was me who lost my mother. I was saved from a complete meltdown only by Hannah joining me, bringing our daughter, trusting me in the outerlands.

I thought of all of that as the boat slid across the calm strait. Dipping the oars into the glassy water, I thought of our existence, as though I was traversing from reality to myth. I imagined what I'd find on the island, the destitute among the ruins, and how I'd deal with whatever and whoever I found. I thought of what to say if I encountered people I knew. Would they even recognize me or remember me? They might decide to shoot first and ask questions later. So I took the assault rifle with me, but I left half the bullets at our motel home. I wasn't going to go full auto and didn't want the extra rounds taken by an islander if I fell. I gave Mom's pistol to Kristen, the shotgun to Hannah, with basic instructions.

"I'm going," I told them one evening after dinner. "I have to go. I need to see what's happened over there. So we know if there are any threats. I can also gather some supplies."

The women did not argue this time. I thought they might worry I could be killed and not return. Then they would be on their own.

"Anyway, I'll have a look, get what I can, and be back as soon as possible."

"You know to be careful," said Hannah, her eyes softening like Mom's did when she feared for me.

In those stories, you see fit guys in camo, carrying guns. They looked well-trained, ready to fight – but that's not how most people will be. Any survivors would be office workers, housewives, factory laborers, teachers and students, store sales clerks, farmers and fishermen, janitors, fry cooks, dentists and nurses, and teen gangs – not so many former military, although the longer you go into an emergency situation the more likely it is the ex-military folks who will be the survivors. The non-military people, however, won't have any particular survival skills, so they will be prey for the few who did nothing but train every day for the final days.

I thought of people on the island preparing to fight. Mom had drilled them like her grandfather, the Marine commando, taught her. They awaited invasion by sea, the island overrun by pirates – just as Mom warned them.

The ferry landing on the island was too high for my boat so I had to pole it around the rocky coast to the beach, then jumped out into the surf and dragged it onto the sand. The morning drew up over my shoulder, made the island look beautiful.

"Diapers, lady things, first aid stuff," I mumbled to myself.

I walked up to the buildings clustered around the intersection where cars lined up for boarding the ferry. Like I was going down to the neighborhood grocery with a shopping list in my hand. Yet the ferry had long ago been moved away. They destroyed the old bridge further south along the channel, too, to prevent others from crossing over to their utopian paradise. They were happy to let the outside world die.

I strode through the hamlet, past the old hamburger shop, long closed and badly damaged, beyond the IGA grocery, in similar poor condition. Not even worth entering to have a look, I decided. My main destination was the community center at the south end of the island, about two miles along the paved road, now breaking up. The concrete building housed the community's office, the clinic in a side room, a library with books people were using for kindling, and the large main hall where they held meetings. That was where Mom was killed. That was where they ordered me off the island for shooting the man who killed her.

I walked the paved road, though it was disintegrating year by year. To my left was the line of dunes. Mom was right: you couldn't see the nude beach from the road. I detoured up one high dune and gazed down upon the strip of beach strewn with hurricane debris, seaweed, flotsam, driftwood, and trash. I knew it was the place where I was conceived, but I couldn't feel anything as I stared at the sand. It no longer carried any emotion. I knew if I walked far enough down the beach I would come to our family's beach house.

With Sadler's assault rifle slung over my shoulder, I took that route, for old times' sake, walking confidently down the sand. I gazed out to sea, seeking nothing in particular, and over at the row of bungalows whose back yards extended to the surf. I watched for anyone watching me. But as the salty breeze blew against me, I slipped back, remembering moments we had enjoyed on the island.

At the caw of a seagull, I broke from my trance, grabbing the rifle on my back and slipping it off my shoulder. Something had startled me, more than the bird's call. I saw ahead on the beach a pair of scraggly dogs. They'd gone wild, which had happened long before we left the island. I didn't want to waste a bullet as either a warning shot or a kill.

Then they bounded off, disappearing between two houses.

I had a gun. I represented force and power. Don't fuck with me.

I was a man, a warrior now. I mean business. I was also stoked full of fear, expecting everything bad to come at me at once. I struggled to maintain control, or else I'd waste all the bullets in a mad fury of confusion.

Continuing down the beach, I arrived at our bungalow and had to stop, had to decide whether to check it out or avoid it. Both good and not good memories. The house seemed intact, although I could see patches of the roof had lost shingles from the hurricane. Most windows were broken. Palm fronds had been thrown everywhere. The fire pit around which we'd had a few *soirées* stood firm.

We were forced to leave, to start our exile; we didn't have time to pack a lot. Plus, we expected to be walking and so couldn't carry much anyway. There were so many things we had to leave behind, things we needed now. So I stepped up the sand onto the ragged lawn, went to the back porch and sat, just like I had with Hannah so many evenings, just the two of us, talking, kissing, believing, and in time me caressing her belly as Isla grew inside her.

I startled at an imagined sound, breaking from the rabbit hole of memory, a dangerous habit I had to stop.

Satisfied my memories were intact, I checked the sliding glass doors, found them locked. I figured other people might've moved in after we left. I peered through the glass, saw the disarray of the interior, like somebody had deliberately trashed everything. Or it could have been the hurricane winds blowing in through broken windows, tossing everything around. It was clearly uninhabitable now and I felt better about leaving this place.

I went around to the front porch, remembering the night Mom kicked Bucky out, tossing his clothes from the porch into the yard, all the time complaining she was crazy and she shouting back her disdain for how he'd tricked her. The islanders had strange rules. Mom played the game and got to be on the council, helped direct island operations. But it cost her a lot.

Debris littered the front yard and the porch, took some dancing to work my way to the front door. It was locked but a bit off its hinges. I forced my way in. I saw the same scene as from the back doors. My attention was on signs that someone else had been living here: food on the counter, blood stains, clothes and shoes that were not my family's, and sexual graffiti on the walls. That made sense! In a pandemic, you must make time to scrawl crude genitalia on the walls. To let the world know you were here, that you existed, that you knew how to draw a penis. No need to insult Mom with a nasty remark and a drawing of her, either.

Angry at the offense but keeping myself tightly coiled, I made my way down the hallway, similarly strewn with debris from the ceiling. Sunlight came through a few gaps where the roof had been torn open. The house had that dank odor of wet things that never quite dried. I paused to look in Mom's former room, the bed where she played with island men to earn her position on the council. I stepped into the room Hannah and I shared, where we'd practiced making love so much. Both beds were ugly now, stained, ruined by the storm breaking through.

I dug in the closets, searched through the bathroom, collected a few things the ladies would want: tampons, toothpaste, aspirin, bandages, deodorant, shampoo, lip balm, tube of sunscreen, hair clips. I took a stack of folded towels from the closet. I grabbed what remained of Hannah's clothes, dismissing a few items which had been ruined in the months we'd been away. I looked for my things, found shirts and shorts.

It was clear I couldn't carry everything by myself back to the boat. I gathered everything by the front door. Probably there would be a cart at the community center I could use to transport them. I smiled, imagining the ladies' delight at seeing what I'd retrieved.

I heard some noise at the back doors.

"Who's there?" I called, holding the rifle up.

When I moved out of the hallway, I saw a pair of children, maybe six or seven years old, quite dirty and forlorn, wearing only soiled undies. They didn't look afraid or pitiful. They had a hard look in their eyes, like I was their prey. I held up the rifle but they were not afraid; possibly they had no experience with guns. They growled as they tried to open the doors. I shifted the rifle against my shoulder, aiming.

Then more noise came from the front door behind me. I whirled around and found three other kids there, glaring at me. They were a little older, maybe ten or eleven, looking as feral as the two at the back door. These older ones carried knives – no, just sharpened sticks, I saw. One grinned, showing hideous brown teeth.

The three at the front door stepped on inside, holding up their weapons. My first thought was to wonder who the boys were. I ran through the list of children on the island when we left but couldn't place them. They had to have been here at the same time. But they were left to their own survival skills because...their parents had been killed?

"Jimmy?" I called, believing I had the name right.

The lead boy growled at me, like a dog, waving his stick.

I could easily shoot them and be safe, but they were humans, boys I should've known from before. Live and let live.

"Hey, boys," I spoke in a gentle voice, feeling the words catch in my throat, "what're you doing? How's it going?"

That drew no reaction. I wondered if they understood me.

"You been on the island long?" I asked, standing firm.

The two at the rear door banged their fists on the glass, but I didn't turn, expecting it was a trick to allow the three before me to attack.

"I have a gun," I announced, aiming alternately at the leader and his two soldiers. "I'll shoot if you come closer."

There was no way for me to know if they understood my words or acted the way they did despite them. I couldn't think what else to say to them.

They charged forward and I shot, straight into his chest.

"I said I'll shoot. Now back off!"

As I turned, the second boy took a swipe at me with his sharp stick. I batted his head with the butt of the rifle, a spin on my heel and a shot to the third boy, upper chest. The second boy came again. I kicked him back. He fell but got up immediately, glanced behind himself as though expecting backup, then ran out.

When I turned to check my six, I didn't see the two at the rear doors any longer.

I lowered the rifle, breathing hard, my heart beating fast as I studied the two boys I'd shot. I didn't feel bad; regret, yes. But in the new normal, you had to do what you had to do to not get killed. I had to make it back to my family. None of that negotiation crap, not now. I'd learned a lot from Mom and from Sgt. Sadler.

Have to stay alert. Wild boys roam the island.

I walked with rifle up, ready to shoot, as I traversed the road, heading down to the community center. I looked over at the houses on each side as I walked, not too fast or too slow, always alert. I saw a forlorn man standing between two houses. He didn't wave at me but once we'd made eye contact, he turned and stepped out of sight. I saw an older woman sitting on the grass in front of one house, appearing lost. I waved; she didn't. I worried about the feral children coming for them. Out on the beach a quartet of children in ragged clothes played – until a pack of dogs ran toward them and the children hurried away.

My nerves tightened as I came to the community center, fearful of what I'd find there. I had tended the garden in front as my main job, my contribution to the community. It was a decorative flower plot originally but we turned it into a vegetable garden. In a way, I felt we owned those plants, although the hurricane had destroyed much of it. I took a few minutes to dig at some of the ones still embedded in the soil, thinking to save them and bring them to the motel's planters. Later.

The double doors to the community center were torn open, both doors laying on the ground. What I could see inside was a mess. The ceiling of the main hall, once a dome, had collapsed, possibly caused by the weight of water. There was a wide opening now, the mangy sky visible above. The plastic skylights had fallen. Around the main hall were smaller rooms. One room had a walk-in freezer which no longer worked, lacking electricity. While Victor's yacht had been docked by the community center, they could run a cable over from solar panels on his yacht and get some power each day.

I wasn't sure if it was worth exploring now. Too much damage. I wasn't likely to find anything useful to take back. I did see, over to the side, an old dolly. I recognized it as what I used to move seed boxes from the veranda out to the garden plots. I removed things that had fallen on it and pulled it free, grabbing its high handle bar. The wheels, though small, rolled fine.

My goal in searching the community center was looking for any food others had missed. This was where the community food hoard was, where we went for our rations. Everyone shared everything, handed out according to a strict plan, based on amount of work we did, but we got by and even started to thrive with Mom's oversight.

So many memories. I froze where I stood. In the center of the main hall, under the fallen ceiling was the spot where Mom died, her blood spilling over the tile floor, and nobody who came for the meeting knew what to do. A pang ripped through my gut, erupting in my heart. But I stood still, wondering if Mom hung around, if she wondered what happened to me.

Outside, at the south end of the island, she lay buried – with my cousin Nathan. I went over there to pay my respects, to say a prayer.

"I'm back," I spoke softly to Mom's spirit. "We tried to save your sister but...well, she had other plans. But we found Kristen. We're all living on the north shore. Not so far, huh? But we'll make it, don't you worry. Oh, and Isla says 'hi'."

When I returned to the community center, the noise of debris shifting somewhere got my attention. I listened for more, expecting wild boys to be following me. Maybe they'd gathered a larger pack to deal with me.

I held up the rifle as I took a step toward the noise. It seemed to be coming from a side room which used to be the clinic. When we first arrived we had to be checked for infection and suitability for pro-creation; it was awkward and embarrassing. Doc Rick, who was a chiropractor before the pandemic, ran it. He lost his wife, a nurse, but found her cousin Bobby on the island as a new partner.

The door of the office was half open, piles of trash and debris keeping it from opening more or closing. The noise came from that room, like papers were swishing over the floor.

I stepped to the open door, feeling a flash of fear, like an attack would come from behind me as soon as I entered.

Inside, I saw a flash of movement behind the table he had used as a desk before, pushed to the back corner of the room and turned on its side like a fortress. Someone squirmed there, cringed against the wall, with a low moan emanating every few moments.

"Doc Rick?" I called in a soft voice.

It could only be him in this office.

"It's me, Sandy Baumann." I lowered the rifle.

More shifting behind the desk.

"I came back."

"Who?" came the strained voice after a few seconds.

"Sandy. Son of Polly Baumann. Remember us?"

"Okay...."

"Are you all right?" I glanced around the cluttered office. It was too messy to be a medical office now. "What happened here? Where is everybody?"

More shuffling. He rose from the floor, pulling himself up just enough to show his face, battered and bruised. He rose higher and I saw he was naked, his body covered with bruises and scratches. There was fear in his eyes, like he'd just been attacked, shaking at the expectation of more violence.

"What happened?" I asked, concerned.

His eyes glared at the door behind me so I spun around but saw nothing.

I had to help him, so I set the rifle down, leaning it against the overturned table. I grabbed a lab coat from a coat rack by the door and held it open for him to slide his arms into, stepping backward to me. He wrapped the coat around himself. It reached down to his hips, not quite enough to offer him modesty.

"Thanks," he muttered like his mouth hurt. After taking a few breaths, he stood unbalanced, then dropped himself onto the chair for patients.

"Don't you have other clothes?" I recalled he lived in his office, but I didn't see any rack of clothing. "Where are they?"

He shook his head, fought back tears.

"Are you all right?" I asked. "How can I help?"

He forced a smile, pretending to be the same as before, always a happy camper. But his mask shattered after a few seconds.

"How...?" He tried to speak, seemed out of breath, so I guessed at his question.

"How did I get here? Well, actually we don't live very far away. We only got as far as the north side of the ferry landing. We tried to go farther but, well, things didn't work out so we came back. I'm just here to see what can be salvaged."

Nodding his understanding, he grimaced as though in pain and shifted his position on the chair.

"Good for you." He chewed his lips, eyes fighting off tears. "You came back. The only one...I want to see. The only good man here."

"Only good man? What do you mean?"

"All the others...fighting, killing each other...."

"What do you mean? Killing? Who? What happened?" I asked, with another glance behind me to check for attackers.

His breathing was raspy, and I worried if he might be infected, but he regained his composure. He coughed into his elbow.

"They killed Bobby," he managed to say, then became overcome with emotion.

"Who?" I asked, but he didn't seem able to answer.

"Them.... Those monsters!" he exploded.

I didn't know what he meant. Monsters? Probably people who acted like monsters, not zombies. People could be the scariest.

"What about you?" I asked. "What happened to you?"

He squirmed, forcing a grin that looked artificial. "Me? I'm still here. But not too well." He twisted his face, tears popping from his eyes. He seemed to be in pain. "Nothing left."

"Tell me."

"People here...they divided over the verdict. Some accepted you being exiled. Others thought you did the right thing killing that man who killed your mother. They thought the by-laws should be changed."

"Oh, yeah?" That made me feel better, that some had taken my side even though they didn't do anything to help me.

"But it got worse." Emotion swept through him and he paused to rub his eyes. "It made everybody choose sides. We got into two camps, everybody fighting all the time. It escalated into violence.

Nobody would listen to reason. But it got way past you. It was about fundamental ideas about life here. They started using violence to make their views known, to defend them, worse than people in the cities—"

"What violence? Like fighting somebody to move up the list?" It was a change to the by-laws the council voted for: if a guy wanted to claim a girl on the list and he didn't win her lottery, he could fight the guy who did win her lottery.

"Jackson picked a fight with Randy for the right to Janice. He lost, so he went after Randy, jumped him, I heard. Jackson got his belly cut open. Nothing I could do. Then Dale killed Luke, then Juan. Two women were killed by a jealous man of the other group – tribe, let's say. Then Amira died, assaulted, poor little girl. More retaliation killings. Vendetta. Assaults, rapes, murders. Everyone trying to get even. They went crazy. They realized there weren't any laws anymore, not even by-laws. All hell broke lose. No one was safe. I hid in here. Tried my best to mend injuries, if I could. But too many of them were too serious for me to do anything. But then...."

I was shocked. I could see that happening, given the way those people were acting before we left, a boiling rage underneath all our interactions. Like Mom said: it was a game everyone was playing, and she had to join in or suffer the consequences. But she seemed to win, and ran the island better than those old men on the council did – and they hated her for it.

"Then what...?" I asked him.

He looked up and our eyes met. "The hurricane."

Tears rolled down his cheeks and he put his head in his hands.

"Some people got away. Made a raft and the current took them south to the marshes. I haven't heard from them since. They were the lucky ones, I suppose. There's good places to settle down south there. Places you can hide away."

That explained not seeing hardly anyone on the island.

"And the others? People that stayed?"

That made him shake. Maybe it was too painful to talk about. I changed the subject.

"So...umm...why're you naked in your office?" It seemed a fair question. Doc Rick wasn't a nudist like Mom. He had to have some clothes around somewhere.

A flash of self-consciousness, realizing he was unclothed, then a blush of embarrassment. He started to speak, choked up, sobbed.

"That's okay. Don't need to say anything. None of my business. But if you were hurt somehow...I want to help."

He raised a hand with index finger extended, the others folded back. In graphic fashion he gestured through a sex act, making it clear what had happened.

"Bunch of thugs. Especially the father. He beats me," said the doctor, and I remembered the ugly marks on his body as he rose behind the table. "Every day. Forces me to give in. If I don't...he beats me."

"What? A bully? Who? Who did this to you?" I thought through the men of the island but it had been too long for me to recall more than a handful of them. Everybody liked Doc Rick.

"Nobody you knew," he said. "They came after the hurricane. Drifted down on a raft. With half of us dead or gone, they took over easily – like a new council. He and his sons. Three of them. They moved into the Seaside Inn, kicked others out. Beat up the council men, killed two who didn't get away. And poor Olivia...."

"Like pirates?"

Mom had warned them to prepare for an invasion, offering to train the men. They resisted doing any physical training but they did make weapons like spears.

"Not really. They came like most do, begging for a place to stay till the pandemic ended. Said their mama died. Said they escaped from a quarantine camp."

"It's not ever going to end," I cut in.

"They came over for the usual testing. Like I did for you. It's standard procedure. But they weren't having it. I tried to explain about the by-laws. Instead they...they pushed me down and...and they...they...." He burst into tears.

"You don't have to say it. I understand."

After a couple minutes he composed himself. "When they were

done, they told me they'd do it again if I said anything."

"That's terrible!" I boiled with anger. "I wish I'd been here. I'd shoot'em all."

"But they kept returning, kept on abusing me. Because nobody would stop them. They bullied everyone. Owen got it the worst, but he's managed to hide from them. They know they can abuse me, so they do. They come here nearly every day. I thought it was them when you arrived."

Feeling pain in my chest and a dull ache in my gut, I wanted to make things right. I wanted to cleanse the island.

"I'll take you with me," I said. "You can live with us."

"Really?" He grimaced in pain. "You and your wife and baby?"

"Well, actually we got more people with us now. But they're all good ones."

"Really?"

"Yes, of course. You can't stay here." I looked around the office, my eyes landing on the cabinets. "Do you have any supplies left? We could really use some of the basics."

"Not much. Take what you want."

"We kinda need everything." I met his weary eyes. "You see, me and Hannah are fine, and our baby, Isla, she's good, too, but now we got Hannah's sister and her kids with us. And we got another woman with us. It's a long story. So lots of lady things needed, if you know what I mean."

He half-grinned, broke into a cough. "It must not be easy living with three women."

"You don't know the half of it, doc."

We shared a laugh, painful for him as it shook his body.

I helped him up from the chair. He had to pause a couple times, feeling pain. He winced but pointed to the closet. I found boxes of medical supplies on the shelves. I gathered them and set them on the side table. Now we needed the dolly.

"It would be good to have another man around to help out." I picked up a chair that had been knocked over. "Can't do everything myself. And you know medical stuff."

He scanned the items I put on the side table.

"I'll try my best," he said, sounding hopeful. "It's so good to see you, Sandy. I never thought I would. I mean the way things are now. You saved me."

"I sure never planned to come back here again. Guess it's just the Way of the Son, always leading me to where I should go."

"The Way of the Son? What's that?"

I snickered to myself. "It's all the stupid things I do."

He tried to laugh but stopped.

The doorway was filled by the hulking figure of a monster with narrowed eyes and fists clenched at his sides. The towering, thickset man leered at us, angry scowl on his bewhiskered mug.

"No! Please, no!" Doc Rick shrieked, cowering behind me.

27

THE SAFETY OF NUMBERS

The brute filled the doorway like he was assuring us nobody would be getting out. He grinned through his scraggily beard, showing where a few teeth used to be. Shirtless and wearing ragged jeans, gut hanging over his belt, he reminded me of the brothers in the camp in the woods. He let out a growl like a wild animal happy to find a fresh kill, and took a heavy step toward Doc Rick, ignoring me. Doc Rick rushed behind the overturned table. I was forced aside, holding up the rifle, safety off, but the sight of a gun didn't stop the brute, so focused on his prey.

He grunted a crude remark to Doc Rick, making his intentions clear. Noticing me, he turned and grabbed hold of the business end of the barrel, tried to push it away, so I squeezed the trigger.

The shot into his side didn't seem to make a difference, like it went straight through him and he didn't feel it. I moved in front of him, as he let go of the barrel and wavered like he wasn't sure he'd been shot. I fired again, one in his chest and another in his belly as I dropped my aim. Splatters on the wall behind him made it real. He dropped to his knees, one hand to his chest, the other to his belly, frozen in wonder. Then he toppled over, falling toward me as I jumped back. He crashed hard against the tile floor.

Doc Rick's gasps were loud, rough, quickly tumbling into roars of joy and relief, then guffaws of satisfaction.

"You did it!" You really did it!" He was practically dancing.

"We live in hard times," was all I could say.

"Thank you, thank you, thank you," he sang.

It was a righteous kill, any court would agree, the kind we have to do in hard times. Hard decisions needed to be made in lightning fashion. I learned that from Mom.

Doc Rick came around from behind the table to check my work. I kept the barrel trained on the monster as the doc worked up an amount of saliva and spit on his abuser. He added a kick to the ribs. I said nothing but he looked at me like he wanted approval for his actions. You couldn't take someone to a court in this new normal. You had to deal with it yourself.

We gathered the supplies and put them in a plastic box. Then, stepping over the fallen body, grinding my boots on the monster's back, I took Doc Rick by the arm and led him out. I held the rifle ready and Doc Rick carried the box as we made our way through the strewn debris and out of the community center into the bright sunshine.

My hand went up to block the light. Doc Rick closed his eyes, like he'd been living in a cave. Except for the destruction around us, it seemed like a lovely day. A family could be going to the beach on a weekend holiday. But then I had to sling the rifle over my head and shoulder, ruining the scene.

"That was Gareth," said Doc Rick, holding the box of supplies.

"That thug?"

I glanced around for more of the same but saw nobody.

"Yes." He also surveyed the area. "He's got three sons. They're rather large fellows, too."

"And I've got three bullets...."

I dreaded carrying the box a mile to the ferry landing. I already had armloads of things waiting at the beach house. I remembered the dolly I freed earlier. Rolling it to the garden plot, I checked the planters. Doc Rick keep watch while I knelt. The sun burned through the morning clouds and warmed my back as the island breeze tried to cool me. I put a few planters on the dolly, then the cardboard box beside them. I told Doc Rick about our situation on the north side of the strait, and how I'd set up planters there and the vegetables we were growing.

"You're quite the farmer now," he said with a grin.

Yes, I was a lot of things now. I'd done a lot of growing up.

"I remember before, a few people used solar generators," I said when I was ready to leave the garden. "They had folding panels to catch the sunshine."

"Oh, yes. I remember," said Doc Rick. "Didn't need gasoline."

"You remember which houses they were?"

"Let me see.... I think that would be the Kesslers and the Lees. Maybe the Hardings. Forgot about them. Hope they're okay after the hurricane. I don't see many people now. Not many of us remain to check on each other. But I recall seeing panels set out and poof: *electricity*. After several hours. Me and Bobby used to ride the bike we set up to make electricity for the office. And, of course, Victor with his yacht, had those solar panels on it providing power to the community center."

"That is exactly what we need." I smiled. "The women will be so pleased. They need some power. Cooking and cleaning, you know. Boiling water is the main thing we have to do each day."

I gave Doc Rick a long look.

"What?" he responded, embarrassed.

"We need to get you some clothes."

He gave a nod. "Well, you see, my place was knocked down by the hurricane. I barely escaped with the clothes on my back, you might say. Then what I had on got torn off by those awful men."

"Maybe you can fit in my clothes. We'll check the house where we used to live. I have other things to pick up there."

"I've lost weight since you folks were here." He blushed. "We all have. Not much food here. Used to be a healthy one-sixty-five. Now probably only a hundred-ten."

"It's just been a year, not even. You don't look that bad."

"With no food a lot of us starved. The hurricane destroyed what food there was. Some died, others were killed for food. I mean, they were killed and their food supplies taken. I don't mean they were eaten. I never saw any cannibalism. Others died from eating rotten food though. I couldn't help them. Didn't have the right meds."

He froze, locked in a recurring nightmare.

"It must've been awful." I paused to give him a soft clap on the shoulder which made him wince. "Sorry."

He sniffled back tears. "I'll be all right."

I pushed the dolly down the path, stopped. I glanced back at the cemetery, took a long breath. Pointing, I left Doc Rick to return to my mom's and Nathan's graves.

Sitting cross-legged on the bare ground, I stared at the wooden board used as a headstone with Mom's name and dates cut into the wood. The bass clef was a nice decorative touch. The hurricane had blown it down but I stood it up again, stuck it firmly back into the ground. Did the same with Nathan's marker. His had a leaping fish on it. Thoughts of that day filled me, making me sick.

I stood and gazed north, recalling all I'd done since. And what awaited me there across the strait.

"You all right?" It was Doc Rick asking this time.

I nodded slowly, staring down at the mounds. "Yep."

Mom's bones were there beneath the dirt, partly swept away by hurricane rain and wind. I wanted to dig them up and take them with me, find a better place to lay her to rest – not on the island that killed her. Maybe on my next trip here.

Doc Rick took my arm, tugged, wanting me to leave.

"She's not really there now," he said. "She's in Heaven, playing her new shiny tuba and the angels are applauding."

That made me smile.

We rolled the half-loaded dolly up the road to our beach house. Inside, we rifled through clothes left there, got Doc Rick outfitted in something more suitable. Put other clothes in a laundry bag. We made a nice pile. I realized it was too much for us to carry, maybe too much for that small boat to bear. We still needed to find that generator and the solar panels to take back to the north side of the strait. It seemed like it was going to require multiple trips.

Before we left the house, I stood in the doorway of the bedroom Hannah and I had slept it, had made Isla in, and I could still feel the love we'd made there. Then I stood looking into the room Mom had used. I surveyed every inch of it, not for signs of her existence not swept away by the hurricane, but to memorize the details for later. I never expected to return, had no need to. Then I checked the nightstand drawer's contents, found her purse with some cash folded in it. And her driver's license. Her face, hair pulled back in a ponytail, had an expression of surprise when the camera flashed – but I couldn't look away.

I put the purse on top of the pile and went to the closet next, found Mom's clothes hanging there. I took a few, thinking Sally might like them. I saw small boxes were stacked on the shelf above the clothing rod. Pulling them down, I found lots of old trinkets in them. Letters folded inside envelopes. A few photographs, some of them very old in the sepia style of that era, and picture post cards – the things my grandparents had collected and saved, I supposed, for whoever among us would survive. That was now me. In one box I found a leather-bound notebook with a broken lock on it. Opening it while Doc Rick waited patiently outside, I leafed through the pages, saw the cursive handwriting in blue ink. Some pages were in German, others in English. It looked like a diary. I decided to take it, save it for Isla. She could read it someday.

I came out with two shoeboxes of things, my tense face putting him off from making any remarks.

"Nostalgia," I responded anyway.

Doc Rick, dressed and feeling better, led me to the Kesslers' old house, which had been hit hard by the hurricane and leaned badly. It wasn't a strong structure to begin with, they selecting a lighter, tropical style. They tried to be self-sufficient, garnering their own power while the rest of us did without or only charged up small appliances from the community center's power when Victor's yacht was docked there.

Picking through the precarious house, we gathered items we thought might be useful. I found a can opener – and several dented cans of fruit, vegetables, other food. We shifted heavy things that had fallen to check for more. After a search we located one of the solar panels. The four-foot board was bent slightly at the end but unbroken. It could still work, I hoped. Where was the other panel? And the generator to hook them to? We searched further, checking every room. No luck. Outside we found the other panel, broken in half among a pile of fallen palm fronds.

"Could it work?" I asked, Doc Rick beside me. "The part that's not damaged could still collect solar energy, right?"

"That's really not my area of expertise," said Doc Rick. "But we need the generator, anyway, or else nothing works."

I measured the angle of the damage to the house, like my mom would, determining the direction the storm had blown debris. One panel was inside the house, the other outside. The generator, being heavy, would be inside the house, so we returned and dug around.

"If I were a generator owner," I said, thinking aloud, "who used it everyday, where would I store it?"

"If he put it away to be safe during the storm...?"

"Right. A closet maybe?"

And there it was: in the hall closet, a safe space, sitting on the floor with towels folded on the shelves above it."

"Grab those towels," I instructed. "The ladies sure like towels. Sheets, too. We cut'em up to make diapers for Isla."

It took two trips but we got everything back to my house, piled them up with the other things there. The solar panels were more troublesome than expected but the effort would be worth it when we hooked up everything. The generator was heavy but 'portable' — meant to be carried by one man.

I surveyed our haul.

"No way we can carry all that up to the ferry landing," said Doc Rick. "It would take four or five goes."

"The dolly is full. I hope it can roll. If we had another cart."

"I remember seeing a grocery basket or two that people staying at the Seaside Inn used. Stole them from the IGA, obviously. Some homeless islanders kept all they had in those carts, pushing them back and forth up the road. We can see if they're still there."

But that was where the thugs lived.

"You wait here," I said, seeing him shaking. "I'll get it."

Slinging the rifle on my shoulder, I marched up the road but as I got closer, I slowed, crouching and hiding behind houses and piles of debris, watching the Seaside Inn. I slid the rifle into my hands, ready to use. This was the place where Victor's three ladies had stayed when they weren't lounging half-naked on his yacht. It was where Bucky lived after Mom kicked him out of our house. Not the nicest of places even before the hurricane, but it remained intact. It was sturdy and didn't look any worse for wear.

A door was open to a unit in the middle of the building but I couldn't see inside it. I could hear shouting from people in the unit. Then one fellow came out, shirtless, belly flopping as he scratched himself. He held something that he chewed on. A wild dog came out of nowhere and growled, and the man kicked dirt at the dog to shoo it away. More shouting from inside the unit. The man outside, big as the one in Doc Rick's office, turned to enter the unit, tossing the bones of his meal. The dog returned to snatch the bones and ran off with them.

I made my way to the back of the inn, found the dumpster filled with garbage, surrounded by a black cloud of flies. I pulled up my collar, got out a cloth to cover my nose and mouth, and went to grab the overturned grocery cart. The wheels looked seaworthy as I righted it. I hurried away before I could be seen. I saw another cart up the road, a still-meaty skeleton beside it, and emptied the nasty things left in it.

After an hour, with Doc Rick guarding the stash, I returned to the house pushing one grocery cart and pulling the other. One cart had a bad wheel that didn't quite touch the ground. But I hoped it would work well enough when full.

Doc Rick grinned as I parked them at the curb.

"Good job!" he shouted. "So you didn't have any trouble?"

"Nobody was there." I thought it best not to agitate the doc.

"They might be out looking for their dad," Doc Rick suggested.

"Then we better get back across the strait."

We loaded all that would fit, careful not to make the dolly and the carts too heavy to roll on their small wheels. The generator and solar panels were the most important. Next were supplies for the ladies, medical items, then towels, sheets, clothing, cans of food.

"Ready?" I asked, slinging the rifle over my shoulder again.

"You got bullets left?" asked the doc, looking concerned.

"Plenty, but I'd rather not have to use them. Limited supply, if you know what I mean. We were lucky to get this rifle. A soldier we met gave it to us...in exchange for a jar of pickles."

"A jar of pickles?" He laughed, then held up a big carving knife he took from our house, admiring how the sunlight glared off the blade. "I'm ready, too."

* * *

We weren't up the road too far before someone called out. An older man in ragged clothes came out from between two houses, waving frantically, saying the brothers were looking for Doc Rick and he'd better go hide. The man seemed afraid.

"Don't worry," I told the man. "I've got a gun."

Taking a look around, we didn't see anyone coming for us but I kept the rifle ready. The wild fields between the community and harbor on the south end and the collection of shops around the ferry landing on the north end was low and the view unobstructed. Billboards inviting someone to purchase and develop the empty space had been blown down by the hurricane.

We pushed the dolly and two grocery carts up the road. When we were almost to the ferry landing, far from the houses, the dunes on one side of the road and undeveloped fields on the other side, the channel beyond, we saw something disturbing and halted our cart pushing.

Doc Rick gasped in shock. I pulled the rifle into my hands.

Ahead on the road was the gang of feral kids.

They were taking their sticks to something laying in the road. Raising the sticks high and bringing them down hard, as though in anger or filled with hate. They cursed at the target of their attack.

"I've seen them before," said the doc nervously. "Saw them take down Tyler, cut him apart. Ate the flesh raw, right where they killed him. That's how they survive."

"Who are they?"

"You don't recognize them? That's the Jones' boys, Charlie and Duke. And the Garrison twins. Hardly recognize them, as dirty as they are. That one looks like Vicky Sanderson. And I've seen the daughter of Mick Forman in attacks, too. Erica Ramos seems to be their leader, kind of like their queen. She's maybe fifteen by now. With parents dead, they made their own tribe."

I stared at them, all strangers now, all wild.

"They hunt the others...whoever's left on the island...."

I switched the safety off, put the rifle butt to my shoulder as I watched their attack. The kids ignored us, focusing on their attack. We were out in the open, no defensible place available. I instructed Doc Rick to keep an eye behind us.

"Hit the pig!" cried one kid. "Piggy! Piggy!"

The others chanted: "Hit the pig!"

They swung their sticks down on the victim, who was way past crying out in pain, too exhausted to defend himself.

Doc Rick stayed behind as I stepped slowly forward. Within a few steps they noticed me, halted their beating of the man. They stood together in a line, blocking my view of the victim.

"Stand back," I ordered, to no avail.

As I approached, they spread out. I could see between them the naked man curled in fetal position on the pavement, dark welts on sunburnt skin. He'd been trying to protect himself as best he could but was almost beyond recognition, so dirty and bloody.

At the pause, the man on the pavement dared to raise his head, looking in my direction.

"H-help me," he whimpered.

I was shocked when I recognized his face, the bald head. I knew him from a few *soirées*, community festivals, council meetings and a lot of hateful dreams. Mom's nemesis. The man who'd sent me away, sentenced me to exile from the island: Owen Boudain, leader of the island council, fanatic reader of dystopian novels, purveyor of the perfect patriarchal society.

"Well, look at you now," I muttered.

His face was the same although beaten badly. His body seemed wasted now – had to be down a hundred pounds, but just as ugly.

He rolled flat on his back, unable to fight. "Please...."

I stood closer and the feral kids gave way, some on each side of the man. They apparently recognized me from before, saw I carried the rifle. I didn't threaten them, just made sure they saw I had it. A few growled at me to let me know they had no fear of me.

The man on the pavement was breathing hard, all of his poor choices running through his mind like a movie reel.

"H-help...me...."

"Owen," I spoke calmly, staring down at the piece of shit. "You big fucking slob. What's become of you? You look so damn skinny now, like you ain't eaten in months. I thought you were supposed to be in charge here."

He tried to speak, but nothing came out. His mouth was dry, blood caked around his nose and lips. His hand went to cover his groin. Dark welts covered his body. A few cuts had drawn blood. It was an appropriate way for a man like this to go to his maker. But we could never blame God for making this one. No, Owen thought he could make himself over and be the kind of man he fantasized being. But in the end, he failed.

"You're really in bad shape, but I guess you know that," I said without a smidge of sarcasm.

"P-please h-help," he begged.

"Nothing I can do. No ambulance to call. No doctors to come."

"I'm a doctor," called Doc Rick from the safety of the stacked dolly and the grocery carts, forming a fence around him.

"No," I replied to him, "not the right kind of doctor." Then down at Owen: "You ever imagine I'd come back here? Like for revenge? And here you are, the same fat slob."

"Piggy!" the tallest boy shouted at Owen. Others took up the chant. They slapped their sticks on the pavement.

He rolled himself into a protective ball again.

"It's not looking good for you," I said, refusing to sneer. I didn't know what feelings were filling me but I understood the feral kids' rage, could see through their eyes if only for a moment. Let Nature take its course.

"Piggy! Piggy!" the kids chanted.

"Guess you'll die soon enough, one way or the other," I said, my voice strong, unafraid, defiant. Like he never could hurt me again. "I'm Sandy Baumann. Polly's son. You exiled me from this island a year ago. But you see: I came back. Not to kill you, although now that I think of it...."

He put his hand up as if preparing to receive the fatal blow. I kicked his hand away and the feral kids cheered.

"This is the Way of the Son." And I put the end of the barrel to his cheek. "To right the wrongs done to my family."

I felt a hand on my arm. It was Doc Rick.

"He will die on his own," he said. "No need to waste a bullet."

I nodded. "You're right."

With a nod left and right at the kids, I stepped back. I waved at them to continue their activity.

But they didn't continue. They suddenly seemed afraid.

Turning, I saw a pack of wild dogs padding down the road, five of them. Three large dogs and two medium, all dirty and unkempt, hungry and vicious.

The feral kids scattered, running off in three directions as the wild dogs charged at us. I fired a shot into the first dog, cut his legs from under him. The others slowed but did not halt at the downing of their leader, continuing toward us.

I rushed back to the carts, preparing to make a stand. Doc Rick was already atop his cart full of supplies, solar panels sticking up. I climbed on top of the stacked boxes on the dolly but it wavered unsteadily. I raised the rifle again, took aim at the dogs.

The dogs ran past us, ignoring us, unconcerned with our carts, and attacked the fresh meat sprawled helpless on the road.

We couldn't move past their feasting. We had to wait as they dined, ripping flesh from bones, growling and grunting, sending blood everywhere. Birds gathered overhead, waiting their turn at a meal. Eventually the dogs, satiated, lay about, too full to move. A few of them took away pieces for later. It was more than an hour before we could move on safely to the ferry landing.

28

THE FERRY LANDING BLUES

Everything changes when you lose your mother, even more if you lose her during a pandemic when everyone is fighting for survival and it is your responsibility to protect her and you fail. I regarded her grave yet felt nothing, like she wasn't really there, like she was walking around on some other island far away and I only had to find the right island to be reunited with her.

"Sandy? Are you okay?" asked Doc Rick, sitting in the boat with me. I'd stopped talking long enough to worry him.

Breaking from my trance, I resumed rowing the boat across the strait. It wasn't far: a quarter-mile. If necessary, like to retrieve a boat from the opposite shore, I could probably swim it. Instead, to keep anyone from following us, we punched holes in the boats we found on the south side and loaded up the boat I rowed across and another boat which we tethered to ours. We managed to get all our salvaged supplies in the two boats.

I put my back into the rowing, my shoulders straining, my will as strong as ever. Everything depended on me now, I realized like a sudden rainshower soaking me. I had to protect my family.

As I rowed, I told Doc Rick about our adventures trying to save my aunt, then going to my wife's town and meeting her sister who we'd thought was dead, and the fence there, and the rebels' attack, then returning to the motel. He nodded patiently at each twist of the plot, chuckled at a few ironies, and seemed to understand what I meant when I called it the Way of the Son.

"The road is finite, and well-marked," I said, "so you only need to go along it, following the path that's already set before you. Yet sometimes it will lead you in the wrong direction. Sometimes you will end up in the wrong place."

"Even that old GPS system would have people driving off cliffs sometimes," said Doc Rick.

I looked up as we approached the shore.

There was Mom, standing tall on the far shore, waiting for me to land with our supplies.

No, it was Hannah, posed on the bluff overlooking the strait. She held Isla in her arms. Both of them raised a hand to greet us and feelings of joy overwhelmed me, swept through me, and tears came to my eyes. I couldn't wait to hug them tight.

"Is that...Hannah?" asked Doc Rick as we bumped against the rocks along the shore.

I jumped into the surf to pull the boats ashore.

"Sure is," I replied boastfully. "And little Miss Isla."

"My my," said Doc Rick, getting out of the boat and climbing over the rocks. "It's been such a long time."

"Maybe not long enough."

"And who's this?" he asked.

Sally, in white blouse and canvas skirt, arrived at the shore as we landed. We unloaded the boats, box by box, each carefully set on the ground, stacked up, with the solar generator and panels laid out flat. I greeted her and waved my arms at all that we brought.

"Quite a haul there, mister," she said.

Gathered among the supplies, I did introductions: Sally, former glamour model. Doc Rick, chiropractor and island medic. Like us, he was a survivor.

"Don't say that," Sally grumbled. She turned to Doc Rick. "I'm a med school dropout, too, if that counts for anything." She grinned.

"That counts," said the doc.

"Mostly I've been a wet-nurse and cook the past few years. You see, some country folk captured me, turned me into their servant. Then Sandy helped me escape."

"She helped us escape is more the truth," I said.

They shook hands, then both paused to consider whether it was a safe thing to do, given the virus that hid everywhere.

"I'm sure we're okay," I said. "We're bubble buddies now. Right, Doc Rick?"

"Call me Rick." His characteristic cheery voice came back, now that he knew he was safe. "I doubt I'm much of a doctor any longer. No more by-laws to comply with."

"Well, I'm pleased to meet you," said Sally.

The others came down to see what we'd brought. Gasps of awe filled the air. Kristen smiled at the haul, her boys curious, asking if there were any toys. Hannah stopped when she saw Doc Rick.

I went over and wrapped my arms around Hannah as tight as I could, and Isla grabbed at my nose.

"See? I was careful," I spoke into Hannah's ear. "I could never ever not return to you."

Parting, she gave me a smirk not too different than Mom's, and asked if I shot anybody. I just gave a nod and left it at that.

She took a big breath, like she was both glad I was back home and disappointed I brought someone else to feed.

"Him? You saved him?" Hannah never liked the doc after the island by-laws required him to examine new arrivals, including a pelvic exam to assure females were suitable for breeding. And me, also getting tested. But I thought that was behind us.

"He needed saving," I said, "the only one left to be saved. Most people've gone or else dead. He was in a desperate situation."

Doc Rick blinked. "I was desperate...."

"Yeah, right," Hannah scoffed. "Well, you've seen my hoo-haw, looked right on up there, so I guess we're kinda family now."

"I only did what I had to do," said Doc Rick, humbly. "By-laws, you know. We all did things we didn't want to do. But it's over."

"Yeah," said Hannah. She thumped my chest. "Your mom made us, just so we could stay on that freakin' island."

"She thought it was a safe place. Weird, yeah, but sorta safe," I offered. "Besides, it sure wasn't as bad as having to give a semen sample to analyze. To put me on the list."

"Not as bad?" Hannah shrieked. "At least you had privacy for your jerking. I bet it felt a whole lot better than mine. I was right up there on that table getting poked. First person ever to look up my vee-jay."

"I'm sorry," I said, genuinely feeling bad.

"Not your fault, Sandy—"

"Please calm down. I-I-I've had quite a lot of s-stress recently." Doc Rick waited as we became quiet. "I'm not here for any of that. I...I just w-want to live. And be s-safe. This past year has been too much...uh...mm...."

I put my hand on his shoulder. "I agree."

Hannah handed Isla to me. "Here ya go. Yer turn, Daddy. She's gettin' heavy."

"But we got this li'l Miss Isla," I said, saying her name the way Hannah always did. I gathered our squirming baby in my arms. The cuteness overload relaxed us. "She's definitely the best part of being on the island. She's almost a year old, and she can say some words."

"If you can understand her," said Hannah. "They ain't no words just yet. She thinks we understand, but we don't."

"That's wonderful," said Doc Rick. "She sure looks in the peak of health, if I do say so myself. You've done well."

"You wanna hold her?" asked Hannah, grinning.

"Uh...okay...."

I handed Isla over to the doc but she got fussy right away, so Hannah took her. She scowled, like our baby had identified a bad person. The doc blushed.

Greetings and apologies done, Doc Rick and I, along with Sally, carried everything up to the motel. It took three trips without any carts. Kristen and her boys followed us the first trip, then stayed there. She helped arrange things in the common room.

The women were pleased with the supplies we found, even as I tried to explain how the solar generator worked. We had to set it up and test the panels to see if they still worked. The veranda behind the motel would be the perfect place to collect sunlight. The only issue was whether people on a passing boat would spot them. Yet getting some power each day could be the difference between surviving and not surviving.

We gathered later in the common room where we stored all our supplies and had our meals. Dividing the feminine supplies evenly between the women, Kristen pushed a few boxes over to Sally.

"Here," said Kristen. "This is your allotment."

Sally stared at the pile. "Maybe I don't need so much."

"Why's that?" asked Hannah.

"You don't need tampons and pads?" asked Kristen.

"Maybe not for a while...."

"Oh ma gawd!" Hannah erupted. "Are you...?"

Sally, most times showing a granite face, broke into a big grin and stretched over to hug Hannah, who shot a glance at me, like I was accused of something. But I never went close to Sally.

I was confused as Kristen joined in the hug, and George asked what was going on. Clay didn't seem to care.

"I think...," then I stopped. Maybe it wasn't for me to announce. I recalled when Mom teased us with that news – right before she was killed because of what she announced.

"Miss Sally's gonna have a baby," said Kristen to her boys.

"Is that right?" I asked, surprised. I counted back and Hannah pursed her lips at my behavior. It could be true. Who else? Sally had only been with Sgt. Sadler, just the four 'extended visits' that I could count. Maybe there were other times.

"That's wonderful news," said Doc Rick. "Congratulations."

"Sadler?" I asked stupidly.

"Who else?" said Sally with a quick laugh. "I ain't no whore. We talked, too. About getting married. When the rebellion ended. If he didn't get killed...."

"Ever'body could see he was sweet on you," said Kristen.

I explained to Doc Rick what happened in Hannah's old town, where we spent the winter. Sally had to correct a couple facts and Kristen added more detail, some of which Sally didn't really want shared. But Kristen only laughed and gave Sally a hug.

"I'm sure we woulda been getting married," said Sally. "So we are legitimate. Not that it matters these days."

"It's all right," I said. "Hard times make new rules."

"There ain't no rules now, silly," Hannah chimed in.

"Yeah, well, uh, that's really not what I want right now," Sally said. "I mean, it ain't the best time to be handicapped with this particular situation."

"But we need more people to repopulate the world," I spoke and Hannah slapped my arm.

"I ain't worried about the birth, although I'm pretty sure we got no epidural available. No, it's more about the next eighteen years I gotta protect her from viruses and vagrants."

"You already know it's a girl?" asked Doc Rick, amused.

"Sure do," Sally replied. "That one said so." She pointed to Isla.

"She don't even talk yet," Hannah countered.

"Yes, she does...in her own way." Sally tapped on her temple. "Sure she can't form the words, but she says a lot."

"And you don't get to pass them off to their own adult life, not even then," I said, earning another glare from Hannah. "You have to keep on protecting them."

"How d'you even raise a kid in this new kinda normal?" asked Sally, wiping away a tear.

"You just gotta be extra tough and extra kind," said Hannah.

"First things first," said Kristen. "There's no way to stop it. Not out here. With no medical care." She regarded Doc Rick. "Is there?"

"Did you deliver Isla?" asked Sally before he could speak.

"No, she came C.O.D.," and he gave the Doc Rick chuckle.

"My mom helped deliver Isla," I explained. That should've been enough, but I had to go on. "But I watched it all, so...I could help, I guess, if you need help. When the time comes, I mean. Unless, of course, you'd rather have the girls help you. Which I can totally understand, but...just letting you know, I'm ready to help in any way I can. If you need help, I mean...."

"Sandy," Hannah called me, "shut up, okay?"

"Okay."

"He's about as much help as a gawdamn cheerleader."

Later I heard Sally and Rick talking as Hannah was telling me all the interesting things Isla did while I was on the island.

"I had a wife," he said, acting shy. "She got the virus, died. So I came down here to get away from all that. You know: to forget. But I got stuck on the island when the pandemic got worse. A new kind of flu, they said. Now this flu season is in its ninth year."

"I'm sorry for your loss," Sally responded.

"Then I met Bobby on the island. My wife's cousin – her second-cousin, actually. We got along, took care of each other. But he was murdered by the same terrible fellows that abused me."

"Ain't that cute?" Hannah was saying in my other ear.

"Sure is," I replied absently.

"I had a daughter," Sally shared with Rick. "She was killed by the same vagrants that captured me and abused me." She got emotional.

"Sorry to hear that," Rick said, reaching out to pat her arm. "We sure live in awful times."

"Don't we, now?" She pursed her lips. "And my ex.... Well, he's gone and turned into one of the rebel leaders. Frank Winston. Ever heard of him? So the soldiers there were hassling me cuz of him. But Sergeant Sadler – Buck – he saved me, got them to let me go."

"That's good. I really haven't heard anything for going on a few years now," he replied. "Uh, there are rebels?"

"Trying to overthrow President Philpot," I called out, getting a slap to my arm from Hannah for not paying attention to her.

"You list'ning?" Hannah demanded. "She's your daughter, too."

"Philpot? You mean the senator?" asked Rick. "The one with a white goatee?"

"Yes," I called back.

"...I remember him saying, when we got married," said Sally, "I wouldn't have to change my initials, with me being a Wilson. But, I swear, nothing's easier than changing initials, lemme me tell ya."

"I know what you mean," said Rick. "I'm Hanson, by the way."

Sally held up her hand. "Pleased to meet you, Doctor Hanson."

"Likewise," Rick responded, firmly shaking her hand.

"You sure it's not Handsome instead?"

As Doc Rick blushed, I returned my attention to Hannah. More anecdotes to demonstrate Isla's cuteness, told in a different voice. It seemed Hannah was talking more like her sister now.

When Sally and Rick finished their chatting, I took out my set of keys and opened a new room for Rick. It was on the other side of Sally's room from our end of the motel, closer to the office. Like our room was when Quinn opened the door, it was made-up, with fresh towels (once upon a time) and little bars of soap, ready for the next guest. It had some hurricane damage: wet spots on the ceiling. Doc Rick said he could live with it. Despite the room being musty he was glad to have it. He pushed up the bathroom window and got a nice breeze to air it out.

"My my, this is spacious," he said. "Like a palace compared to my little cubby in the community center. I don't know what to say."

"You're welcome to relax. No clock to follow. We can figure out what to do tomorrow. Just don't drink the water until you boil it. We have plenty of already-boiled water in the common room. Help yourself."

"I will, thanks."

Then Doc Rick stepped up to me, extended his arms for a hug. I recognized that and let him hug me, wrapping his arms around me and squeezing me tight. His face rested on my shoulder. He began to sob.

"Thank you, Sandy. Thank you. Thank you. Thank you."

"It's okay," I replied, giving his back a pat.

He gave my cheek a big wet kiss as we parted.

"The Way of the Son," he said through sniffles, "is you saving all of us."

✳   ✳   ✳

We saw three men standing on the south shore of the strait, gazing northward at our hamlet, perhaps understanding we lived here or pondering what resources they could get from here. I didn't think they knew we saw them. Either way, though, we had to be ready. They were not young men like me or less strong men like Rick. They were brutes, the sons of Gareth, thug-in-chief, who I killed in the clinic inside the community center without apology.

"Shit," I muttered, peering over the rocks at the figures on the opposite shore. "They're getting ideas."

"That looks like them," Rick confirmed, laying beside me on the rocks. The shadows of the rocks hid us from their view. His voice shook. "But we have guns, right?"

"Yes," I replied, "but do they?"

"I saw them carry a pistol for a while, until we found out it had no bullets. Then they stopped carrying it. Didn't need it, anyway. They prefer using their hands. They like to punch."

"You're safe with us," I said.

"I hope so." He choked up. "If they find me again, they'll put a world of hurt on me. Especially that Beau. He's the worst. Dexter's not as bad. He has a son named Jeb, about sixteen. Clyde is almost normal, I'd say. He tried to hold the others back one time. But they shamed him into joining in with...uh...*that*."

"I won't let them come near you, so don't worry."

After a moment, he spoke: "They might find a gun in one of the houses. If they thought to look."

We tried to go on with our lives. We gave our hamlet, which we had been calling 'the north side of the ferry landing', the name of Ferryville officially. Then Hannah, with Isla's approval, respelled it as Fairyville. Perhaps those mean men wouldn't want to go over to Fairyville, not to die in a sissy place like this.

Hannah even made up a song: "'We're sailing off to Fairyville / Gonna steal some hearts / Gonna let out farts / You'll get the bill / In far away Fairyville / Pay it on your way out'." She called it the *Ferry Landing Blues* and sang it in bluesy style. Kristen joined in, adding vocal *twang*s as accompaniment, imitating a slide guitar. "'Why, you've got the blues / Them ferry landing blues / Oh, yeah / Longing for home / After you roam / Yeah, any ferry landing'll do / To save poor li'l me and maybe you'." I told her it should be '*those* ferry landing blues' not 'them' but she never changed it.

We all clapped. Too bad Quinn's guitar got broken in the ceiling collapse. No glue strong enough to repair it. We still had Mom's tuba, I reminded them.

"Huh-uh," Hannah voted, shaking her head.

I went ahead and checked Mom's tuba, oiled the valves again, blew some air through it, had the urge to play a tune. But I had to worry about the men from the south shore hearing me playing and knowing for certain people lived over here. Mom would've played anyway, daring them to come.

The next week, with Rick's help, we got the planters growing again, and fixed the water catch and the rainwater barrel system. We needed a lot of water. The Scout manual I had said we needed a gallon per day per person at a minimum. But we needed more for cooking and cleaning. What came from the tap now was no longer good: colored and smelly, worse than before. The pressure was low, too, and the toilets wouldn't flush. I had to empty them and then set up an outdoor long drop on the bluff which the ladies weren't very happy about. They had to go in pairs: someone to keep watch while the other did her business. Of course we still kept a bucket of water in the room for use with simple tasks.

We needed to boil water for drinking, but that was easier with the hotplate we powered with the solar generator. Although some of the solar cells on the panels were broken, the ones that weren't collected radiation and fed it to the picnic cooler-sized generator. It took all day with both panels spread out on the veranda to charge up a couple hours' worth of power – depending how sunny it was. So each morning I took the generator and the panels out and set them up, and each dusk packed them up and took them inside. I didn't want someone to come by and steal them. It was enough for cooking dinner, boiling water, and most of all recharging Hannah's MP3 player. I wanted her to have her tunes. I charged my cell phone weekly and checked it daily for a minute, but I got no new messages. I sent out a standard message to my contact list. I wasn't sure if any cell towers were in operation or if my message just went to the clouds and was lost forever.

We also could have a lamp on for about an hour and I used that time to write in my notebook – Quinn's notebook, with his Will in it. I wrote about our adventures. Or I could read a book, but all we had was the Scout manual.

"Remember when we used to read together?" I asked Hannah.

"That old book from the library?" she replied with a smile.

"Yeah, *East of Eden*. But we never finished it."

"I kinda got the story though. Life is tough. Maybe you get a moment or two of something good, but then you die."

"Well, I guess that's what all books are like."

I told her I missed us reading together, a page at a time, then switching readers, like it was a sacred ritual. She said the only books she found were Bibles in the drawers of the nightstands. Isla would need to learn to read so she could understand what I wrote in the notebook.

"Don't worry, I'll teach her." She grinned at me, then continued in her sister's voice: "Yessiree, we gonna be learnin all them kids their readin n writin, and some rithmetics too."

"And the history of our world," I added, "and how it all went to hell in a viral handbag."

"Don't worry." She laid her arm over my shoulders. "Everything gonna be awright."

I thought a lot about what to teach Isla, especially while I stood fishing. Every other day I took out the fishing gear and managed to catch a fish, working from the rocky shore below the motel. Rick had better luck, having once been a fishing buff up north, working the streams for trout. Fishing from the surf was a new experience but he caught on. Between us, we did all right. We all were putting on some weight. We were happy in our little clan.

However, I knew it was only a matter of time before the thugs on the south shore would want what we had and come to get it. So I took stock of our defenses. The M-16 rifle still had 46 rounds in the long magazine and 10 in the short one. We had six shells for the shotgun. Mom's pistol had seven rounds. A box of ammo with twenty. We had a good spear Quinn made from a golf club, cutting off and sharpening the handle end, saving the club end as a...a club. Some of the tools I saved from the van could be weapons, too. We also had good ol' kitchen knives.

We arranged an escape station, where we would run to if we needed to get away from the motel, and stocked it with supplies. We talked through the plan if we were attacked. Everyone knew their role. Hannah would take the kids, along with pregnant Sally, head to the escape station. They had to be saved. Kristen, being tougher in my estimate than Hannah, would help us fight. I would take the lead. Doc Rick would be our backup, watching our backs, prepping weapons. We made a defensive line using iron fence rods that had arrow-shaped points on them. We put them down among the rocks to prevent anyone from landing. They would poke into the boat's hull, making it take on water. Maybe they would stop to take care of the boat instead of attacking us. If they scrambled up the rocks, the spears might catch their legs.

We rehearsed tactical movements like I saw Sadler do with his squad. We started in a basic position. At my signal, we retreated to our designated spots and hunkered down. I liked how they looked to me as the leader. That made me work harder to be responsible for them, earning their trust. That made me more nervous being responsible for them. But this was the Way of the Son, I knew. I had to do it. It was a lot more than making Mom proud of me. It was saving our share of humanity.

* * *

It wasn't long before they were standing on the opposite shore each morning studying us, marking our daily routine, looking for a way to get to us. That scared me. Knowing there were no serviceable boats on that shore didn't give me much comfort. The strait could be swum, but maybe those fellows didn't know how to swim.

"It's only a matter of time," I told everyone at our evening meal in the common room. "They know we're here. They'll find a way to come across. With just me and Rick, I don't think we stand much of a chance."

"We have guns," said Kristen confidently.

"So do they," I said. "Probably. Have to assume they do."

"We wait for them, then blast them when they come ashore," Hannah suggested. "Then it's done."

"Like that?" asked Sally.

"That's the only way," said Rick, hesitancy in his voice.

"It's not like we gotta be fair," I said. "They won't be fair with us. I'll let them live as long as they stay over there on their side."

"That's fair," said Rick with a sigh.

I cleared my throat. George thought it was funny and tried to imitate me, much to Kristen's amusement.

"Look, here isn't a safe place. Maybe nowhere is safe now, but here we definitely have some bad people close by who know we live here and mean to do us harm."

I looked around at everyone, making sure they were taking me seriously. I had their attention.

"People will come here – like we did – just follow the road down the hill to the ferry landing. They'll decide to see what's here, what this motel has to offer. Like we did. Or they'll come down the coast on a boat and even with the rocks they'll find a place to land and go searching for anything useful. And they'll probably find us. Or people from the island will find a way to cross the strait. Maybe those feral kids or, worse, those thugs. So...."

"But we got guns," said Kristen.

The room fell silent as we all understood how precarious our situation really was. We were like sitting ducks, waiting for a wolf to come by. Even Isla stopped squirming in Hannah's arms and focused. *What are we gonna do?* her eyes seemed to ask. I heard faint words echoing in my head.

"So we must leave," I said, and waited for rebuttals. None, so I continued: "Anyone who sees our light in the darkness – God bless the solar generator – will want to see who lives here, see who else has survived the pandemic. Then they will want to take what we have. 'They got a solar generator; we want it' – and they'll kill us for it. Anything we have, they'll want it."

That stopped even the crickets from making a sound.

"But where else can we go?" asked Hannah, looking at me with a half-smile, like she thought I might be joking. "You had your li'l excursion already. That didn't go too well, did it? Or too far. And here we are: back to the same place we started from."

"That's not what I mean," I responded.

"Ain't it?" she challenged.

"What he means is any place leftover from society is a target," said Kristen. "And people gonna come. Marauders gonna maraud."

"We need to go someplace where nobody can find us," I said in my most serious voice. "Not any place where people would usually go, like a motel or a house. Not a town, or village, not even a small collection of buildings like here. You would expect to find people in those places. No, I mean a place no one would look."

"What're you saying?" asked Sally, her hands resting over her belly, which wasn't yet showing any curve.

"We should go someplace where no one can find us. I mean hide away for a while. Be completely away from anything looking like civilization. And come out only when the world has settled down."

"And what if it never settles down?" asked Hannah, an edge to her voice. Isla picked up her seriousness and began to fuss in her mother's arms.

Kristen's boys squirmed, sensing the adults' fear.

"Then we stay hidden forever." I swallowed hard. "Because the alternative is far worse."

29

THE DEFENSE OF FAIRYVILLE

I walked my route among the buildings of Fairyville, checking if anyone might've sneaked down the hill in search of food or people to harass. I walked it twice on most days, first before lunch time – though we usually had no lunch. I walked it in the evenings after dinner. Each time I passed by the landing I gazed across the strait. Sometimes I saw figures standing over there, gazing back. I made a show of having the M-16, raising it, putting it to my shoulder, aiming at them, so they would see it, hoping to dissuade them from thoughts of coming across.

"You're making me nervous," said Hannah when I turned in at last after sitting among the rocks late into the evening, always on guard duty.

"Don't be," I said in a weary voice. I hadn't been sleeping well, being more nervous than her. But I couldn't tell her that. I had to be the strong one. "We have to be ready."

"Ready for what?" She sounded scared.

"You know. The threat from the island."

"But are we still gonna be leaving?"

"Yes, but when is the question. We need to decide where to go first. To a place nobody would look for us."

"There are maps in the office." She tried to chuckle, failed. "You mean like a cave back in the woods? Or a hole in the ground? Like a badger. Or prairie dogs."

"There're no prairie dogs in this part of the country," I said.

301

"If Mother could see us now," she sighed, "how damn grown-up we are now. Just as worried as she was. But she had real reasons to be. Not us. Okay, not as much as her."

I nodded. "I'd rather we didn't have to grow up, not have to do all this shit. I want to stay teenagers with you."

"But we do, Sandy. Even if everything was normal again."

"Yeah, but I'd rather have a normal job and come home to you and Isla at the end of the day. Not be on constant guard duty."

I was so tired, working all day long, then sitting up most of the night guarding our hamlet. All I wanted was a good hour with my wife, my lover, and some playtime with our little girl. Then I could endure anything.

We were working hard at it when a knocking on the door made us stop. I got up and peeked out through the curtains, saw it was Kristen. It was evening but well after dinner. I slipped on shorts and opened the door as Hannah pulled the sheet up over herself.

In stepped Kristen, carrying Clay with George following.

"Sorry to bother y'all," said Kristen, giving us a quick grin then turning serious, "but we was down by the shore and we saw them fellas from the island. One pointed right to us. I'm afraid they saw us come back to the motel here."

"They already know where we live," said Hannah. She let go a big sigh like the interruption wasn't worth the news.

George decided to climb up on the bed as I sat on the edge. He happily jumped up and down until his mother told him to stop it. Hannah wrestled him into her arms, teasing him.

"Thought you should know," said Kristen.

"Thanks," I responded, forcing a smile. "I'll go out and check on them. I doubt they'll try anything 'til after dark."

Kristen and her boys left but we didn't return to lovemaking, unable to get in the mood again.

I got up about seven every morning, my body clock working too well. I hauled out the solar panels, set them up. I collected what water had gathered overnight, brought it into the common room, started boiling it. One of the ladies would be up by then, getting breakfast started. I checked for messages on my recharged phone.

After breakfast I worked on whatever project needed work. Rick or Sally helped. Or I'd go down to the shore to try to catch fish in the morning. Then a general tour of the hamlet before lunch. Caring for the planters in the afternoon. Another tour of the hamlet after dinner. Then maybe some free time to rest – or something better, if we weren't interrupted. Or a short nap, if I could get it, then I'd be up half the night watching for danger, the rifle at my side.

Every day, it seemed, I did whatever I did as though Mom was watching me, judging me. I worried that I wasn't doing enough, or doing the right things, to make her proud of me. I'd always tried to make her proud of me. What I was doing now was protecting my family, like Mom had protected me.

Thoughts nagged me as I lay among the rocks in the darkness, clouds overhead letting through an occasional sliver of moonlight. I felt more certain than ever the thugs from the island would come for us. Why tonight? More like *why not?* I tried thinking as they might think: How would I get across to that shore without a boat? Swim, of course – if it wasn't too far, or current too strong, and there were no sharks. I hadn't seen signs of sharks in the strait or the channel but they could swim in any time they wanted.

Another dull night with no threats....

I rolled onto my back, gazing up at the stars, waiting for a lone cloud to drift by and carry me away. Why wouldn't this pandemic end? Yet, even if it did, everything would still be in ruins. Nothing like it was before. People would need to work together to rebuild society, not be fighting each other. Why couldn't everything return to the way it was nine years ago? Life was good then.

Eventually you become jaded waiting for trouble to come night after night, then you can't respond when the threat does come....

We'd lived on the island almost two years, long enough to learn how to run a small community of pandemic survivors, to learn how fearful people would act in atypical ways to save themselves. And long enough to learn how every kindness had strings attached. It was long enough for me and my pretend wife to have a baby. But our stay was too long ultimately, or else we would still have Mom and Hannah's brother with us. We would probably still be there.

I imagined going to a dark wood, as Hannah suggested, a place where nobody would find us, where we could make our home, be our own town, and do things our own way. Like Sgt. Hendricks told me about his plan. Hide out, wait it out. One day after that, we would emerge and find we actually were the only family left on Earth. That thought made me shudder.

And there, sitting on the soft moss in the dark of the forest I would think of Mom, imagine her playing her tuba, with no special occasion, just her love of music. Being a young unmarried mother, we grew up together, just her and me, and I loved her playing and took comfort in her songs. She was a music professor, the tubist in the Symphony, and in younger years she toured with a rock band called the Tubafonics. I had to write about her, to leave a record.

A faint noise disturbed the quiet night. A slight ripple of water coming from the channel, like an oar dipping in the water trying not to make a splash. I looked out past the tall buttresses of the landing which cradled the ferry when it docked. Something was out there in the water.

The shimmer of moonlight that streaked the water when clouds parted caught my attention. A small boat slid silently through the water, coming up to the shore on the opposite side of the landing, hidden by the concrete supports for the ramp cars drove over to board the ferry. The boat was coming from the channel.

I got up on my knees, keeping low among the rocks, and stared through the darkness, waiting for clouds to move and let moonlight down.

Two large figures looked around as the boat reached the shore. One stepped into the water to push the boat up to the rocks. It was obvious they were trying to be quiet, which indicated they had an objective, didn't want to be detected.

Here they come. My heart beat fast and I instinctively switched the rifle's safety off.

Yet before I could decide what to do, they slipped away in the darkness. I couldn't see where they went. I listened for footsteps on the concrete of the landing but I wasn't sure of the direction. They just vanished. Of course, they probably rushed behind a building, hiding there, but I didn't see where.

I cursed, knowing I had to catch up. Where were they? Where were they going? I guessed they would be heading to the motel. I wondered if I should go after them, sneaking around the buildings in the dark and risk confronting them, or stay put where I could keep an eye on the motel up the slope.

All was dark at the motel, as late as it was, looking abandoned and not giving away our presence. But these men from the island already knew about us. They were out for blood. Better to get to them before they could circle around to the motel.

I stood slowly, expecting the night to hide me. With rifle raised, I stepped lightly over to where they'd landed. The boat was empty, no supplies or weapons. I released the rope from the rocks, kicked the craft out into the water, away from shore. The current would take it out to the ocean.

Watching Sgt. Sadler, I'd learned to imitate his movement, the way he stepped, the way he held his rifle, looking down its barrel, always aware of what might be to his right and his left. I affected the same stance, moved like a soldier on patrol, playing the role, and I could imitate his gruff voice giving commands. But a few minutes later I felt silly. I wasn't a soldier and I likely would make a mistake and that would be that.

Stay focused. This wasn't a childhood game playing army with the boys in my neighborhood. Those boys had plastic toy guns. I had to make do with a good stick. Mom wouldn't allow me to play with guns, even as toys – while she owned a real pistol once used by her grandfather in Vietnam. Look, Mom: now I'm carrying a real gun, a rifle I've already used to kill bad men—

Dammit, stay alert! My thoughts overwhelmed me and I had to stop and shake them loose. I had to catch up to the men, too, so I hurried through the streets between buildings as quietly as I could jog, soon breathing hard as I went up the slope to the motel.

There! Two shadowy figures appeared between buildings across the road from the motel, where the road fanned out to become the motel's parking lot. Mom's old car was parked there, marking our room, I suddenly realized. How stupid!

Posed just outside a splash of moonlit pavement on their side of the road, they planned their attack. One checked with the other, pointing ahead, apparently at our room.

I crouched in the shadows of another building with rifle raised, equal distance to where they stood and to the door of our room. I could pop them off right then – assuming I was on target. But if I missed or got only one, the other would flee. I thought of how to distract them, get them off their plan, maybe lure them away from the motel.

I saw debris nearby that would make some noise. A long board with two nails in the end laying there would make a good weapon. I set my rifle down, leaning it against the wall, and grabbed the board, stood up straight and held it like a baseball bat. I kicked the pile of debris, pieces of metal and wood, pleased with the noise it made. I saw them halt at the noise, looking at each other.

"Come on," I muttered, "come over here."

One man took a couple steps, paused to listen and look around. The other man was going ahead, crossing the parking lot. He had a long-handled axe in his hands as he stopped to look inside Mom's car. His brother took a few more steps in my direction and I noted the big knife he pulled out from a sheath on his belt.

I kicked the debris again, made more noise.

He came toward me, knife in his hand but arms down like he wasn't expecting anything to happen—

Wham!

I swung the board at him as hard as I could, sure that one or both nails caught his cheek.

He fell back, lost his balance and dropped to a knee. The knife clattered on the ground. He felt his cheek, found blood there, and got mad. He sprang up, fists clenched, grunting at me. He held up an arm to catch the board if I were to swing it again.

Before I could take another swing at him, or reach for the rifle, I saw beyond this brute that his brother had gotten to the door of our room – a hundred feet away from me.

The big brother, holding the axe in his two hands, put his foot to the door and threw all of his weight against it but didn't force it open. I was glad I'd taught Hannah how to brace the door with a chair. Like Mom showed me.

I threw down the board and grabbed the rifle. My plan was to run out of the shadows, sidestep the brother I hit, and race across the parking lot with rifle firing. But this brother stood in my way. I tried to go around him but he moved to block me.

I shouted out as loud as I could, no longer afraid of drawing attention to myself, wanting to warn Hannah and the others.

The doors to Doc Rick's room and Kristen's room opened, a look out from the doc and a hand with a pistol from the sister.

The man trying to kick in the door halted at the sight of others looking out. He cursed at them.

Growling his rage, he tried again to kick open the door, put his boot heel to the latch plate and with another hard kick, broke it apart. The door swung open and he stood in the dark doorway with the axe in his two hands, ready to swing it—

Boom!

His eyes must've gotten real big in that final instant before the shotgun went off. Then he fell back like sawn timber, crashing flat on the concrete walk, arms and legs splayed. The other brother I'd been dealing with froze. I could've shot him then but he started for his shot brother.

Hannah stepped into the doorway, shotgun aimed at the second brother as he dared to approach her. Wearing her usual t-shirt and panties, she barked harsh words at him.

I stepped toward her and she switched her aim to me.

"It's me," I called, holding up the rifle like I was surrendering.

Recognizing me, she lowered the shotgun. But in that moment the other brother took off at a full run, stomping down the parking lot, slipping into the darkness. I didn't care. More important for me to check on my family.

"Got'im," said Hannah, neither proudly or with any sadness in her voice. It was a statement of fact.

Inside our dark room, Isla was bawling. Doc Rick and Kristen rushed down to us. Sally came out and followed.

"What the heck?" said Sally.

"George," called Kristen, realizing her boys were watching us, "you and Clay stay right there, you hear?"

We stood over the fallen man, as nasty as the blast left him.

"I think that's Dexter," said Rick, looking down at the shotgun-savaged man on the ground. "Hard to tell with his face like that. The other's probably Clyde. I'll bet Beau's waiting on the other side—"

"He's getting away," I grunted and hurried after him.

The man was running as well as he could for his size and with a wound, escaping. I took off after him, keeping my rifle ready. He might return and try again, bring his other brother with him. He could gather more thugs and attack us. I hated brothers. He had to die, I decided. My anger roared inside me. The threat had to be removed once and forever.

I saw him lumbering toward the shore where they left the boat. He stopped short, seeing the boat was now out in the strait. With a glance back over his shoulder at me, walking with determination toward him, he dove into the water.

I rushed to the edge of the rocks, located him in the water, and took aim. He splashed loudly as he swam to the boat, fifty yards out. I waited for a good view, not wanting to use more than one bullet. As his arm rose from the water, taking a stroke, I shot at where his shoulder blade slid against his spine, then waited.

He went under, didn't appear on the surface for a while, and I thought I'd gotten him. Then his body popped up, floating there. I squinted, trying to see if he would move, if he were still alive. The body remained unmoving.

I relaxed, taking deep breaths, the deed done. As I sat back on the rocks, letting my heartbeat return to normal, a splash of water got my attention. I saw the floating body jerked under. It popped up, then jerked down once more and never resurfaced. Evidently there was at least one shark deciding to enter the strait.

30

THE SCATTERING

When I returned to the motel, Hannah had lain a soiled diaper, dirty side down, over the hamburgered face of the intruder, rather than wash it out for reuse.

"Don't look," she said.

It was also my job to remove dead bodies, apparently, so I dragged the big lummox by his ankles away from the motel. I took the body to another building where I could leave it for someone else to deal with. I didn't want to expend energy digging a grave.

Returning and washing my hands, I hugged Hannah, her fist clenching the shotgun, her breath on my neck reminding me how we were partners.

At the first noise, she immediately grabbed the shotgun, as I'd instructed her to do, even if she thought it was me coming back. I reminded her I would have a key. If I lost the key, then I'd knock on the door, call out to her so she'd hear my voice. I wouldn't be trying to kick in the door. So she knew it was someone else. She was ready when the door finally broke open and the lummox stood malevolently in the doorway.

"You better take your baby," said Hannah, handing Isla to me. "She's quite upset at all the noise."

I set the rifle down inside the room and gathered crying Isla in my arms, looking her eye to eye, seeing the fear there. I held her tight, rocking her, until calm returned to her frazzled nerves.

"So much for adventure," said Rick later, sitting in the common room for breakfast. "I've never actually ever used a gun before."

"I have," Kristen boasted, patting Mom's pistol on her hip.

"So have I," said a dark-voiced me.

As we ate, the obvious topic hid from us. They came to kill us. More would likely come. Any collection of buildings might harbor survivors. Survivors had food and supplies, and that would attract desperate people. With no laws now to prevent them from acting violently, they would try to get whatever they wanted.

"We are a target," I spoke as we finished eating. With so little food to distribute among us, a meal didn't take long. "And now the door's busted. Can't be locked – or even shut tight. It's not enough to take another room. No, this is an obvious place: the end of the road. People will find their way here."

"Then what'll we do?" asked Kristen. Hannah's eyes asked the same question. Sally and Rick focused on me. George got serious as the adults became quiet. Clay and Isla were content to sit in their mothers' laps.

"We have to leave," I said. "We have to go some other place. A place outside of civilization. At least for a while. A while longer."

In the silence came nodding heads and grimaces.

"Okay, Sandy, I get it," said Kristen.

"Likely fighting some marauders every week," I added.

"No place is safe now," Sally clarified.

Rick cleared his throat. "Before the hurricane, lots of folks went south from the island. They took boats or made rafts. To get away from those council bullies, you know. Even before those Tuttle boys arrived."

He looked around our group but only I met his eyes.

"After the hurricane," he continued, "people that survived, they also went south. They thought it must be better down there, with the hurricane hitting north here, turning inland like it did. They thought south of here must've been spared. It's easy. The current sweeps you that way."

"And what's there? In the south?" I asked.

"More islands, I suppose. But they're uninhabited, not like our island. Lots of marshes, almost thick as a jungle in some places.

Not a tourist area at all. But fishermen like it. Oh, there's a town eventually. But I guess you already know how towns these days."

"Hit or miss," said Kristen.

"It's not too big," said Rick. "Haven't heard any bad news about it, so it may be a safe place. Seems all the trouble is up north."

"Have you heard *any* news from *any*where?" asked Sally.

He shook his head. "Not really. When we had some power," and he looked over at me, "from a yacht docked beside the community center, we could check the signals, find any news being broadcast. Last I recall before he sailed away was news about this country invading that country – and other countries lining up on each side, and talking about missiles being fired. Meaning nuclear missiles – as though that's exactly what we need now, with this pandemic hanging on and the country already in tatters."

"Geez," muttered Hannah, and Isla squirmed.

"Sorry I asked," Sally grumbled.

"He's right," said Kristen, looking at me.

"Right about what?" asked Hannah, trying to get Isla to stay calm, putting off nursing.

"About a safe place for us to go." Kristen checked with each of us. "A place to hide out for a while. I don't know nothing about no marsh, other than I heard that kinda place kinda refreshes water naturally. Lotsa living things, too, I hear. So lotsa food. It could be good. And nobody gonna bother us."

"Makes sense," said Hannah.

"Or...." I started, then got everyone's dagger eyes. "What? I was gonna say we could go north, or northwest, up into the mountains, and live in the forest. A lot of food resources in forests. You can fish in the marsh but we could fish in the streams. And hunt."

"What's this *you* and *we*?" asked Sally. "Aren't we all gonna go together?" She gave her belly a pat. "I can't do this alone."

"Of course we'll be together," I said. "You're part of our family, Sally. You and Rick, both. Our clan...our tribe."

"Well, thank you very much," she responded and regarded Rick sitting beside her. He smiled at her.

"You can come with us," said Kristen, her eyes shifting between

Sally and Rick.

He chuckled. "Are you sure?"

"Absolutely," said Kristen. "We'll go together. We'll take the boats and whatever we can put in them with us, and just let loose from shore and the current'll take us to our new home."

"That sounds wonderful," said Rick, with Sally saying the same thing at the same time. The two of them laughed.

"Heck, I don't mind you joining us," said Kristen. "Even though we got a thing going on." She winked at Sally.

Rick blushed. "I had a wife I loved, and...." He shook his head. "Shouldn't matter. We're trying to survive. Who you love doesn't matter as much as where we can get food."

"It's like Mom used to say," I said, perking up: "'I'm hungry and I'm going to burn this food to make it easier to digest, and I don't give a damn what goes into the air to make pollution for tomorrow – because today, right now, I want to eat.'" I chuckled to myself, then saw everyone staring at me. "Okay, that was Mom. She was like that." I felt my heart rumble and I had to shut up for a while.

"It's okay," said Sally. "I'm me, you're you, she's her, and the boys are whatever they wanna be, if it'll be possible one day to do our own thing. Let's just try to get to next year."

"Sandy's still missing his mom," said Hannah to everyone, as though they didn't understand. She always knew what to say. "She was the only adult in his life. And then she was murdered. So cut him some slack, okay? We all lost somebody in this pandemic, and more from violence than virus." Heads nodding around our circle. "Now it's time for us, the new generation, to take charge and try to make it to some kind of a better world. It's up to us. There's no one else. We hafta."

✳ ✳ ✳

Lost in random thoughts, I startled when I noticed a figure behind me on the rocks as I stood minding the fishing line on an overcast morning. It was Kristen, knees pulled up, chin resting on them.

She sat up when I called back, wishing her a good morning.

"I guess I know you well enough by now," she said, raising her voice over the noise of the waves hitting the rocks, "well enough to be frank with you."

"What is it?" I worried what she was going to say.

"I know you love my sister, and I sure as hell know she loves you back. So I just wanna tell you you'd better take real good care of her. Yeah, sure I know you will, but I gotta say it. Men can lose their way, get stubborn, and they go off to someone they think'll be better. But lemme tell ya, y'ain't never gonna find nobody good as her. So don't you even try thinking of switching her for somebody else. You hear me?"

I never had those thoughts. Of course, I never had the chance to meet anybody else. Yes, on the island they tried to put me on a breeding list. But they exiled us before my turn came up.

"Don't worry," I replied, forcing a chuckle like she was crazy. "I know she's the best. I wouldn't ever do anything to hurt her. We're partners."

"See to it, then. I gotta trust you to take care of her."

"I will. I promise."

"You know I was in the quarantine camp. Had to make do with whoever wanted me, make them want me just to get food. I had to figure out how to survive, and it weren't easy. I did things I didn't wanna do, ya know? So I wouldn't wanna hear my sis gotta do the same somewhere, because you didn't protect her."

"I swear I'll protect her. Her and Isla. It's job one."

"And you protect that li'l girl of yours. Don't let her get taken away and made to do things she don't wanna do. I swear if I had it to do over, I'da stayed in that hospital instead of running into that there wood with the homeless camp. Maybe they woulda given me the jab, who knows? But it sure woulda been better'an what I been through. Maybe I woulda died from that jab, but that sure woulda been better'an what I had to do the next few years of hell."

"I'm sorry you had to go through that," I said, the only words I could think of saying.

"I didn't have to go through that, I was *forced* to go through all that. And I never even had the virus."

"I know what you mean," I offered, giving her my full attention.

"Naw, you don't know what I mean." Her face was tense, daring me to speak. "You guys had it pretty easy. But I don't envy you for it. Now I got two boys and they're near perfect. God's blessing, you could say. But when the time is right, years in the future, if we can make it to that day, you ready to let my boys get with your girl? I mean to repopulate the world?"

"What?" I was surprised, Mom's famous word stuck in my head. "What do you mean 'repopulate'?"

"Hannah was talking about it." Kristen smiled at me. "And we agreed. So I just wanna get your permission. She said I should."

"To...?"

"If it's only us, are you okay with Isla getting with my George or Clay, whichever she like, or maybe both, to repopulate the world like Aunt Polly always talked about?"

I felt a tug on my line. "I guess so."

"You guess so?"

I reset the line, letting the fish escape.

"I mean, I don't have anything against it. Just kinda shocked to hear you talking about it."

I gave her a long look. She was pretty like her sister, but with some scars on her face – more under her clothes, I guessed. She'd had a rough life already.

"In the future we gotta do whatever we can to survive," I went on. "We can't be picky about who makes babies. If we can make a baby in the future, the way everything's going. The virus, maybe the vaccines, left a lot of people unable to conceive, my mom said. We'll be lucky to have new life anyway we can do it."

She grinned then, satisfied. "That's all I need to hear."

"But won't they be cousins?" I asked suddenly, my mind filled with scripts from the past.

"Guess so," she laughed. "Worked out for you and my sis. Didn't it now?"

※　※　※

In the future we will forget the past. We will forget that there were days when we didn't need to wear masks, didn't need to line up for jabs. There was a time when we didn't need to hide at home, afraid to go out and breathe the air. That there was a time when we could embrace each other, even put our lips together. We wouldn't cover our smiles but clearly show our teeth, letting other people know we were happy to be close to them. And store shelves were still full, then half-full, then empty.

We were simply happy to be alive, survivors of a nine-year long flu season with no signs of ending. Every sneeze, every cough sent us into hiding, yet without masks, vaccines, everything to combat the virus used up by now, it was for each of us to carry on as best we could, making do with what we had or what we found. We were roving bands of survivors, hoping to get to the next day, with no destination, scattering like clouds of pollen on the breeze.

We stood by the ferry landing. I held the end of the rope tied to the boat bobbing there, filled with supplies.

"Gonna miss ya big time, sis," Hannah said through streams of tears. She and Kristen hugged.

"Miss you, too, sissy." Kristen kissed her sister's cheek. "I'll be sure to write."

They tried to laugh.

"Yeah, sure ya will," said Hannah. "Like the post office's up and running. Like ya got any stamps, like in old times, huh?"

"Someday it'll be open again. And cell towers will be lit. Check your phone. I'll send you a message." She laughed.

Another hug, more tears. When they parted, Kristen took Isla from my arms and bounced her, got her to giggle. Hannah squatted before the boys. She hugged Clay and shook George's hand like he had been taught.

"Gonna miss this little one," said Kristen, holding giggly Isla in her arms. "One year old. No birthday cake anywhere to be found. We'll make it up to you, sweetie. Promise."

"These boys're gonna be so big next time we see'em," Hannah said. "Hopefully, we can visit each other. When things are back to normal. Not too much longer, I hope."

We laughed at that idea. I gathered Isla back from Kristen as Hannah gave George a hug and kissed him, then Clay.

"If y'all get tired of living in the woods," said Kristen, squinting against the glare off the water, "you can come live with us. Only we don't know yet where we'll be. Sally'll pick a good spot. Rick can chop wood, start a fire. We'll get by. Fishing is pretty good, I hear."

Hannah grinned, understanding.

"Or you can visit us," I said. "Up north in the mountains. I'm not sure where exactly, but I have an idea. Mom took me camping there when I was a little boy. It's a national park."

"Sounds lovely," said Sally.

"Maybe we can plan to meet back here in a year," I suggested. "Same time. Around Isla's next birthday."

"Let's make it a plan, then," said Rick, and we shook hands.

My wife held her smile until it sagged, no longer real. I sensed she wanted to go with her sister, but she chose to go with me, like a punishment she thought she deserved. She kept saying Mom told her to look after me. So I would do everything I could to make her life as comfortable and pleasant as possible. That would be my life: protecting and providing for my family.

That is the Way of the Son.

✳ ✳ ✳

Up through the trees I gaze at a trio of passing birds flying in a triangle, and my chest tightens. They are quickly lost beyond the treetops. We live in a cathedral of tall oaks and pines, their thick trunks rising like marble columns, the ground below soft with moss or protected with brambles and undergrowth. No one would dare come up here, too far to be worth the hike. We are safe here in our dark wood.

I think of Mom, our life on the island. I stare inward at the sea stuck in my mind's eye, the surf rolling up the beach, calm once more. I take a breath, remembering the view.

I ponder my wife and daughter sitting outside our little dug-out home, mother teasing child, imparting some kind of lesson. Did I do the right thing? I listen to them enjoy the afternoon. Was this place the best for us? Would we be able to survive here?

As Mom liked to say, hard times require hard decisions. And I will have to make a lot of hard decisions as we enter the future. The Way of the Son is fraught with hard decisions, after all. So I made one and we left our home in Fairyville and trekked into the mountains.

I carried Mom's tuba on my back. For now, however, I dare not play Timmy in the forest or someone might hear it and come our way. Music had to be put away for a while.

Smiling, I recall the way Mom talked about how anyone would decide to make a tuba. "Are they going to make one to test it, then make another with adjustments to the length? No, it's all math. Of course they calculated the length to be able to get the notes they wanted. Then they added the valves and extra tubing to be able to change the overall length to play other notes. Who would've ever thought of that? I'll tell you: people who had security, and the time to think of it. People who wanted to be able to make sounds that were beautiful and comforting, to make music." She would go on listing the specifications of her precious tuba, her voice brightening with each sentence. "Because music is the height of civilization. Oh, I suppose you could say that some kind of technology made our lives easier, but music makes our lives more beautiful. Music is what makes us the best we can be as humans."

We would hide out here until some sign let us know it was safe to come out, to see what the world had become. Then I would pull Mom's tuba into my lap and blow loud and long, calling everyone to rise again, to start over and build anew.

Nine years ago people thought the world was ending. They watched the skies, stared across the rooftops, waited in fields and by shores, some hoping it would happen soon. Instead, they got a little death, impossible to see with their eyes, a flake of a mote from a bit of crumb that decided to eat us from the inside out. And we made up games that would help us beat that little death. A few of us won and went on.

It wasn't that the world was ending. No, it would always exist –

until either the sun expanded or a good-sized comet struck. No, it was the sober realization that *we* would be ending. A clean sweep. A necessary refreshening. Some people sang praises for that end while others couldn't endure the wait and took matters into their own hands. Same result. In that way, we hastened our transition to a more wild world, one bearing fewer of us: the unlucky ones, they said; we were supposed to envy the dead—

I break from my trance at the sound of Isla's babbling down the slope. They sit outside our dug-out home, a burrow I constantly repair and improve. That is my daily job. I also hunt and fish and we gather fruit and seeds, nuts, and whatever herbs grow in our forest. I make use of the Scout manual to determine the edibility of what we find. I recall how to tie different knots, how to purify water, how to make a fire, how to fashion traps to catch animals for food. And my dear wife helps, takes care of our daughter, keeps the dug-out as clean as a dug-out home can be kept clean. We do what we have to do, sharing everything, always working together to make a good life for ourselves. We are partners.

With Isla's cute babbling increasing, we decided it was time to start teaching her words. Although Hannah enjoys it, I hear only nonsense. I wish Mom were here to witness this new phase of our family history: the dawn of a daughter.

One day in the spring, after enduring a winter that was mild for these parts, being safe and warm in our snug burrow, I hear Isla speaking out. It's what I consider her first true speech, saying real words that I can recognize.

She says: "Da-ba-doo. Da-ba-ba-wee."

"You hear that?" My smile spreads. "I think she said 'daddy'."

Hannah scoffs. "She did not say 'daddy'."

"No, she did." I hold Isla up, face to face. "Say it again."

Actually I was trying to tell my mama and my daddy what to be careful of, the things they could not see coming. I did not have all the words yet but I knew I had to warn them. However, I had little patience for these baby-talk games they so enjoyed. They may have contributed some genes to my creation but they were not the bosses of me. Whatever they thought they were, it would be me who carried us forward.

"Say it again, Isla. Go on now."

"Da-ba-doo, da-ba-ba-wee."

"See?"

"That ain't 'daddy'. That's something else completely."

"No, it's 'daddy' – definitely." I gaze into Isla's beautiful eyes as she squirms in my arms. "Daddy what...? What're you trying to tell me? You need something?"

She wrenches her hand free, points across the slope.

"Dee-dee," she says, and we turn to see the whitetail doe and her fawn quietly feeding between the trees, unafraid of us, like it is the most natural thing in the world.

ACKNOWLEDGMENTS

A lot of influences came together randomly to initiate this story idea and then to propel the writing forward.

I can determine some of these influences, such as the film *A Boy and His Dog* (1975), a sardonic adventure set in a post-apocalyptic landscape, based on Harlan Ellison's short story. I would have done it differently, of course, but I did give my novel the working title "A Boy and his Mom and her tuba" – perhaps a little too obvious. (Later, well into the writing, I saw a meme of Ellison's story online that suggested making a film about a woman and her cats.)

At the start of the SARS-CoV2 ("covid-19") pandemic, I sought to write a novel on this end-of-the-world theme, thinking I could draw on real experiences. However, those early days proved too serious for me to focus on fiction. Nearly two years later, when I was ready to write, I wanted to focus not on the initial days, when everything was immediate and real, but further into the future, when the worst we experienced had gotten worse still, say, six years into the future. As Book 2 continues the story, we have gone through two more years; by its end, another year has passed. Everything is irrevocably broken by then.

While preparing for the writing, I read a few post-apocalyptic novels. *Earth Abides* (1949) by George R. Stewart, a classic of the genre, was definitely ahead of its time. While the hero finds himself alone at the start, with not much mention of the cause of humanity's demise (hints at it being a plague), his construction of a new society became a helpful manual and I leaned on that for the second half of Book 1.

Other works with a near-future or post-apocalyptic setting were well-known to me (e.g., *The Handmaid's Tale* by Margaret Atwood) and I tried to avoid any resemblance to them as much as possible. However, I do have characters refer to a book or two. Throughout the trilogy, I consciously tried to keep to realistic, probable activity

321

rather than what may be plausible yet more far-fetched, away from the fantastic direction some writers have gone in the 'post-apocalyptic' genre.

My own experiences during the two years of our real pandemic (2020-2022) got into the story in Book 1. A character tells what happened to him, based on my experiences in the earliest days. As usual, I tend to put some elements of my life into the story. I am a tuba player – used to be, but never a professional. My mother is in no way like the mom in Book 1. Neither is my father. I did have a Schnauzer and lost him in a similar way. My parents had a home on a barrier island but only upon their retirement. My father did enjoy fishing there. We did stay at Tropic Isle motel on our first trip there.

I always select music to help create an appropriate emotive soundscape for my writing and revision sessions. The aural support is necessary to unlock my muse. I found an ideal soundtrack in the music of Otto A. Totland, Peter Sandberg, and Gavin Luke. The mostly piano music from several albums and EPs, which I played over and over during the months of this project, provided the perfect background. I also listened to some tuba music for writing Book 2.

A special thanks goes to those who worked the front lines during the pandemic, some of whom lost their lives alongside their patients. Our gratitude is immeasurable.